DRINK FOR THE THIRST TO COME

DRINK FOR THE THIRST TO COME
First Edition

Printed in the United States of America

Published by Silverthought Press
www.silverthought.com

Cover art: "Home" © 2011 by Anton Semenov

"At Angels Sixteen" was first published in A DARK AND DEADLY VALLEY,
Silverthought Press.

"A Very Bad Day" was in TALES FROM THE PET SHOP,
Twilight Tales Books.

"Then, Just a Dream" appeared in STARSHIPSOFA STORIES, Vol. 2.

"So Many Tiny Mouths" was published in Feral Fiction.

"Cordwell's Book" first appeared in TALES FROM THE RED LION,
Twilight Tales Books.

ISBN: 978-0-9841738-4-6

DRINK FOR THE THIRST TO COME

— the short fiction of —
LAWRENCE SANTORO

[silverthought]
Philadelphia | New York

CONTENTS

A few words…

Five of the fifteen stories in this collection have been printed elsewhere. Two were made to-order for anthologies that never came about. That happens. Three were podcast. Two were submitted and rejected. That happens too. The rest were written then put aside. I do that. The earliest piece in the book is "Rat Time in the Hall of Pain." It sounds like a title from a writer just setting forth, doesn't it? It is.

Because I always want to know where things come from, I've done short post-mortems on all the pieces in the collection. That can be tricky. I once told a guy who'd sent me a complimentary note that the story he'd liked was based on a real event. He was disappointed. "I thought you made it up," was the crux of it.

So if you're not interested, forget the afterword.

As with almost everything I've written, I hope you'll read these stories aloud. They were written that way, me typing and talking (and getting 'looks' from people in cafés, on trains, wherever). So read them to a friend or to yourself. I'd like their voices to be yours.

Now go. Enjoy.

DRINK FOR THE THIRST TO COME

...summer day and mild, mild weather, a day like no other, a day of sun and warmth, of swimming, friends and beer, a day of just-up corn stolen from the field above the quarry, cobs wrapped in mud, roasted in fire-ash, butter rubbed into the char till it dripped down the fingers.

Later, black clouds rolled across the green-forever. A thunder-anvil filled the world above with miles-high darkness and the smell of how a penny tasted. Late day rain cleared the midsummer heat and brought a chill before the night, a crash-down bang, beauty and wonder, a wonder at the fury of it all, a bombardment, personal, from God in heaven to Chris Harp from out Haul Road, Dolph Station, Texas. As they clamored up the slope, down-rushing mud washed the earth from beneath their feet and hands and they all slid back to the shelf above the water below. Trapped and laughing. At the next down flash and bang, the girls, Lord bless them, Sally Wayne, Jaycee Dogton, Sarah Gonzales, Winnie Border, wriggled, squealing, beneath the blankets. Trapped! So what the hell? Chris dove into the water. Height of the storm, lightning strikes and thunder coming flash/bam and down he dives.

He cleaved deep water, down to where the world was cold and green and the thunder pressed his whole body with terrible immediacy. Little fishies in a mass, shuddered, turned round by regiments.

Perfect.

The guys, Tex Acre, Billy Madeira, Marty Mundt, dove in after. Let them follow, let them not. This was for him, his perfect day, all a game, not for forever. Forever? Hell, forever was inside him, Chris Harp. He carried forever in his every grunt and drip.

Later, with no expectation, Jaycee Dogton was under the blanket with him, in his space and he in her, in her good and sweet, long and quiet so not to be heard, and wholly without preparation. And ah, the smell of sweat and wool and them.

Later, when they hit the diner, the day begins to bleed away. They still roll with joy. When they order, a dozen voices call; as they wait, they rock the eyes of the Sunday folk who turn Methodist stares upon them. Sure they're the center of attention. And, as this is a dream of perfection, *he* was the center of that center. They bit old Eulie's ass, they surely did, but even she smiles as she takes their orders, brings the grub. Had to love them, Chris Harp and friends, Lords of the Earth, holders of forever!

By the window, Chris watches night seep from the trees that fence the joint. Texas night shines the rainslick macadam in the lot. Their pickup kicks back orange glitter from sodium lights.

And as always on the road, walking from nowhere, going who knew where, barefoot, white hair flying ahead, shirt, open, flapping, ragged jeans gray with dust, there comes Walkin' Will, the Old Guy. Grandpa'd told of Will from down in '34, told of Walkin' Will who walked the land preaching judgment at the end of times, who shouts out scripture and who takes offered rides on truck or wagon, then somewhere, nowhere, cries, "God says, *walk* here!" and out he leaps to walk wherever, down a road, into the fields... Now here he comes, same one, same as always. Looking back at those left behind he calls, "You! Drink, you! Drink for the thirst to come!"

Chris watches. Beneath the table, Jaycee Dogton takes his hand. Day has bled to memories, beer and thunder, chill water, butter, corn, and her. And with that memory, his final convulsion and the tingle as he flows from himself into Jaycee and into the world, the perfect day becomes one more dirty morning and night is gone with the dream.

And there lay Chris Harp: dirty little man of more than middle years, and those years hidden unto his own-damnself, he waked into a dark and ugly morning, as always. He breathed stench. Everywhere, the reek of mold and ash, of long-drowned fire and rust, of rotted teeth and unwashed pit and crotch, his and hundreds more. One bunk above, the One-eyed Kid from Nowhere still cut wood with the rest of the rink.

For seconds Chris held the dream. When he shoved it away, time it was to rise, shinny down the bunks and be.

Johnny's Icehouse flop was cold. He shivered into shirt and pants, wrapped the static chain around his waist, thin metal, fine and supple as yarn, let it curl in his pocket with his breathing silks. His jacket was balled beneath the blanket. Leather, fur trimmed, it had come all the way on the Walk. In the pocket, his cell. He stroked dead plastic, touched the numbers of home.

He shook his boots over the edge, wagged his socks and threads. *Let floormen worry about stray critters*, he thought. Slipped into his socks. *The Old Guy's socks!* "Remember me," the Old Guy said *(A couple months ago, was that all?),* said before he gave his all to the Vendateria. The socks were warm, a little stiff. Chris wiggled his toes. No holes. Good tubes, tight wove, thick.

"They're new," the Old Guy'd said.

New they was. By some miracle, bag-new. Survivors of The Day, the socks—a miracle of all the days between The Day and the Old Guy's finding of them—found in plastic, three pairs full.

"Chicago's gone but my socks survive. Found outta that mess below the collapsed ceiling, mixed they was with skates, pucks,

5

and bust-up junk from Gunzo's pro shop at Johnnie's. In the blastshadow the place was. I believe Sears's' Tower saved them socks!" The Old Guy pressed his socks into Chris's hands. "Remember me. My name," he said.

Chris kept the socks close. *Thank you Sears Roebuck and all things in between. Thank you, Old Guy. Never was no good with names. Sorry.* Socks were pure *worth.* Chris had his own worth, too. He still ate thistle, but was that/close to the Boss table. *That/close.* He'd get there. Can's bottom, maybe, but something *from* the can at least, a little fat, a bit of...

Fuck you Harp, Chris told himself, *there's* this *day to do.* And the next and so it would go until he heard, "Chris Harp. Rise." *Then* he'd move on up ("...to that de-luxe apartment in the sky-y-y!" *What the hell was that from? What? Cripes, so much gone*). If he didn't rise to the Boss table, well hell, tumbleweed sprout—called *thistle* in Texas—stayed in him, stayed down anyway, gave him juice to run on. Not everyone was that lucky.

Time to motivate. Early worm gets top weed.

Chris smacked the slats above him. The Kid's snores gurgled before turning to tears. *What the hell? The Kid? What's his name? Worth plain nothing and that was fact.* Chris wondered why the Boss...

No. Shut down that Goddamn plink. He did not wonder *why-the-Boss* anything.

Down the pole went Chris, by the Mex, past Fireman Bill and the Drooler. He hit floor where tucked last night's TV Johnny, snoozing still. A celebrity and still on the floors. *Lost: the series premiere* this Johnny'd been last night. Maybe Chris'd be TV John tonight. He was a tolerable *Simpsons* but no one—*not a one!*—was *My Name Is Earl* like Christian Harp. Now that was one ace shitload of worth.

Watch your hiddens, Harp. Damn hiddens kill.

Gray light shafted through the roof thirty feet above. It lay busted on snoring lumps that quivered and farted across the floor of the rink. Time to move. There'd be shadow today. The Long Season *was* ending, Boss had said. So there it was. Sky *is* clearing, five-year Winter verging on Spring.

And then?

Then earth returns, bears fruit and…

…*and enough of that!*

In the lobby, more light knifed through the curving wall and ceiling. For a second he watched the beams crawl. They licked floor, folded over trophy cases, caught the once-glassed pictures of men on ice. One hell of a spot must have been the Icehouse lobby back in the day before The Day.

Fuckit. He skittered, crunching glass and beams of dirty light that cut through pulver-dust. It was a spooked out place— though none spoke of spooks or living dead. "*Ain't no living dead,*" Boss had said. Still, sometimes, late, dragging back from a worth-hunt—be it folly or for the Boss—Chris felt shivers in the neckhair. Just wall crackles or creeping skitters among shards and busted brick, sure-sure. But when shadows flickered in tallow flame, yeah, he scooted, ahead of thoughts of Walkin' Will barefooting the busted earth. *Them nights*, Chris shinnied to his bunk, wriggled down beneath his blanket like a girl and let the snoring ease him…

Goddamn! Plinking again!

The tin sheet over the doorway thundered as he wiggled into morning. Light cut through the stumps of buildings, Wetward. And there! His shadow, a sun-shade falling through the dust. It dragged westward from his feet, toward the Outskirts and long-gone 'burbs. He felt like dancing his shadow. He did not. And there was the gong, the always and forever *bong-bong, bong-bong,* distant, tolling out of the Wet. One day he'd like to…

No-no, not his business, them *bongs*. Still he wondered, in day, night, wind, or none, *bong-bong, bong-bong.*

Even in light the Icehouse was a black mass, bomb-baked brick swiped gray with pulver. A bob-wire path led, there to the Center. The Boss decreed it: a path of prongs to keep you straight in deep dark, in swirling dust or driving snow. This morning, even poles and wire threw down shadow. They made a choppy lane a hundred yards to the Center. Chris could barely see it now, in the pitch, but it was out there, more char-black brick, more sheet tin, more gray, the forever dust here at world's-end.

Ditch that, duster, he told himself. He gripped a bob to punish him. *Best not plink upon that "World's End" shit, Harp!* The prong dug flesh down to the blood! *Boss hears discouraging word, spies an eye in downcast plinks, and Boss will lunch upon said eye and* that *for him who spoke or plinked it.*

A sudden wind from the Wet raised a wraith. A little'n. Vaporized steel, pulverized brick, flour-fine cement, wee shards of beast- and folk-bone raised from the earth, twisted skyward, caught light, reared three, four hundred feet—who could tell? Dusted wind caught hollows in downed walls and busted buildings; it sheared over sheet tin corners to raise a reedy howl. The Icehouse faded. The Center was gone. The wraith matured from pup to wolf like/that. Out of the moan came a crackle. The Boss's bob-wire fence flickered. Starry static snapped electric blue on every prong and post. Chris wrapped his face in a breathing silk, drew cleaner breath. He dropped his static chain down his leg to trail and drain electric fire into the dust.

And here comes Lenny.

And there Lenny came, limping, leading with his shoulder, head, and elbow, out of the wraith. And there Lenny went, gimping the other way from breakfast, mumbling.

Lenny had smoke again. What was it about that old Kicker? Son of a bitch could flop in a can of turd and come up smoking! Lenny'd been somewhere, not here, two days back. Doing Boss bidding, something Chris would not ask about and did not need to know, no sir. Anyways, since he's back, Lenny's worth is up, up, up. Up with the Boss, up with the Kickmen and the Bits— even soft and fragrant Bits glommed onto gimpy Len, begged to suck him dry or be just *his own* Little Bit for the night. With *everyone*, Lenny's worth is through the clouds.

Now, he's shoving wind, Chris realized. "How's morning thistle, Len?" Chris hollered against the wind, letting pulver flake sneak by his silk, suck up his nose, scour his eyes.

Lenny swatted the question back at Chris and put his ass to the wind. "I ain't ate!"

A Boss job, sure. "What! Haven't had your breakfast, Len?" Chris shouted.

Lenny shuffled sidewise, plinkage filled with mumbles and murder. "Fuck no, ain't ate yet."

Enough. The man's doing for the Boss. Son of a bitch'll be back with more weed and... "Hey, Len. Len, I gottcher back," Chris called above the moan.

Lenny's limp. Good and faithful kicker he once was, Lenny took a bolt from the Wet. Who knew? From a Niggertown kink, from 'Tweeners, from somedamnone, but he took it for the Boss! Good Lenny. Boss himself dug it out of Lenny's thigh, first chance he had! Chris helped a little. He'd flopped across, held down the big lug's bottom parts so Len would not disgrace himself in jumps and kicks, not jolt the procedure or the Boss.

A good kicker before that bolt, Lenny'd snap a neck like/that! One windmill twirl from standing still and *crack*! A thing to see!

The bolt was rusted rebar, probably shot from a leaf-spring cross'. Not dangerous eventually. Might have been a poison bolt or one soaked in sick but it healed. Still, his left leg, his kicking leg, was fucked. So Lenny now cannot kick. He is slow coming when called and is certainly not the kicker he was. Being too damn dumb to admin others, his worth is seriously shit-lined. So now the presh is on. "Deliver or get you gone!" the Boss might have said. "Thanks for taking that bolt, old Len, just the same…"

But he sure could dip that smoke! And smoke was *worth*!

"I'll dip grunts for you, okay Len? Be back soon, yeah?" Without waiting for a "sure-sure" or "fuck y'self," Chris dodged the slanting shove of the wraith wind and grabbed the Gimper's tin, forgetting—

…a *whack-crack* static shot and—

…Chris was down hard. His drag-chain saved him the worst of it, but a *snap-slap* arced from Lenny's plate to Chris's mitt, walloped like the old kicker might have done himself and Chris, who should have known, was down. An old Dust-Walker like him!

Lenny leaned against the wind and appreciated the moment. He laughed and laughed. He shook his paw—he'd caught a clout of static, too—but Chris's flop was just that damn funny and worth a tingling mitt.

Rising from the dirt, Chris joined, laughed at his own damnself. *Better,* Chris figured, *take a clout offering a worthy thing.* And he'd pry smoke from the old kicker. Sure.

Then Lenny stopped and stared. *He's thinking, 'What's this? He gets my thistle, saves me space, and what's it cost me?'* Chris almost smelled Lenny's brain working.

"Nice," Lenny said, not looking at Chris, his stare fixed on the rising beauty of morning.

Len's looking at light and don't mind hunger, Chris realized. Chris peeked. Sun-up was making dustbows, the color refracted from particulates wilding in the air. It was all so damn pretty! *Old Lenny!* Then it was done. Strands of wispy gray hair whipped Lenny's face and he was off, a galloping limp. *Boss work.*

"Sure-sure." The wind tossed Lenny's words to Chris. "I'm over the Jordan! Back in no time!"

Chris waved Lenny's tin above his head.

The Jordan? What the hell's the Boss doing with the old stadium, now taboo, off limits, stay out, this means you? Well, huh?

Chris dug another bob into his hand. *None of your business,* he told himself.

Another couple tons of pulverized city kicked high and hung 'round whilst sunbeams split the clouds. A couple strakes of light reddened, then goldened the Goddamn air. Shit, it *was* damn near pretty. Until you wanted to breathe.

Chris snugged silk across his nose. *Yeah. The Long Season* was *ending.*

The Boiler ladled out the grunts. "Salt your thistle, Dusty," he said. "Sparse picking so we're stretchin' with don't-ask-won't tell!" Paste gray tumbleweed stew hit Chris's tin like mealy buckshot.

"Cheer up, brother. See the light?" Chris slinked his smiley words by the Boiler's shaking head. "Season's ending. Boss says."

"Feed me Boss stuff. Moveit!" The line growled with late snoozers and the shiftless. "C'mon, c'mon. Next!" Boiler yelled.

Chris lay down Lenny's tray. "For Len."

The Boiler squeezed his eye on Chris. The line grumbled all the way downsteps into the World.

"Hear it, brother!" Chris leaned near the Boiler's ear stump. "Lenny's on a run." He pitched his voice just so. "Jordan's House!" as though he knew what! "Time he's back," he waggled his thumb at the growlers, "this'll be done-'fer."

"Yeah?" Boiler said.

"Yeah. So?"

"You getting suck, ain't you, Harp?"

"I hope to and that's honest!"

The eye squinted. "You let the Boss to know I'm serving twice-to-one here and tomorrow you go beg. Tomorrow and tomorrow forever-more you beg!" A slop of stew hit Lenny's tin. "And I take some suck sticks." He held up a three-fingered hand. "For risk."

"Three sticks. Done."

"Full hand's *five*!" Boiler yelled.

"Five then! Absolute!"

"And because I'm so pretty!" The Boiler opened mouth and laughed.

Burnups who'd got better were not pretty: flash-flesh, scarred white, bald, a wee black hole where once an eye had peeped. Laughing made it worse. Least he could cook. Saved Boiler from turning 'Tweener.

Chris found a sit to eat his tumbleweed upon. The thistle needed salt indeed, more salt. Never salt enough.

"You." The Boss voice came over the bent necks in the Round Room where Chris ate. Not a shout. No need. "You," meant Chris, meant now.

Goddamn! Chris downed his spoon and scurried, let his breakfast to the tender care of Whitey, the One-eyed Kid from the rack above him. Whitey'd care for, touch neither his nor Lenny's grub, not for himself nor give anyone else taste, touch, or smell. Whitey needed worth.

"Yeah, Boss?" Chris twitched. His body wanted to get doing, doing whatever.

"You need some work, my man."

He surely did and glad to have it too. Chris was middle pole. Stuck. Another twitch would help.

"Got you a task. Think you're up for it."

"I'm up."

"Didn't ask, Duster. You're going to the Wet. You get yourself out to the Heath and Hollows and see a man. Señor Temoco. He'll have something for you.

"Yes."

"Wait! The something will be a box."

"A box."

"Small box." The Boss showed him. A foot by a foot by a foot.

"Mm."

"You'll be careful with that box."

"Yeah."

"You'll not open, bounce, drop, or break it."

"No I won't!"

"Wait! Cripes. You'll bear it back like it holds a Boomer. A big bad Boomer!

Chris smiled.

"You'll treat it like your only pair of balls."

"Mm."

"'Cause it will be."

"Yes."

"You'll need trade for this box. You draw you some goods."

The Boss and Chris let that hang dust.

"Yes. Okay. Mm." *Sees me sweat, feels me shake, knows I'm...*

"What's done with the goods, here to there, that's your lookout."

"Yes!"

"Just... Cripes, I'll nail your dick to a wall you start hauling before I give you leave! Just make sure the goods is fresh upon delivery. It's for sure Señor Temoco will want fresh for this most valuable box."

"Yep."

"And how will you know Señor Temoco?"

"I'll." He was nodding but that was all Chris had. Some eye passed between the Boss and Chris. *Cripes. He's having fun.*

"You will know Señor Temoco by his bearing."

"His bearing. Yes." This time he waited. The Boss's look?

Could have been friendly, might have been a smile, could have been pity, never could tell. You also never took for granted. And the Boss never pitied, so that was out.

"And you'll do what when you get the… what is it again?"

"Box. This big. I bring it to you."

"And you look."

"Hell I do. I treat it like my nuts."

"And you wonder what it is?"

Chris blinked twice. "You'll tell me if I need to know."

"Okay, Duster. Haul."

Chris lit out, spring-shot past his bench in the round room. *Cripes, cripes, cripes.* There was Whitey and what was left of morning grunts, his and Lenny's. *Cripes.*

"You grip that grub, Whitey." He gave the kid a plinking eye. "You give it all to Lenny and you let him know it's thanks to me he's eating. Got it?"

"Yeah!" the Kid said. "From you. And you…?"

"Are working Boss stuff."

And Chris was down the torch-lit stairwell, tallow-black smoke spinning in the suck, rising to the busted roof.

…to the Vendateria. Early. *Good.*

The Girl stood out.

Vendors lazed, looking, scratching. A couple kickers leaned by the door, giving little heed—slinky pricks! There were newsons come from here and there looking to make a name. There were oldsters and Eustaces looking to ramp their worth, hold on a few more. They milled, filled the 'coves and looked plain miserable. The air was full of sweat and need.

When the place had been just the City of Chicago Office of Emergency Management Center, the Vendateria was a long low room at the far end of the first level of the pie-shaped building, the spot for soda pop and candy, machines dispensing goods and change. There were sofas to lounge on, alcoves where to sack out through long shifts, when snows, floods, riots were managed there.

That crap went crash on The Day. On The Day, the Center fried and died like the City. Now the Vendateria was a grotto off the main floor, the machines stripped and long gone but the place still vended. Newsons gathered there, women, Bits and boys, whoever the hell, those who'd been traded off by little Daleys of the 'hoods, folks who'd wandered in from north or south, from West or Wet. An occasional kink from Niggertown showed, or those who'd just dragged it in from the far Dust like Chris (*Christ, what was it, four years gone?*). They all showed there, wanting.

Chris could about tell for looking, from where a newson hailed. Didn't matter, newsons were for sale, for use, for gathering worth. They were grabbing root like everyone.

The 'teria was for goods too. The left-outs. Whatever crossed the border, after the Boss and his kickers, admin boys, and special bits had dips, what was left was left-out for vending. But, hell, after The Day, everything had some worth—in the dipping or the vending—and everyone needed worth.

The Girl was fresh. That alone was worth. Third alcove in, there she was. Sitting. Calm. Waiting. Like someone had told her, just go there and wait. Chris couldn't peg her. Not out of Wrigley or the Heaths and Hollows, not from the 'burbs, surely not from Niggertown. Didn't look like from anyplace he'd seen except Dolph Station, Texas, day before The Day. First, she was damn-near plump. *Where's a girl get her plump these days?* It gave Chris pause.

Then the threads. She was wrapped in style, good stuff and mostly clean, tough wearing but nice. She looked, cripes, like the bunnies on the bus back in old Dolph Station. Pretty girls, the ones who rode, same times, to Perrytown Mondays-through-

busy, white wires trailing to pretty little ears, pretty faces stuck in the news, pretty shoes in jimmy bags and sneaks on pretty feet. His bus, the street, the town, not good enough for pretty shoes and *Cripes!* He was stroking the busted cell in his jacket pocket.

Boss must have had a good peek and plink over her. Boss had looked but had not bit. Nor had let his kickers bite. Chris strolled by, didn't gaze, didn't sniff. To the far end of the room. He picked and touched at nothing much, fingered stuff he'd no notion what. In the meander he gave kicker Stosh a peek.

Stosh gave a snort.

Snort's good as a nod. Chris shopped some, then wandered back. No care, no goal till there he was at the 'cove where the girl was propped, showing color, style, and self.

She was not a bit. Might be one who'd do it for love or fun or if you were someone special, like what Jaycee was studying to be back... *Enough. Fuck them and Jaycee too.*

"You," he said.

She didn't blink.

"Where the hell'd you come from, you?"

"Why, you are charming!" she said, almost a little bunny song.

Close-to, she wasn't so young, thirty maybe, hiding age. Like him. Knew how, too. Kept her skills. More amazing, she still had stuff to do it. And now he sniffed, girl had an interesting stink to her. Not bad, not like him, but sweat and something else.

"You're a newson, ain't you? Fresh meat?"

"Utterly charming man."

"You a walk-in? Duster? Where you from?"

"A place you've never been." The back of his neck quivered with the look she gave him, up-and-down. She let it hang. "I found my way. My own way, yes." She leaned closer. "Do you have," her breath was clean, "*baths* here?"

Damn near snotted himself. "We do. You don't."

Again the look, the smile. "So your excuse might be…?"

"We get baths when we get water. You get water when you're worth your water. You ain't worth."

"'Worth,'" she smiled the word, "I hear that a lot."

"You're coming with me."

"And I would do that because?"

"Because I say."

She looked at the rest of the 'teria. She eyed kicker Stosh, others. Then looked again at Chris. "Are you a father?"

"What?"

"Have you ever been a father?" she said.

"I got a working pair, that's what you mean!"

Again, the look that tingled.

She's figuring! I tell her she's coming and she figures! "Look, I say 'you,' you come. I get the kicker over—him you're eyeing—he'll decide you, toot sweet. I'm jobbing for the Boss; he's the Daley here. You come with, be part and pick you up some worth maybe, maybe you get that bath and…"

On "bath" she slipped her butt off the stool and snaked out of the 'cove like a slink, like he'd dipped her from a vendor bin! "Coming?" she said.

They drew grub and drink, pulled cleaned-out breather silks. Chris dug out a pretty good flashlight, bats, and carry bags.

"Use up them bats, Harp, and I use up you!" the admin said, handing out the shit.

Chris nodded. "Give a kid a list and a lock and he grows him kicker's balls."

The girl looked at the admin boy and followed Chris.

The sun was as up as it got. Long Season might be ending— *was* ending, Boss'd said—still, clouds were thick and day was barely brighter than old-time Texas winter twilight.

"Where to, boss?" she said.

He about decked her, calling him Boss, then figured her ignorant and let it slip.

"There." Chris tipped his chin across the miles of pulvered deadland toward the ragged line of crud and masonry, toward the forever *bong-bong* that was Chicago.

They weren't 100 steps Wetward when she put it out there. "And where were you on The Day, Prince Charming?"

They made another 50, 60 steps into the deadland. "Driving bus," he said.

"Sorry, what?"

He raised his voice above the wind and pulver hiss. "I was driving my bus. Perrytown to Dolph Station."

"Oh. Not Chicago. I know Chicago." She chuckled. "Knew it when."

"Most who knew Chicago-that-was are pulver," he said a dozen steps later. He kicked ground. It rattled like old bone.

"Right you are, Mr. Driver. Most. Not all. Bet you didn't know that. There are a few left. Yep."

"Okay!"

"And you? You're from the south? Yes? Somewhere in Dixie?"

He'd known her half an hour, best. Already he cherished the memory of silence.

"Dolph Station. That's Texas."

"Huh," she started...

"Nobody hit D.S. Nobody hit Perrytown. I was between them, anyway." She drew breath. "The Panhandle! 'No Man's Land' old folks called it."

"Missed the war?"

"Maybe." He'd missed it, hadn't heard the warnings, hadn't caught the news, never saw a flash. Maybe something. Maybe the earth jumped, maybe he'd caught a flicker in the sky. Maybe he thought a thunderstorm was coming and kept looking for rain. He liked driving in rain. None came. Time they got to Perrytown, Wave One was over. No more Austin, Houston, Dallas, Galveston, no more much of anything. No TV, radio, no electric anything. Everything had gone silent, "Pulse-Dead" folks said. The Day had come and gone. He'd missed it. "Okay. Never even seen pictures."

"So all this," she spread her arms, "is just hearsay!"

And she laughed, a real nice laugh, a running brook, close to the heart. She talked too much, said shit made him want to deck her, but her laugh. He hadn't heard that in a time.

He kicked some pulver into a little whirly-wind that stirred alongside the path. "Yep. One day maybe I'll wake and find it ain't so! So, where were you on The Day?"

Slipped out. *Stupid. Stupid. Everyone asks. But everyone doing don't make a thing not stupid.*

"Right here." She pointed down. "I'm a Chicagoan and lived to tell." There was another laugh. "'Course, I never saw it, either." Just a giggle, this time. What the hell, he'd heard that giggle a million times, bunnies on the bus. Never understood it.

"'Course not," he said.

"But you? How did you get here? From Gulf…?

"Dolph."

"Dolph, Texas, then?"

"Dolph Station."

The day darkened, the air chilled. From the brightest morning in years, the clouds layered one sheet atop another. Little winds rose here and there, whirligigs of pulver climbed between them and the horizon. Not enough to raise a wraith but distance vanished. Rain coming, snudfall maybe.

He picked up the pace. "Walked," he said.

"Hm."

He gutted the urge to smack her and picked up the pace

again.

He could have told her, would have been something to do, walking. Why bother, why talk? The Walk took a year. Before that they'd waited. Waited for the government. Waited for the Long Season to end. Waited for someone to say. Month on month, night and cold, wind eternal from the north raised whole counties of Oklahoma, Colorado, Kansas. The wind rolled them down Dolph Station way. Blowing ice cut like knives, and the dust, forever dust, filled his guts.

When Chris'd been a kid, Grandpa told of dusters down in '34. Mutt Harp had seen them.

Christian Harp saw them now, living mountains of breathing black where God's blue sky and far horizons ought to be. He saw twister winds descend, bow down, lay on their sides, become miles-long rollers that sucked earth, sand, houses, lives, into the black rising giant, then drove it down, grinding, pulverizing.

They left no food or power. No cars, trucks, planes or trains. No buses. Gas was done. The wind drifted roadways, runways, railroads under—under forever. Hell, where's to go anyway? And there was Chris Harp, a roller where nothing rolled, a man without worth.

After a year, maybe more, there came a lee. A few were left. Some put wind to their backs, headed south toward the Gulf. *Fuck that.* Chris had seen the Gulf pissed-off! He and the worthless rest, a hundred, maybe more, headed into the wind, Panhandle to the Chicago Waste, east and north a thousand miles, maybe more.

They walked another year of Long Season. Nobody knew *what* but winter had come forever. Along the way there'd been a dozen dusters, dusters that stretched as far as there was of east and west across the night dark plains of No Man's Land.

The Walkers knew the storm was always with them, knew there only was *one* storm, that monster who lived in the earth and waited for the wind to wake it. They hid from the worst and walked in calms between, but even when the beast lay down, there was no stillness, just a dark moan that rolled, and kept rolling until the beastie rose and filled a walker with Himself. Dust pneumonia, they called it, dust cancer, sometimes. Touched by it, you kept going or you didn't. Most didn't. No heroes in the walk. How many reached the Wastes? Of the hundred? Five, six? He didn't know. He didn't know them. They were just dust on foot, just them that hadn't dropped. He was one.

Fuckem all.

"And?" she asked again.

"What? Nothing. Winter came and didn't end. Grub was gone so we walked. Took a year. Most died."

"You didn't."

"Apparently."

"I see." She walked. "After Wave One, you walk out of Texas to Chicago?"

"Pretty much."

"And on your way you dined upon?"

"Thistle. Butter. Rabbit."

"Thistle…"

"What you call tumbleweed. Russian thistle! You never…?"

"Butter…"

"Never took roach butter…?

She swallowed a puke.

"Rabbit's rabbit! You never seen a Jack stamp?"

"Jack?"

"Rabbit!"

"A jackrabbit stamp?"

"Pede. Stampede!"

"Bunnies on the run? A fearsome sight I'd bet."

What she don't know, he thought.

Chris and the girl pointed noses toward the *bong-bongs*. They crossed from Center turf into the deadlands. *Funny,* he thought, *just this morning, I thought to find that bong-bong's reason...*

The air was clear enough so that jagged stump of the Monadnock and a few other buildings marked the Heath and Hollows on a hazy horizon. Señor Temoco, he'd find them, sure.

Thinking *bong-bong* and deadlands, Chris considered the rebar bolt that had fluttered out of the 'Tween place and buried itself up to its sheet-tin fletching in the meat of Lenny the kicker's leg. The day had been a common one in a quiet time. Then someone shouts, "Incoming!" Head's-up, Lenny throws the Boss aside. There's a meaty thunk could be heard forever and Lenny's scream tops it all and there's Lenny, his good left leg—his kicking leg—pinned to the standing part of a fallen wall. Lenny's wails went on until the Boss dusted off and shut him down. *Len had nuts, say that!* The rest followed: a dozen shift-work scrabblers and a handful of newsons hung around, leaning and licking lips at the looking while the bolt's hacksawed then drawed out of Lenny's meat. All of them were thinking *who'll dip what of the kicker's stuff when he gives it up?*

He didn't give it. The Boss cut and drew the bolt, his own hands, Chris, sitting on Lenny's legs as Lenny bucked. Ribbed steel pulls out rough. Still, he made it through.

Now there they were, Chris and this girl, walking plain across the land from whence the bolt had come. *Señor Temoco hadn't fired that bolt. Not he, himself, pretty sure. Someone out here jerking off, was all. 'Tweeners, Niggertown kinks.*

"Tell me more about your walkabout?" Chris jolted off his think about rebar bolts, the casual jerking off of 'Tweeners, Señor Temoco, about the box to come and about that plump and fragrant girl critter herself who'd just jolted him!

"Quiet," he said quietly, "'Tweeners," he added to be nice. She stayed quiet for three steps.

22

"'Tween...?"

"Shh."

Another step.

"Okay. What's tha—

"Sh!"

"...that gong?" she whispered.

"You'll tell me," he whispered back, "being a Chicagoite and all, you tell me what's been out here bonging, long as I remember."

She listened for a few steps. "Well..."

"Hsht..." he said.

"...wind, loose metal, maybe... something...

"Sh," he said.

"'Sh' why?" she started.

"Shh the fuck up is why!" He shouted his whispers now. He stopped long enough to give her one good plink, let her know it meant a busted lip, maybe, if she didn't *Shh* real good. He didn't like stopping here: deadlands, 'Tweeners, *bong-bongs*, hell! Yeah, he was thinking 'Tweeners scared hissowndamnself! And he wished he had the Boss's way with plinking looks and steely nerve!

Out came that wet little laugh. She raised her hands in surrender and took the lead, patted his shoulder as she passed.

That shit never happened to the Boss.

Hell, maybe there ain't *no 'Tweeners by.*

With her ahead the walk went quiet. The ground beneath, they moved inside a gray dome, chill dark above and nothing all 'round. Easy walking, but when Chris figured it noonish, he was ready for a breather. *Old,* he thought, near *old at least.* "Grunts," he said—too loud—and slipped his pack by a hollow drop. The Girl perched her rump on a heap of brick and stared at the grub from her pack.

"What's..." she started.

"Sh, don't," he said. *Doesn't recognize butter. Didn't know thistle, never heard of jack. What the hell's she been grunting since The Day?* If she didn't know roach, he wasn't going to explain roach, not here. *The noise alone*, he thought.

"Don't eat it, you don't want it."

She dipped a yarrow leaf in the pale yellow paste then touched it with her tongue.

"Ah. Lovely," she said. "For the conversation portion of the meal you'll tell me more of your hero's journey?"

Torqued his jaw. "No, you'll tell me. Don't know butter, don't know thistle. Don't know much of nothing. Where the hell you been?"

"Why am I alive?"

"You might could start there."

"That is what it means, yes? 'Where were you on The Day?' means 'How come so-and-so's dead and you're not?'" A moment's quiet. A gear shifted behind her eyes and she slipped the distance between them, sat at his feet. She was warm. He felt her warmth through his leggings and slacks. Her eyes were green.

"On The Day, I was in the Deep Tunnel. You're not from here, okay. The Deep Tunnel was an engineering project, to cut flooding, keep effluents out of the Lake."

He stared.

"Think sewer!" she said.

"You was in a sewer when."

"Think *big* sewer. Think *really* big sewer! Think Gargantua, King Kong, Godzilla. The Triple Trump in Vegas. Think that. The Deep is tunnels 40 feet in diameter, 400 feet down there." She pointed to the ground. "Two hundred and seven point three miles of tunnel. That's a world down there.

"The Tunnel was going to keep Lake Michigan clean… where we got our drinking water, Chicago, back then. Thing was begun…" She squinted. The squint was kind of sweet. "I don't know project history. I was engineering assistant to a Commissioner, Metropolitan Water Reclamation District. They started digging in 1980. By The Day, the thing had spread about everywhere there was under the City. Probably below us, right here."

"So, so! On The Day?"

"So on The Day. I was adjacent to one of the South Calumet catchments, four hundred and twenty eight feet below grade wrapped in solid limestone and damn near Indiana. My Commissioner, world-class cocksucker that he was, you see, knew it was coming, The Day. Well, everybody did! Didn't we all? I mean, it was in the air, right? There was this feeling, the whole race had it, the big kill off, 'Let's just get it done, do it, right now!' You know?

He did not.

"I mean, more or less. You did? I mean, you felt it in the air?"

He'd not.

"Well my guy, Commissioner Cocksucker Michael Acciari, was prepared! One of the few. Well, he had the chops for it. I mean, give a man a 7-billion-dollar hole in the ground, he can hide a few private scratches.

"Mike had a whole side section excavated, sealed, finished, provisioned—the works—water, food, fuel, tools, books, *movies*. Civilization enough for a hundred people for 20 years! More." She was panting. "A little world. And all for himself." Her eyes locked on Chris. "And a friend."

He couldn't see in the near dark but he knew those green eyes were wet.

"So. We're working, doing what we do, Monday-through. Suddenly Mike's 'going to the field' he says, 'contractor needs verification, yadda, yadda.' And I, I don't know from The Day because it's just another day, it's work, and I don't know the end of the world's in motion and I go with my Commissioner because that's what I do and he needs me to verify, for the record, a testament, you know, attest to the fucking record to bring before the Board of Commissioners." Her voice dropped. "The Goddamn humping mother records and the board of socktucking Commissioners. You know? And that's where we are. Specifically, that's where I am and Commissioner Cocksucker is on The Day—at the Moment that day became *The* Day and it all went! You know? Dead. I am checking flow rate, one catchment to another and, boom. It went.

"Ever hear a nuclear detonation a couple dozen miles away through 428 feet of limestone?"

Chris stared.

"Don't. Bad for the sinuses. Feels like you opened the door on Mars 2. One big suck, then slam! Like an underwater explosion. The pressure blasts up your skull like it's the inside of a hydraulic ram and someone shoved the drive pipe up your ass."

"Underwater! Yeah!" Chris said.

"When you realize you really are alive, you notice everything's dark and dead and has been for, well, since that first big suck. And you're there, alone, at the bottom of the world. Alone meaning him and you, Cocksucker Adam and Ms. Fucking Eve. Which has been his thinking all along. Stick to the books, kids: I was hired out of IIT, third in my class, to be fucking Eve. Emphasis on, well, you know?"

He was noticing her wet green eyes when the 'Tweeners showed.

He smelled before he heard. He caught the whiff around the time he remembered underwater thunder from his dream-memory. Deadlands were full of every which-kind of stink, so he didn't think too much about this stench until scrapes and grunts started coming from the shade and haze, Wetward. Without a "shh" he wrapped his arm around her neck and covered her mouth with his gloved mitt. She wiggled and blew snot but caught on when he eased them into a quiet slide down a dozen feet of shattered brick and pulver into a cellar hole. At bottom was a three-foot drop into the muck. It oozed but didn't splash and he shoved her against what had been a basement wall five years back.

It had been years since he'd had to duck and cover from slinking scum—thank the Center's kickers—but it came back. He pressed them to the tangled roots sprouted from the wall. She'd *shh'd.*

The 'Tweeners were having a good old time, no trail discipline, probably hadn't reckoned anyone but themselves being in the 'lands. Cripes, he should have heard them a good half-minute earlier but he'd tuned to the girl being fucked on The Day or whatever. The 'Tweeners were talking some shit he didn't, *greaser, nigger, Polack! Walking burnups, Christ...* Who knew what they talked or what twitched their nads, if nads they had?

They passed in shadows above. Chris knew more than he could see. Dreams and imaginings filled them in, made the picture whole. "They live to fuck witcha!" the Boss had said. Hate a Wrigleytowner for his airs, a greasy Mex from the Heaths and Hollows, maybe, bastard Soxers, absolutely! But 'Tweeners? Well, you deal. Hell, they're there to fuck you, fuck you good so you fuck them sure! Chris knew they had no teeth—or just a few, but them few filed sharp as hell! He knew they were more scar than skin, and never enough limbs, no hair except white and straggling thin stuff here and there. Eyes? A few. That he knew though he'd never seen. Among 'Tweeners, Chris knew the Boiler would have been a pretty man, his smile, Christmas jolly, his laugh, sugar sweet! That much Chris knew. Now, he strained to see.

Shadows passed, above. The clouds had thickened in the

nooning of the day and the dark was near to night. No matter what the Boss said about the Long Season, today was dark, cold, and Seasonable!

One, angles and humps, stopped near the edge above. He stirred the air and shouted a whiskery hush. The stench it spread, the sound it kicked from gut and throat gave Chris the willies. Then it waited, stumps on hips, like a Boss, while the others slid their shit. Spalls and bits of pulver rolled down on them. Under 'Tweener babble was a rolling crush. They were moving something big.

Bolt-shooter. Bolt shooter, yes.

The girl wiggled under his hand and pointed. A dozen yards along the wall, the brick showed black. A cut, a hidey hole maybe. They worked toward it. Four yards, six… Chris's eyes on the 'Tweener by the edge.

Boss, Chris figured. *Watches them others do the work.* Caught himself. A plink like that! He wanted to punch himself! Decided to wait.

The black crack in the cellar wall had been a coal bin. They eased inside. Waited. The 'Tweener's grunts and giggles seemed farther off, had less edge, but they were there, still passing.

Took time before he realized the girl had been punching his arm. Her eyes were wide and white, her face dark. "Yeah, well," he whispered and eased the pressure on her mouth and nose.

She sucked air.

'Least she breathes quiet!

Time hung. There was noise. Some noise. He couldn't see worth shit, *stuck down here, what the hell, what the hell to do… You almost choke her? Responsibility!* His responsibility. He felt himself shaking.

She tapped his arm again, held a small thing under his nose. Took a second, dark as it was, but no shit, a watch! No band, just a round old watch. Its face glowed dull green.

"Five minutes!" she mouthed the words against his ear, pointed to the dial. The tick, tick, ticks were loud in close—like that news show he never watched. He stared at the damn thing like it was a blessed TV Johnnie, itself; couldn't take his eyes off. The ghost-thin hand swept the dial like he hadn't seen one do since, cripes, since forever. Five years. No! Longer! Not since Grandpa Mutt's Waltham-Ball Railroad watch with the radium dial! Little gears and springs unwinding. Mutt once pried the back off, showed him. One thing moving another on that windy watch! Windy watch still worked; mechanics, not batteries, something you could see move, no magic crap. The minute hand flowed, disengaged from the 7, headed into space toward 8.

The rolling crush of the 'Tweeners' passing peaked, grew faint as the glowing hand crept. In three minutes the noise was near gone. Four minutes and it was. The rot-meat stink of the 'Tweeners thinned, the hiss of pulver tumbling down the bank dissolved to wind-sigh as the last seconds passed and the hand touched, then covered the 8.

"Okay?" she breathed.

"What?" Close her smell was different. "Yeah."

He leaned out of the coalhole. Not a sound, nothing moved.

"Shall we?" she breathed.

He held up his hand. He was, by God, gonna let naught happen! That was sure! "You wait. I slither," he said with his hands.

"My hero," she whispered.

Up he slithered. He was still a fair creeper but it took breath. He was winded by the time he peeked the lip. No denying, he was getting on. On the deadland flats, the world was a close ring of pulver and busted brick. In the few minutes they'd been below, the sky had darkened and the gray dome around them had narrowed. Two new tracks cut the dust where he stood. The 'Tweeners—five, six of them—had rolled or shoved something large and heavy by.

When she touched his shoulder it about sent his spine through the top of his head! "Gone?" she said.

"Hsshh," he hissed and snatched hold of her.

"Gone?" she mouthed.

He looked at the narrowing world around them. "Guess."

"What was that they were pushing?"

"Cross', I reckon."

"Cross'..."

"Big crossbow dealy!"

She shook her head.

"They set them up and shoot bolts into where there's folks. For fuck's sake. Pins someone, sometimes, mostly not."

"Those people made a ballista?" she said.

"What?"

"'Big crossbow dealy,'" she said. "A Roman thing. They built a ballista just to harass your group?"

He stared at the path.

She looked around in the haze. "So? Which way?"

"Well," he said. "Well."

"You have a compass?"

"Well, we find where we was and I figure where from there."

They backed along the edge of the hollow and the girl suddenly perked. "There!" she pointed.

Their packs lay by the tracks of that—what'd she call it? A ballster? Before he could say, "shh," she was running to them like a tip-toed coyote.

The thought hit him like thunder. 'Tweeners passed. They'd seen their stuff.

She snatched up her pack, turned, and her eyes went wide.

Saved his worth. Realization—and the 'Tweener—kicked him in the nuts at about the same time. Nut-pain, fierce and chilly, shriveled him blind! He dropped like a shot as a hollow whoosh from a length of pipe moaned the air over his head. The world was a dusty sudden mouthful. He rolled, grabbed himself best as he could, reached for whatever. Life could be over in three, four seconds and he worried over his nuts! All that growing and school, hanging with the guys and Jaycee, driving bus, the walk to Chicago—everything he saw, did, knew and wanted, done forever.

He skittered sidewise.

The pipe whooshed again.

He'd been out of the swim for a time, this kind of thing. The big 'Tweener's stink gagged him as he grabbed dirt, reached for rock, brick, anything to hand for a weapon! Nads hurt like he'd never known nad-hurt. His eyes wouldn't stay sharp and his gut wanted to ralph every chew he'd grunted that week. Topping that, he heard the Boss saying how much this trip was worth, his only pair of nuts and all...

Another bass whoosh and a thud as the 'Tweener's pipe smacked pulver where his head had been. Things moved too fast for figuring. *Keep moving, stay lucky! That's enough.* The critter-man trying to nut or brain him was a blur of greasy gut, a pair of bare legs, a quick blink at mismatched chukka boots (no socks), grub-white flesh, smooth like a baby's. Rolling past, his eye caught a scratch on the critter's right ankle. Small. An "ah shit" thing you might could get brushing a rock. How'd he notice that?

Another whoosh!

Didn't know. His head pounded. *Head pain from a shot to the nuts, what the hell...?*

He rolled...

Hollow whoosh, muffled thud... The 'Tweener grunted. Chris felt its breath, smelled its sweat.

Roll! ...and the world skewed sideways. *Keep grabbing for...* A brick swept by as he twisted in pulver that filled his nose, mouth, eyes, ears. He grabbed.

Missed.

Another stinking oink and the pipe shattered the brick Chris had missed. Broken shards sprayed the back of his head, nicked his ear, caught the corner of his right eye. *How long?* Chris wondered as he tried to roll upright, gain a weapon, stay off target. *How long do I stay lucky?*

It *was* luck! Scary. He'd never been a lucky son-of-a—

The world buzzed like an alarm clock. Life went herringbone...

...and she was standing over him. Then kneeling. She touched him. His face was numb where it didn't hurt like hell. A glancing blow, like they say, otherwise he'd be dead.

...and he was still dodging. The girl was talking but he was twisting, rolling. Finally, he snagged a pair of bricks, rolled to his feet, stood ground, looked every way for the 'Tweener, the 'Tweener's moaning pipe, and what the hell, there was the girl and she? She was standing over a pile of skin and cloth, blood and white thin hair. It was over. Then she had him by the elbow, steering, carrying both their packs!

"Wait, Goddamn, wait!" It was the top of a whisper. Chris tried to stay with her, keep his bearings, not let every 'Tweener in the deadlands know they'd survived. When he got moving on his own she let go his arm. She took off like a rabbit into the pulver mist a dozen yards ahead, leaving the probably dead 'Tweener at the edge of the basement hollow. *Hell, she done him; girl done a 'Tweener!* He knew he hadn't; hadn't even seen him, except for that little cut. *And now she's running*, probably, toward the Wet, toward the Monadnock.

The whole thing? Ten minutes. Less, he guessed: one or two, sliding and slinking, five waiting, another couple, three him damn near getting cocked stupid by a 'Tweener ambuscade! Ten minutes ago they'd been having a bite. Now his nuts throbbed, the side of his face was starting to buzz, and she's running. What for? Not for life!

He caught up, grabbed her arm. "Wait!" he whispered. She spun toward him and...

The world came back into focus. He was on the ground. She was leaning over him again. He hated the taste of pulver. "Cripes," was all he had.

Her voice chittered. "Collateral damage. It's instinct. Jesus on a stick!" She snuffled, "World War's what, five years old, and I just now make my second kill?" She offered her hand. "Almost my third. Sorry. Not a good American, I guess." She was babbling. She looked at his face, touched it. "Look, as Big as it is, there's not a lot going on in the Tunnel. Once you fuel the gennies, clear the vents, clean the filters, make sure the batteries are charging, there's not a lot to do for the day except walk past each other from time to time and get ideas. We had different ideas, Mike and I.

"Anyway, he'd made sure there was a gym. Important his Eve keep fit. Me, that is. I did. Unarmed combat Blu-rays were to my taste. I learned a lot. In theory. Mike had other tastes." She pulled Chris to his feet. "Don't like being grabbed, I'm sorry. Mike found out." She shivered, looked at her hand. "That's irony," she said.

He didn't ask any more. Her "plump" was mostly muscle.

The *bong-bongs* were close.

"Funny," he said. He winced. Talk hurt. "Woke this morning thinking 'I'd like to find out about that...'" His face hurt as much as his nuts. His nuts felt better, though. The over-sky was still swirly black, but the air had settled some. No wraiths. No static. Good seeing was a hundred, hundred and fifty yards. In the last quarter mile, the ground had flattened. Blast and firestorm had blown it all to flinders, reduced the residue to ash, left only pulver ground and basement holes and they walked a graveyard of neatly spaced holes.

"Man," she said, "that's, I don't know, it's familiar."

"What?"

"That gong! Jesus. Drive you nuts or what?"

"Been there's long as I been here. Almost don't notice it no more."

"Like living near the 'L'"

"Like?"

"Never mind. That tone. It's so..."

The ground was rising.

"Fifteen minutes," she said.

"What?"

"That." She cocked her chin at the *gong-gong*. "Every fifteen minutes. Four *per* hour." She looked at the watch. "Like clockwork."

"Someone keeping time?"

She shrugged.

"So it ain't wind..."

"That is *really* familiar," she said.

"Coming up on something," he said.

The rising ground resolved into a gray mass that blocked the way.

"The Kennedy," she said. "I-90, I-94. Collapsed."

A solid ridge of blasted concrete and fused metal, eight, nine stories high, stretched north to south as far as sight took them. The highway supports had dissolved in the blast, girding, signs, arches had evaporated, been blown away. Roadways, clover leafs, on-ramps, interchanges, overpasses, vehicles and people had tumbled, pancaked, one atop the other. What had been a highway was a gray-green range of cliffs. Rivulets of black water emerged from it, caught the dim light. The runoff chattered and rippled. Here and there waterfalls cascaded from halfway up the face.

"What's sourcing that?" she said.

He shook his head but she was talking to herself.

"Artesian? Hydrostatic pressure?" She was shaking her head.

"You wanted a bath!"

"Smell. You don't bathe in that," she said, "you test for it. Come on, this is your trip."

Smelled like too-long dead.

Took a nasty hour, meaty water washing their feet most of the way. Mosses and wild toadstools had gone to grip along the seeps and runoffs. The slick masses, inches thick in places, made the climb difficult, made Chris look clumsy. Here and there, the ground gave way as fissures opened or the cliff face collapsed inward. Echoes of falling debris came back. Lousy stinks oozed from the interior.

Just short of the top, a crevasse six, seven feet wide cut their way. From what seemed deeper darkness came a hollow rush of distant running water interlaced with questionable splashes, chatterings. A yawning groan sounded as Chris leaned over to look.

"Like a mama lion with cubs."

"Don't wonder at it," she said. "I spent five years below. There are things you want to stay away from."

Chris gave the expressway a good plink. "Guess we'll work back a ways," he started.

The girl landed easily on the other side. "'S okay. Just a long step, really." She held out her hand.

He hardened his plink on her. "I wasn't asking. I said we scout another way."

She reached a little farther.

The jump *was* easier than it looked, even for a guy near fifty. He didn't need her help!

"By the way," she said, "what's down there? They want to stay away from you too."

As they neared the top the clouds opened some and Chris's shadow preceded him. The air cleared. For a good three minutes, it stayed that way. What had been a river cut along the base of the Kennedy ridge. Ahead, hollow ponds caught daylight like silver paddies. Bright pools dotted the landscape, north and east. The stump of the Monadnock and other masonry ruins rose from the waters like jagged islands. Between the ponds and the buildings spread flat heaths of brown and green.

The *bong* tolled from the peak of a shattered building directly across the river from where they stood. The sound gained detail. Each peal arose from a soft impact, not metal on metal like bell and clapper. Each stroke quivered pure but ended as a ragged buzz that emerged from under the main tone.

"*Turandot!*" the girl said. "I knew it was familiar. The gong!" She pointed to the source. "It's the Lyric Opera's *Turandot* gong. I saw it a year before The Day. They—whoever they are—hauled that thing up and mounted it on top of what's left of the Civic Opera House."

The gong was a good fifteen feet in diameter and hung from a frame. When the man struck the quarter hour the sound reached them a good two seconds after. "A half-mile," she said quietly. Her voice quivered.

They stared, gathering the sight. Not wanting to.

"Hm," he said.

The thing wielded by the ringer *was* soft, and for the first few strokes, still alive.

A dozen or more people surrounded the gong and frame. Men, women, hard to see detail, harder to figure what the hell.

"What are they?" she said.

"What you think?" he said. "Yep. Taking pieces. Just what you think."

The shattering buzz that lingered on the end of each tone was a voice. Next toll, he thought, the voice would be different.

The ringer would probably use up his hammer.

"But what…?"

"Religion, I guess," Chris said.

The girl ralphed.

She is *a girl*, Chris thought.

A rubble dam blocked the slow dark river upstream from their position. The nearest crossing was directly below.

They waited for sinking light to pitch shadow darkness across the Wetward face of I-90/94. Even in near dark, the descent was easier than the climb. Two toll cycles and they'd reached the ford. Day was falling into the west and the girl was squirrelly to be away, far as possible, from the *bong-bong.*

"Religion?" she spit it. And took off.

The pour began when they'd cleared the river and skirted the Opera Tower. The gongs never slacked through the Wet, marked each quarter hour with certainty. They pressed until the Opera was in the dark, then they sheltered in the base of a building that rose from one of the mossy heaths and a now-gray, rain-pocked pond.

"Willis Tower," the girl said. "Maybe not. Hard to tell." Chris wiggled his toes and thanked his socks, the Old Guy.

The girl shook. From the walk, the kill, the climb, the *bong-bongs* from the Opera? Chris didn't know. Maybe she was cold, tired. Who could tell about girls?

The pour became a downpour, the downpour wanted to be snow then damn near was. Each dirty drop, a slushy mud ball, fell hard. They sheltered in a stairway landing above a basement pond that stank of green rot. Looked pretty from on high and in the light. Girders overhead sagged like candles in July. Chris dipped a metalized polyfiber tarp from his pack and strung it over them. The snudfall drops drummed inches from their heads. It was true dark, now. She was there. He could smell her, feel warmth, hear her... *What the hell? Crying.*

Chris didn't like where masonry remained: the flash-black walls were thick with white niter, bearded with pale roothairs curled into a near-living mat. Leaves and stems bound the shattered foundation, held it against falling in. The walls chattered and crackled, as they did at the Center, elsewhere. Goddamn, he'd eat the butter of them but would not to see the critters, did not want them to touch! Sheltering in these living shells on the Long Walk, Chris had felt the spooks in the ruins. As a newson, sleeping unclaimed and rough, he thought the City was haunted by those evaporated on The Day. Night brought dreams, that much he knew. The folk he carried living in his head, Mom and Daddy, the guys, Jaycee, others, dragged their clean bright pasts from his dark and dirty now. Came to life as he slept, clawed the walls.

What an ass I was! He looked at the darkness where the girl was. *An ass and likely still remain.*

She squeaked, a mostly quiet little noise, unheard, but by him. He felt her jump, knew she was looking wide. "What's..." she started.

"Sh." He dared a moment's drain of the Center's batteries. Yellow light flickered on the wall. Where they'd always been, what they always were, the ghosts of Chicago, of the days past The Day: palm-long roaches, fist-thick 'pedes, their million footfalls rustling hairy white roots.

"Oh," she said and scooted from the wall. He saved the bats. "Okay," she said. The next bonging peal rasped over them. "Okay, here's the deal," she said. "That Adam and Eve thing Commissioner Mike was thinking? Didn't work. Not with him. In retrospect, not a bad notion, what with racial suicide and all, but not with him. Anyway, he's gone and his little Eden 400 feet below world's end? It's still operational, still stocked, still enough of everything there for hundreds." There was a moment's quiet.

"For now it's empty."

"Yeah?" he said.

"It is. Yes."

He might have been shaking. "So, you what? You have any suck down there?"

"Suck?"

"Weed? Cripes, smoke? Cigarettes?"

Her liquid chuckle came from the dark. "Sorry," she said. "He didn't smoke. Neither do I."

"Oh."

"So?"

Cripes, Chris thought, *she ain't going to ask...?*

"Look, I came up to see if there might be someone. You know?"

He knew. She touched him, in the dark. What the Boss had said? What? *"What's done with the goods, here to there, that's your lookout."* What did that mean? Shit. Deciding was never his strong suit.

"I mean," she said, "you have a better offer?"

He thought. *Hard, this kind of stuff.* He touched the cell in his jacket pocket, keyed his number, the number of home. Just a thing, a meaningless thing.

"You know," he said, "all along that walk from Dolph Station to here, I kept seeing Walking Will."

"Walking...?"

"Will. Grampa talked about him. Something folks saw in Dust Bowl times: this old guy who walked the world giving warning, gettin' rides, jumpin' out. Saying stuff. One thing Grampa said he'd yell: 'Drink! Drink for the thirst to come!' No idea what it meant except maybe 'Fill up now cause tomorrow you go dry!' I dunno. Maybe that and something more. Maybe..."

He could only smell her, feel her touch. "One thing I been

wondering," he said to the dark. "What's that smell?"

Silence. "What?"

"That smell. You got a smell."

The water-running laugh again. "Chanel," she said.

"Chanel. Okay. I got to tell you stuff," he said. He could feel her waiting. "I got hiddens, a lot of hiddens. First, I'm older'n I look. I'm 47. I look younger and I let on I am."

He went on. Told her everything there was. Everything he'd wanted to say but didn't for five long years, maybe longer. That was that.

Snudfall stopped. They struck out for the Monadnock stump. An easy half-mile and they were there. The *bongs* behind them, every fifteen minutes, still buzzed with screams but they were behind.

The Monadnock was a gutted shell. The Heath and Hollows people? People. Mex's mostly. Chris was used to Mex's. Like home.

First, the people wanted to string them up, him and the girl, grab their worth. Like at the Center when newbies oozed in all strange. "*Al carillón, al carillón,*" they shouted.

"Señor Temoco!" Chris yelled. "We got Daley business with Señor Temoco!"

Down they were put for a few dark minutes, everyone muttering, plinking hard. Then there came Señor. Heard him before he saw him, a little *squeak-squeak, squeak-squeak* and the Mex's parted sharp. Out of the shadows rolled Señor, a fat man on a chair, a legless fat man on a chair with wheels, big wheels, rolling on the paths across the pulver that had been packed down smooth for him. *Squeak-squeak.* The chair was topped with torches dripping burning fat or tallow. Puddles of liquid fire trailed back the way he came.

Chris laughed when he caught on. He wanted to slap

someone's back—the Boss's back for a matter of fact—and shout out, "Why hell, that's the best I've heard since The Day! You'll know him by his bearing! His Goddamned burned out bearing!"

Squeak-squeak, squeak... And the Señor stopped and was looking, his eyes bright flames behind ridges of fat. He looked at the girl, plinked Chris, looked at the girl again and licked a lip.

"Señor Temoco," Chris said.

"*Jefe*," the Señor said, little sharp gleams behind the eye fat.

"*Jefe*," Chris said, "I'm here from the Boss, my Daley from the Center, to pick up a thing he says you got. A box he says. This big." He showed.

"This is arranged, yes," *Jefe* said.

From behind Señor Temoco's chair came a guy. The guy carried a small wooden box. A box like the Boss had said. The box buzzed a long drawn-out humm that never drew breath.

Chris smiled and made his trade. The smile was not deep.

"'Spected you yesterday." The Boss looked at him like he'd forgotten something. "What's your name?"

"Harp. Chris Harp."

"Harp." The boss looked him up and down. At the mud, the blood, the pipe-smacked face, gone to shit. "Fun out there, Angel?"

"Some."

"And?"

"Box." Chris handed the buzzing thing to the Boss. He'd kept it clean all the way back.

"Yeah." He handed it to Lenny. "Leonard?"

"Yeah," Lenny said.

"Something for our Angel Harp here."

Lenny tucked the box under his arm. Passed Chris a hand of smoke, a full pack of suck. *Marlboro.* Cellophane, tab and all.

Twenty weeds sealed. A week of suck.

"Lenny," Boss said.

"Right," and he was off with the box.

"Wonder what that is, do you?"

Chris looked after Lenny. The old kicker was gimping toward the old United stadium half-a-mile 'burbward, No-one's place.

"The future, Boss?"

The Boss smiled. Put his hand on Chris's shoulder. "Hell, probably not. Just bees. Some say they're necessary. Well, you gotta try, right? You're wondering, 'Was it a good trade?'"

Chris kept eyes on Lenny until he disappeared into the dark and pulver mist. "Not so much."

"Stop by my table tomorrow. Have a bite." Boss said. "Fresh meat."

The Icehouse was dark and stinking. He'd missed night thistle. *Better grunts coming, anyway!*

He'd missed TV Johnny. That hurt.

He climbed his tier. Second from the top. His muscles ached. Near fifty. Still looked forty. Good. He still could climb but fifty's coming. *Me, an old guy! Imagine that!* Still. Climbing was... nothing to it. He stepped on the Mex's meaty paw. Guy grunted like he's gut-kicked. Fuck him. This might could be his last night of being too, too high on this particular shitpile. Boss'd hinted; Boss said: good trade. And he touched him, gave him a name. Cripes. Luck. Maybe he was lucky.

He eased into the sack, slipped off boots, slipped off socks—tucked them in his pockets, one each side. Careful. Jacket off, shirt, there he was, not looking forward but here he was with a night to go, facing them: the living of his dreams.

The bunk above was empty, the One-Eyed Kid from Nowhere was nowhere. That's the way. No point thinking about. Whitey'd been his name.

It had been?

He thought about darkness for a little. Darkness was close. From the walls around came the chatter of the 'pedes, the roaches' crackle. At least his bunk wasn't by the wall. It hadn't been a bad couple days! Been to the Wet and back. Seen the *bong-bongs*. He'd met that girl and did what he had to, his job. She said her name, but it did not bother him. No. Had a job and he'd done it: brought the box. She'd not be in his living nights, there to kick his dreams. No. Let someone in, that's someone there to lose. He'd told her all, given his hiddens. *Now she's gone,* and the Boss had touched him! Invited him to grunts tomorrow! Cripes, worth-up. And smokes! Holy Cripes, that's how Goddamn good the days had been: he scored suck and hadn't remembered. Luck. Still, he wished: *Wish I could have gotten that* tick-tock *watch.* Would have been...

Wouldn't have been right. Señor Temoco's by rights. *Shit,* he'd wanted to tell her about the jack stamp on the Walk; always wanted to tell someone but hell that was just an old folk's tale. Sometimes you had to step back a little, see how much one thing or another... something to think on later when you couldn't do nothing else. And maybe someday when he was old, he'd find that hole, the Big Hole where were lights and movies and...

He was slipping, now. In his sleep, he fingered the cell. Keyed the number, *the* number. Home. What would he ask? If someone answered? What should... He almost couldn't keep the days, the times he'd had, in mind—and he wanted to! No! Christ. That's the thing. Close it all! *Pray, maybe.* The dead cell, the silence of home filled him. He held on. If he could remember something else about how he'd spent... He'd seen the Wet. Seen the Hollows... Seen Walkin' Will... No, no. He just told of him. And he'd had a choice? Not so good that... He'd had a job. He'd said what? Old Will'd said, "Drink! Drink for the thirst to come!" *What the hey?* There was something else that could've meant! *No,* he thought, *no. Don't sleep. You sleep, you'll dream.* Those dreams of the living, of Dolph Station and Jaycee Dogton, Tex, Marty, the others, the living. By then, day had bled away and Chris Harp of Johnny's Icehouse slept. The dream-day was bright blue and gold and went on, oh God, forever, a summer day and mild, mild weather, a day like no other...

ROOT SOUP, WINTER SOUP

Cordelia and trees. She saw in the still water of the pond her silly old face and no one else. That funny old face smiled up. She wiggled her finger in the cold water and Cordelia was alone, excepting the trees. Leaves floated lazy, half on top, half under the water, hardly drifting. Afternoon air was cool, heading to cold. Cold nights were coming.

Soon them leaves'll be cotched up and froze-in, she knew. *Cotched good.* The pond would be an ice sheet, then covered with fallen things, leaves, acorns and little branches, more leaves and other goods as fell. *A person don't know it's there might could fall right in,* she thought. Well, she knew it was there. The critters that wandered there for a drink knew it too. They would have to *tap, tap* by hoof or claw on the icy shell to water there. Soon after they'd eat snow or perish to the thirst. She knew that.

The pond water stilled and there was that old Cordelia face again, minnows swimming through. Why, there she was. Couldn't see the scars, not like when she looked in a peering glass. No. Could see how one eye was a little sagged, could see her funny crookback nose, could see...

"Oh fuss!" she said. *What's the point? His season's over. He is gone and done with and good riddance to him.* He who'd given her that eye, that nose, that curly lip.

She stirred the water again, chased the face away. Her minnies scattered. She laughed.

Walking, Cordelia gathered the wooly hunting jacket around herself. *Real cold coming.* Time, indeed, for her root soup, her winter soup. She looked forward to the good smells as filled her cabin, winters. She wanted to run and do it quick, hug the comfort, the wonder of the forever pot, the pot going down with eating, the pot filled up again with bits added, an essence from the stock pot, more chopped roots and other pieces from the cellar. The forever pot of root soup, God's good winter warmth.

Another year and no one found her morel patch, where it lay sprouting. The season's 'shrooms had been fine and plentiful, big headed, tender and clean-grown through the rot. And all hers for taking. A time gone, someone had felled a stand of tree where the morels sprouted now. Someone building, maybe. *Someone who give up and moved on,* she figured. Maybe a long time gone. New growth had sprouted since and filled around the wasted logs.

Good. This season hundreds more morels had spread across the moldering stumps, between old cut-and-fallen logs. A thousand more had spread onto the damp forest floor where decay made a wet and fragrant bed.

She'd shown that hunter, but none had found the place on their own, not a one. None would.

The season was over. *Cold come, picking done,* she thought. Even these last smelled good as she added them to her sack. Long things, they were, thick-brained and heavy with wet.

The roadway parsnips she'd cultivated another place back in the deep woods. They, too, had a good season. Each fat root had burrowed way down. Rich they were within the earth, their long finger-ends reached deep; deep hairy roots spread wide, held place in the ground. They didn't want to come up and out, but up and out they'd come and she'd stocked her cellar.

Cordelia loved the burlap's prickle on her shoulder, like a game bag swinging with her walk, heavy with her potatoes, onions, her carrots and 'snips. Near home, now, with the last of the season's sweet things heavy in her bag, Cordelia couldn't wait to make a start. The chopping was first, a long part of it, but the heart of winter soup. Scrubbing, making it clean for the stock. The careful scraping, paring and cutting, the pieces shaped just right for the pot, the broth, the savor of the thing, each thickness, just right to release its flavor.

God loved good soup and Cordelia made a good, good winter soup.

At home, now, she stoked the stove with seasoned logs, last year's cut. She built sweet, laid the bed for slow, steady heat. She watched as the old logs, the large ones that had lain in porchway shade through summer and early fall, caught flame by their ends and barks. Daddy-leggers scampered into the fire's winking hell, spiders twitched and ran, old cocoons opened wiggling. Not nice, maybe, but all those little lives, she figured, added to the savor, gave favor to the scent, the earthy scent of God's good soup.

She chopped into the dark of night; she scraped and parboiled, shaved, halved and quartered. The scrapings, the bits, heads and tails, thin parsnip fingers, she added to the stock pot. She crushed the herbs to free the essence and added them to the mix. Then one more thing.

The black iron shears hung heavy on her apron tie. She held her lantern ahead. The picnic basket swung free, crooked in her other arm, the busted-withered one. A bottle of whiskey sloshed, safely nested in a mess of torn rag and sphagnum. Fall leaves hushed in the dark; the *shush, shush, shush* of her footsweeps spread among the trees. Night critters went quiet as she passed. She stepped off a hundred paces up the hill and counted a little more to pass the pond. Another count took her beyond her 'shrooming patch. Except for her, the forest was still.

She didn't need light for the walk. Light was needed for the work. Down the cellar, in the dark of the cellar, the root cellar, was where light was wanted.

The oak plank door lay across the hole in the hillock. A Civil War lock hung cold against the boards and hasp. Covered with leaves, it was, and near invisible, days, part of the world at night.

The lock snapped open. As she raised the door the earth smell from below breathed over her. Earth and more. She descended the four steps. The light led her, then came the noise. Iron against rock. The clatter cut the silence, a body moaned and rattled his iron bonds against his rock, his earthbound rock.

She hadn't known him, just a huntsman as came walking through the woods. Lost. Asking. She offered a drink of whiskey and pointed a way. He came back, still lost. She said she'd lead, then asked his help, *A little thing, please. So good to be a help.* God gave to those who helped. Some more whiskey and he was in chains. Like that!

Those chains and more held him now to that rock below the world in her cellar.

No man she knew. Her light caught him, now. He was white like a grub. And naked. She'd left him blankets, but no clothes to wear. He hung naked, hugging his rock. He looked up. He cried.

Why, yes, oh Lord. Yes. He did live underground like one of them things as wiggled under the rotted logs that fed her morels. She had to chuckle.

His head was long and thin. Not much face to him, narrow hook nose, a thin yellow beard she hardly could see in the yellow of her lantern. His head was flat on top. His teeth were busted, crooked. He cried and tried to stand. He stood and dangled. She laughed again. Up top on the world, he wouldn't have cried.

But she had things to do. She rolled the whiskey jar to him then sat to watch. It took a time. He yelled. He cried. He made to throw the jar at her head.

She laughed. Sweetly. Cordelia had a pretty laugh. Funny face, but a pretty laugh.

The man blubbered. He shouted, "Why...?" Other things, but the heart of it was, "Why?"

"Drink," she said, "an' it won't hurt."

By and by, he drank. Long pulls, tears coming between gulps and runny-nosed blubbers.

In less than an hour the screams were only hoarse bubbles. She clipped three fingers and some hand meat from him; a couple toes from his left foot. He screamed and bled. She caught the blood in a Mason jar and capped it. She wrapped his hand and foot with sphagnum and left more rags.

She almost left, then returned and scissored off a rasher of fat from his gut, the flabby place. He screamed and bubbled but by then it was over. *Leave the man-oysters for later*, she figured. *Take them now, he'll lose spirit. Men, so silly and so sweet*, she thought, *believe in their hearts—way down—their lives, their God Spirit comes from there, down the root and sack between their legs.*

She left a few more rags and the bottle.

The blood smelled rich. The thick warmth pillowed the earthy scent of the cellar. She hoped he'd be all right. She liked the blood-aroma of this one.

Later that night the cries came all the way to her cabin. Sobs and curses. She heard even as the pot came boiling, even later, so much later, the screams. Long far'way echoes, as from a mountain across a valley, all the world's trees between.

Must hurt, she thought, stirring soup. *Aww, hurt don't last.* She knew that.

Night was over and light was through the trees, God peeking white through black, He touched His ground with His Mighty Eye.

The pot had bubbled night-long. The perfect heat she'd made had concentrated the liquor of the soup; thin soup was now thick soup, rich soup, winter soup, dark and earthy. Smelled so pretty now.

Cordelia took another swipe with her spoon. Dark broth swirled among the roots and other things. She breathed its rich essence as she stirred. Turnips, potatoes, the spinning joint-bones made dull taps against the iron pot, the carrots and parsnips swirled. She tasted with her nose. *Mmmm.*

The cabin air had gone winter. *Just that one night. Imagine.* Fire warmth, and blessed-God quiet filled the place. Her room was fragrant with chopped wood, spices, and the bite of soup and winter.

Excepting the morning whippoorwill, the woods were quiet. The cries were gone, all gone.

She added the morels last, fried up in the fat. She tasted the tip of the spoon. She sucked a hot spray of broth, her first savor of Winter Soup.

It was good.

After dark she'd maybe take a jar to him in the cellar. A little. She wanted him to last. It was going to be a long, long winter. She felt it in her bones.

WIND SHADOWS

"We owe respect to the living; to the dead we owe nothing but the truth." —Voltaire

2:50 Ack Emma. Crickets. Finally, morning birds among the crickets' stillness.

3:10 Ack Emma. General Plumer said, "By damn."

Bill thought of the shamblers in the dark as he and Welly groped for the tunnel lift.

Then, someone closed the electric gap, a spark gasped. Off went nineteen charges, one voice, a million and more pounds of HE. In friendly trenches up and down the lines, nine and a half miles along, the ground shivered, compressed, shattered. Men fell to earth, the earth quaked, collapsed, ears burst. A half-mile across No Man's Land, a ridge nine and a half miles long rose slowly—or so it seemed, so vast was it, horizon-to-horizon—and rose and rose and rose.

"The mouf of hell!" someone said.

Beneath the German lines, nine and a half miles of them, nineteen mouths of hell opened wide and the 3 a.m. dawn darkness vaporized in roaring light.

Across the Channel, 130 miles from the Messines Ridge, windows rattled in Maida Vale and Mayfair. In Downing Street, tables set for breakfast quivered, crystal tinkled against crystal.

The shiver of silver against silver was deadened by thick white linen. Eyes opened.

3:10 a.m. and some moments. Along nine and a half miles of British lines, whistles blew and the men were over the top advancing through the still shattering dust. Fifteen seconds after zero, the cloud continued to roil upward. Germans, parts of Germans, machines, weapons, and other things began to rain among advancing troops. There were casualties. A blockhouse big as a railcar fell among them. The creeping barrage leading the men toward the blazing craters faltered here and there, shells fell short. There were casualties. It was the beginning of the day. Some men never remembered dying.

The man remained on deck for the Channel crossing, Dover to Calais. He might have been Old Bill of the cartoons, Old Bill himself. He had been, thirteen years before. They all had been Old Bills, all of them decrepit, stinking beyond belief, scratched raw, sucked by louse, dined on by rat. Old Bills by the hundreds of thousands, 1914 to 1918, citizens of those temporary lands: Verdun, "Wipers," Passchendale, the Argonne and the Somme and others, worlds without end, amen.

Thirteen years on, Old Bill stood on the deck of a Channel ferry. France rose from the morning ahead. He was old, but who could tell? Bill was old at seventeen, he was. He was old from waiting, from seeing too much or burning too brightly. At eighteen, his eyes were craters in his face, sun-creases radiant from them, a walrus mustache curtained a grin going toothless. That was a boy's grin grown too sure of death and worse. At nineteen his skin was waterlogged and scabbed, hands cracked, feet shocking. But ah, those cheeks, scraped to the skin by razors two-years dull, morning stubble softened by cold water and equal parts mud, old bone, blood, piss and shit, those bright red child's cheeks put the lie to his age. All their sweet young faces, plucked whisker-by-whisker for morning turnout to quarters: inspection on the firing step, heads down facing No Man's Land, rifle at the ready. Ready for the Hun (should the Hun come today) and, worse, the Lieutenant (who came every day). Worse yet, the Sarge, who was always there, taking names *("You two! I'M LOOKING AT YOU! You and you shall walk the Dixie down to 'Bert today and fetch the water back! Chop-chop!" Sarge screamed. "Can't the niggers hop it, Sarge?" Welly'd said. "Their turn, I'm sure…" Sarge's mouth engulfed Welly's nose and he give him what for: "The Nig-gers? Them Niggers ain't yours to detail. Sing me not that hopeful song, you horrid little man! Them nig-nogs got another job, a task of never-you-mind, you dirty bugger! Now you two 'op it, you and you!" And Welly and Bill made the two-mile saunter from the front, down the zigzag to the reserve, guessing all the way—this time lucky—where and when to duck and wait the sniper's eye, then another mile rearward along the muddied duckboards and into Albert. "Whatcher fink, Old Bill?" Welly said, pumping water at the well. He pointed at Albert's pocked and potted steeple. The Madonna sagged, barely hanging on, her arms raised, baby God held at 9 o'clock in the shell-singing sky. "Fink she's gonna topple or fink she'll stay? What say ther, Bill?" And Bill, he'd had no idea except to reckon if the steeple fell one day, it would fall on him, a cert. Him, detailed by the Sarge to sit beneath and "wait for it, wait for it!" Then, with pranged and tinkered Dixie full, Bill and Welly made the same miles back to the line, ducking snipers at the crossroads of their luck/his skill and, slipping on the muck-soft duckboards—Welly remembering at one place along the way, "I sawr him go, Bill. Ol' Ned. One minute there, then zing he scratches at a rabbit in his pants and orf the boards he slips and down he goes into that ther shellhole—that'n ther—and thas the last anyone seen Ol' Ned, drown he was wiff all his kit. You remember Ned?" And Old Bill laughed and laughed remembering Ned. Welly, too. And returning with the Dixie barely half sloshing full of water. "GOD Damn you two! I'm watching you!" Sarge says at the nearly empty Dixie can.)*

Ahead, in France and beyond, more memories. Inspection

mornings: faces scraped, clothes dried and brushed as mudless as could be, their weapons ready.

"Wait for it. Wait for IT!" Waiting for the Sarge's whistle and the call to stand down. *("You there!" Sarge yelled, plain and simple this time, no trench poetry to color it. "Munger! Keep away from that Loop, you! Hans'll have you in his sights and I'll be down another fool!")* Waiting for it. Waiting for it.

Then the call, "Staaand. DOWN."

Morning. Each morning: cold water tea and the bouquet of shit, of all things redolent of the body, life steeped in piss and blood. Trench life, a heady marinade of rotted corpse brewed in No Man's Land.

"It's *between*," Welly said. He was peeking with Munger through the sniper's loop toward the German lines. "*Between* is what that is," he whispered, looking at the sea of bloodied khaki that stretched from here to there. "No shelter, no trench, just holes and holes and holes blown in holes."

Bill peeked. Some khaki bits moved but never for long. Sometimes the bodies were blown and buried by artillery, then resurrected from the muck and water-filled holes, their parts pounded, mixed and buried again by the shells. Over it all a spreading mist of night and death, gassy, gangrenous, heaving or jostled by amyl nitrate and steel. Here and there, tiny sparks of life flickered, or here and there they screamed. There was that. Since One July, screams licked day and night. The screams were of men and (he still had to laugh) horses. Horses! Mud-drowned horses. The cavalry, up for one last charge, *for the old century's sake, don'tchaknow?* Haig's urge, "Soften the Hun with HE and steel, pound 'em week upon week, then a steady walk 'cross the green to the German's lines. Who'd survive that barrage, eh? Punt a football, why don't you lads? A prize to the first goal in Otto's trench, eh. And, oh yes, let's have horses. Big push, eh? Cavalry to drive through the hole, enfilade the Hun and crush him, what?"

So: there remained a moaning, seething carpet of pounded khaki and horse bodies dusted pale, yes, and Munger (the peeker at the loop), Munger among them, he and others, Riley and others, others by the thousands all in a few minutes chopped, churned, and added to the pot, stirred with mustard gas, and phosgene spice. Then sprinkled with the hopeless hope of quicklime—lime to dissolve it all, wash all away, but lime left to lay and fly, white and drifting in any breeze.

At night, tucked below the trench lip, night shone green in the downfall swinging brightness of the Very pistol's flares descending like God-rays through drifting powdered bone, gas, and dust.

Old Bill remembered: the eleventh hour of 11/11, 1918. He remembered that other boat. How he had a drink with Welly on that boat back then... Going home to Blighty.

Now, thirteen years on, he'd come across the Channel again (like he said he'd never), unarmed, a fiver in his pocket. He squinted at the water washing the rusting prow. *Blackout drill?* Years ago. Tonight? Boat lights laughed across the black water. *Silent drill?* The band played on the promenade tonight. Tonight, the boat danced, shameless splashing, shining bright, cutting through moon and stars. There was music and light, men and women danced, whites and wogs, Frog and Hun, Brit and Black (he stared at African faces sweating in the white and blue and red lights).

All them muddled together in jazz and night, Welly. Crikey, what a world we made!

No U-boats below reached out. Not now. He knew that much. *What U-boats there are, are drowned down there. And if they wait, they wait in the dark, alone forever, torpedoes rusting with the wait.* But the boats? Unmoving, dead, the boats. *The crews?* Ah, the crews in the dark, in the dead drowned boats? *Them? Who knew? Who knew?* He did not, that was one thing certain.

Old Bill blinked. So long. Thirteen years on. The water beneath them? So much of it. So much *below* to this old world; too much *beneath* for any man to see and know. He tried. And couldn't. He blinked again.

The band had finished. Short numbers. It was on the cheap for this day-trip crossing. A lark for the young who'd never been, echoes and shadows for the widows who came across to wonder. For those among the still-living, those who returned to walk in the sun and seek to find where IT had happened—whatever *IT* was carried: a fragment in the leg, an armless sleeve, a missing mind. All this? Less than a lifetime ago, a few years only. Thirteen, just.

The IT Bill carried: Welly and Bill in the *estament* at... Where was it? What town? Albert? The chantusey ("Oh, weren't she a piece? Whoo *Parleyvoo!*") Musky, dark and (*"There*, right there!") on the stage, ("Two meters away, Crikey! A woman!") singing. And in tears. Who knew what for?

Later, they waited in the narrow hall behind the piano to have a genteel squat.

"Imagine, Billy lad. A loo!"

A door there was, to close your privacy within. A dozen or two waited in the narrow place. The place was filled with blue smoke and scorched and boiled serge.

Then she burst from the W.C., the chantusey, hands balled, shouts and no more tears. The manager of the *estament*, a big man on Civy Street, old silk and braces, he eases through the waiting line, plunger in hand.

"Lookit. Such a dainty fing." Welly nudged Bill, pointed at the plunger. "Who's seen such a fing as that in years?"

There she was, the chantusey, shrieking, fists tensed to fight.

They met, manager and woman, she took and held the ground not a foot and a half from Old Bill's face. Shaking fury, her eyes blown wide and mad, she held up one foot then the other to the manager, her dainty shoes sloshed, sogged with shit, stockings soaked and smeared. French words blew past Old Bill, shrapnel blasts of spit, tabac, whiskey, garlic, tooth decay and other things he didn't know what.

Old Bill breathed her clothes and her. Her smell was apart from theirs, a thing from another world. Here were their bodies. The familiar: the trenches disinfected. There was she…

Well, apart, she was one with them. She had voice, sweat, piss, shit, passion.

Then he realized, of course, no, she shared nothing. A mere foot and a half from her, he wasn't there. Not leastways for her. Yet there she was: breath, life, woman. For her, Old Bill, Welly and the rest might as well have been home in Blighty, might well have been dead for all she knew, and her just a foot and a half from him.

A blink: They were hauling their fool selves and a hundred pounds, each, of trench supplies back to the line. On the way, they passed beneath the muzzles of their guns. At intervals of four, each piece—six yards apart and ten miles of them—spit flame angled at the night. Their fires cracked and roared away, rolling down the line. Each gun by numbers, the Gunny Sergeant chanting his count: "If I wasn't a gunner, I wouldn't be HERE. Fire now the GUN!" The piece shouted again and again and again as they walked. They walked below, ducking unnecessarily, beneath the elevated mouths.

"You know, Welly," Old Bill said as they passed beneath the nitrate breath and downfalling thunder.

"No, what?" Welly shouted as the 8-incher clicked and blew another thundering cough to the Hun, five miles out.

"That's her!" He cocked his head at the gun.

WHOOM the gun said to the night.

"Who?" shouted Welly.

"That chantusey back there," Bill went on. "Them civilians. They don't know we're here neither! None of 'em even sees us passing..."

"Fire now the GUN!" chanted the gunner.

WHOOM said the gun. And the next to it. And the next. Ten miles on.

"Yea," said Bill.

"But wasn't she a piece? *Parleyvoo*."

The guns spoke on, and on.

Old Bill disembarked with the other day-trippers. He wandered Calais then, finally, took the train to Wipers.

"Ypres!" said the station agent. "Belgique!"

Not a long ride, Calais to Wipers, but farther than Dover was from Calais.

Wipers was still rebuilding. Thirteen years on and Cloth Hall was still rising from the rubble, a meandering medieval blockhouse, stone icicles melting upward, Bill thought. He had his look. The place was new. Ugly. He wondered about the steeple in Albert.

Precious few buses to be had and all that were were filled with smiling trippers.

"Oh well, oh well. Oh, oh, oh what a lovely day," Old Bill said, and walked.

Flanders was flat, green, small trees now grew here and there. More amazing, it was dry. As he'd known it, Flanders had been wet brown runnels, naught but holes and mud. The trees had been crooked stakes, solitary or, here and there, forests of sticks arising from the muck and drifting mist.

Welly said it: "Holes and holes and holes blown in holes."

A motorcycle and sidecar passed, going like 60MPH, and Bill

stepped off the road. Warm day and Castrol fumes washed him. He stood on the dirt. The dirt was warm and giving. He took a handful. The war in miniature, dirt, steel bits, bone chips, old powdered flesh, all that, more, sifted between his fingers. A gust of wind carried his thinning hair into his face. Dust breathed across his neck. A wind shadow rippled the pale green grass. *The grass come quick, hasn't it, Bill?*

It's been years, Bill thought. *Years, Welly.*

Ah, right you are Billy lad.

Grassy places had remained in No Man's Land, a tuft here and there, *the between,* Welly called it, where a rabbit nibbled or a flower came red and sudden one morning till Welly or he or Munger or Riley took it with a shot and a laugh. Looking across the rolling green wind, his old eyes dissolved the day down to the earth as he had known it. Down below, under the grass, the day was still 1917. In 1917, the world was mud down to the chalk. Holes in holes, chalk scooped by steel and high explosive, stone turned liquid by rain, a fluid like flesh rendered by jellied petrol...

Another wind shadow rolled the field; the waves spread.

1917: Concussive ripples spread as shellfalls walked like giants in the wet wild land between armies... or the shadows, rising, nights.

Sarge said, "You two. That's you and you!"

"Me, Sarge?" Welly said.

Bill stared. "Me?"

"You want to see them nig-nogs work? Why, aren't you the lucky lads? You're going to go an' join 'em. Grab your kits, you two. Chop-CHOP!"

That was that.

"Never look 'em in the eyes," Welly said. He and Bill and the rest walked the zig-zag to the rear. "Never, in their eyes, me ol' ma'am sez. Steal your soul, them Niggers will."

"An' yer kit," Bill said, giving him a shove. A face along the side shone black with sweat, dull with mud and dust. The face watched them.

The blacks were sappers, diggers. Their dig began five hundred yards to the rear of the line. The mine entrance was wood-framed and shored, a black hole in brown earth. A ladder down to a stage, from the stage a lift dropped into the black.

They rode the lift together. Sixty, seventy feet and more. The world winked shut above. With the sun went the stink of dead men, shit, cordite, quicklime and filthy life. They breathed humid earth. Day was yellow bulbs.

The tunnel began at the bottom of the lift. It descended, running east, toward the German lines. Electric lights every ten feet gave edges to the darkness. Their kits clacked as they walked until a voice from the dark said, "Halt." Not like Sarge, a whisper, yet every man of them went still.

"One by one. Advance."

One by one, they advanced. The whisper in the dark was a black, a sergeant nonetheless. A five-foot sergeant, no less. He met them at the entrance to a side gallery, just a hole in the wall and darkness beyond. One by one the sergeant shoved each man into the hole, whispering as they passed.

Welly winked at Bill, ducked and entered. Bill waited. When he came out, Welly winked again and headed down the line.

The sergeant grabbed Bill and pulled him to his mouth. "Go in. Drop kit. All of it, quite. Then come."

"For a cert?" Bill said. He looked the little nig-nog in the eye. He felt a shove and in he went.

The gallery was cooler than the tunnel. Naught but a slick of light that snackered in from the tunnel lit the place. From the sound that pressed his ears, Bill felt the room around him was large. Around him lay a dozen kits or more. He unslung his gear, all he'd carried and treasured. The weight of iron, steel, canvas, rubber, leather, and webbing slid from his body. And wasn't that better? His feet barely held him to the earth.

"Sss." The corporal hissed from the light behind him. Bill rejoined the column.

A dozen feet along, Bill caught up with Welly. "Still in the trenches, us, eh Billy?" Welly turned, a smile on him. He spread his arms, walking backward. His hands brushed each side of the tunnel. His smile flicked on and off as light and shadow crossed his face. "Trenches, eh?" He reached up, ran his hand along the fresh air pipe that led them down. "Just a trench wiv a lid on it?"

They walked another dozen steps east and down. "And quiet, eh?" Bill whispered.

The pipe exhaled a breath from the world above.

"Phew," Welly said.

"Hshh. No talk," a voice ahead said. "No talk. Here on. Hshh."

They went silent a dozen steps or more. The pipe exhaled another gasp, rank with death and life too long stewed in sweat and filth.

"What a pong," Welly said. "Is that us up ther? No wonder we ain't had no lovin', word nor touch, since dunno when, eh Bill? Remember that chantusey…"

From dark by Welly's side stepped a black fellow cloaked in canvas and dirt, all eyes and teeth. His paw took Welly by the shoulder and dragged him into the shadow of a side passage.

"Oi!" Bill said. "My mate!" He stepped out of line following Welly and the wog.

"Hsshhh." The black man turned and took Bill and Welly together by their shirts, drew them together, spoke to their ears. "They above a little. Little-bit above." He showed with his blistered fingers how far above was the enemy.

"We're 80, 90 feet down, mate," Welly whispered. "Who'll hear us, 90 feet of muck and war between?" he whispered.

"Right, Sambo," Bill said to the darkness. The detail had passed, still heading downward, forward, still toward the German lines.

"Not soldier. Not above. Digger. Them diggers." The African let go. When he did the tunnel was truly still. Their mates had passed them. Now the war was Welly, Bill, and the nig-nog sapper alone in the shade of the war, in the black, black earth and silence.

"Hshh," he said again.

Then Bill heard: first, the wheeze and momentary stench of the pipe's breath from above. Then the now and again rumble, a grumble on the chest, a tap upon the eardrum, the guns above, far, far away, too far to reach. After, there was stillness and the rich loamy smell of the quiet earth. Subtracting all of that, what remained was something else.

"Whaa?" Welly's breath in Bill's ear momentarily erased the something. Then, a scratch. The smallest scrape, as of something soft moving above, ahead. A little ahead, not far above but insistent, a scratch and a small fall of sand and earth, like through an hourglass. Persisting.

"German dead, they dig too," the nig-nog whispered.

"Whisss," Welly...

Later. Much later, after it all, November 11: There came a final volley from the 8-inchers in their rear at 10:59 Ack Emma and a little more. A round went over like a fast express, thudded somewhere beyond. Then all went silent. 11 Ack Emma, the eleventh day of the eleventh month. Along the lines, 800 miles of everything went still.

Bill and Welly stared at each other. Rain drizzled as it had since… Since, God love it, 1914. Bill was shivers and shakes in the silence. Then his legs held him no more and he fell. Welly caught him. They stared at each other. Then a million men sighed. No joy, just noise.

Others, below, did not shout.

Bill and Welly were ordered back the way they'd come. They knew. They dashed. They rose from their lines and walked the way they'd come four years before, the churned earth and charnel world behind.

"She fell," Bill said to Welly as they passed through Albert. The Madonna of the steeple lay in the rubble that was the rest of the town.

Finally, a train, the train to Calais: cattle cars for them—forty men per car, or ten horses ("Horses," Welly laughed. "Horses!" He laughed and laughed and didn't stop, Bill thought, until they boarded the boat).

They waited and waited aboard until things were right, just right, for some officer or other. Welly smiled at the sea, the horizon. He wouldn't look back, not at France, not at the ruin of Europe. No. He would not.

Someone—many, actually—had a bottle or three. When they cast off for Blighty it was dark. The boat kept blackout. Regulation.

"Oi!" a hundred shouted at the captain. "Give us some light 'ere, won't ya! U-boats ain't hunting no more!"

The lights stayed black.

"Some'them submarines down there may not have got the word, eh, Welly?" Bill said. He took a long pull on a bottle a mate had handed him out of the dark.

"Down there, right!" Welly said. "Asleep in the deep, eh Bill," and he took a long haul on the bottle. "All that *down*, down there, eh, Bill. All that *below*! Holes in holes and what else in the holes?" He laughed and drank some more.

"Home for Christmas, Welly!" Bill shouted. "This year, home! Come on, let's inside, out of the air, out of the cold. Let's us have some warmth." He steered Welly toward the blacked out salon bar.

A hundred bodies, a thousand for all Bill and Welly knew, a million survivors and them, gathered, singing in the light of a hundred candles. Welly showed what was left of his teeth. "Horses!" he shouted over the singing. "Horses!"

Bill laughed with him.

"Gotter go!" Welly shouted over the song.

"What?" Bill shouted at his ear.

Welly made an arc with his hand, pointed to the deck.

"'ave a piss for me," Bill said and let him go.

Much later, someone said someone, one of the Lanc's he reckoned, had gone over the side and into the briny. "I shouted but over he went and down, like that," he said with a snap.

They didn't stop the boat.

Back then, when Welly and the war still lived, the nigger in the dark took them by their arms and led them. He pointed and slipped away with not a sound. Back in the tunnel and lights, Welly and Bill listened as they walked toward the mine face.

"What'cher fink ther, Bill?" Welly whispered.

"Germans is digging toward our line, we're digging to theirs. First one there gets to blow t'other off the world, is what I think."

"'Th' German dead's wot he said. Howzat you fink, Bill?"

"Who knows what they mean, Welly?" Bill whispered. "Their way of talking, is all, I reckon."

Welly snorted. "Yea. All uv us is dead men, eh Bill!" He snorted again.

Scratch, scratch, scratch, said the darkness overhead.

Bill sat by the road. The sun settled into the earth behind him. His shadow rippled across the field as daylight drained from the sky. From sunup on the boat until now, he'd had a day in

France and Belgium. Thirteen years ago, life, the war, all of it, was the narrow strip of land he now stared at in gathering dark.

"Sun setting in England, too, Welly," he said.

No answer but gentle wind. Across the fields toward Messines the grasses rolled, dark shadows chasing light. In the last of the light, the wind settled to earth. Bill closed his eyes and whispered to the night.

Once down, they didn't leave the mine. Day, night, all the same: day was work.

"You here. You carry." The African corporal threw an empty sandbag at Welly, at Bill. The nig-nog marched down the line tossing sacks to the fifty blokes detailed to the dig. White blokes. "Soon dirt gone. When then, we lay big boom. You carry boom stuff. Then Boom."

Welly shot Bill a look. "What's that, mate?" Welly said, cocking his head, his hand to his ear. "Couldn't quite catch'er ther, Womba…"

The corporal turned. A low growl came from his chest. He looked far into Welly's eye, laid a black hand across Welly's mouth. Welly's eyes widened, he started to speak, but the corporal pressed his left thumb on Welly's forehead. Pressed and pressed. The thumb entered Welly's head. Seemed to. Of course it did not, could not. Then the corporal let him go. Eye to eye, the corporal said, "Some carry. Other some dig. Now, you carry. Sometime… sometime you dig. You hope you not dig."

The shiny corporal's eyes scanned the line of men. They rested on Bill, the eyes, gold and shot through with brown. "Now carry." He walked away and the men followed.

"He hurt you?" Bill said.

Welly spit and wiped his mouth. "Nuh," he said.

"What'd he do, then?"

Welly twitched and wiped his face, touched his head where

the corporal's thumb had pressed. "Dunno. Dunno. He mark me?"

No mark, none that Bill saw.

"Ah. I always been a bit touched, eh Bill? Touched! Get it?"

They kipped, wrapped in wool blankets, huddled in a side gallery.

"How long you fink, Bill? 'Fore they trick orf this lit'le home o' ours? Blow it to hell and let us get back up to the real fight?"

"Dunno."

"Nor me. Questions mate. Questions is what I got. You too? Yea. Them nig-nogs, now, they're in charge. They got answers. I reckon we're here for the duration, like. Here till we're done!"

Skitch, skitch, the silence said.

"What do you fig'r?" Welly whispered to Bill. "Fritz or us, who'll be first?"

Bill shrugged. "Dunno," he said. "Corporal said, so, yeah, I figure," Bill said.

Skitch, skitch, said the silence.

"Fig'r we'll see Ol' Nick soon? Eh?" Welly laughed.

Skitch, skitch, said the earth.

"Yeah. Fig'r."

"Nig-nog ain't talking big, is sure."

Bill thought about it. "Well…" Bill started. The darkness suited thinking. "We gotter get there first," Bill whispered, "that's a cert. Dig under No Man's Land, get to th' Hun's line, under his trenches. Then our digger niggers rout out a gallery. For the explosives, you know, a nice tight chamber. Then we haul the blasting stuff, bit by bit. Pack it in…"

"Yeah. That's us, I reckon… Hauling HE. Packing high explosive?"

"Reckon."

"Don't fancy that, Bill. Packing explosions like a bloody horse? Ain't what me ol' mum raise her lit'le Welly boy for."

"Oi! Hshh..." from way, way down in the dark. One of their own.

"Hishh, yersel'..." Welly whispered back. There was silence for a minute.

Skitch, skitch, skitch... said the silence.

"Them Africans," Welly started.

"Wha...?"

"Africaners. They know somefink. I been watching..." Welly snugged up close. Bill felt Welly's breath in his ear, smelled their supper of boiled spud and thin horse gravy. "Cookin' somefink for us all, oh you know they are. Why ain't we seen sun since we come here? Eh? Why ain't no one else come down for helping since? Saving us for somefink special." A gentle breeze came from the darkness beyond. "Hsh," Welly said.

They lay in silence.

"Oi," Welly said. "Bill? Reckon the Huns is got theirs digging their mines, too?"

"Their what?"

"Africaners. Well, whoever. I dunno. Who's digging fer us, Bill? I ain't never spoke to no diggers. We do the hauling. Them black boys do the telling. Dunno. I never seen no one dig! Must be blokes up there, past them tarps, niggers maybe? Or what?"

"Shamblers," Bill said before he thought about it.

"Eh?"

"Nothing, Welly. Old Suffolk tales is all."

Beyond the gallery's low opening, the tunnel lights went dim. Then out. Then there was nothing anywhere, except Welly's breath and his own. Then something else. Something moved in the near distance, a shuffle at the very bottom of Bill's hearing. The darkness rippled and from the ripples came a...

What is it? Bill thought. *What?*

"Wha..." Welly began. Bill stopped his mouth.

Suffolk tales remembered: Da's silent house, Mum's white,

white sheets, him, just a lad, lying abed between sleeping brothers, darkness all 'round, above, below, outside, oozing up from the ground. He knew darkness then, Little Bill did, the dark, so full of hairy things, man-things and bigger things, he knew, than Da, things that breathed and shuffled on hard feet. And Bill, a little lad, pressed his palms against his eyeballs, blotting all out. And with the press, explosions of color bloomed behind his lids. Little Bill knew, he did. The shufflers carried the smell of rotted meat on them, a stink like down where Dad butchered hogs and for two days after. There, between his brothers, Little Bill pressed his hands into his eyes and waited for the shufflers to pass.

They were there now, shambling the tunnel. Shuffling toward the mine head. Not the same, 'course not, but the same smell of dead flesh oozed from them, those man-things, their black hairs and hard dark feet. Probably. They moved through the same silent explosions of color that danced in his eyes behind his hands. Little Bill once thought the shamblers ate those colors that lived in his eyes. They ate them colors and shat dead pig-meat, made the stinks that lived up his nose when Da butchered. He knew them to be hairy, knew them to be black, black as the inside of his head. He knew they ate boys' dreams and men and all. He knew that, all right.

Now, they were out there. Now, he was glad he couldn't speak, now.

"Whassat, Bill?" Welly said.

"Nothing," Bill said. He'd have told Welly about the shamblers but that would make them real.

Old Bill woke. He hadn't slept by the roadside, not exactly. He hadn't slept. The moon lay edge-on along the line of trees on the Messines Ridge and constellations filled the sky. The air was still and still warm. More warmth rose from the earth. In the bright darkness, Old Bill saw the world as it was at that moment and as it had been, the British trenches cut in chalk and mud. He saw the great Between of No Man's Land, the rolls of wire accordioned out for mile on mile, the broken trees, the stirred dead and rotted horse. Farther off, on the Messines Ridge, he saw the German lines and zig-zags. The shadows of the craters, the great depressions where the mouths of hell had yawned that chirping morning, 3:10 Ack Emma.

And further, his watery eyes and youth reached down to the dark tunnels, the galleries and mines he, Welly, and the others had scraped and carried from the living earth.

There it was. The last of the moonlight showed him, before him, beneath him: the Is, the Was, the Always Will-Be. Through collapsed and burned out galleries, below, still moved the shuffling shapes, those shamblers still digging beneath the fields of Flanders. They prowled, they swam in dirt, rock, chalk and mud, pale fish in the depthless oceans beyond the watery moon and turning stars.

Hun sappers broke through in Bill and Welly's night (above, it may have been bright, bright Sunday, sun and silence, or drizzly Friday, nothing doing but the wait-'n-wait). Welly had just whispered a Welly sort of whisper. After, neither remembered what, but when he whispered the world went black. From the ceiling of the small side gallery (little more than an underground storage shed) where Welly and Bill were nabbing a kip, a rain of noise and guttural shouts fell on them. A cascade of dirt, first, then bodies. Then the light went out. Something shoved Bill aside. With falling bodies came the smell of strangers, of air from a different part of earth, bodies drenched in different sweats, breaths from different lungs, it poured from above.

"Oi!" Welly shouted in the din.

"Crikey!" Bill yelled.

A gramble of German words spewed into his left ear.

Something hard pressed his ribs. Flashes here, there, around. He grabbed the hard thing and twisted it from himself. Another flash and gunpowder thunder lit the space. A grunt from nearby. Other flashes, thunders. He and the other rolled in dirt, clattered among tools, coils of wire, lengths of pipe. Empty sandbags attacked his face, caught his arms, legs. More shots, more grunts. A pickax came to his hands and a blood-cry rose from inside him as he pushed the darkness back to gain swinging space. He swung. He swung again. And again. With each swing he screamed. A buzzing riot shot through his nerves. He stepped forward, swung, took another step and swung again. Ah! The pick connected (*the wall*, he thought—the pick bit softness and the soft something hadn't screamed). Again he connected. The pick dug in and wiggled.

Beyond the gallery, Welly shouted too, a voice brought from his depths. More shots, soft thuds of bullet strikes. Grunts. No screams.

In a minute, maybe more, others arrived. Some, from the break-through above, rained down, more dirt, more stench. Others. Their own reserves, from the tunnel, other galleries, wherever. English, German, Welsh, maybe, African jabber-jabber, Bill didn't know, it all exploded in darkness: words, shots, now screams and a continuing rain of dirt, a dirtfall, an avalanche of bodies and steel filled the space. More muzzle flashes, reports. Bill dove face-down, flattened himself in the dirt. He tried swimming deeper. He crawled. He screamed as he did. When he reached a wall, he wriggled, farther, still screaming, no idea, not a notion where safety was, if safety was at all where hell poured from above and death stank everywhere.

In a minute, he'd crawled beyond, beyond cordite flash and grunts, the clash and sparks as shovels met picks or found softer ground in dirt or flesh. He crawled and crawled. He screamed. In another minute he realized he was calling Welly's name. He shut up.

It seemed he'd escaped the battle. His heart thudded against his eardrums, his breath came in, went out. His hands shook. He felt it all. If he bled, he bled small. Life tingled, filthy, smelly, fucking sweet. He rose, his hands clawed, dragged himself upright. His hand found steel: the pipe, the pipe that breathed from the surface down to them, the pipe. He was in the main tunnel and still the dark held him, the blind dark.

Bill wedged himself against a wooden brace. His body screamed for clear air, for light, for silence, for some open place where nothing pressed him into himself and where he didn't dig into darkness.

He took a moment.

In that moment something shambled by. He pressed the tunnel wall. Another something passed; it spread a chill of... What? Of old meat, of piggie two days dead. A whiff from Suffolk childhood. Another darkness shambled by, and another and more, more.

They were advancing from the mine head, from the face, beyond the veil. The diggers. They were coming, shuffling to the rescue.

He held himself close. He sank, his face between his knees. He whispered quietly to himself, kept the prayer inside so they wouldn't hear. He pressed his eyes so the colors blazed within him. *Give them something to digest,* he thought. *The colors in his head. Vittles for the fight.*

From beyond, where the small war clashed and grunted, he heard a wet tearing, a soft cracking. Screams, now. Not the enemy, his mates giving voice to pain, to terror, to life leaving. The clash of metal on metal or into flesh, the crack of pistols faded one by one to nothing. The soft wet shredding of flesh and the soft crackle of bone went on. And whimpers from the darkness, they increased.

Soon the screams ended but the whimpers lingered.

Then, in the near silence of sighs, the darkness shambled by again. No rush, no need, just darkness rippling past him again and again in the dark, back toward the mine face, back to the veil, dragging, carrying the moans, the whimpers.

Something touched him and he screamed. "Bill, Old Bill!" the thing shouted and embraced him. "Welly!" Welly wet and shaking. Welly screaming him, his name. And Bill, of course, shouted his.

"Bill!" he shouted. "Oh Bill! They're us, them is! Them diggers at the face, them behind that tarp! They're us!"

Bill held Welly. A sticky wet covered him, but Bill held him, let him sob.

"Old Ned," Welly sobbed. "He's here! Old Ned what slipped orf the path and drownded wiv his kit! He's one. I sawr his face in a gunflash. Sawr it, Bill. He's down here, one'a them! And Riley, Munger. Uvers, so many uvers! All down wiv us!"

The moon set. Morning was close but star-night filled Old Bill's eyes. He thought better, heard better. Old Bill heard the grasses stir. The windless night was full of wind shadows and rolling earth. He stood and began walking across the field toward the ridge.

Later, Welly said, "You believe in God?" He whispered to Bill's back as they carried their dirt to the lift.

Bill shrugged. "Dunno."

"I never. Fig'red this was it, wa'n't it?"

"I reck'n." They reached the lift and dropped their loads onto the stage with the others. Welly rubbed his forehead. The rest shuffled past, dropped their bags and trudged back toward the mine face.

Above them, the tiny circle of day cast white silence and

flickering shadow as the load of bags rose.

"Nothing stirring. No war today," Bill said.

"Always somfink happen'in', I reck'n." Welly kept staring at the bright circle above. His body shook. Tears showed in the dirt of his eyes. He rubbed his head again. "Billy, I al'ays figured, 'God? None of that guff for old Welly.' I dunno. Scares me, Bill, but there may be a God'n all."

"Could be…"

"No. Fink of it! Them fings diggin' down there. I reckon them is us. You know? Them blokes as gone before. The dead. Figure them…" he leaned close to Bill's ear, "them Africans— ours, theirs, who knows—is jigabooin' the dead to life. Some nig- nog jinxin', mebbe. War's making lots of dead for all the work down here, somewhere's else. Maybe everywhere. I dunno. I mean, I saw Old Ned. I saw him. That was him. Sure as I'm me. Old Ned coming after them fings as was falling down from the German mine… An' Munger… Him as was always peekin' out the loop to No Man's Land…"

"Welly," Bill started. He started to say it was all a load of old cobblers, that he'd gone shell-shocked, rounders. He didn't. "Welly," is all he said.

"Yea. An' he din't even know me, Bill. Ol' Ned din't know his old mate. Nor Riley. No."

Bill let it go. He looked up at the dim circle of light. A cloud across the sun, maybe.

"So, I fig'res, Bill… They all gone and snuffed it. And there it is. They's somfink else, now. Something from after death! There's that much about what we don't know. You know? If that shite's out there, then, what the hell? Bad shite means there's good stuff, too. If ther's the devil, you know, there must be God." He was crying. "God, Bill. If there's God, then there's… Y'know? I been a bad'n. Y'know? We bof been. Crikey. God means hell…"

The wind shadows rolled past Old Bill like waves. Grass caressed his legs, his thighs. The stalks played him like a billion dust dry fingers. His palm played across their tassels. They rasped with small, edged teeth. He walked toward high ground between craters at the ridge, the place that hadn't opened its mouth to the 3:10 sky that June morning, 1917. He crossed what had been the British lines, stepped into the Between, No Man's Land.

Morning wake up. Bill, Welly, those left, in a line down the tunnel, empty sacks in hand. Twenty men of the forty that had come down with them. The shining black corporal with the golden eyes walked the line in shadow and light: light, dark, light, dark passed over him…

"You. Here!" The corporal pointed to Welly.

Welly looked at Bill. "Wha?" he whispered.

"You come."

"'S alright, i'nnit?" Welly whispered.

"You come." The corporal pointed to another man, and another and another. Five in all. Bill was left, one of fifteen.

"Soon done," the corporal said and pointed. Welly went last behind the veil.

Bill stopped where the ridge rose. Either side of him, the line of craters stretched for miles. Where he stood under the stars and in the still gently roiling earth, nothing had happened that morning 13 years ago.

At 3:10 Ack Emma, General Plumer said, "By damn!" and someone closed the electric gap. Along the ridge, 19 mines had blown. The world shouted with the voice of one million two hundred thousand pounds of HE. Ten thousand men died that second, more, later.

Two mines failed.

Bill knew why the one. The other? Not a clue.

Life went quiet when Welly left. Bill had watched men die. He'd known the men who were the empty places in the mess, on the firing step. Things went on. But the silence of Welly's going was complete. Part of Bill went too. He woke to silence. He carried his loads, a stranger's back ahead. He went to sleep without a dozen questions, no answers to consider.

The earth, the grass, reached out to caress him. The earth beneath the silent stars breathed. He felt the swimmers in the shadows rising.

"Know one of your own, don't you?" he said to the rolling runnels that tipped him back and forth.

Time came. The ten who remained carted HE down the tunnel. A nearly endless supply squeaked down the lift from the light above or from the darkness, in rain or dry. It came and came. Tons of it. Carried, one charge at a time, and left at the canvas wall, then back to the lift for more. When they returned, their previous load was gone.

They rested.

The corporal watched.

When they rose, the corporal pointed. "You," he'd say to one. "You go where charges go. You pack. I show." And another went behind the canvas curtain.

Finally, only Bill remained when the last charge came down the lift. Bill and the corporal.

"Wire come. We get."

Bill followed the corporal to the lift. Down it came: a cable spool unrolling, trailing lines to the surface. Together, Bill and the corporal rolled the spool to the canvas wall.

"You go," the corporal said. He pointed to the canvas flap. "I show."

Past the canvas was a narrow chamber lit by several bulbs, at the far end, another canvas bulkhead. No men. No explosives. Here the electric lines, the air pipe, ended. Beyond was darkness. Above, the Hun.

Bill turned. "Where's Welly?" he said to the corporal. "You done your dig! Where are the diggers? Where's my mate?"

The nig-nog's eye swam toward Bill. The brown swirled, the gold of it burrowed into him. Bill's chest went empty. The corporal's hand barely twitched from his side, the thumb caressed the edge of his forefinger.

"Where're the other blokes!" Bill shouted with the last air in his chest.

The corporal closed the space between them.

Bill's ears went dead. The damp wet smell of the earth drained from him. A pale shadow, the scent of pig two days dead remained. The corporal reached toward him, his thumb pointed at Bill's forehead. Bill staggered backward into the shade between bulbs. As the corporal approached, Bill's vision faded, flickered, shrank to a bright center. The black thumb reached toward the single warm point, all that remained of Bill. Bill was swallowing himself, darkness, the earth, the night, all time, forever, were becoming him. One point remained. One movement remained to him. He swung the pickax by his side, swung toward the pinpoint place on the surface of his sight.

Then...

The corporal's hand flew in a spray of bright, bright red. With it, the call of a thousand voices, a sound from beyond the dark, beyond the walls of the tunnel, from above, below and everywhere, filled Bill like air, like light, like space.

The corporal continued to stare at Bill. The black flesh of the corporal's arm ended in a ragged red place that filled the air with wet. The dark hand lay in the dirt. The thumb tap, tap, tapped the ground.

"How?" the corporal asked. "How I touch you now?" His brown and golden eyes flicked from Bill to the hand. He spoke more but Bill didn't *parleyvoo*. He did not care to. He didn't care to resolve the corporal's problem.

"Welly!" Bill shouted. "Welly!" he screamed. The corporal continued to stare at the hand. Bill ran to the opening at the far end of the chamber. "Welly!" he shrieked. "Oi! Welly!"

Part of him knew he screamed a woman's scream, a child's. The screams continued even after he'd gone through the canvas wall. There, where the electric lamps stopped, he stopped running. No place to run. He sensed rather than saw the light beyond. The rational part of him knew, surely, here was insufficient light to see. Nonetheless he saw. Imagination, maybe, but a misty luminescence filled the space, a pale green glow, more anticipation than sight. An assumption of light, perhaps, but around Bill, floor to roof—and the roof here was high, two, three man-heights, more, into darkness—here were the charges they'd carried and the space was filled with light. The wooden high explosive cartridges were stacked row upon row.

The smell was that old, old smell from home: the reek of pig, of blood and death.

The green dark swam like tadpole fishies in his head. He knew the men who sat upon the boxes. There they were. The lads, his mates. The shamblers in the dark.

"Welly! Welly! Welly!" The name was noise without meaning. In a moment or three, there was Welly.

"Wot?" he said to Bill. He clambered down the crates, like walking down a stairway from the sky.

Bill still screamed his name.

"Hshh," Welly said. "You'll wake the Huns."

Bill hushed. The others of the detail—the fifty that had come and hundreds more—stared at him, shadows among the crates, their bodies and faces an arrangement, high, low, wide and deep, in shadow, flesh and dirty serge. A thousand eyes, unblinking but flickering in the pale and drifting light, fixed on him. They were at rest. Not curious. They waited. A thousand eyes perched above, to the sides, down the cavern. Everywhere, eyes, eyes waiting, eyes at rest, done.

"We're leaving," Bill said to Welly.

"Right," Welly said. His eyes, too, were finished.

"We're hopping it," Bill said.

"Right," said Welly. His eyes didn't flash or flicker.

The corporal waited at the entrance to the chamber. He'd solved his problem. He held his right hand in his left. He pointed the thumb at Welly like a revolver. "You stay," he said.

Welly stopped.

He turned to Bill. "You connect wire! I show."

The world narrowed again. The haze of hoarfrost light from behind faded; his vision narrowed. The corporal advanced. The black hand with its gored thumb filled his sight. The fingers curled as they reached for his cheek.

The world collapsed. The world collapsed on Bill. Another world collided with his head and pressed both eardrums through his nose... or so it felt. The earth fell on his chest.

After a second or so, what remained of Bill thought the mine had gone off. He thought death, considered, yes, this, this was the first moment of hell. Four, five, six seconds later Bill knew that, no, the tunnel was intact, the lights had gone out, the corporal had, well, had vanished, had gone, was dead, maybe, maybe crushed, flattened, torn to pieces. And Welly... Well, Welly held Bill's hand.

Then he knew he wasn't dead, not exactly, not precisely dead, but the other mines along the ridge had gone off...

3:11 Ack Emma.

"Le Pelerin failed," the colonel reported. "And another."

"Damn," said General Plumer.

"Will it matter, sir?" the colonel said. "Nineteen will do."

"Damn," the general said again. "One prefers perfection."

De-mobbed, in London, Bill eventually turned up, back in Ouze, back in Suffolk. Da's place opened its arms to the returning warriors. Bill among them. His sleeping brothers not.

He lay on their bed for a week. Longer. Alone. No one said much. They fed him. He didn't eat. They smiled. He nodded. *Be fair,* he thought. He tried to eat his old Ma's food. Too salty. Too rich. Just too.

He walked among Da's pigs.

"Don't forget your Wellies," Ma said.

"What?" He stared at her.

"Your boots!" She handed him his Wellingtons. "We knew you'd be back. Kept 'em for 'e!"

The muck and shit sucked at his feet. The boots felt heavy. But the stink, ah, the stink made him remember home: the grunts and rumbling snorts of boar hogs, the squeal of shoats so comfortable, and the long crookey smiles of mother pigs in sun, ahh. Home.

He watched Da at slaughter. He helped and all. Naught was right, though. He knew. Da and Ma knew. Naught was quite right. He slept poorly. He waked in the night. Alone. He covered his eyes and pressed. Nothing. No light and color licked the darkness behind his lids. He held his breath, seemed like hours, holding. He waited for the smell, the breathing of the shamblers. No, no. They stayed away. He rose and walked the narrow halls past his parents' room, down around the narrow steps, the remnants of the evening's fire and the draining warmth of the kitchen. He wandered here and there. Naught to be seen. No shamblers here.

What he was told, he did. What he did, he did poorly. Nothing filled him.

"Your mind's not in pigs. Like you're not all here," Da said gently.

At the Plow in Ouze, he'd lift a pint or two. Every night. Folk did that. He did, too.

"Howzzat, Mikey!" he shouted to the landlord, arriving.

Mikey Alsop always pulled a pint for him, on the house. "Least the house can do 'nall, right lads?"

Bill smiled and leaned on the bar. He listened to talk of test matches, innings and overs, to farm chat, to word of work and prices and of who was back, who wasn't, who would never. He spoke of all things right and proper: Plow talk.

Nights at the Plow he leaned on the bar, his spot, by the window. He'd watch the evening rise. When a fellow'd come by with an empty sleeve, a knotted trouser leg, some other notice on him jotted off from the recent war, Bill turned away to watch the sky. No empty parts to Bill's kit, no sir.

10:00 Pip Emma, prompt: "Time Gen'lemen, please!" Mikey'd say with a whispered smile. "10:00 lads, Constable Grimm'l be by and by on his little bikey, by-n-by. Shut the door, our Stanley! Dim them lights." And the life of the pub would go forth blacked out, hushed when the constable's bicycle squeaked past the door, through the village, on to Lakenheath, beyond. And all the gathered lads and men would smile their beers and jiggers and whisper more of cricket and of pigs.

In the street and tramping up the way in the cool or in the warm mud of spring, Bill watched the sky and counted sunsets.

"High latitude, us," Stanley'd say walking 'longside Bill as far as the fork in the path. "Look a' that," pointing to the sun's glow that lingered on the horizon, "an hour shy o' midnight'n all. Day stays well into night, roundabout, you know. Oh yes. We're a northern country, us."

"Oh, aye, that we are," Bill said. And saying it, he felt…
"Feels like I'm practicing at sommat," he said. Surprised he spoke aloud.

"Eh?" Stanley said, perched on the branch of the road his way. "Eh?"

"I walk and talk, I work. But it's playing scales, you know? Practice. Ma's parlor piano when I was… Crikey, six years gone! Imagine that and all? I was a lad, these six years back. Crikey. Up and down, up and down."

"Oh, aye," Stanly said, and cocked a goodnight wave.

The wind blew and the flat, flat land rippled in the stars and moon, when moon there was. Wind shadows rolled the earth.

He didn't fit. He was the *between*, the hole in a hole. Beer didn't taste. Work brought nor sweat nor joy. Old Da, his Ma, the sister girls gave no home that settled him.

"You ain't come back," Ma said. "I heard of other lads like you. Likely lads'n all, fellows who left sommat of the' selfs out there."

"I died," he said one day, looking at her.

"Ahh, nor did you!" she said. "You hear that, Nels? Our Bill says he died over there in France."

"Oh, aye? The Yanks say, 'How're you gonna keep 'em down on the farm now they seen Paree?'" Da said.

"No, I'll never," Bill said, "never go there," he said. "Never back."

"No. Says he died, like. Like Charlie done and Rafe. For real an' all!" Ma said, staring at him, as though trying to see below his skin and into him.

"I don't know when it was or how," Bill said.

"Ah," Da said, and puffed his pipe.

"Mustna' say them things, now Bill!" Ma said, crying. "And your brothers dead and buried somewhere over there."

"I didn't die?" Bill said.

"Mustna'!" she said.

"I won't," he said.

Da collapsed hoisting up a pig to stick him. The pig hung screaming while Bill went for help. Da's heart, doctor reckoned.

That was ten years after he'd come back.

"That were quick like," Stanley said after the funeral. "He went in the glory of his time, I'd say. Wouldn't you, Mikey? Say old Nels went in the glory of his years?"

"Oh, aye," Mikey said and set the house for Old Bill.

Ma faded after. The girls were gone and married, the brothers, just a pair of pictures. Bill had no marker to her deterioration, none he could say to, "Ain't Ma favoring that leg, of late?" or "She takes a time goin' up them steps, eh?"

He noticed she would start a thing and not finish. Not that that was strange. Just that Ma never had done it. Or if she had, Da had finished for her. Now she lingered in the silence. Or times were she couldn't make an end to something. She'd start chopping onions at the board, times were, and wouldn't stop when the thing was done. Just kept at it. Chop, chop, chop.

She died. One morning, there she was, on the steps, stopped, coming down, stopped and seated, leaning to the wall.

That was twelve years after Old Bill came home.

After that, well, there was nothing left. No one left to tell him he was still alive, no one to say, "Ach!" when he said the best of him he'd left in a hole below a field in Flanders. No one left to tell him "No."

He watched the earth, nights, homing from the Plow. After leaving Stanley at the fork, he climbed the gentle rise. He'd start across the fields near home and watch the earth ripple in the still, still air.

"When'd I die?" he said. "Who took me?"

Nothing.

"You think I'm the only one left walking in the air?" he asked Welly.

Welly, drowned and gone in the chops of the Channel, never said a thing. Nothing at all.

"You went and drownded yourself because! Ain't that right?" Bill said. "Because why? Because you din't want ter go unnerground no more, ain't that it? You were dead, too, and knew it and wanted no more crawling in the mud, ever after. Right, am I, Welly?"

And nothing spoke to him, but the questions seemed complete. The air winkled in the field and shadows rolled in the starlit grass.

"Down there, Welly? Well there's dead below the waters, too, old son!" Bill shouted to the night. "You dancing in the deep are you, Welly?"

Maybe it was the beer but the next day Bill put a fiver in his pocket and took the train to Dover.

Messines Ridge blocked the eastern sky. Dawn was a way away and the moon long gone. The ripples in the earth raised, became flesh, flesh and bone and urges. The urges grew fingers and the hands from the earth stroked Bill's feet. They reached upward. The emerging arms shed earth and flesh as they gripped and climbed his legs. The weight of their bodies, unbuoyed by the dirt they displaced, staggered him. They didn't hurt. They meant no harm, Bill knew. What harm could they do? He didn't know them, not by name, not yet, but they knew him. Heads and shoulders lifted from the dark that rolled beneath. They only wanted him.

"I'm watching you, you horrid little man," one said, his voice, a whisper at Bill's ear. Others spoke. Whispered French twittered at his nose, German rolled around his face, other words and ways, Bill knew, but didn't know what.

"Wanner come down and 'ave a swim wiv us, Old Bill?" another said. Munger. "You're one o' us, there, Ol' Bill, right enough!"

"Am I?" Bill said to the face that had climbed his chest and stared up his nose. "I'm one o' you lot?"

"Wait for it!" called a familiar voice. "Wait for IT..." another. So many familiar parts and places swam and rose in the field around him. Bodies by the hundreds lifted from the dirt and from the holes in the holes around the Messines Ridge. Bodies broke the surface in the starlight, their world glinting from the bone between the flesh and serge and wool and rusted steel. They hugged him and the scent of earth filled his nostrils, the scent of old explosions, of shit and piss, of gunpowder and dead horse, of blood and garbage, of old gas attacks and the eternal smell of men and sweat and breath and fear and life near the edge of the great hole.

Their bodies were not heavy, light as dust, in fact. Just so many of them. He waited, though. Waited for it.

"Now lads," Sarge shouted, "over the top!" His whistle blew across the morning and Bill went forward, falling, swimming, digging, crawling; crawling down to glory.

IN A DAINTY PLACE

I was a magician when the old hallway returned. Just *a phase*, Mother said. Still, the doomed deer, the flying dog and weeping women, the whole world I'd imagined, returned to the upstairs hall. Magic? Not mine. I'd paged through *The Big Book of Malini*. I'd memorized a few stories to distract the audience—patter, we called it. I knew gags that could confuse my kid brother. "Alikazam," a quarter drops out of his nose and he grabs for it or "Shazam," his rubber duck vanishes and he starts squalling. That was it. The hallway? No. The hallway was beyond me. Way beyond.

We lived in Grandfather's house. Grandfather was "Pop-pop." In Pop-pop's house there was a hallway on the second floor. The hall ran between Mother's room and mine. The floor was splintery wood, a worn maroon carpet, from one end to the other. Nothing hung on the walls. They were wallpapered. The paper felt like thick fabric, fabric with pictures, *a* picture, same on both sides of the hall. The thing that almost caught your eye first was the dog, flying. That wasn't the first thing because just below the flying dog was a dying deer, a stag, taller than my father had been. The stag's antlers were huge, thirty-two points to be precise. Magicians need precision. The stag was surrounded by hunters, men on horseback, on foot, with pikes, bows and arrows, dogs. The dogs' fangs and claws had raked cruel stripes across the animal's flanks and he bristled with arrows. One of the mounted hunter's pikes had pierced its shoulder. The horse had reared. If the light was right and you watched for a time, the hooves seemed to move, but only if the light was right. The hooves mixed with the stag's tossing antlers so the deer's head seemed to move too.

The hunters were not cowboys or Indians. "They're of a different age," Pop-pop said, from long-ago and far-away. Not Americans, they came from where Pop-pop's stories had come.

Seven women stood on the outskirts of the clearing, eyes and faces turned away from the killing. They wore tall pointed hats; veils streamed from them. Two clutched their hearts.

The deer's eyes, the eyes of the pikeman's horse were wide and wild. Terror, I guessed, both of them, maybe anger or other things I didn't understand, the sight and smell of bleeding dogs, the whinnies of a downed horse. And there was that flying dog. His howls. He must be howling. I could hear. Terror. Wide terror. Terror of being tossed by those antlers, of flight. Dogs aren't used to flying. The kid always looked there first, always laughed at that flying dog. Not at everything, but at that.

I don't remember the whole of the picture, not exactly, not anymore. Whenever I spent a rainy day sitting on the floor, watching it, I continued the story, on my own. I heard the animals, the shouts of the hunters, the women's sobs; all of that became part of the little world. I felt the heat of that day on my face. I smelled the blood, the green richness of the forest, smelled smoke from campfires beyond the picture. I don't remember the whole picture because so much of my memory of it is conjured, the story I made up that began, went into the broader world, and ended in that clearing. I heard voices. The men, the women, then others, close by, then distant ones. Voices meant lives lived. Lives lived in there. It was me, of course it must have been. And so I made stories of what had come before, what happened after, what was happening in the trees or through them, in the castle that must be beyond the woods, in the town around the castle. Where else are those hunters from? Details. I made details I knew weren't there but which had to be somewhere.

I'd never hunted, never even been to the woods. My father was a hunter. He was going to take me. Always said when I grew this-tall he would. But he went away before. And other than at the butcher shop, I'd never smelled blood. I'd squeezed a few drops from the kid's poked finger once, tasted it before putting on the Band-Aid, but that was it. Yet in Pop-pop's hallway, I heard the forest murmur, what I know to be cicadae, wind in the trees, small brooks, the rustle of animals.

I remember the feel of the wallpaper, like narrow cords on stiff cloth. Like tapestry, Pop-pop said. Close, the smell was of the old, of wheat paste, dried and cracked. Like the inside of a scrapbook, maybe.

The only light in the hallway was from a lamp Mother kept on a small table with a marble top. The table legs were claws that clutched clear glass balls. Dragon feet, the kid called them. "Yeah," I told him, "the feet of a dragon Dad killed."

He said no, but I think he believed part of it.

The upstairs phone also sat on the table. A heavy black affair, the thing smelled of Pop-pop's pipe and kisses. The lamp was lit day and night. A yellow cone of light spread upward across the picture, washed the deer's face, his wounds and blood and, at its limit, kept the flying dog from tumbling upward into the dark.

At Mother's room and mine, the picture disappeared into forest—a world wooded. Beyond those woods? Again, I made so many nearly good stories that they became real to me.

Rising from Mom's room, the morning sun lit the edge of the picture, the ladies clutching, weeping. The sunset, from my end of the hall, sometimes glowed the dark trees and washed the women in red.

On the other side of the hall was the same picture, reversed. There were interruptions, the bathroom door, the stairway to the living room, the side hall leading to the attic steps, Pop-pop's room. Pop-pop's room was at the center. His door cut the deer's head and shoulders from the picture so, no wound, no blood, no wild eyes there. The horse reared, the huntsman's pike disappeared into the frame, half the flying dog emerged.

When the war came, Dad went. He died and my kid brother was born. Dad was killed on the day Raymond was born. My guess. That made it kind of perfect anyway. We got the letter in the middle of winter just after Mom came home from the hospital with Raymie and I came home from Aunt Erby and Uncle Mac's, where I'd been stashed until Mom could cope. Her word. Pop-pop was not to be trusted with the entirety of me, I guess. I was five when the kid showed up. It was Raymie's fault the wallpaper went away. Here's the story:

Picture Mom standing in the hallway early one morning. The kid could walk, but she's holding him anyway and he's screaming. Here's why: the phone rang at 6:30. I was up and in the bathroom but I never answered the phone, not mornings or late at night. Mother's rule. Raymie ran out of Mom's room and to the phone. He always did. Then he stood and stared at it like a pointer until someone came and answered it. I guess Raymie caught his foot in one of holes in the carpet and fell. Mom came, picked him up, like always, and held him in the crook of her arm, bouncing him quiet as she answered the phone. Simple. He always stopped crying when she held him. Now he didn't. He didn't so much that I came out of the bathroom, toothpaste slobbering out of my mouth, to see what was going on.

Dull morning light poured out of Mom's room. Deer, dogs, spear, blood, women, everything blue or green or yellow or any color was soaked in deep red.

Mom was on the line bouncing him but the kid would not

shut up. I didn't know why. Then I did. Raymie was nose-to-nose with the bleeding deer, its wild wide eye, maybe six inches from his, flying dog above him, sticking spears, arrows, rearing horses. He twisted one way, the other, another; everywhere was blood pain.

Mom didn't notice at first. She kept bouncing the kid on her hip and trying to talk. I was laughing my head off—quietly, so not to disturb. Raymie looked at me, saw toothpaste foam on my mouth I guess and upped the screams to where Mom finally realized the kid wasn't going to shut up.

"Excuse me a second, okay?" she said. Then, "Raymond. Raymond? Ramie, what? What?" She looked at me. "Is it your brother?" I wiped the paste off my lips and shrugged. I didn't know. The kid kept it up. "Is it what? What, honey? What?"

The kid pointed at the wall and screamed.

"What? The paper? Is it this, the wallpaper?" She looked at me. "You think the wall is scaring him?"

It seemed stupid.

"I think. Are you? You afraid of this?" Mom laid her hand on the deer's face.

Raymie doubled the volume and buried his eyes in her hair.

"He is. He's afraid of the wallpaper! Huh! Listen," she said to the phone, "have to go."

Pop-pop had been born in the house. The wallpaper was there when he was a kid. Never bothered him, so far as he said. Mom had been born in the house. She didn't say so, but it probably didn't scare her. I was a baby there and it never made me cry. Then on, Raymond went through the hall, eyes shut. He fell at least once a week, with consequent screaming and flailing, right under the stag's head, the horse's hooves.

Finally, Pop-pop started taking estimates for redoing the hallway. One guy wandered, looking. He wanted to scrape and re-plaster, said that paper was on there darn good; even with the steam she was gonna rip out a lot of that old plaster. "That there's horse-hair binder, that there's holding it to them lathe strips under there," he said. "Gonna be rough, that job, and gonna lose some them lathes, too. Then there's the wire's gotta go over them voids and the new plaster." When all that was done, he could put on some pretty new paper over it. "Something ain't scary, you know, something, say, with flowers, nice flowers," he said, smiling down at the kid. "Or them puppy dogs and bunny bears. Something'll come off easy when the kid's growed, you know?"

The kid stared. This was in the living room where there were no horses, stags, and hounds.

Another guy figured the same, wrote it on a piece of butcher paper with a stubby pencil he kept licking, then sat down alone and did some quiet arithmetic. He finally said the walls would probably have to come down and go back up. Then he could hang some paper. Or not. Her choice. He gave mom a big book with lots of samples. She could choose, choose anything she wanted. Most of them had flowers, stripes, or both. He left the paper with it written in wet pencil lines and numbers.

Another wanted to just scrape, plaster and paint. Some nice paint, he thought. White would be good, people are doing that now, paint. "Wallpaper? That's horse and buggy days."

The kid whimpered about the horse and buggy stuff.

Everyone wanted to scrape and plaster first.

"That costs what?" Pop-pop asked. Three times he asked.

Each man said. They said different figures, but numbers so high Pop-pop's eyebrows went up each time. Each time he made blow-face noises.

Pop-pop died early one Sunday morning. He dropped down in the hall on his way to the bathroom and lay there until Raymie tripped over him. There was screaming.

Then it was up to Mom. Six months later she painted. Over

the wallpaper. She'd had it. She had a guy in, none of the ones from before, a guy she found in the phone book. He started pretty much the same as the others and Mom shut him up! If the damn stuff is on there so good, it can just stay there and he could paint over it.

The guy didn't like that and he left. Said it wasn't worth his time.

The next guy in the yellow pages was a one-armed vet with a limp. He looked, touched the wall with his one hand, ran it along, felt the texture.

"Seventy-five bucks," he said.

"About right," Mother said, "seventy-five dollars. About right."

"The paint on top of that," the guy said.

"Seventy-five and paint."

Color?

"White. Not just white, off-white, an almost white but not quite white white." Even Mom laughed when she said it. I did. The one-armed guy did too. When he laughed, scars showed on his cheek and neck. Raymie just stared at the guy.

The vet did it. He laid thick paint-spattered canvas along the hallway floor.

"Don't worry," Mom said, "I'm getting new!"

"Still," he said, and put it down anyway. Ran tape around the woodwork and baseboards.

He laid down a thick first coat. "Impasto!" he said, producing the word like a magician would. There went the picture, mom's side down to mine. The brush slapped the nubbly paper, erased the women, the woods, the horses, men, flying dogs, deer, blood. Then down the other side, my end to Mom's. The whole world from when Pop-pop was a boy disappeared stroke by stroke. All the darkness from Pop-pop's stories, the shadows that crawled, evenings, from beneath the trees and from under the houses, the castle, the world we couldn't see, the rasp of crickets, the whiff of chimney smoke and the smoke of dragons, the cold touches in the night, all the fears and holy wonders that came to life in my head, I had brought them out, emptied me of them and put them there to live in the story on the wallpaper, beyond the forest where I couldn't see them, gone.

Sitting in the hallway, alone afternoons or evenings, I knew the terrors were real as my dad had been, real but far, far away, unable to touch me.

Now it all disappeared and I went out of the house and down the block and sat beneath a tree near the mountain and cried. I was old enough to cross streets but I still cried! I never told that before.

The house smelled of paint and three days later the one-armed vet came back. He sanded and sanded until he was sanding with paper so fine it felt like velvet. He wiped the walls, sweeping in long smooth strokes. White dust filled the air. The air smelled like dry sand, damp oil, and old wheat paste. Then he came back and painted, let dry, sanded smooth again. Then he came back with the not-quite-white paint Mom wanted.

"Yes, that's it. Just it!"

"Old lace," he said.

"What? Oh, yes. Lace. Old lace! Yes."

This time she laid on smooth, the vet said, and when she dried that wall was smooth as a baby's bottom. What he said.

"Old lace," Mom said again, "white but not quite."

Mom's new carpet sat in a roll at the bottom of the stairs waiting for the vet to finish. The morning light from Mom's room bounced down the not quite white walls. The back and forth reflection lit, slightly, even the dark side passageway to the attic stairs. At sunset, the walls still looked like blood.

Through the work, Raymie left dust and paint trails everywhere. Mom cleaned, told him, "Be careful, you'll get paint everywhere." He wasn't, but at least he didn't cry every time he had to pee. Every day the vet came she told him where Raymie had made a mess, left footprints on the stairs, on the bathroom linoleum, the living room rug. The vet stuck his tongue in the corner of his mouth, patched, cleaned and never seemed to care, just did what he had to.

Then it was finished. Mom handed him seventy-five dollars in fives, extra for the paint and a little more for him. She got red in the face when she handed it to him. His face got red taking it.

Two minutes after he'd folded his drop cloth and was putting it into the trunk of his car, the kid ran a sliver into his big toe. He was running barefoot back and forth up and down the hall, shouting *hooray, hooray, yea!* When he got the splinter he flopped on his face and wouldn't stop screaming until mom tweezered the sliver out and mercurochromed his toe.

"You want for me to roll that runner down for you?" the vet asked when he came back for his brushes and buckets.

"Oh, I don't know. I think I can."

He ran his hand along the rough pine floor. "Should run a sander on these planks." He flipped a long sharp piece of wood with a fingernail. "Buddy of mine's got one he don't use so much and he owes me so it wouldn't take but an hour. Them splinters, it'll take the edge off 'em. Maybe two hours. Maybe seal the edges along the baseboard there with a little varnish." He touched Raymie's head. "Whole thing," he looked up and down the hall, my room to Mom's, "say, twenty bucks. Probably do it tomorrow, day after, depending. Little extra for varnish."

"Sure," Mom said.

"Raymond. Wear your shoes till then. Okay, Chief?" The guy waved a finger under the kid's nose. Raymie sniveled and stuck his face in Mom's leg.

The kid cried again that night. I awoke hearing screams. Mom was in the hall, holding him.

"Splinter?"

Mom shook her head. Raymie kept screaming; she held him. I stood. Finally Raymie looked at me. "Too big," he said.

"What is?" Mom said.

"It's too big!"

"What? The hallway?"

"Too big!"

"Yeah," I said. Mom gave me a look. But the hallway did look longer, now the trees and story were gone. Now there was nothing, nothing but walls and ceiling and that long run of splintery wood, just a little lamp to light it. I never thought our house was big, but it was. It was especially when you're just three feet tall as Raymie was. I remembered.

"Well, it's only as big as it ever was, Raymond," Mom said, still giving me the look. "Just exactly. No bigger."

"Hiding," he screamed, "in the woods. In there. And it is bigger. It wasn't this big before. They're hiding!" Then he looked at me and smiled. Cried, terrified and he smiled. His smile gave me gooseflesh. And I hadn't thought of it but maybe they were in there, the picture, the men, women, horses, dogs, the bleeding stag, the trees, the forest, the world beyond the forest, all the stories I'd built. My stories were still there, behind that nice not quite white paint. Maybe you'd have to be a magician to get it.

Mom didn't. She thought it was just the kid being like he was. "Just watch your feet, Raymie, okay?" is what she said.

The vet came back the next day. Mom didn't say anything. She didn't even tell it, laughing like she did when telling a Raymie story. The vet's buddy's sander was big. I was amazed the guy could get it up the steps with one arm. Mom offered to help but he just smiled. He hefted, balanced the thing, one handed, like he was, and limped it up the steps. I can't imagine.

"You guys get yourselves downstairs," he said to Raymie and me. "This thing starts up I gotta keep her going or she'll dig in and cut right through the floor." He winked at Mom. "No, really, get on down, she kicks up a lotta stuff."

We did. The sander growled around the hall for an hour. The vet walked behind the machine, let it have its way carefully, like dancing with it. He wore a wet bandana around his mouth and nose, looked like a holdup man in the westerns. Raymie had never seen a movie, cowboy or otherwise, didn't know about that stuff. Still, he giggled, looking at the one-armed guy but made cry-faces when the sander growled and ground.

I sat on the bottom step and breathed in the smells. Mom and the kid sat with me. She talked. I don't remember about what, but she talked. Every time the vet passed the upper landing, she stopped and watched. Every time, he looked down and his eyes smiled at her. She waved, every time. He nodded.

"Swifty," Mom said, sniffing the dust. "That's Swifty."

"What?"

"Smell that?"

Yes. Something at the heart of the smell coming from upstairs was not wood, not paint or varnish. It smelled like…

"Doggie pee," Mom said.

Piss. Yes.

"That's my Springer spaniel. Swifty. When I was your age, a little older, he used to…" She laughed. "When he was a pup and every time there was thunder and lightning, Swifty would pee himself. He'd run down by your room, the corner at the bathroom door? And he'd tinkle. It got so the wood was soaked black from pee. That's when Dad put that old runner down. That's what you smell. You smell him? Swifty." Her mouth was open a little and she smiled across it.

Raymie stared at Mom as she told the story. She got into it, remembered this and that about the pup, the dog, the old dog. "He died up there." She arched her neck toward the buzzing sander. "Right about where Pop-pop…" Then she started to cry and Raymie was on the edge. He had that look of something not right, something pushing him to cry but he didn't know what.

I breathed in the hot wood and piss dust of the long-gone Swifty. That was enough.

When the sander stopped, the hall floor was smooth as a baby's bottom. We all stood in that long near-white corridor.

"I'll dry mop it now and let it set for a little," the vet said. "Come back tomorrow, if that's okay with youse, and lay down a coat of varnish. Do one side then come another day and lay down the other. That way you can walk around up there so long's you remember to keep to the dry side."

"That's fine," Mom said. "Yes. Come back tomorrow. I can sweep. You've done enough for your twenty bucks, for goodness sake."

Mom never talked like that. "Twenty bucks."

The vet came back and varnished half the hall; he waited a day, then did the other half. On the Saturday he returned to roll and tack the new carpet. If anything happened between or among those days, I don't remember.

Mom paid the twenty bucks, something extra for the varnish, and put a little on top for him. She blushed again. That was that, we thought.

The new carpet was soft and thick, a pale gray, like pearls rich with body heat. The not-quite white white walls were already familiar. Through nights and dark parts of day, the lamp on the phone table made the corridor glow warm, yellow. I loved how my bare feet sank into the carpet like they did into dry sand. And no holes. The kid shuffled up and down, making sure nothing would grab, make him flop. Nothing did. Nothing did, but sparks cracked when he touched the brass doorknobs or the lamp. He cried about it at first, but soon he enjoyed making small lightning snaps. For days he slid along the hallway, leaning, taking a long lead on the sharp crackle that jumped between his finger and the brass lamp. In the dark, he watched as the spark jumped, yelping a little, laughing at the tiny pain. Of course I did it, too, touched his ear or nose. Of course! And, of course, he cried and growled at me.

During the time the vet worked there, the place had filled with amazing stenches, paint, turpentine, old wheat paste and horse hair, pulverized wood dust, Swifty's pee, the varnish. These and other things, things without names, smells damp and dry, steeped the house. This was summer and, while Mother kept the windows open so to catch the breezes, the air hung dead outside, so the smells of the veteran's work lingered and settled.

The first storm changed that. I missed its approach but awoke when a white flash and simultaneous thunder kicked the world to life just outside my window. It was that close, close enough so that when the sound awakened me, the lightning still lingered at the black edges of my room. Air, finally cool, breezed across me, sucked the heat of my body through summer sweats and carried it away. For minutes I was afraid to move, afraid another smash would blast the porch roof outside my window to flinders and me with it.

Finally, something about the rain, wind, and the stillness of our home made me tingle. Lightning and thunder were coming regularly, but none with the immediacy of that first shock. I got up.

Raymie was in the hall. The lamp threw a dull yellow cone up the wall. The kid stood between it and me. His cheek and body were pressed against the not quite white wall, as though he were floating on it, peering beneath. I assumed he was…

Truth is, I had no idea what he was or was not. I'd never seen him at anything like this. A tide of white lightning washed the hallway. The light froze his shadow on the wall for a flickering moment then it was gone. Raymond didn't move then he did. His fingertips walked his right hand a few inches nearer his head. His left hand slipped higher, higher, then stopped. He shifted his weight, tottered, shuffled closer to me, turned toward me... then he sang. No tune, no radio melody, nothing from memory, a kid's floating hum trying to find itself. The thunder rumbled below it.

Then the lamp winked and was gone. The storm hung fire and there was nothing, no light for seconds. Then distant lightning from Mom's end, dimly, then once or twice brilliantly, quietly lit us. Each time, the kid had moved closer, flash by flash, each time, he was in a different position and nearer. His small voice and songless song grew louder, his bare feet hushing the carpet, my way. Distant thunders but no lightning, nothing but my brother's voice and the closer, closer shuffle of his small bare feet.

I wanted to fill the place with daylight, jump, yell. I didn't. I knew there was a danger, waking sleepwalkers. I didn't know what, but knew there was, so I backed toward my room, keeping darkness between us.

I didn't remember closing my door, but suddenly my back was against it. The wind, likely, the wind that now blew through the hall must have eased it shut. Now I noticed the wind; it flowed over my feet and toward the crack beneath my door. Cool storm air from the side hallway, from downstairs, from Pop-pop's empty room, from our mother's room, sighed along the hallway and brought my brother toward me.

"Raym," I whispered. "Raymie," I said louder. "Raymond!" I shouted, but the shout was like one those thin screams made in a dream that's nearly over. The lightning came bright and silent and Raymond's face was inches from my chest, his eyes were wide and wild, his mouth open, every tooth he owned showing in a silent cry lost in the thunder. The lightning held the hallway flickering in a semblance of movement as shadows came into being then collapsed one on top of the other.

And that was that.

I screamed us all awake. Mom came from her room with candle. Raymie cried. I tried it, but the bathroom light didn't work.

"Raymond, oh, honey Raymond, it's okay. It's just rain and thunder. Can't hurt you." She looked at me. "And what're you yelling at?"

I was still flicking the light switch. "Power's out," I said.

"Get Pop-pop's whatever... his fish light." As though I were an idiot.

When I returned with the camp lantern she was holding the kid in her arms. He was snuffling and looking sheepish, like he did. I put the lantern on the table. It threw a bull's-eye of light on the ceiling. The outer rings ran down the wall and spread a little yellow on the hunt.

"What were you doing? Where did you think you were? Oh, honey..." She cooed while she petted Raymond's wet hair back from his eyes.

He looked at her and, this is funny, the cry oozed out of his face and was replaced, I swear, by a look, one of those 'I have a secret' looks. I had felt that look cross my face from time to time. Raymie tossed it away in less than a second...

"Raymond?" Mom said.

...and he replaced that look with a smile so beautiful.

"I was in a dainty place," he said.

"...a what?" Mom said.

"I was in a dainty place."

I almost dropped dead away.

The power was back next day. That day, Mom hung the first pictures in the hall. Family photos. Raymie's episode and the photos were not connected. I don't think, anyway. Mom simply came out of her room that morning, stretched, looked down the long white hall. "Little bleak, huh?"

That was that. After breakfast she tap-tap-tapped a couple pictures of Dad and us on the wall, a few of Raymie and me, two of her with Dad from before the war, one with him in his uniform, a lake in the background. Mom blushed when she hung that one. She sniffled when she touched it. Going into the walls, the nails sounded soft, as though they were being driven into thick nothing.

"Better?" she said.

I shrugged.

She started bringing home frames, plain ones from the Five-and-Dime, beat-up things from junk shops. Into them she fed photos that had been around for as long as I'd been alive, shots of Pop-pop, Nanna and Mom at the shore or on a mountainside, them sitting in clearings in the woods or by lakes. There were photographs of family I didn't know, or of us in places I'd never been, pictures of me held by people I never knew or those I knew to be dead. There were pictures of young Pop-pop and pretty Nanna and other dead people in prickly clothes from horse and buggy days, Mom's people, slicked and unsmiling. There was none of Dad's people I think. Some pictures I asked about and when she explained I still didn't know.

By the start of school, the old lace walls were black and white with pictures and frames.

"I want you guys to know where you came from," she said at the table. Dinner had been cleared and she was matching pictures to frames. "You know, those people," she flicked her head upward. Raymie followed the look through the kitchen ceiling. "They all lived, had lives and did, well, whatever. Now..." she sniffled, "now, you're them."

Raymie and I looked at each other. His mouth was open.

I guess she looked at me because I was squinting. "I mean, you're what's left of your dad and me and Pop-pop and Nanna, all our people. You're it, what's here." She stopped talking and went back to framing.

"Family," she said smiling, touching my neck.

Okay. Why I almost dropped dead that night. It goes back to the picture that lay beneath the almost white paint and a bit to the mostly dead family that was gathering in the hallway. Beyond the hunt and trees, there was a castle. Could it be seen? No. I put it there with my head, built it through days of sitting, reading to myself or remembering Pop-pop's stories, bringing forth all the stuff that scared me in them. I put the castle on the far side of the woods. It was a huge stone thing on a hill on its own sunny plain, a little Sleeping Beauty, some of Prince Valiant, a bit of Rapunzel and some of the White Castle, downtown. The place was white, anyway. White in the sun, at night it was black and pierced a thousand places by candle-lit windows and torch-bright arrow slits. The place wasn't well thought out. I'd pictured a lot of towers, portcullises and drawbridges, a moat. Inside were feasting halls with house-high fireplaces, torches, banners everywhere. The halls had pine boughs spread across the floor. Pop-pop said they did that, that it made things smell good, like our living room at Christmas and after. Below were dungeons and passageways, one secret place to another. There were high rooms of stone and tapestries. And here and there were rooms for just me and the friends I'd have.

And another place, a small place. No windows. Whenever I saw it in my head the room was yellow with candlelight, filled with the scent of hot wax mingled with spices—Pop-pop's tales always had people who risked the world for spices and riches. The room smelled old. Old like the mummy-room at the museum. Yet this was a room of small things, fragile this-and-thats. There were shelves and cupboards, chests and boxes, small vaults and built-in safes sealed with cunning locks and demonically clever traps—more Pop-pop words—that were filled with cogs, gears, springs, spools of wire, with limbs and digits, hearts and eyes for mechanical people and clockwork beasts, of gadget bits, parts of toys and tick-tock whimsies to amaze and delight. There was a table of instruments, tools that warped space with vorpaled edges and measured the impossible with verniers of light. Things waited here and there, for repairs for building, just for so, for nice.

This place was the heart of it all, what I always thought of as a "dainty place." A Nanna-name. Nanna never saw the room, of course. It was only in my head and she was gone long before it existed even there. In life, whenever Nanna saw a precious thing, a lady-watch, a tiny cup, a spun-glass animal, or wooden balls within rings inside boxes, she would cup it in her hands, hold it to her eye and breathe, "Oh, isn't this just what whimsy is? Isn't that a dainty place?"

I was young. That look, the move, her eye, those words are almost all I remember.

Raymond, of course, had never known, never heard, and I'd never spoken it, not to him nor anyone. Yet, that night, he was there, awake and back from some place, that dainty place at the heart of my castle of terrors.

He asked me about Nanna soon after. Half a dozen pictures of her were on the wall, photos that spanned her life from when she married Pop-pop, a bright hazy beauty next to him, a straight-haired, horse-faced, hard-collared boy, younger than Mom was now, all the way to her last days, skin dried to crinkles and not a lick of spit in her.

"Who's she?" Raymie said, pointing at the bride.

"Nanna," I said. "Grandmother. Mom's mom."

"And that? Who's that?"

"Nanna, too. She's old there."

"No!" he yelled, looking from one to the other. Then he laughed. "No."

The pictures opened doors. We'd meet in the hallway. He'd point, "Who's that?"

"Dad," I'd say or whomever.

"Tell me about your dad!"

"Your dad, too..." I'd say.

"No," he said, and looked again. "No. That's your dad. Where's my dad?"

"Same one."

Then he cried.

Or I'd be in my room working tricks from Malini, making balls disappear, reappear, and the kid would drag me to the wall. "Where are we there?" or "Who's that?"

I'd answer if I could. If I didn't know, or tried to put him aside, Raymie wouldn't stop. "Well is that our mountain?" "Well is it our another Granddad?" "Well is it Pop-pop's brother?" "Well is that their house?" "I guess *that's* your dad, too?"

Sometimes I'd ask Mom. Sometimes she knew, other times she'd shake her head. "Pop-pop knew what that was, but..."

On one picture a woman posed by a steam tractor with spiral sprung iron wheels twice the woman's height. A dirty man perched on the machine's high saddle. "No. Pop-pop told me who and what, but darned if I remember." She had another squint, ticked her tongue and gave up.

Raymond always seemed sure, always gave me a look as though I held back some truth I didn't want to share. Ignorance was never enough so I took a hint from the Big Book of Malini and made things up.

That great iron and steam thing once had been a fearsome beast. Alive and raging, it was captured in the forest. "Yeah, the forest on the wall. Before." When captured, it had been changed into a machine. "Yep, that one." A mighty witch, our great, great-grandmom from the old country, cast the spell. "Her in the picture. There!" I pointed. "She used the machine with her Imp,

Igor—him, up in the saddle, cripes!—they killed Nazis in the war with it. The mountains? No, they're not our mountains, those're mountains beyond our mountain, they're mountains in a place you've never seen. You might. One day."

It was like that.

Raymie nodded his head, touched the picture, looked at me, smiled. That would be that. Much easier than a thousand questions after an "I don't know."

In my one of my tales an old guy, a stiff black suit standing to his shins in mud in the middle of a field, was an escaped priest from far away and over the seas. He'd fallen in love with a peasant girl who came to hear him, the young priest, serve mass. He left the monastery, where he'd been under a vow of loveless silence, to woo her. The monks chased them across the land. Along the way they'd become robbers just to earn their living.

It went on.

Finally, their backs to a cliff, out of bullets, the two decided to leap into the sea rather than surrender to the ravaging hordes of monks and nuns. In their final moment they were rescued by a crew of Barbary Pirates who climbed up the cliffs, set to and slew all the holy people, then offered the robber priest and his peasant love a place on their jolly ship. They accepted immediately and sailed upon the seven seas—the Atlantic, Pacific, Mediterranean, Superior, Arctic, Mississippi, and Titicaca—where they laid waste to many towns and collected precious jewels, mountains of gold, countless bolts of fine silks, and spices galore from all around the world.

When the pirate priest and his corsair wife grew tired of blood and treasure, they retired to a farm near Philly. They built a castle—gone now—and raised a bunch of kids. The only photograph ever taken of them—"this one"—was snapped by one of the children—a school-chum of Pop-pop's who gave it him just before he marched off to war, making Pop-pop swear never to tell the whole true story, ever.

"He died in the war, of course," I told Raymie.

"How do you know it, then?" the kid asked.

"Pop-pop talked in his sleep," I said. "Didn't you know that?"

There were dozens of other tales and the next noise in the hallway came in late summer.

I woke. There was a cricket's insistent buzz at the heart of the house's silence. I had heard crickets in the yard, in the park. This was inside. Summer had lingered into deep September. Still, wet heat wrapped the nights. With windows open, this thing had come and settled into the walls I guessed. It played an insistent, metallic chitter.

I lay not sleeping. What if the bug chewed the wires, made a short? What if the constant sawing of cricket legs heated them to kindling and he burst to life inside the walls, set the house and us on fire?

Stupid? Yes. Possible? Well...

Into the hallway with me. And the chirrup, chirrup, stopped. Still, a bug could chew and chew so silently... I waited. Listened. Nothing, nothing. Nothing. To bed and moments later the chirrup-chirrup began again. And I was back. That pattern continued. Finally, I surrendered, slept. We lived.

I said nothing the next day. Raymie did.

"Woods're back," he said, his fork burrowing into his mashed potatoes. "Ch, ch, ch, ch, ch," he said, a tolerable impression.

"What?" Mother said.

"The forest is coming back. I heard." He did his noise again.

"There's a cricket in the baseboard," I said. "Must have come in a window. Something. It might eat the wires. Probably not, though, huh?"

"Well, some people think they're lucky," Mother said. "So, third grade? You like it better?"

I didn't. That's all she said about it. That's all I said about chewed wires. The kid smiled.

That night they were back: the heat, the ch-ch-ch and sudden silence. I became familiar with it, insect conflagration. Night-by-night the fear of flames became ordinary.

Top to bottom, it was a long stairway, fifteen steps, three more to the living room floor. That summer I had grown long enough in my legs and arms to feel that I'd be able to make the jump, eleven feet and three inches, top step to bottom landing. I'd tested my reach, leaned out from the top, walked my hand down the banister on the right, inched-down against the wall on the left. Long arms. I reached nearly halfway down by the time third grade started. Saturday morning, I leaned farther than ever, body horizontal. I said a prayer to Dad and committed. I swung out on a whim, kicked my legs ahead to proceed the fall, enough, I hoped, to miss the last steps and land flat on the landing. I landed flat on the landing. Almost went head-first into the wall, but didn't. I was alive and whole and it never hurt a bit and the world was wonderful.

"Do it again!" The kid had been watching from the hallway. "Then me..." He came down a couple steps, grabbed the rail with both hands, looked at the space ahead. He was thinking.

I yelped, ran, grabbed the kid, and dragged him to the landing. "You're too little. You'd bust your noodle." I tapped his head. "I've been waiting since I was your age to do that." I mussed his hair.

He gave me the look, the *I-can-do-anything-I-want* look, the *you-can't-tell-ME* look, and shoved his hair back.

"Breakfast," Mom called from the kitchen.

Raymond relaxed in my arms.

"Okay?" I eased off. "Okay, you won't?"

"Before it's lunch, guys, come on." Mom came in from the kitchen. "What?" she said, looking at the two of us facing off.

Raymond smiled. His cut-glass laugh squeezed out and he ran to the kitchen. That was that.

A week later I awoke. Another storm was coming. The cricket—cicada, whatever—had had a family. It was now locusts and other things, things I don't know what. Mom had to be awake, she had to be, but when I went into the hall, no, she wasn't, or if so, she'd ignored the night, gone back to sleep. They were behind the walls, both sides. Above the ch-ch-ch and lingering metallic buzz was a meaty, furry chatter that bounded back from the side passage to the attic. When the full downpour settled across the house, the buzz almost disappeared into the storm. Driven rain scoured the walls and windows. In the lightning, the old people on the walls licked in and out of being, flickered between storm-brightness and the yellow limbo of the table lamp. Four times, I went to the hall to look, to listen. Raymie was there on the fifth, asleep, as before. He walked with blind confidence. His fingertips slid the walls like electric brushes gathering a charge. His hands tipped the pictures. The faces, places, stories tick-tocked back as he passed. His eyes were open but he slept. Awake, he never had the face he had now. Now he was not here, he was there, inside, beyond night and storm, beyond the hunt, he was through the forest and into the castle, in the castle's still wax light, in the dainty place Nanna had breathed on and Pop-pop and I built with stories.

Raymond's eyes were on me. As the lightning chattered up and down the hallway, I saw... How to say? I saw figures, dark, familiar shades, figures of men, horses, dogs, deer. They rose from beneath the old lace surface to the flickering hall. Forest murmurs drove them upward. And with them arose the sure but distant voices of men and horses, dogs and sobbing women.

At the heart of it, Raymond, Raymond in the dainty place, so far away. I knew he was there.

And finally, when I could call, call him awake, call for help, for Mother, it was morning and I was in bed and the sky was blue and washed and my call was a whisper.

At supper Raymond sang.

We sat at the table, Mom's meatloaf and the last of the season's corn on the cob in front of us, a single bulb overhead. Nothing much was said about the night, the storm before, just that it had been one doozy of a downpour, huh, guys?

Yes. I'd heard Mom. Earlier, on the phone: Well, we were just kids, you know? *Kids'll be kids. No, he's never been afraid of lightning! Why now? Well, kids will be kids! It's something new, always.*

This to Aunt Erby, whose only kids had been dogs or glass figures on mirror shelves. I was the "he" Mother meant had never been afraid of lightning. And I wasn't. I didn't think so.

Raymond had forgotten walking the hall, his hands sliding, tipping the pictures. He didn't remember the dark shadows of horses, men and dogs and the near-dead deer surfacing. "Vast dark echoes rising from a deep mountain tarn," Pop-pop's Poe might have called it.

Raymie smiled and rolled his corn in butter and sang the same songless tune. He used both hands. He ate, singing.

"Raymond..."

His eyes swung, lazy, to Mom...

"Singing at table, Raymond?"

He smiled and chewed. Raymie had just begun eating cob corn by himself, buttering, gnawing the ears. The kid slobbered, smeared butter across his cheeks, up his nose. It dripped up his arms to his elbows. I hated watching. Corn is one of those things...

"Mom..." I tried.

"He's learning," she said.

"He's disgusting..."

She smiled. "He's a little boy."

"Cripes. Can't you eat evenly? That's disgusting, strands and pieces, your mouth everywhere, over the whole ear! Look." I took an ear from my plate. "Fifteen rows. Eat them three rows at a time, one end to the other, or four at a time three times and have one left of three rows."

Mom was laughing. So was Raymond.

"You don't eat 'em side to side and all around at the same time..."

They were rolling on the floor.

"Well, Jesus damn Christ!" I yelled. "Little bastard's a pig!"

That was that for me that night.

That night Raymond broke the hallway light. Knocked it off the table then tripped over his feet and started screaming. I have no idea what he was doing at 3 in the morning. I didn't care. Mom handled it.

Two days later the vet was back. He limped up and down, staring at the hallway ceiling. Mom stood aside. "Oh, heck, yeah. We could," he said. "Maybe." He was talking to himself. "Yeah, a small one. Right there." He pointed. Mom nodded. "The joist should be there, I guess, coming off that side hall." He tapped the ceiling three, four places with a broom handle. "Yeah. There't is. Then I run your wire down, cut a channel, tie it into the same circuit as that there lamp..."

He drifted away, mumbling, tapping, listening. Finally, "Sure. Nice little chandelier just there. A little spackle. Switches down there and over there." He pointed. "No problem. You know what?"

"What?"

He looked right at her. "This is gonna be a whatchacallit."

Mom smiled. "No? What do you call it?"

"You know…"

Her smile became a laugh.

"A showplace. My calling card, you know? This hall. I ought to take pitchers, bring customers to see youse. Heck, I ought to just move in!" He laughed in the middle, his words still running.

The kid laughed with him and the vet ruffled his hair with his single hand.

Mom went red through her chuckles and put her arm around Raymie.

That night, the photographs came off the wall and went into boxes in the living room.

Next day the vet was back. He came back every day for a week. The chandelier was not so simple. Scaffolding moved in, permanently it seemed. Dust and buzz, rolls of wire were everywhere. I was in school most of the time but Raymie, Mom, and the vet were there. He was there when I left in the morning; he was there when I returned in the afternoon. Every day the hall looked the same: no further along. No, I lie! Every day it was a little worse, maybe. Every time I heard the vet working, he grunted, cursed, dropped things and dragged them, the walls shook, he pounded and said words! Words I couldn't.

He ate with us sometimes, then went back to work. Doing whatever. That, or he sat with Mom and Raymie, listening to the radio and laughing along. Sometimes Mom played music and danced. He'd sit and smile.

"Dance," the kid said, pushing the vet. "Dance like this!" And Raymie showed him.

"Naw," the vet said. "I don't."

"Leave it be, Raymond," Mom said.

"No, no. You can dance. I can. You can. See." Raymond hopped from foot to foot, arms out like he was holding Mom.

"Now Raymond, let me tell you," the vet said. He leaned forward and rolled up his pants leg just above the ankle. "See, I have a funny leg." And he did, a leg of metal and wood and hinges. From the top of his sock, his leg was metal rods encased in wood, sheathed with tin plate. Steel cable ran up and disappeared.

Raymie looked at the artificial leg and smiled.

"It only goes to here." He showed where, below the knee. "But it leave me so I don't dance so good no more. Not good as you, anyhow!" The kid laughed and the vet scooped him up in his one arm and swung him round his shoulder. Raymie screamed, laughing. "I sure ain't good enough to boogie-woogie with your mom!"

I had no idea. No idea what else wasn't real?

The chandelier was up. The wire runs were patched and painted, the switches set—one at the bottom of the stairs, one outside Mom's room—and we had "a little ceremony" Mom called it.

"Turn off! Turn off the lights! Everything!" Mom shouted. We did. We stood in the old lace hallway in the dark. In the dark, I felt I might fall. I touched the wall. Just to hold. I swear something. Something moved beneath my hand, like the floor when a truck goes by, like thunder against your chest. Mom said, "One... two... THREE!"

The vet turned the switch at the bottom of the stairs. The chandelier came on. The hallway was four-bulbs-bright. Hot damn. The rumbling beneath my hand stopped.

"Hey." He came up, admiring the work. "Hey, not bad," he said. "Hey. Try the night setting!"

Mom minced down the hall to her bedroom. "Okay!" she sang. "One, two three." Click, click, click and one, two, three, the lamps went out, leaving a single bulb glowing dim yellow. Shadows of the other bulbs and the chandelier arms stretched across the ceiling. Yes, it looked like a spider. It wasn't. The kid whimpered but the vet put his arm around him. Raymie gave up the whimper and laughed. "Spider," he said, giggling.

Mom and the vet drank some wine.

"Perfecto," he said.

"Perfecto," she said and clicked her glass against his. "Yes."

"Alikazam!" Raymond said.

I went to bed and heard the vet's truck leave, I don't know, midnight maybe, maybe later.

The cricket came back. The bugs had been silent while the vet had worked. Now to hell with them. I slept.

The vet kept showing up. He did no work. He ate with us. Sometimes he and Mom went places, restaurants, movies, wherever. When they did, Aunt Erby came over and read the paper until they returned and had stupid stuff on the radio. "They dancing?" Raymie asked Erby. He showed his dance.

"I think so, Ray," she said.

"Shazam," Raymond said and pointed at me.

On the last thunderstorm, I woke and there was nothing. Nothing in the house, nothing outside. That was it. Nothing. The cricket was gone. His friends the locusts, the others, the ones of meat and fur, they'd left. There was a distant bumble. Just something felt, like your ears feel, going up the mountain. The hallway light was on "night setting." I lay in bed feeling nothing from everywhere. A thin slit of light crept through my mostly closed door. It swayed a little. Just a little. Finally, I got up.

The pictures were back on the walls. Mom, the kid, and the vet had replaced them right after the chandelier ceremony. All the dark family was silent in the silence around them. I went to the bathroom and peed. As I did, I felt cool air slide around my ankles. A storm gathering. I could hear it now, distant. I washed my hands and turned off the light.

The kid was in the hall, just outside his door, Pop-pop's door. He stared up at the spider-shadow on the ceiling, down the wall. The chandelier was swaying in the breeze that had freshened in the last few minutes. He was talking. I couldn't hear what, or what he said made no sense, like his tuneless song at the table. With his voice, though, the wind picked up, the chandelier moved quicker. Without taking his eyes off the shadows crawling across the ceiling and wall, he walked backward toward Mom's room. Her door was open. Raymond pulled it shut. He turned toward me.

"Raymie…" I said.

"Shh. You'll miss the magic!"

"What…" I started.

"Alikazam," he said and flicked off the light. The hallway went black.

"Raymie!" I yelled. I knew Mom would be up by then. I knew it. And of course I was wrong.

The first lightning flickered and Raymond was halfway between Mom's room and his. The next flash, and Raymond was beneath the chandelier. He touched the wall. In the lingering flicker I saw shadows rise through the near-white. They stretched themselves into shapes, the shapes I remembered from my earliest days: deer, men. With the thunder's rumble, I heard dogs. For the first time, I heard the clabber of horses, hooves and whickers, the shriek of the downed mare.

Raymond was still speaking, saying nothing, and his hand reached through the surface of the white. He smiled and waved goodbye. He reached into the far-away place with his other arm. And was gone.

I shouted something. I think one of Malini's magic words. I yelled to leave a word behind for Mom and reached for the wall, touched it, felt its old lace softness, its tapestry thickness and suddenly I was not. That was all: I was not.

113

Where I was, where I am, is here. This side. Where the images float. It is not what I remember. Not exactly. Looking back to where the wall was there is more of here. But it is dark, very dark; it is blacker than the deepest mountain tarn. And no light from here goes very far, there.

There is no Raymond. Not here. I arrived and, for a second, saw him, face and body. He was flattening, sifting through, returning through the darkness to the other side, Pop-pop's hallway. Our mother's. The one-armed veteran's showplace. Raymie turned, folded like a paper doll in black and white, and said something, "Shazam," I think and, whoof, he was gone. I reached for him but where he was, I wasn't, and where I am, the darkness just goes on.

This is a quiet place. The sounds of horse and dog? That was a trick. Of Raymond's? I don't know. A trick of the place? Perhaps. But the world is quiet near the stag and horses, the dogs and men. It is most quiet nearest the deep darkness where the horse's hooves have not moved for years. Not that I've seen. The dog still flies. He's not risen nor fallen a quarter inch, not in my time, and that has been long. The women sob but the tears do not fall, have not inched a fraction down their downy cheeks. Farther from all that is a small pond at the edge of the woods. I couldn't see it from the hallway, or maybe I never noticed. The surface almost ripples. But it extends into the trees, away from the sunlight. There a person can sit and from time to time skip a stone across the still black water. The stones spin slowly, touch the surface gently and do not penetrate, not precisely. There, the air is fragrant—and I know fragrance implies movement, a movement, at least of air and particles in the air. I don't understand it, but there it is.

The temperature is mild. Miles away, at the far edge of the woods, it sometimes rains, gently, slowly. I think farther away there are quicker rains because a river flows from the mountain and it rolls with a thunder I sometimes hear in my sleep.

There are birds in the woods beyond the stag and men, nearly still and almost silent doves. I can pluck them from the branches or the air. They're clean. Pressing my face into their feathered breasts, I smell sunlight and dust. They must, once long ago, have flown where sun shines. What's best, I can make them vanish at will, vanish for real, no trick to it, no gaffs or patter: I hold them up, I let them go and say, "Alikazam" or "Shazam" or just "Go 'way," and they're gone. The words don't matter; it's the will that makes it so. Where they go? I don't know for certain, but I think I do.

I've seen the castle, beyond. It is large, larger than our town. Things move on the battlements and, in windows, things dance, people, I think. There are voices, distant. I can't understand them. Someday I'll go there. Some night I'll be a monster from a far-off land or an invisible thing and find my way to that room at its heart. My brother will not be there. He doesn't need that dainty place, its cogs, wires, and gizmos. He has his father. By then, Mom may be there. Dad, Pop-pop, Nanna, the dark suited man, once the pirate scourge of the seven seas, his peasant wife, they'll be there and others and me, invisible. Then we'll hunt.

AT ANGELS SIXTEEN

"Old wars is mainly lies," is what Daddy said. I got no reason to disagree; he was almost always right. So let me tell you one. An ancient critter, I still don't know what to call him, saved my shot-down ass in the air war over Europe, 19-and-43.

A lie? Matter of fact I don't know about that one myself. Might could have been it was Miss Duchenne, my teacher, eighth grade, who taught me a waltz and fox trot and who I fell in love with. Maybe she saved my plummeting butt, or it could have been science like the Germans said, but it happened like this:

Pearl Harbor was my sixteenth birthday and I wanted to go fight. Daddy said trenches is no place for kids. Said he ought to know, having been a kid in the trenches himself, the last war. But he kept thinking. That same Sunday evening we walked into the bottomland and watched night gather and scoot out from under the trees by the Red. Ground crackled underfoot and sucked my boots like it wanted to draw me down. Our place is rich loam and always keeps a little damp under an early freeze so nothing strange there. That night smelled so pretty, a little charred hickory in the air. But we're talking about Daddy, who was still thinking. I held my breath.

"That Old World's a strange place," he said. "Europe's got things in her soil, up her airs, probably under her waters, too. I won't speak to that; I never been under them waters."

I didn't know what Daddy was talking about but seemed like he was changing his heart. He didn't do that much, so I stood quiet.

"I learned things in the mud of France what I wouldn't have got nowhere else." He chewed on his cheek. "You can go," he said. "But." He looked at my eyes like he was sure it was me busted the kitchen window, which it was. "You watch now, y'hear?"

"I'll be careful," me being agreeable, figuring he'd already changed his mind once that night.

"I ain't saying be careful. Cripes, careful ain't for soldiers. I'm telling you, keep your eyes open and your ears clean." He beaded down hard. "I'd tell you about the old ones as cares for earth and air, tell you about them things in the fire. Water too I guess, cripes. I'd tell you, but then you'd think your daddy'd gone crazy with fairy ways and Santy Claus." He spat on the ground. "You'll see. Maybe. Maybe only us folk sees them." He looked at me. "Farmers—part spit, part dirt, and all hot air." He kicked the place where his spit fell. "We got old ones, too. Old Folk here go back before the white man, so maybe they're less partial to you and me…"

The dark had crawled up to his face. For maybe the ninth time in his life, Daddy smiled. He shoved my hair around, then, "Anyways," he said, "old wars is mainly lies."

Next day I ran across them fields to enlist. I lied about my age. Daddy confirmed the lie on a paper he wrote out, saying, "My boy is oldern he looks and smartern he seems."

Being small, I had nothing much to work the lie upon, but what I lacked in height and muscle, I made up for in face hair and brass, so they took me.

Boot camp shaved my head and ran me ragged. We lifted, jumped, pushed-up, polished, threw, crawled, and fought. We got yelled at, told not to think Goddamnit and to jump when someone says to jump and quick too. When I got past thinking and got big where it mattered, the Army declared me a soldier then sent me to the Air Corps. Which would be all right, I figured, flying a plane of hurtling silver, shooting down my enemy man-to-man.

They shipped me to gunnery school where I sat in wheelbarrows and shot broom handles, which is how I learned the .30 caliber and the .50. Sergeant Bugg said in all his days he'd never seen one so deadly with a broom as was I.

My buddy was a guy from the east called Socrates. He was smart and told me Sarge was ironic—making fun. Soc and I took turns running the barrow while the other aimed the broom.

When they gave me shooting guns that was better. I could write my name with a caliber .30—if what I aimed at wasn't dodging, diving, or shooting back. Shooting, diving, and ducking—that was war, seemed to me. Soc laughed, shook his head, and wrote down what I'd said in a book he was making.

They assigned us to the B-17, the Flying Fortress. Soc learned waist gunning. Being small, I became a tail gunner.

Let me tell you about the B-17: The 17's a hair off 75 feet long. Tail gunner sits less than three feet from the dead end.

Let me tell you about the tail of a B-17: The plane skinnies from the waist on. Heading back, first you stoop, then you duck, then you waddle. You try not to bump your head but, naturally, you do. You watch grabbing anything along the sides because on the skin and between the ribs are breaker boxes, conduits, wire bundles, oxygen bottles, there are hydraulic lines everywhere, control cables that squeak through struts, roll over pulleys, and dip into secret places. All that keeps the plane flying or someone alive. Anyway, you never touch anything metal with your bare hands, not at Angels Sixteen and up, because the cold burns your skin right to it. That's why you've got a flight suit and gloves.

Flying, the plane shifts, creaks, and chatters, she bends,

twists, flaps, moans, and shivers. Can't tell you all the sounds she makes.

At bulkhead seven, there's a caibo can to the side. It stinks but so much of the plane does in so many interesting ways, I didn't mind. Past the can, you crawl; you crawl around the hump where the tailwheel snugs into the fuselage. You crawl and eventually there's an armored seat. Above it is a glass box big enough for your head. After that is the air. Twin .50s poke between your legs in case you want to kill something means you harm. In woolens, flight suit, helmet, gloves, boots, and parachute, you barely squeeze into that iron-bottom seat. Even I had trouble. After a bit I started leaving my chute back by the tail wheel. An easier crawl that way. SOPs said not to, everyone said not, the gunnery sergeant, pilot, everyone, so I figured everyone must do it so I did it too. That wasn't exactly thinking—which I knew not to do—but without the chute, I could at least move a little, look around, get some idea where the targets were coming from, the notion being you kill the target before the target kills everybody.

That's the tail of the B-17.

When the Army graduated us to the war, Soc and I shipped as cargo on a flight of 17s being ferried to 8th Air Force, England. Replacements—ships and us. No one had to tell us what we were replacing or why we were required.

At Angels Twenty-five—that's Air Corps talk for twenty-five thousand feet—it's three hundred miles an hour and forty below zero outside the plane. It's not much warmer in.

Soc and I hunkered down forward of the waist guns and talked. Keeping warm, you know? Soc talked, anyway. He talked about the war, the world after the war—"geopolitics" he called it—he talked about the next war, about the big sciences of life and death and, well, he talked about Socrates things. For warmth, you know.

"Next time," he said, "it's going to be science. New wars will be numbers and engineering."

Couldn't help laughing. I remembered what Daddy said about old wars.

Soc didn't notice. "Look here," he said. His voice was rubbery through his O-mask. "Soon it'll be just our machines fighting theirs. Our brains versus theirs. Men won't even see the battles they're in." He pulled his mask deeper into the fur hole around his hood. "Science won't make war obsolete—just the warrior." The voice came out his O-tube.

"Might have a point," I said.

"Huh?" he said.

I pointed my face at the plane around us. There we were, I told him, sailing the mighty ocean in a single night, freezing our soft asses behind thin metal at Angels Twenty-five. I was trying not to think, see? At least I wasn't thinking science, but you look at a B-17 on the ground. There is no way it flies. A 17 is sixty-five thousand pounds of Mother Earth, mined, smelted, poured, shaped, fitted and tuned. It could not, no shade of doubt about it, fly. It could not but that everyone agreed it could—pilot, crew, folks at home, the enemy in Berlin, everyone knew a B-17 flew—so fly it just naturally does. Science? I didn't know; Soc would have called that superstition.

"Yeah," I said, "the plane's the warrior, huh?"

"Yeah, yeah, sure," he said and went on thinking aloud. "We'll pave the world, dwell in buildings of the mind, all be part of a vast electric..." His eye poked from his parka. "You know what?" his rubber-voice asked, "we are priests." Oxygen hissed around his words. "Yeah, you and me, acolytes of the new rites of combat. Yeah, that's going to be my book, *Priesthood of Mars* it's called." He squinted. "Or *In Holy Orders*... Well, something like." He pulled his head back under the fur and said something I don't doubt was important, but which I couldn't hear.

On the ground in England another bunch of pilots—they seemed like pretty happy guys, mostly drunk I think—took the planes and flew them off to bases all over what they called Anglia. That was still England.

Soc and me shipped in a beat-up bus to our assignment base, Cranwell Hall, Suffolk, the Air Corps having more important things to fly than us, for Christ sake. I was used to least tit by now.

England's air breathed different. It tasted. Smelled like Granma's place, old and smoky. The air and that cold night flight might have put me to sleep because on the way to Cranwell I dreamed. It was full night when Soc nudged me awake. Our headlamps were blacked down to little slits and the bus crawled behind a little squeak of light on the road ahead.

"German night raiders!" Soc whispered and pointed overhead. Gave me a chilly thrill. Here I was in the war, history all around. I got used to it in a few minutes.

Fields rose on steep hills, both sides of the road. All along those up-and-down meadows the harvest ground-stubble was afire. Low flames tumbled in long weaving lines. They rolled uphill, wriggling and whipping like deep blue worms in red and yellow rut. Between the fires and our creeping bus, dark shadows danced; people and animals, I guessed. The shadows herded the flames across the leas and over the crests!

"Farmers?" I asked Soc.

"Don't know," he whispered, and kept writing his book.

"Incendiaries?" I asked.

"I don't know," he said slow and plain. "Ask the driver."

"Bombs?" I asked the old bloke driving. He said nothing.

"Sir!" I yelled above the engine. "Was it bombs made them fires?" I guessed he was deaf.

When we cleared the burning hills and rolled into flat land

and darker night the driver piped up. "Not bombs, Yank," he said. "You be in Anglia, now. This be sea-born land 'n' all here'bouts." He hunched the wheel, his chin pointed ahead. "All the land here be claimed from the sea in King Charlie's time." He gave me a wink. "Them folk," he cocked his head at the glowing hills behind us, "crazy with country ways, they are. After harvest, they dance wi' th' eelymen'als, give 'em their way about, you see? It were their old farthers as stole the warter's land, they reckon, so pleasing them Undeens makes fer good crops—good wars, too, I reckon." He coughed a saw-grass laugh my direction. "Eelymen'als like a good to-do!"

"Eely whats?" I shouted to him.

"Eel-e-mentals!" he hollered back, straining on the word. "Old folk! Them of earth and air, the fires and the warters. Them farm folk there be lettin' the Sallymander play, I reckon. But what's the point, I arsks? They'll be fire enough anon, little Yank." He laughed, then laughed again.

I listened like Daddy told me, but had no idea what the old bloke was saying. When I came back to the seat Soc was asleep. Soon I was too.

Let me tell you about Cranwell Hall and Lakenheath. At this time, all England was under arms. Cranwell Hall was one of hundreds of bases along the North Sea all aimed at the Continent. Every day, our planes from Cranwell and the others rose, rendezvoused over the Channel, and headed for Hanover, Bremen, Frankfurt, Brest, and a thousand places. We were taking war to the enemy.

Three miles from Cranwell was another farm town, Lakenheath: a street of houses, a monument to Daddy's War, two pubs, a church—all flint and balance—and a chips shop.

Between Lakenheath and Cranwell Hall was a common meadow. On Lakenheath Lea, what the blokes called it, the Air Corps had built a dummy base. The figuring was that from three miles up and lit by marker flares, wood and canvas, painted lines and staked-out squares would look enough like planes, flight lines, and barracks to convince German night raiders to target the Lea and not Cranwell.

That was the idea. It frequently worked.

The Germans showed up at Cranwell about the same time Soc and I did so we spent our first night of war in the brig, a solid place and mostly empty.

Soc was shivering. "Ironic," he said between waves, "our lives, plans, my future depends on the Germans being perfect. Planes, pilots, bombardiers, bombs all have to be on the money. We expect they'll miss us because they'll be on target for the decoy." His eyes flickered in the winking dark. "What about Kraut fuckups? Our ruse is perfect but some Heinie sad sack misses by a mile and kills the real thing. Us! Ironic. So damn ironic."

The night went flash and boom distantly and Soc said "ironic" again. I figured war had lots of irony.

That night the ruse and the Nazis worked swell. I slept. Sleeping, I dreamed fireworms crawling the fields. I heard musical voices in the flame. Maybe this was what Daddy'd said to listen for. But this was England. He'd been in France.

Next day, we met the First Sergeant. He said we were mostly useless and sent us to get assigned. We got driven to the crew area in a jeep, which was as much help as we got. Nobody liked us. Like the first shirt said, we were useless and probably already dead, so there wasn't much point in fussing.

Eventually we got assigned. Soc got sent to one plane. I went to another.

My pilot was Shorty Doas—Captain Doas—from Kentucky and taller than me by just that-much. He looked hardly any older but must have been. I walked in, he took one look and grinned like I was a long-missed baby brother. He wrapped his arm on me and said none of the guys could now rightly call him Shorty. He said it again, louder, ran his hand from the top of my head to the middle of his so everybody got he was an inch taller. They all laughed. Then I was one of them.

Our plane was the *Gallopin' Gremlin*. The other crews hated the name. Called us bad luck. Doas loved that. That was him, twist the devil's tail.

The *Gremlin*'s crew had just formed up. None of us—the plane either, for that matter—had seen combat. The guy I was replacing was dead before anybody met him. Nobody knew him, not even his name. His gear was still in the first shirt's office and Sarge was waiting for the guy's orders to catch up so he could find where to ship it all back stateside. The pain-in-the-ass hadn't been killed by action. Drunk when he arrived, he walked into a spinning prop on the flightline.

"All of him walked in, half of him walked out," First Shirt said. That's how Soc put it down.

"A lesson to us all," Doas said and passed the bottle.

Soc was riding *Gale's Wrath*. He loved her. That was going to be his novel, he said. Gale was his pilot's girlfriend. Soc wanted to meet her after the war. His pilot said, "Sure you do."

We flew practice, high level, low level, made phony bomb runs. We did night flights, day raid simulations, threw up together through maneuvers. We got used to each other, the plane, the Bomb Group. Our first mission would be a piece of cake. Headquarters said so.

In the tail, you're alone. At Angels Sixteen your breath freezes your mask to your face, your head is in your glass box, and sky is everywhere. The world is contrails streaming aft, above below. The war being fought by the rest of your plane and your nine buddies is a rumor on the headset. Except for the engines, everything you hear is on headset. Seventy feet up front, everyone knows everything. They're yelling, "Watch for it,

Shorty! Get him, Ern! Get it, get it... Come on, oh Jesus Christ take him, Brandon, oh fuck, five o'clock low, that's LOW, Goddamnit, nononono!"

Like that. The 17's a Sunday drive with nine backseat drivers.

From my seat in the tail, I watched backward. Now and then something flew by or came rocking in from the side, swinging back and forth trying to kill me. Felt that personal. I shot back until they went away. I don't know if I hit anyone. I tried.

Sixty-five thousand pounds of *Gremlin* bumped and quivered whenever all thirteen .50s spit short chatters at the MEs and F-Ws that rammed past.

We neared the target. The fighters disappeared. For seconds it was just us and quiet. Then the air opened up.

Let me tell you about flak: It's high explosive wrapped in scrap-metal. Big anti-aircraft guns throw it up to where we are, then it explodes. Thing about it: It's beautiful. In the big emptiness all around, white, black and pink puffballs blossom, blots of color bump the air. You see it wrinkle, the air. When it's heavy you can smell it. The smell is like a fired off 12-gauge: hot powder and burnt metal. Flak chews your control surfaces, peppers your hydraulics, it can whip your belly open like-that, unravel your guts around the plane, spin your head clean off—all while you watch in wonder and breathe that back-home smell of duck season on the Red!

I sat in my glass house and waited to explode.

Doas ignored everyone, did his job, drove us to the target, released *Gremlin* to the bombardier, whose Norden bombsight inched us over whatever we were trying to kill that day—I disremember—and loosed our load. We bounced up, light and happy, and *Gremlin* and *Gale* returned to Cornhole without a scratch.

Soc and I got drunk because everyone said we'd stand down till headquarters evaluated the fuck-up, why intelligence promised a milkrun and the Germans fed us a buzzsaw. Sorry, Soc, I'm mixing what you call your metaphors.

And we didn't stand down. Next day we were up again. Again, *Gremlin* and *Gale* came home untouched and Soc and me decided drunk was lucky. Maybe Soc was starting to believe in superstition.

As a reward, we got sent back the very next day. Hungover, boozy, focused by pain, we clobbered the target that third time. Whatever it was.

Three missions and the *Gremlin*s and the *Gale*s were untouched. Not one piece of flak, not one bullet, not one drop of blood. It shit-scared us.

On Gremlin's fifth mission, a pair of Focke-Wulfs stitched us across the middle and took out one of the waist gunners. Burdette. A big guy. Quiet. Always a little smile like something funny had... Well, that was that.

On seven, we took a burst in the gut and the ball-turret was gone, the ball-turret gunner just a smear along the underside almost to my ass in the tail. What the hell was his name, the ball turret gunner?

Okay. What I didn't tell the debriefing crew was that during the mission—okay, all the missions—I'd heard things. First, I thought I was picking up Kraut radio on the headset. That happens. Don't know why. Listening, I knew I heard no radio and what I heard was not on headset. The voices were in the air, in the flames and noise, cripes, in the smell of the plane, the caibo shit, oil burning itself at pressure, flak and cordite fumes whipping back from the waist. I know a little Kraut and the singing words were not *Deutsche*, they were... Okay, they were older. Older like Daddy'd said older. On the headset, I hear Doas's Kentucky drawl, the other guys' shouts, what's-his-name, the ball-turret gunner's final chirrup before he became a streak of grease down the belly, all that was there. And I hear it. I hear engines, guns, I hear the flak. But wrapped around all that is a tom-tom chorus and a bull-roar hum. I hear the air itself and the air's flames. They're all a choir at some old, old church. The voices are explosions and the flak that peppers us, the engines, our guns, theirs, the fighter's buzz and the rushing air, all seem to be... No, it all is... it all was liquid music. Music and laughter.

I said nothing. Not to Intelligence, not to Doas, not to Soc. As I said, tail gunner's pretty far back there.

Anyway, we were blooded and felt better. Not happy Burdette and what's-his-name, the ball-turret gunner, were dead. No. But we didn't have to worry about what was going to happen first, because the first thing had already happened.

So it got to be routine: missions, stand-downs, scrubs and rainouts, losses, escapes. We were combat vets.

Mundt! That was the ball-turret gunner.

Soc and I were working our pre-mission hoodoo at the Ploughman in Lakenheath. Soc had fallen to the wiles of a country girl still with all her teeth from somewhere by the River Ouze. He'd told her about the book he was writing. *"By River Ouze,* I call it," he said. She was impressed and when they closed the boozer, he and she were off talking books. They left me without even a bike to pedal myself back to base on, so I walked. I liked walking fields. Day or night, I liked talking to the critters, to the noises in the earth. This is best done alone. The time I did so in Soc's hearing, he wrote me down and said I was colorful.

At Lakenheath Lea, I considered risk: cross the decoy field or hoof the long way around? A lone cow sat in the mist under the wing of a decoy plane. I asked what she was doing, out.

Left behind in someone's haste, she said.

I laughed. A rabbit, then another, leaped the painted lines and went dodging among wood and canvas shapes in the fog.

I thought to risk it.

When the night raiders showed it was like a movie director said, "Lights and action!" Searchlights like ice fingers shot into the mist. Sirens sighed from low to high and back. The drone of radial engines sifted through broken sky. Anti-aircraft—what the blokes called "ack-ack"—bloomed among the stars.

The ruse must have worked because Lakenheath Lea heaved. Earth filled the air. I did the dodger's run, left my own staggering drunk behind running till I ran out of field and was over the fence without climbing. I flopped up one side of a little hill, then rolled down the other and ate mud like Daddy done in his trenches.

When I peeked over the crest, the booze must have jumped back inside because I was drunk again. It was all so damned beautiful, music, light, and song. Wave over wave of air washed out from the bursting bombs like wet wrinkles. I would have stood to conduct if I'd had that talent, but I didn't so I lay and breathed it.

When the old guy next to me in the dark ditch howled like a steel-cutting saw, I about jumped from my skin. By bomb's light, he was hairy and old. Black, see? Not like a Colored man, he was old iron black and the dark of rich loam. He was all the shades of the world black. Except for that he could have been the bus driver bloke.

I thought he was drunk as I was and said something like, "What're we doing here, mate?"

He answered like a yard full of geese. Well, I was just learning the language there in England, and that night's lager had settled back in me after my dodge. Thing was, I understood. Got that he'd come up to the Lea for this. Come up, special. As if he'd been, well, down somewhere. Don't know where. Him and the others—he waved his arm—they were here for this. This special thing we were doing.

A stick of incendiaries threw bright heat and I saw the hillside filled like a stadium for homecoming. The old guy and the rest howled like a steel mill chorus at a midnight pouring.

On the Lea was more of him. More, different, their shadows danced with the flames.

Soc would have loved it, hundreds of little hairy critters. They ran, spun, tornadoed the dirt. A bomb whistled. I looked. Foolish, but damn if there wasn't a girl on it. Okay, not on it, she slow-danced it down the sky. Which is why I could see it at all. Behind her, a whole rack of Kraut 500-pounders cavorted in the arms of little women. Okay, not women. The *idea* of women. They sweet doe-see-doed those clumsy iron bubbles, something Walt Disney could've made in that *Fantasia* picture. When the bubbles burst, they blossomed, yellow-white and rose-touched. Snake flames licked the ground and skittered, rolling, growing, growing so fast, twisting into the air with wood, canvas, and painted earth. The howl of blooming steel washed over us and I know, I know, a dozen, two dozen of the folk were pulverized in the blasts, pulverized and shot aloft where the spray of parts and pieces rejoined and laughed down as shadows, black shadows, against the heat and shock and thrumming strings. Sounded like it anyway.

Then it was over: bombs, planes, ack-ack. Drifting smoke, air-tossed muck, skittering sparks remained. Then a lady-rain came to clean it all. The rain was part of it and fell like light. As if all the fire and light, all the burning planes and men that had fallen from the sky in steel and armored drops, the glowing bits of bone and chary rags and spatters of liquid plastic, were distilled to hazy mist. All that dropped gently in a cleansing rain. Wondrous.

My old black bloke said something to me and rolled his head back. I thought he'd laugh. He did and came apart in joy, then sank. That was it. He sank into the hillside. The music of rain and air, wrinkled and was gone. All was gone, waiting for the next…

What?

Festival is the word I'd caught. This Festival we were making just for them.

When the all clear sounded I was sober again for the third time that day. I stood. Common mist rolled across Lakenheath Lea. The surviving flames were ordinary fires, dying in the wet. In the light, the carcass of my friend the cow lay opened, burning. I didn't see rabbits.

I was in my rack when the Sergeant rolled us out, calling "Wakey-wakey!" like the blokes.

Jammed into the briefing room, we sat in body heat and wool, staring at the curtained blackboard on the stage. The place was blue with cigarette. When Col. Cawdor came down the aisle, the air parted and we came to attention, coughing.

"At ease," he said. He looked at the officers, looked at us. "Gentlemen, your target is Schweinfurt." Then he left. The Air Exec conducted the rest of the general briefing before we separated into crew briefs.

Let me tell you about Schweinfurt. That October, the 8th Air Force lost a quarter of the planes it sent to take out the ball bearing factories of Schweinfurt. Ball bearings, now, ball bearings are the soul—the heart, anyway—of modern war. Without ball bearings, you're fighting the last war's war.

Since that bloody October, the 8th had a grudge against those ball bearings and be damned if we could knock out the plants. We kept going back.

There were the usual hoots, whines, and whimpers, the fake screams that covered real ones. In the end, we were going back to Schweinfurt, its two thousand ack-ack guns and crack crews and where half the Luftwaffe waited for us to come to try to kill their ball bearings.

Schweinfurt. Shit, guess I DID want to live forever.

We jeeped to the perimeter and ran preflight. Just another

pretty day of dying. HQ teased us with a hold while meteorology waited for the numbers to say the target skies was clear. I was hoping the mission would stay held, get scrubbed, go away. It didn't.

Some of the guys from *Gale's Wrath* and *Gremlin* tossed a baseball 'round a circle, others stood and laughed or lay sacked out against the landing gear. Soc wandered across the pad and squatted on wet grass next to me. We were quiet. I wanted to say nothing about last night's Festival, figuring it was mostly booze, anyway.

"About science," Soc said, "see, you should be able to know—to figure, anyway—when your number's coming, well, not up, but around." He looked at the sky. "Gotta say, I'm feeling it's close."

The day was sunny and cool. Last night's rain lay in thin sheens across the tarmac. Behind the perimeter fence, cows grazed like they had forever. Nothing had changed for them. Or me. Hell, I was still a farmer, mostly dirt, spit, and hot air. A while ago I was doing what my folks had done for as long as those cows had been in their line of work. This flying in the air, flames, tearing metal and spraying blood, that was a just something to be done before getting back to the earth.

Soc didn't say anything, then he said, "You know, I've seen things." He tilted his head back. "Up there…" He looked at me and laughed. "Nah. No such thing."

"Yes. Yes, there is," I said. "Socrates. There is!" I grabbed his arm. I was going to unburden me about last night, the voices, the music.

Then Ops popped the Very pistol and it was time to go. The engines revved and prop blasts blew last night's puddles away.

Soc smacked me on the leg with his flight gloves. "Got to tell you about my book! I think I've got it! Finally got it!" And he was off to die. I knew that.

He did. After the fighters left us to fly alone into the flak of Schweinfurt's two thousand ack-acks, *Gale's Wrath*, leading on high approach to the drop point, caught a shell in a soft spot. There was a puff and the plane folded, wings, tail, nose. The whole thing drifted apart and rained people and pieces over the low-level flights, rearward. It was almost artful. Soc could have done it justice and maybe would have appreciated the numbers of it all. No chutes.

We made the run, dropped our load, and then were on our own. I hoped there were ball bearings all over Schweinfurt.

Gremlin was light and bouncy without bombs and a good part of its fuel. Her tail was frisky. We dropped into the coffin corner, the number five slot in formation, and were the first hit from the rear by fighters. Sitting in my nest, chute stuffed in the tunnel behind, I had time to think as I popped tracers at the 109s that swept up and past. I was thinking about the novel Soc wouldn't finish, about numbers and how I didn't believe this thing, this B-17, could fly, not for real, so how could we be here?

When the little hairy guy behind me started singing, I barely had time to yell what the hell's a civilian doing on a combat mission? He laughed and the tracers laughed with him, said I was right, the damned thing couldn't fly, not if I didn't believe it. He didn't speak American but I knew what he was saying. He told me to get on with it; he was none of my worry. I was there to give them their Festival, the fireworks.

Those are my words. His were something older. Finer. He laughed and laughed. I didn't believe in him any more than I did in the ability of a B-17 to climb to Angels Twenty-five, then soft as a bird, come back to earth.

The headset was jammed, everyone shouting at once. The bombardier and navigator were on nose guns, yelling. Jens, the radio guy, was on dorsal. The waist gunners were doing the port and starboard dance as the F-Ws and MEs swooped over, under and past us. The two between my legs were working and I was doing my share of yelling. Our thirteen guns poured streams of half-inch steel-jackets in divergent cones of fire. We surrounded *Gremlin* with a shell of shielding metal.

Except from what slipped through.

The Messerschmitt dropped into our slipstream. My tracers reached for him, but he was below my cone of fire. Then a funny thing: A haze of—I can only call it "female" light—flew down, flew up, flew in, surrounded him, danced him up, up so softly, to be pecked by my bullets. They swam him back and forth; my 50s tapped along his engine cowling. Smoke streamed. When the bullets reached the canopy, it vanished in a spray of blood and fragments.

My kill.

The plane didn't realize its pilot was dead, though, and kept to the mission. Slid itself under us, then, in revenge or maybe for fun, peeled up and into our starboard wing. We lost the last ten feet of wing and the 109 spun flaming away and down.

Gremlin waggled but flew. When we lost the outboard engine, we banked into the stream of fuel pouring from the broken wing. I was believing less and less in this 17's ability to fly.

There was music behind me. The space aft of bulkhead seven was filled with, well, "people," I guess you'd call them. Some had stuck their heads through *Gremlin*'s skin. Watching the show, I guessed. A few slipped outside for a better look at the broken wingtip. They dissolved their way along the vapors that vented from us.

We plunged into a cloud mass and sky raced past my windows. The intercom was solid sound.

Our war was over. We might could limp a bit, but *Gremlin* was not going back to Cornhole. The old guy behind me was having just the best time about that.

We popped out of the thunderhead into clear sky. Ahead, the sun would be going to ground. My view was behind. Way back, Schweinfurt was a pillar of smoke rising to catch the failing light. Below was night where thunder licked the clouds. Smoke and fuel poured from the inboard engine, gas vapors filled the air in our spiraling wake.

Doas ignored the headset screams and feathered the inboard portside engine and pulled the bottle. The extinguisher did its job. We drove along struggling to stay airborne. After the bomb run, our altitude had been close to our operational ceiling, near Angels Thirty. In the last—Christ, it had only been about ten minutes—I reckon we had dropped to eighteen, twenty.

Not that I wasn't already scared, but when the old guy leaned over my shoulder and shoved, well, through me—the only way I can describe it—and pushed his face out the bulletproof glass in front of my nose, it upset me. He pulled the rest of the way through me and out of the plane and stood on my twin barrels. I knew he didn't really need them guns to stand in the air.

He called. A wave of others like him, and some a lot prettier and others, different, flowed up from below. They came so easy, no effort...

...leading a flock of ME 109s. The Messerschmitts peeled off to bypass my tracers. I yelled to Doas that we had company but a stream of tracers buzzed through the ship forward my position, and that was it for the rest of the world.

Gremlin seemed to stop dead for a second, then she eased side-wise, wobbled, and went right again. The sky was beautiful, blue, gold, and red against the towering column of Schweinfurt. Hundreds of little guys and their thousand friends sat in the air outside; they watched like we were a movie.

Black smoke streamed past my face. Thin at first, it grew thick in a second or two. I felt heat behind me. I turned...

Saw...

Red flame and pretty young people. Fire wrapped them like love and they sang it. They had my parachute. It blossomed and the shrouds were ribbons of white and dancing heat snakes, the silk bubbled red and gold. The pretty people poured the light of my chute from hand to hand. My eyeballs sucked dry with the heat.

I guess it was another piece of the starboard wing. Something rammed back along the fuselage and spun by like an echo. Soon the fire would be at the fuel and we'd go up like a bomb.

I thought I'd jump, take any way to go but fire death. Another part of me said do nothing. A moral conflict, Soc might have called it.

The Old Guy stuck his face back through the glass and into mine. In pure joy he sang. In his words was the stench of war. He sang in ways I didn't know. He sang, "Why are you waiting? Walk with me." Maybe it was, "Be with me." He wanted me to be with the air, with him. That was my place. The plane was of earth. Dirt made metal. Metal made to fly. No sense, but there she was.

Then he was Miss Duchenne, my teacher whom I've dearly loved these years and have mentioned before. I considered. She gave her arm, an offer to dance, and said she'd tell me, there, of metal ores and plastics made of oil from the deep, and rubber from jungle trees a world away. We'd dance and learn together.

I reached behind, released the emergency hatch. My hands blistered, but I didn't care. Doas, the others, were gone or going. Way I saw it, my post was deserting me. I said goodbye to the war, the world, let go my belief that steel could fly and rolled out slick, Miss Duchenne on my arm.

The air was liquid ice and washed me away from *Gremlin* and its smells. I danced a cool bee-bop turn with warm Micheline Duchenne. On my back, *Gremlin* dropped away above, then dissolved in flame and parts. The air wrinkled and pieces scattered, grinding finer and finer, ripping past us, then falling smaller, smaller than dust.

Miss Duchenne laughed at my concern. She said, "They don't like left-behinds." The air, the water, the fire would cleanse it all, she said. When she said it, the sky above us went clear with night and stars. I fell, believing in the people of the flames, in the cleansing air, and probably the waters too, I didn't know about that. Micheline thanked me, bid *adieu*, and slipped into the night. I spread my arms and leaned into the thunder below. Earth opened up to take me, laughing with me, at my fall to home.

I remember nothing, after, but singing voices and an orchestra of machinery that ground down, forever. And when I woke, everyone was talking German. I knew they did not speak German in heaven so figured I was elsewhere.

I was: Berlin. After six hospitals, I'd ended in Berlin. To count it: I had two broken legs, a shattered arm and collarbone. Other things internal. Spleens and such. They thought I'd lose an eye, but I kept it. I had burns where my flight suit had flamed as I fell. According to one Kraut, a doctor, S.S. officer, whatever he was, the fall should have extinguished me. And where was my parachute, he wanted to know?

"The old folk took it. I left it in the plane," I said.

He nodded. I could not survive a fall from three miles without a parachute. Could I? Would I care to try it again? 16,000 feet? Show them how I did it, would I, would I?

I said no. I said I didn't know. That maybe I was borne aloft, that flights of angels had sung me to my rest. Miss Duchenne taught me those words, oh, years ago. Even I laughed at it with him. I never told that I had danced to earth.

The final report was a beaut. In scientific German, complete with numbers, it said falling I'd blacked out from lack of oxygen, from cold, from pain. That, unconscious, my arms and legs had spread. That I'd pancaked down, buoyed by an updraft from the storm. That, while the terminal velocity for my aerodynamic configuration would have killed me on impact, I had fallen among evergreen trees; my fall was broken by branches, and, farther down, by underbrush, that when I landed, I fell into deep snow and loamy soil. Like on Daddy's farm.

Finally, the Germans said I was brave, a soldier who did not accept death as given, but trusted to the elements of air, earth, fire, and water. I think that smiling Kraut doctor put in that last part. Maybe he was right.

"What your English comrades call 'Gremlins' perhaps?" he said with a final smirk.

Or maybe it was Miss Duchenne.

The Germans traded me, with honors. The Air Corps was suspicious. Finally someone figured it would be better to celebrate than punish me. They sent me home a hero, an American miracle.

I walked again, learned to use my arm. I can almost see from the eye the Germans thought I'd lose.

One night after the war, walking our land looking at the night, the mud got to sucking at my boots. Daddy was next to me, also looking at the dark. He talked about weather, about crops. Then he was quiet. There was more he wanted to say and he said it. "This is the one time I'll ask what happened," he said. "If you're ready, you can tell me."

I did, told him more or less the truth. When I finished, he smiled for maybe the tenth time in his life.

"Tonight I was thinking about Socrates," I said. "Them books he'll never write. I was wondering why I lived and he didn't."

Daddy nodded. "Every man comes back from war is that question: 'Why me, not them; why them, not me?' You got an answer?" He looked at me and waited. I believe that was the first time Daddy ever asked something he didn't already have an answer for.

"Maybe because I'm part dirt and spit and all hot air. Maybe because this is magic every season, every year." Mud sucked at my boots. Fireflies winked as far as I saw. Rain cut the distance, and lightning. For a moment, I thought I heard the voices that were not speech or noise, but more and older, music without sound.

"Good reason as any," Daddy said. He looked at me then watched the fireflies too. "Like I said, old wars is mainly lies."

The thunder thanked me. I turned up my collar. Big rains and more were coming.

SOME STAGES ON THE ROAD
TOWARD OUR FAILURE TO REACH
THE MOON

The trip to the moon did not happen. It failed because of a hat. As with most things the failure arrived in stages, the end-point of many details. Of course it was not the fault of the hat.

Stage One: DeAngelo was born.

Stage Two: DeAngelo's dad died. Korea.

Stage Three: DeAngelo found the dead cat three weeks after school started. Fifth grade. Luck was all. As usual he was dodging Keegan and Niewig after Release Time at Saint Sophie's. As usual they got him. This time he came to earth by the peony bushes along the rectory wall, his face in the dirt, arm wrung behind. Niewig twisted, Keegan giggled.

Two feet from DeAngelo's nose, lying in the tangle of stems and peony petals, recently dead—within a day, DeAngelo figured—was Father O'Doule's cat. Its grinning head was angled stiffly; it screamed a silent yowl inches from DeAngelo's face. Its paws stiff, tail going bare, muddy skin showed beneath the fur.

Pain from his twisted arm shot from his shoulder to the back of his head. He shoved pain and Keegan's giggles to the background. When he did, what had happened to the cat became apparent: the thing expired, probably snoozing on O'Doule's windowsill, directly above. Struck by sickness, nastiness, age, or poison, God had come to it and it had fallen three stone stories into the peonies that ringed the building. The cat was dead on landing, DeAngelo was sure, but getting it from alive on the sill to dead in the bush, that was the thing. He ran the stages in his head: the jerk of croaking death, that first. Then, propelled from the sill, already stiffening (bouncing off an imagined parapet which DeAngelo knew that falling bodies always struck in slow-motion), the cat body tumbled slowly, fell between stems, hit the ground, adjusted to place. The peonies rebounded, swayed, then were still with all evidence of death, fall and cat, gone. Then, forever begins.

Meanwhile, Niewig and Keegan knelt on DeAngelo's back. They twisted and giggled until he grunted into the dirt, yes, yes he was queer, one big queer! He said it, said it again, whatever.

Whatever DeAngelo was at that moment though, Father O'Doule's cat lay there, rotting. It would continue in that course. In *Encyclopedia Britannica* time-lapse he imagined: cat shriveling, collapsing, white grubs blooming, wriggling in quick time, devouring until.

And DeAngelo knew where it was happening. Better: no one else did, certainly not Reinhart.

Stage Four: DeAngelo showed Reinhart the drawings he'd made over a week of watching the animal disintegrate. Reinhart shrugged.

"Wait'll you see," DeAngelo told him.

The day he took him there, two things happened: the cat disappeared and Sputnik went up.

That quick, DeAngelo stopped caring about cats or drawings made on-scene, improved by flashlight at night and kept in his box of secrets beneath the bed. A cat? Who cared? Not DeAngelo.

Stage Five: DeAngelo made a poem. The poem was:

Twinkle, twinkle little Sputnik
How I wonder why you Wink-nik
You dirty little Russian nudnik,
How the heck'll I get my sleep
When all night long you beep, beep, beep?

DeAngelo read it aloud. "I like the 'heck'll I get my sleep' part," he said. "'heck'll I…' That's good."

Reinhart snorted. "That's dumb," he said.

"Dumb because you didn't make it."

"Dumb because 'Wink-nik?' Dumb because you mean 'hell' and you say 'heck'…"

"'Heck'll I!' All right! 'How the HELL can I get my sleep' then."

"Dumb because the lines have too many syl-ables. And there are too many lines! And A-A-A-B-B? Come on!" Reinhart sang his complaints, as though talking to a child. "And you can't hear Sputnik, not without equipment. It beeps on the radio and gotta be tuned just right. And you have the right kind of radio."

"I heard," DeAngelo said. "And Sputnik makes me not sleep."

Everyone had heard it and seen it. Television. The picture was from Russia. And Channel 10 carried it. Worse, they played the beeps, the awful beeps, Russian beeps from a Commie moon that circled overhead, every hour and a half. John Facenda voiced doom: "This," he said, "is the sound…"

First silence, then a hiss. From space, a rhythmic beat approached within the hiss, something, a ship calling in distant night. It neared, then faded, then was gone.

Facenda went on: "That is the sound from outer space tonight. It is courtesy of the Union. Of Soviet. Socialist's. Republics." Channel 10 had a scratchy animation of a round nothing in space, "the size of a basketball." Facenda spoke of it as though the game of basketball should be ashamed.

The speed, DeAngelo thought. "Wow," he said.

Reinhart shrugged. "Eighteen thousand miles an hour."

"It's crazy," DeAngelo whispered.

"Any faster, it escapes. Twenty-five thousand and whisssh!" Reinhart's hand shot past DeAngelo's ear. "For good'n gone!"

"Nuts." DeAngelo was mad. "Why didn't we do it?"

"We will. For IGY. Vanguard's going in what, a couple weeks. Criminies, DeAngelo, it's not the end of the—"

"But we didn't. We didn't do it. Forever, we didn't."

"So we will. And better. And your poem still stinks. And you can't hear Sputnik in bed. You can't hear beeps. It beeps radio."

DeAngelo had heard. He couldn't sleep. And "heck'll I" was better than hell! The hell with it, he thought finally. It was stupid, the poem. Now on anyway he was a science guy, not an English guy.

Stage Six: Vanguard collapsed. A slender pencil, the rocket quivered on its tail, smoke rolled, it rose, what? Two feet. Collapsed on itself and blew. DeAngelo and Reinhart decided if the country couldn't, they would. They'd go to the moon. They would. Not now, not tomorrow (they were kids!). But they would go, and go soon. They were scientists. Would be. In stages over the next... Well, over the years, however many, they would gather *materiel* (Reinhart's brother, a mechanic in the Air Force, sent letters home using words like that). Materiel was out there. Military surplus. Good stuff. They saw it at STAUFFER'S ARMY-NAVY on Railroad Street: parachutes, bayonets, helmets. The government must have too much other stuff: missiles, probably. Old ones, anyway. V-2s from Germany after the war, shipped to New Mexico, tested, stored and now were useless around Nikes, Jupiters, and Redstones. They'd get one, fit it out to carry a different payload—them—then...

As Pop-pop saw it, the problem was not that they didn't have money enough for a war surplus shovel much less a German rocket ship, it was not a question of them building a missile to go to the moon when the whole American government couldn't even…

"Wouldn't!" DeAngelo groused.

…put a basketball in orbit. The problem wasn't even that they were kids for crineoutloud, "The problem is nobody's going to the moon is the problem. Now you get one of your rockets up too far there, and it's falling right back."

"Russians' didn't."

The old man lip-farted. "Sputnik, not out. Not in whatchacall Out-of-Space. Sputnik's just…" he pointed to the ceiling, "UP. Going 'round around the world up there. You can't go into out of space." He leaned closer. "What's your rocket going to push against? Answer me that."

There was an answer. DeAngelo knew there was but the old man made a point. He did not bring Pop-pop's point to Reinhart during design meetings in the back of Klein's Pharmacy. Even when first ice silvered the trees, Klein's Pharmacy kept its Kool Konditioned smell from summer. Their heads together at the marble-top table back by surgical supplies and bedpans, the scent of creams and ice and rubber tubes, varnished wood and flypaper filled DeAngelo. "Going to the moon smells like…" he sniffed deeply, "cough syrup and rubber tube."

"Huh?" said Reinhart.

On paper, one surplus V-2 had become three, one atop the other in stages. Each stage latched to the one below, each chopped and tucked, the assembly tapered to a point a hundred feet above the desert.

In plan the journey was beginning to look… Well? Possible.

The Nazi rockets were now atom fueled. At least the first stage was atomic, the one that had to lift the whole load off the desert earth. Only made sense, DeAngelo argued. Atoms were

more powerful than chemicals. Of course they were. *Bah-OOOM!*
Everyone had seen the movies.

Reinhart squinted. "More than gunpowder. If you're blowing
something up."

"More than red fuming nitric acid!"

"*And* hydrazine," Reinhart added.

Atoms were certainly safer than the powdered zinc and sulfur
compound they'd actually made and tested. DeAngelo tingled at
the memory. Powdered zinc. Sulfur. There it was in Reinhart's
chemistry set. They mixed them, packed the compound into one
of the empty .30-06 cartridges DeAngelo's dad had left with his
hunting stuff. When he'd held his dad's Zippo under the shell, it
spit hot stuff all over him and whip-cracked across the yard and
alley. If anyone had seen it, that would have been it. If it had
made it to Hebhart's house it would have smashed the kitchen
window. If that, it would have buried itself in Hebhart's grandma
or baby brother, always in the kitchen. DeAngelo knew, he just
knew as he watched the thing streak and fizz. If... If it hadn't
thwacked the wet sheets Hebhart's mom had hung on the line, if
it hadn't dropped, hissing, onto the rump of Hebhart's mutt, it
would have been... It didn't. The mutt woofed dully and looked
sadly at the world. So much of the world was "if," DeAngelo
realized. Thank God. Still, DeAngelo and Reinhart ran their
separate ways.

And Reinhart agreed, atoms were probably best. Still, he
squinted at the sketch, at the now triumphantly radiating atomic
pile in what had been the hydrogen peroxide tank.

Stage Seven: They practiced for flight. Mahler had a new
refrigerator. The carton was dragged to DeAngelo's basement.
They painted gauges, buttons and switches on the inside walls.
DeAngelo drew more buttons and dials on a pair of shoebox
consoles they carried on their laps. The bulb hanging at the far

end of the basement shone through the porthole.

"That's where we're going," he told Reinhart.

Reinhart squinted.

For the test flights, DeAngelo began to wear his dad's garrison cap. The silver captain's bars seemed right for a trip to the moon. In the dark crew compartment, light from the bulb touched the bars. Reflections swept Reinhart's face, flashed across the instruments, touched the red FIRE button as they counted from 50 to Zero.

They made the trip a half-dozen times.

"Rods!" Reinhart yelled one day. DeAngelo had reached 28.

"Counting! Cripes! 26, 25..."

"Cripes yourself, you need rods."

"What? 22, 21..."

"Thorium rods." Reinhart pointed to the red button on the shoebox.

DeAngelo's captain's bars flashed in Reinhart's eyes. "19, 18..."

"Thorium controls the chain reaction. Don't you know about thorium?" Reinhart sang his stupidity song.

"I know! 13..."

"They have to pull out... withdraw." Reinhart's hand fluttered over dozens of imaginary rods sliding—or not—from the atomic pile below.

"One, zero." DeAngelo didn't push the red button. Nothing happened.

Later at Klein's, DeAngelo drew ropes and channels. The ropes and channels climbed in elaborate ways from the atomic pile through all the stages. They met the top where he, DeAngelo, lay strapped in the cabin waiting to pull a darn lever.

Cripes, he thought, *pull out a rod*. He imagined nuclear fire funneled in a rage through the rocket hole in their tail: thunder, flame, the thrill of a lifetime and a long space voyage, a forever adventure, begun with the pull of a rod.

Reinhart squinted.

DeAngelo made more pictures: their rocket and its gantry, the rocket in space (Pushing against the what? What!) and descending on a piston of fire to the cratered moon, his rocket parked among the moon's sawtooth mountains. Pictures of them: climbing the gantry, waving good-bye, strapped down surrounded by gauges, switches. DeAngelo made pictures of Earth spreading below them as small as the bulb at the far end of the basement, pictures of the moon and of him steering them down the fire as the moon rushed toward them. He didn't show these to Reinhart.

Reinhart bailed out, screaming, the afternoon a large black water bug crawled up his leg. Five minutes to touchdown, and Reinhart tore the hatch off the ship and ran swiping at his crotch. He danced, screaming, beneath the moon, still brushing.

DeAngelo went into space alone. Half the crew meant twice the air, fuel and sandwich. Alone between basement and moon, DeAngelo survived (or did not survive) meteor storms and engine failure. He'd lost (and sometimes re-found) his way between worlds, or, pushing the limit of his ship, ended on Mars or dodged asteroids all the way out to Jupiter, sometimes on to Saturn. Once, he'd set foot on the sun (The sun! He tore those pages from his log, almost hearing Reinhart's singsong smirk). He made pictures of the possibilities (remote, but potential) of attack by monsters, by meteor beasts that caught him, passing in space. He wrote and drew descriptions of the dinosaurs that lived in the jungles of cloud-sheathed Venus. He met wise star folk who did not want Mankind in space because we could not be trusted among peaceful beings. He made pictures of alien ships that were hidden behind the moon, waiting the moment, which might be any moment, to spring.

Crazy Lenz came along a few times. With Lenz, the journeys

lasted rarely more than a minute before meteors hulled them and they tumbled across the basement or before Lenz hushed with, "You hear? Listen! Y'hear that?" At every landing, it was them against Martians, Russians, Germans, Chinese Commies, whatever might lurk down the alley or lay hidden in the gangways between houses on Perkiomen.

With Lenz they always carried guns and always had a ball.

Even so, when DeAngelo drew two explorers standing, finally standing, on the moon, the Earth in the always-black black sky above, the tiny ship far away and behind, the second suit was always Reinhart's. DeAngelo and Reinhart, the flag between them. After all that had come before, whatever it had been, whatever would come between them in the years that were to follow, they were there and alive, DeAngelo and Reinhart, on the moon, first on the moon. Famous forever.

Reinhart shuffled the pictures. "You're nuts."

"What about them?" DeAngelo said.

Reinhart got it then giggled.

Still, that was the last time he showed Reinhart any but technical drawings.

Christmas. For no reason he could fathom there was a Junior Engineer's drafting set under the tree—drawing board, T-square, pair of compasses, dividers, French curves, architect's scale, kneaded eraser, mechanical pencil, real drafting paper, book of projects. DeAngelo looked from Mother to Pop-pop, to visiting aunts and sleeping uncles and back.

"Still got nothing to push on. But you can make better pictures," Pop-pop said.

He made different pictures. He spent hours drafting the ship's hull, making both sides just-so.

Reinhart nodded, no squint.

DeAngelo threw it away. The lousy drawings were better, the dozens where one edge bellied more than the other or where a bulbous extrusion lumped crazy from the nose. The more the differences, the better it felt.

"The heck's that?" Reinhart said. He was squeakier each time they got to work.

"Looks better," DeAngelo said. "See?" He traced a softly curving ship's underbelly in the air. "Then..." He traced a humpback topside above Reinhart's head. "Cool, huh?"

"Yeah?" The question hung. "And by the way," Reinhart poked the detail drawing of the ship's atomic pile, "you have any idea what a reactor weighs?"

DeAngelo shrugged.

"Well, it's mostly concrete and lead!"

"So?"

"Well, no atomic pile, no atomic pow-er." Singing. "Anyway, what're you figuring's the reaction mass?"

DeAngelo shuffled drawings. "Mass, mass. Reaction mass?" he said as he paged.

"What's the 'pile' supposed to heat up? What blows out the ass to make us go? Newton's law, you know? Action? Reaction? It's what makes us go. What's our action, DeAngelo?"

That was almost it. Not quite.

Stage Eight: Finally, it was about who would lead. DeAngelo was DeAngelo's choice. To Reinhart, there was no question. "What's pi?" he asked.

"Three point I don't give a crap."

"Three point one four one five nine two..." He strung the number to a dozen places. "What's orbital velocity?"

DeAngelo couldn't say.

"Escape velocity? What's the escape asymptote? Where's the optimum launch place?"

"New Mexico!"

"Equa-tor! Dummy."

Reinhart capped the questions. He pointed at the tiny final stage. "Okay? That gets us to the moon. What gets us home? You forget that? You and Lenz ever make it back? Or were you too busy shooting mon-sters?"

DeAngelo had not worked it out; he had not forgotten. There were reasons. Secrets. Nothing to do with Lenz or being too busy. DeAngelo didn't say. He stared at Reinhart. Who knew pi, asymptotes and orbits; Reinhart was a book of knowing. He picked at problems but never drew solutions.

"Your buddy carries a trunk full of *not* and never has a pocket full of *why*," Pop-pop said.

Reinhart never burned with the joy of not knowing, never seemed to feel lovely terror. He never saw monsters in shadows because he knew there were no monsters. Water bugs from basement drains? They were. He wasn't sure, but DeAngelo was pretty sure, Reinhart had not said prayers to be first, the first to set foot upon the moon, to be that first forever.

Reinhart's asymptotes and numbers made the moon possible. Reinhart leading, the trip could happen. DeAngelo could counter with nothing that would make sense. Not to Reinhart. How could he say, "Who'd want to go to your moon?"

What DeAngelo had was a cap and the Old Man's captain's bars. That was it. Captains led. No question. The trip was his. He'd wear Dad's rank and be first. Simple. The journey to that moon was a trip of joy.

The fight was simple and terrible, fought at St. Sophie's playground in April. Mahler was there, Hebhart, Hebhart's dog, Crazy Lenz and others. It was about something, a game, a game of no importance. But it was about mankind's first journey to the moon, no mistake about it, not for DeAngelo. Did Reinhart know? Who knew?

Reinhart insisted he should coach the game. DeAngelo said no, no, no, no, no. "I have the Captain's Cap."

"That makes you a Captain?" The Reinhart giggle followed.

They hurled at each other, grappled, rolled on the grass. Nobody hurt.

Smoking over by the pavilion, Keegan and Niewig laughed and punched each other like sissies to demonstrate how little queers fought.

DeAngelo's nose bled a little, but it did that anyway, no punches needed. Reinhart's glasses were knocked off his face. Lenz grabbed and held them until. After tussles and grunts, DeAngelo got Reinhart turned on his stomach. He knelt in his back, twisted his arm. He looked over at Keegan and remembered how that hurt.

"Who's Captain?" he shouted in Reinhart's ear. "Who leads?" Reinhart dissolved. "You do, you do, you do you do!"

When they separated and stood, snot ran down Reinhart's lip and made mud with the dirt there. He squinted away tears. Lenz handed his glasses back. They were bent. Not much. Reinhart twisted them to shape as he walked away. Niewig and Keegan hooted.

Reinhart and DeAngelo didn't talk until seventh grade. By then, it was too late.

Touchdown: Vietnam. DeAngelo in the NCO club, Da Nang. The tube above the bar flickered black and white. Hisses. Cronkite shut up. What the hell was the time? The club was open. The war was on. Armstrong flickered past the camera, a slow-mo leap, touched the surface, rebounded. *Looked like*, DeAngelo thought. Sound cut in, out, breathing.

"Armstrong is on the moon…" Cronkite said.

"Say what?" someone down the bar said. "What'd he say on the moon?" guy said over Armstrong's first words.

DeAngelo sucked his beer. He'd heard. Slick but what the hell? Everyone knew they'd make it.

"Think they'll make it back?" guy said.

"Figure you will?" another voice said in back. "Any us?"

A thousand-yard laugh from another corner of the dark.

DeAngelo drained his beer, called in another. Tipped it to the tube. "I wouldn't," he said, "wouldn't come back."

"Say what?" someone said from the side. "Why not?"

DeAngelo snorted. "Hell, getting there's the fun."

THE BOY'S ROOM

Everybody loved Rafe Tozier. Who wouldn't love a boy so filled with mischief and life? First she saw of him, though, Melissa Patricia Tozier thought he was awful, just awful. Later, considering her Mississippi cousin from the distance of her home in Chicago, Melissa Tozier realized he was the handsomest boy she'd ever seen, if awful.

Then Rafe went off and died in the war, still only a boy, so everyone loved him forever. "That's the way," someone said. "Live beloved, die lamented."

Sixty-some years after, Melissa Patricia realized the ghost story she had held to since childhood was not about "why"— hauntings always are about unfinished life, aren't they? No, the ghostly business served up that one night in the Boy's Room turned on the "who" of the haunting, not "why."

Her first night sleeping in handsome, awful, cousin Rafe's room, the so-called Boy's Room (called so by the southern Toziers), had been during the war, 1943. That first night, Melissa had lain, tingling, ready to jump. Bugs and such worried her, but her heart's fear was centered on what the family'd say, their looks, knowing she and Barbary Ann (who should have known better) had assaulted the sanctity of that old Boy's Room. Melissa lay in darkness, imagining scowls and squints on rawboned Tozier faces. Those folds, dewlaps and jowls worried her more than the thought of creatures creeping over her in sleep. *Phooey to it.* She shoved fear aside. *That's me*, so she thought. Maybe she ought not be there, but Criminies, cool air pleased her so. Seen from the heat of the big house, the rotting curtains of Spanish moss that draped the twisted oaks hung determinedly still and far off in breathless night. In that little shack, though, further even than the old outhouse, small breezes could be seen to stir the moss. From there, the air gathered some measure of chill from the shadows of those trees, then sighed across her body.

Melissa spread herself in damp moonlight. She crowded Barbary Ann into a sliver of bed. Lying wide, night breeze drew the sweat heat right out of her.

Well, cousin Rafe was gone, after all. No, she ought not to be there, Melissa Patricia knew, but phooey to sleepless night under the hot roof of the big house.

She dozed.

The shack at the foot of Tozier land always had been the Boy's Room. There never was more than one boy per generation, but always the place was where Tozier—that is said "TOE-zher" with a voiced z-h—it was where boy Toziers lived when they came to an age to be by themselves. "Gets them out of the home with their smells," Gran Nana said. "No man should be to home all th' time. Livin' there saves them a walk to the back building."

She meant it. If Old Strog, her mostly crippled husband ("One arm and no reliable leg."), chose not to use the back house down the property, why he or any man Tozier could certainly use the "Whites Only" at the Cities Service to do their uglies. ("Just a short quarter mile 'long Bay St. Louis Road, down by the Five Corners where Boulevard Parfume brushes the canal, 'long the near edge of Monocle? There you see the Cities' sign and cannot possibly miss it.")

Gran Nana Tozier hated a grown man, any man, all his scents

and ways, living fully under her roof. She was firm on the issue. Never mind she was not Tozier-born, roof, house, and land hers by Christian ceremony only. Never mind Old Strog had had the indoor facility made so he might not have to hobble all the way to that old back house. No, the indoor necessity was for ladies. Even if the indoor facility was hardly more than an indoor back house with a chain-pull flush and was barely indoors at that, being on a closed porch right by the kitchen window.

Understand, the Boy's Room was not a sanitary facility. It was a shack where a boy could grow and do things, things boys do coming to manhood. Those things. And from there a boy could use the back house, only a couple dozen feet away, for his necessaries. Washing up he might do in the big house. That might be all right, depending.

Toziers lived beyond the edge of the town, Monocle. To Melissa Patricia, Monocle was a sagged-down affair, a busted old town in a land full of the dead.

"God," she thought aloud when first she stood at the end of the dirt road that widened from country-breadth and opened into that dusty corridor of scabby white buildings and flopped-down dogs that was King's Road, Monocle, "this place was born dead!" She may not have said it for cousin Barbary Ann to hear, but so it seemed.

The land was steeped in ghosts, parched by tobacco, and vexed by reality. The town seemed fed by the same charred, eerie reality. The old barge canal lazed across Tozier land, its surface thick and green, its only business that of frog, fish, and mosquito egg. Closing on all sides were twisted oak and magnolia that seemed to arise already rotting from pale earth.

The Tozier home was pure white-folk. Not grand and antebellum, just a house that was built then grew by rambling during the years between Secession and sharecrop days that followed. Coloreds had lived across the old canal that connected

Tozier fields to the world.

When Young Strog—whose proper name was Captain Strother G. Tozier—came home from Over There, still a boy, he limped horribly and his right sleeve arm was pinned to his shoulder. He stumped around the house a few days, then took residence in what had been the nearest Negro shack. So not to be a burden and to be closer to the back house and not have to limp so far.

He continued there even after his mamma died.

When Daddy Strog, the original Strother G., passed, Cap hobbled up to the big house and took command. He married soon after and sired the boy, Bindle, who, at 12 year's age, went down to the Old Shack by the trees. Which is when it got to be called "the Boy's Room." By then, the canal had been abandoned in a burst of enthusiasm for road building, caught from Huey Long next-door in Louisiana. Where it crossed their land, the Toziers absorbed the waterway, towpath, and bridge across. The Boy's Room became just a nice little walk from the house.

In his time, Bindle grew and moved up to the home place and married himself a Wallace.

And so on.

Over decades, Cap Strog's war limp gave way to higher and higher amputations. Soon he was Old Strog. It was Bindle's son's boy, Raphael (Rafe), who was growing in the Boy's Room when Melissa Patricia—called by her southern kin, "M'lissa Trish?"—first came visiting from Chicago. There always was that hint of a question whenever any of the southern Toziers called her by name. "M'lissa Trish?" As though they could not quite understand just what she meant or where she was. Just a bitty-thing at the time, M'lissa Trish remembered pieces of the visit. What she remembered, she did so vividly. One memory was peeing (and worse) down at the stinky awful falling-down outhouse her cousins called "the back house," a thousand miles at least, and across a rickety bridge from where they lived. This was before Old Strog built the inside toilet.

Melissa remembered that long walk, crossing a trembling bridge. She remembered her cousin, the boy, Rafe, at whom she had just plain stared at the station and later at the house.

That memory had help. The day she'd arrived, Rafe came sneaking up to lean his long self against the back house door to block her in, trap her among smells and bugs. Rafe even covered the sickle-moon cutout in the door with his hand and made the whole black stinky place blacker and stinkier yet.

Trapped in dark, M'lissa Trish positively knew those million-legged things she knew skittered under the too-big wooden hole under her bony bottom would take this opportunity to come crawl between her legs.

"They gon' getcher," Rafe whispered through the dark, "black Woof spider gon' getcher little tee-tee place down there. H'll climb up inside 'n wringle out y'nose."

Melissa yelled and yelled. No one heard. A long acre smothers much on a buzzing summer day.

In a minute, cuz' Rafe got anxious about a game of toss-ball being missed. He left off covering the hole, propped a rake head against the handle and went off to do boy things.

Melissa banged and yelled and even then did not get free until her other cousin, Rafe's younger sister, Barbary Ann, came to use the facility. Ten, twenty minutes was all.

"That old Rafe, he does the same to me, cuz," Barbary Ann, sometimes called B.A., said, "same doggone thing! That Boy's Room place of his is so close, he knows every time you and me are, well, let's say he knows when."

That was one of Melissa's vivid memories.

Another was of heat. Her first night, she lay dying under the tin roof of the big house. Mississippi heat was a fierce something, a whole country, real and hard and mean. No breath of air crossed her body (nor, she gathered, was it likely to for the whole long August of her announced visit). Resentment fumed from Melissa as she shared a hot bed with cousin B.A. Rafe's "hospitality" indeed, and her, a guest, made to walk so-far just to you-know. Wretchedly awful (tousle-haired, golden) Rafe, beast-boy that he was (aglow in wriggly southern light), his awful smile (that dazzled her) that did not fool her put a pretty face on a dark, dark heart. "A boy like that." Melissa shook her head. "Southern hospitality. Hospitality indeed!"

Barbary Ann cooed, asked what she might do.

M'lissa sat up. How was Rafe permitted? Phooey on hiding her feelings, how could he lay asleep and comfortable by the trees? Why'd he enjoy that comfort when she, they, did not?

A moment of sympathy, perhaps, or maybe B.A. sought to soothe her guest's natural northern impatience, but Barbary Ann sat up and began the tale of Lady Ophelia, the Negro woman who, once upon a time, had lived where Rafe now spent nights doing only God knew what.

By all reckoning Ophelia was one scary old woman. First, she was a former slave who had lived almost forever. Second, she was a conjure-woman of great power. Most important, she had no kin or friend, no one knew where she was from. No one came by to say, "Ophelia! Why of course, she's from up in..." or "Yassir, she's kin to them folk down by..." then speak the names of known Negroes in another town or county. Barbary Ann told the tale as though the story came through her own eyes, that she'd seen the magics writhing in night-smoke, right there!

She had not. Ophelia may have lived almost forever, but of course was a woman dead by the time of B.A.'s great granddad's boyhood. B.A.'s tale told that hot night had been embellished by time and whim by others and now were further festooned by Barbary Ann's hospitality.

The Lady Ophelia had been the last woman resident of the

place that, after, became the Tozier boys' Boy's Room. Already run down by life and hardship, she simply moved in one night. "Just as like it was her natural right! And no one, not Toziers, Wallaces, nor anyone dared say her nay! Some tried, none did!"

She never left, not ever again, not once in life. Folks did for her. And her, a colored woman! Toziers, other folks, white or Negro, town or country, anyone who came visiting, brought food, water, wood to burn in winter, they made up, cleaned out, kept the place repaired year-round.

"For her?"

"For her."

"Why?"

"Why? She was a conjure-woman for goodness sakes is why! The most pow'ful conjure-woman maybe ever. Folks feared and required her. A woman who works the darkness is important, for goodness sake. They protected her, did for her."

The Lady Ophelia dipped from the waters of Old Africa and made certain a bull was calved if a bull was needed, or a child was a born a boy if a boy was wanted. She cast darkness before despised neighbors, foretold time, dispensed futures, and unraveled dreams.

She died one day. "When next a visitor came bringing gifts and bearing secret need, he took one look into that old dark shack and ran himself all the way to Monocle calling alarm."

The colored pastor came and behind him, his congregation. They dug a hole in the forest. Nervous Christian words were said over the little dark bundle. "And folks were content only after she'd been lowered into the ground and certain things thrown in after."

"Things? What things?"

"Power things."

"What?"

"Never you mind. Things! And red dirt and dead moss scraped in and over it all. Even us Toziers attended, can you believe?"

"Well, what of it?" Melissa said. She was still hot and now tired of the story.

"Well, for goodness sake," Barbary-Ann said. "Ophelia says, 'When you set to study revenge for wrong, what you must do is take the vera' thin' done-you, and turn it back on the doer!' It's what she says."

"Yeah?" M'lissa started slowly.

B.A. was near asleep. The story was silly. To her, a hot night was nothing. In consequence she was somewhat irritable when she said, "I mean we could grab us one of those jumpin' spiders Rafe locked you with, and of which you are so afraid, silly you. Catch it by moon's full light and, before mornin', make it into old Rafe's breakfast chicory drink, and…" She yawned.

M'lissa shuddered, barely able to speak the eight-legged word. The thought of catching, grinding, drinking… Well, she shuddered. Thank Goodness there was no time for wait and worry. There it was above, full yellow moon rising, wet-hot and burning her eyes. She was too soaked-hot for sleep anyway. Worse, M'lissa knew by-and-by she'd HAVE to use the thunder mug under the bed, then have to carry the hateful thing, sloshing, across the lawn, over the bridge, past Rafe's Boy's Room, just to empty it into the hole in the back house *and* cousin Rafe watching what she carried!

In the minute it took Melissa to resolve to act, cousin B.A. was asleep. Melissa lay waiting. Moon heat and the metallic buzz of cicadas made sleep impossible to catch and hold. *Jaspers*, she thought, *it has GOT to be darn near dawn*. It was a mere hour after the tales had been told, but the awful moonlight barely crawled. The stars that survived full moon brightness wriggled along the rippled windowpanes above their bed. *Criminies*, Melissa thought, *they move!* Every few seconds a mosquito sang in her ear or stung the edge of an eyebrow. She whacked herself a crack every time and still the thing lived to sing again. Melissa was everywhere sweat-wet and skitter-bit. Between dozes, she rolled to and fro, angrier and angrier.

"Wake up!" Melissa finally said aloud and shoved her cousin off the bed.

"Criminies, M'lis' Trish?" B.A. said. "What. Are. You. Doin'?"

Melissa peered over the side of the bed. "Time to get us some, you-know, spider. Time to make us a revenge!" She was glad the moon was at her back, knowing she did not look as sure as her voice sounded.

With imagination, the wet grass in the long yard felt cold between her toes. M'lissa Trish's lady-nightie (her mother's, cut down, pinned up) dragged in the dew. Barbary Ann, in Rafe's left-back and snugged skivvy shorts and undershirt, shuffled behind. She hugged herself for shame. Bugs were now still in the hours between midnight and sun. A horse snickered in the distance. Somewhere there were frogs.

Barbary Ann carried an empty Prince Albert tobacco tin fished from her treasure box under the bed. The little red tin was about half the size of the hip flask Old Strog kept filled with bourbon whiskey and hidden among the *Argosy* and *Police Gazette* magazines in the raw attic next to the girl's finished room at the top of the house. Their way 'cross the yard was lit by the electric lamp Bindle Tozier used to hunt night-crawlers. They danced across the towpath road, following the lantern's yellow circles, M'lissa's city-soft feet cut to fancied bloody ruin on gravel spalls. The black canal water below the bridge stank of life and death and Melissa couldn't help but think it flowed too, too quiet. They gave the Boy's Room a wide pass and whispered through the long grass off the trail. Their way took them near the old trees and their weeping Spanish moss.

"In there," B.A. nodded toward the trees, "is where Ophelia lies buried!" Her whisper stirred the hanging moss.

"Hsssh," Melissa said. By full moonlight, the bare wood of the Boy's Room shone pure white. "Hush, can't you?"

When they reached the back house, Melissa's hands were shaking. Thoughts of spider, yes. Thoughts of Rafe, surely. They were about to begin eternal things, things she didn't altogether believe, but...

Barbary Ann stuck the tobacco tin into Melissa Patricia's hands.

"Huh?"

"Your vengeance," Barbary said. "You harvest the spider bug."

"I am not grabbing crawlies from a crapper. Not alone!"

"Oh, you are. You are, indeed," her cousin huffed, "and you gonna grind and mumbo-jumbo it. Feed it, too, like Lady Ophelia says." Barbary Ann leaned forward, her voice, old and witchy. She breathed sleepy breath into Melissa's face. "'Onc't you set forth 'pon a c'reer of revengeance," she squinted one eye, "ain't no back-turn to't. You are Vengeance hisself,' she says! Ophelia says."

Melissa Patricia's head tingled. She shivered before. Locked in darkness by Rafe, daylight, a wooden door away and only daytime thoughts of hairy things to worry her, that was as nothing. Blame Rafe before but now she stepped by choice into darkness, sunlight, a quarter-world away. Melissa Patricia Tozier, 117 East Oak Street, Chicago, Illinois went alone into the back house. Her eyes and the lantern light went busy with fear. Jumping yellow circles from Bindle's lamp made the unlit parts of the crapper seem darker still. Generation upon generation of Tozier outpourings exhaled from the earth-pit beneath the sagging wood floor. Melissa Patricia's toes curled at the touch of soggy wood beneath bare feet. She hopped foot to foot. Every creak and gasp returned an echo from below. Absolutely, without a shade of doubt, she would NOT stick her hand down that hole, would not reach down where daytime air had been thick with flies (Who knew what else?) and which now was hideously silent. She would not look there. No! She scanned walls, rafters... She looked for... She did not wish to find... But she looked for that thing she sought...

Then saw. One. A big one. A leg twitched from the pages of the Sears book hung by the seat. The leg was thick as a pencil lead and bristly with hair.

"See one." A bare breath, hissed to her cousin.

The leg twitched.

"A rightly one?" B.A. whispered back. "It has got to be 'propriate. By which I mean it has got to be B. I. G., big."

The leg became two and, attached, the body.

"Ah. Ah. Yeah. Yeah-yeah. Big..."

M'lissa Trish opened the flip-lid of the Prince Albert can. She wished the opening were wider, the can longer. She stuck her hand toward the spider that now squatted on the edge of the catalog. For all the world, the critter breathed.

"Get him quick. If he's a wolf, they jump!"

Shaking more than ever she had in her whole little life, M'lissa wiggled the can below where the spider quivered. She nudged the edge of the book with the can. The critter clamored. One leg, one long, thick, hairy leg brushed the tip of M'lissa Trish's finger. Where it touched, she tingled. She shrieked a little then whooped the can's tin lip over the twitching beast. The leg tried to grip her finger, a claw dug into her flesh, another leg grappled her skin, tried to climb her hand. She felt it cock itself for a leap. She shrieked again and the whole fat hair-covered body—a body with a pretty little light brown spot on its belly—went tick, tick, tick against the metal can, and, *snap*, M'lissa clicked the lid shut.

"What the *hey're* you two doin'?" The door opened. Cousin Rafe's boy-voice darn near ripped her spine getting to her head. He filled the night behind Barbary Ann. Both let a shriek could shatter glass and tore a wet streak through the black grass in white moonlight.

Rafe, candle in hand, was left at the back house door, scratching.

By the time they reached the kitchen, first fright was off the adventure and they could not stop giggling. Even so, Melissa was well aware the can she held was filled with spider. Through their giggles and shushes, the critter scrabbled, *tick, tick, tick,* against the sides and bottom. *Tick, tick, tick.*

Cousin B.A. gritted her teeth. "I endeavor to keep from peeing with the laughter," she said. Melissa made sure Prince Albert's top stayed good and tight-snapped. Every few seconds, she banged the can against her other hand, then held it to her ear. Each time, she heard skitters and scrabbles inside and whomped it again. Each time, she giggled less.

"What *are* you doing?" B.A. whispered.

"Stunning the thing." *Whack.* "Killing it," M'lissa whispered. *Whack.*

The flashlight's dome lamp threw yellow and dark circles on the kitchen's varnished lathe ceiling.

"You cannot kill your vengeance spider like that, M'lissa Trish. Criminies, don't you know a thing? He's the haunt-catcher, don't-you-know?"

Feeling, at just that moment, bigger than herself, Melissa looked her cousin right down. "I did not. And I was not *to* know such a thing, now was I, cousin?"

"Well it is a spirit-catcher," Barbary Ann whispered. "That there in the can is waitin' to be told what life it's gonna catch and what it's to become in the next world. You treat it with wishful respect, now."

"And that would be how?" Melissa gave the can another *whomp*. "How might we kill a thing respectfully?"

"Why, you say worshipful words over him, alive. Then you grind him like you might could do a han'ful of cumin seed and make a pasty meal of him." B.A. leaned and spoke words direct to M'lissa Trish's ear. Her lips touched the hair that hung in sweated hanks from Melissa's temple. The whispered words will not be repeated.

"Ready?" Cousin Barbary Ann breathed.

M'lissa Trish stood by Aunt Wallace's mortar, the pestle poised to pulp the beast. "Ready... No, wait!" She retreated from the table and held the marble rod one-handed in front, drew her other arm away as though balancing with it.

"You fixing to walk tightrope or wreak your vengeance?" B.A. whispered.

"I am ready," Melissa said.

Barbary flipped the lid and whooped the can upside into the bowl.

The spider flopped then scrabbled all eight directions at once. Melissa's second or third downbeat whomped it. In fairness to her grit, her little grunted shrieks were quiet enough to not wake the house. The grown Toziers, above, therefore, did not hear Negro conjuring whispered in their kitchen that hot night. The *whomp* that first got the critter, knocked a lump of pale yellow jelly from the fat brown body, the loss of which did not improve the spider's mood nor, it seemed, impair its ability to scramble the slick sides of the bowl. Another few strokes of the pestle, though, ground her up, legs, spider-hair, jelly, and eye-clusters. With each stroke, M'lissa tried her best to say the words her cousin had whispered. She squeaked them. Cousin Barbary prompted from behind. In 20, 25 repetitions of the short Negro verse, the back house spider was a gray paste in the bowl. By then, the effort had taken on the scent of cinnamon and cumin and cloves.

That nearly was it. They ground it together with a measure of dry roasted chicory from the can then poured the mix in a packet M'lissa Trish carried with her as the two giggled quietly up the steps by the creep of morning light.

Who could sleep after that? Anyway, the night was still hot and horrible. They waited until they heard Lady Cal, the colored lady, come to do for the Toziers, preparing breakfast, firing the stove to full heat for the day's hot meal at lunch. The girls jumped to their clothes and ran down for the grits to be set to boil, the coffee to be perked, and cousin Rafe's chicory to be steeped. Barbary Ann set a while and talked with Lady Cal. She talked about Lady Cal's son, about the awful hot weather, about the best way to make poultice…

M'lissa Trish hovered by the stove. Finally, Lady Cal turned and said, "Give that pot a stir now, so it don't thicken to a lump!" Into the chicory Melissa poured the contents of her envelope. *If this is a film*, Melissa thought as she poured, *today, just today, someone else'll decide for that stuff. Someone else'll get struck down by my revenge.* She swallowed hard as she poured. *Maybe even my own self.*

But that morning it was just Rafe tucked full of chicory and swallowed down the charm of spider taken in the full of the moon. By that his soul was doomed to come wandering. The girls knew it. They giggled through breakfast, bit the insides of their cheeks so not to bust with laughing. Rafe stared and made faces, no idea in heck what those darn girls were about.

M'lissa and B.A. cringed at one another other during the noon hot-meal and by cold supper were half-asleep and had pretty much forgotten it all. Except that evening, M'lissa Trish noticed a knothole in the wall above the stove, high up near the lathe-work ceiling. From the varnished pine knot, a pair of furry brown spider legs dangled into the dim light of the kitchen's single bulb. The leg stayed through the meal.

That's right, Melissa Patricia remembered, *that is right. SOMEbody's soul has been caught. SOMEbody's.*

Then there was that awful war, the Second World War. By the time M'lissa Trish returned to the south, grown into a lady (but not by much), Rafe Tozier was gone and dead, killed in the Pacific Theater of Operations, a U.S. Marine Corps Corporal, battlefield commission to Second Lieutenant pending. A terrible thing, the last boy gone from the Boy's Room, gone from life, and no more to come bearing the Tozier name.

The south to which 15-year-old Melissa (she now was just Melissa; a month before, she had favored Pat) returned was booming. Booming maybe, but it was a somewhat sadder place, a place of so many newly dead. In addition to the loss of Second Lieutenant (pending) Rafe Tozier, the passing of Old Strog (the oldest person Melissa had ever known) now further diminished the family. A year before, Strog had the last portion of his second leg cut off. He never fully recovered and certainly was not able to make the trip to the Corners where the Cities Service Whites-Only would welcome him. He now lay buried in pale red-earth alongside Rafe and a passel of Toziers, Wallaces, Preckwinkles, Leblancs and other older names and branches that braided the family back into the dark shadows before time had gathered them all together on this continent.

Cousin Barbary Ann was inconsolable over the old man's passing and about her brother. That surprised Melissa. B.A. seemed never actually to *like* the boy as others had. She always made faces, spoke unwell of him while others smiled and said loving things. B.A. spoke unwell of Rafe even in her short infrequent letters to Chicago, always found space to make firm-footed complaint of her brother, complaint that continued to the day he left for boot camp.

In her even less-frequent replies, Melissa mentioned Rafe once, and that in benevolent observation of the news of his loss. She was shocked, of course. Maybe not shocked. Who is shocked over a single death in so vast a war? In a way, isn't it expected, Death? Isn't it magical, somehow, when someone *doesn't* die? Still, she was surprised. To her credit, Melissa was touched by it. And, of course, she lamented the waste. *So good-looking a boy being, well, wasted like that.* She remembered his hair in the sun, the gold of him, his smile, the scent of…

In further truth, however, Melissa could not say Rafe's passing grieved her. Of course she had not the experience of the boy, day by day, an entire life-long. All she knew was the nasty summer boy who lived below the big house in the relative cool of the Boy's Room and, once, had locked her in that damn smelly outhouse that one awful hot day. Then ignored her.

There had been no summer visit for years. Thus, the cousins hugged tight when hugging was going around at the train station. Barbary Ann, who still liked that name, or, sometimes, just B.A., Barbary Ann had grown pretty and soft. Her face was matured by grief, Melissa thought.

But, damn, if her tears weren't fresh. And Rafe Tozier, months in the grave. But when Melissa thought the long close hug was over, B.A. clenched her again.

"Buried a suit is what we did, cousin," she confided to Melissa. B.A. expanded upon that as they settled into the same room at the top of the house. The house seemed smaller and bigger at once, the paint peeled more like scabs than ever. "Oh, cousin, we buried a uniform of clothes. And not even his, just Marine Corps dress with the medals he was owed and the officer bars that came awarded after he was gone." She spoke with an edge of sweetness and horror, a question hanging in her voice.

"Why?" Melissa barely said.

"Nothing left for burial, the gov'ment said. Can you imagine?"

"Imagine," Melissa said. She looked at the floor as she shook her head. She did not want B.A. to see how dry her cheeks were. Dry not so much about Rafe, but over B.A. *That cousin of mine*, she hated to admit, *is just a silly, pretty thing! Girl'll never amount to anything.*

"Imagine? Nothing left of a whole human being," B.A. sniffled. Then and there, looking at her cousin's wet pretty face, Melissa remembered the night the two of them had spelled Rafe with that old ground-up spider.

"Remember," Melissa began. And she remembered that silly night.

"Sometimes, you know, M'lissa, sometimes the best times we've got are the back end of the worst, darlin'!" Melissa couldn't quite grasp that thought, but agreed to be nice. "So we all wish for a happy, happy end, some happy day." With that, B.A. assembled a brave and miserably happy face.

The visit's second day was hotter. Bright heat hugged Melissa, every breath felt drawn through a steamed towel. "You're young women now," Aunt Wallace said. "Yes, and old enough to go shopping to town by yourselves." With silent gravity, the War Board ration point-book was entrusted to niece Melissa from Illinois ("'Land of Lincoln,' indeed!") and the girls were sent walking to Monocle.

The heat rose in snaky waves from Mr. Roosevelt's half-mile of Kingfish-inspired asphalt. Monocle was not so far as it was. The town had spread up that straightened WPA road and now covered over most of the old canal. Passing through the wartime bustle, the girls shopped for yard goods and notions, for canned and fresh and the weekly meat ration from Talifierro's. Mr. Talifierro pointed with his long shiny chin as he weighed out their ration of bacon on the big white scale. "Look a'that nigger's

168

stroll, won'tcha?"

The cousins turned to look. Crossing the busy main street, a small colored boy walked. He was deliberate, slow, looking no way but ahead, not frightened, paying heed neither to the uncertain clomp of horses and wagons or to the huge military vehicles as they cleared their big-geared diesel throats, downshifting. Sweating uniformed drivers swerved and cursed in rippling midday.

"Niggras don't care 'bout death, hisseff," Mr. Talifierro said. "*That'*n at least! You'd think he was a haunt or something, 'stead of just a spook. Haw-haw."

A man or two picked up Mr. Talifierro's muley *haw-haws*. A pair of small white boys leaned noses against the shop window. Some ladies shook their heads, fearful for the boy.

Melissa bit the knuckles of her right hand until he reached the pavement and turned the corner. *Stupid*, she thought. *Stupid, stupid boy.* On the way home, their purchases dangling in a cotton web-bag hung between them, Barbary Ann grumbled. "Now I want you to know, Mr. Talifierro, there, was pure mush-mouthed ignorant," she said, "calling that Negro boy a 'nigger.' Even, 'niggra,'" she said. "Why, nobody—nobody—calls them that anymore, the coloreds. They are colored people, for goodness sake. Negroes."

The tale was brought out at table that evening. B.A. quoted butcher Talifierro on the subject of "spooks."

With the word "spook" raised twice in one day, the notion of "haints," of ghosts, "spirits of air and waters" came to Melissa. Around her, in the silence between the still-sad adults at table, through the dark house and outside in twilight, there drifted the enduring dead. *A suit of clothes, indeed*, she thought. So thinking, Melissa remembered the night she and B.A. caught, killed, and ground that old wolf spider, fed it to cousin Rafe to vengeance his spirit for having locked her in the outhouse dark. They'd done it right there, right where they sat. Melissa laughed into the hungry circle.

"Why, what is tickling you, M'lissa Trish?" Aunt Wallace asked in the expectant silence. "Something amuse you?"

"Just something," Melissa said. "A little nothing long ago."

Everyone smiled and waited.

"No, that's all. Just a silly thing, something of no matter. Pay me no mind."

They stared until more important concerns arose. Of course she could not speak of cousin Rafe, his spirit caught and taken by the dust of a wolf spider. She couldn't wrap a story of one so recently dead into a memory of silly girls shrieking in the night long ago. Of course the story was more about how the spider had nearly leaped on her and crawled over her hand in the outhouse and, all squished, had yet tried to run at her up the marble side of Aunt Wallace's mortar bowl. Even so, no, she could not speak of curses and the beloved dead in one breath.

Melissa smiled again when she noticed the knothole above the stove, where wall and ceiling met. She wondered if a small, hairy spider leg would show.

It did not.

Sweltering in bed next to cousin B.A., Melissa asked why, in all this heat, why had she not moved down to the Boy's Room.

"Silly thing. It is the *Boy's* Room."

"But it's private..."

"No buts, Missy Melissa!"

"But," she said, leaning on the word, "there are no boys." Darn but she hated saying that. "And, I bet it is cooler and lots more comfortable."

From the dark, B.A.'s voice was straight, stiff. "Th' idea. Rafe so soon in his grave."

"And with the Marines and boot camp, gone more than two years—two years gone in all, cuz."

"Th' idea!"

"And I am sure he wouldn't mind us sleeping in that old shack. No disrespect, B.A., but under this hot roof there is no breath of air. For me, it is sleep in the Boy's Room or on the porch by the 'facility.'"

Thus, Melissa slept her first night in the Boy's Room. They carried bedding and pillows. In a few steps, their feet were wet with dew. As before, the earth seemed cool, steeped in shadows that soaked into it from the woods. Melissa tingled but boldly trod, leading with the light from the same old night-crawler lamp.

B.A. hung back, unsure of the propriety of the enterprise. "Th' idea. I cannot imagine what Mother and Father will want us to say, Rafe so soon in his grave."

Rafe's MEDALS so soon, Melissa thought. *Some suit of Marine clothes so soon.* She did not say that, of course. "We'll think of something appropriate after a good night's sleep, Barbary," is what she said.

The Boy's Room smelled old. A hint of something else hung there, but did not smell too bad, not exactly, not after they threw the place open to night air. There was a little of dry leather to the scent, much of dust and moldy paper. The lantern revealed piles and piles of mildewed magazines, newspapers, funny books, illustrated periodicals of sports and crimes. Maybe there was something of dead animal to the air, too, but in a few minutes, even that had pretty well cleared. It was cooler.

The old shack leaned like a dog straining its lead; it drooped away from its wattle and daub chimneystack. Even so, the place seemed to have remained tight against weather and the windows didn't stick too badly to their skewed frames. A push and a shove and they swung open. When they did, air flowed through from woods and field.

"Oh Barbary, feel the night breathe!" Melissa said.

"Yug," B.A. said. She pointed the lamp at a stack of

magazines at her feet. In the sudden light, silverfish swarmed like short bright words deserting the paragraphs of THE POLICE GAZETTE. "This was NOT a good idea, cuz."

"Objection noted," Melissa said, quoting a war film she had seen in Chicago. She put her back to the night. "But feel the air!"

Cautious as to the placement of her feet, B.A. stepped away from the piles. Closer to the window, she sniffed and hugged herself through a shiver. The lantern flickered. Outside, wind-sifted moss swept a quiet whisper through the grass. Dry catalpa pods clacked. Something, some furred critter most likely, cracked a branch along the edge of the trees. Another something ruffled one of the piles of paper in a farther corner of the room.

"Boo!" Melissa said loudly, jumping at her cousin. B.A. shrieked a quick yelp. As did Melissa, who had frightened herself.

Then the cousins laughed, made up the old spring bed by the quickly failing lantern, lay down together and soon, sooner than they realized they might, they slept.

Then on, the visit was pleasant, considering the sadness of its occasion. By permission unasked, word ungiven, the girls continued sleeping in the Boy's Room.

The visit was a short one. Melissa's daddy had to return to Chicago in a few days, return to work, his work of the war. Mother, too, had duties: volunteer war efforts, other duties, duties, if not of family, then of life, life back north in Chicago. "'Land of Lincoln,' indeed!" Barbary Ann said of her cousin's home, and no more was said about it.

That was on the last night. That night the air was filled with lightning bugs. Glowworms lit the trees, their cold stars winked to life and faded between the shack and the big house. They drifted deeper into the woods and across the land beyond Tozier property. B.A. cried a little at the thought of Melissa Trish leaving, of her being left alone in that place, in that house, in that family, alone. Would she go back or sleep in the Boy's Room?

She cried half about her brother and nearly half about her cousin chugging away in that train, the train going so far north. "North to the Land of..." She sniffed. Lying in bed in the Boy's Room, the shack where the conjure woman Ophelia had breathed her last spells alone, where the boy, Rafe, had spent his last night in the bosom of his family, the cousins hugged and talked far toward morning and, suddenly, they slept.

When the bright spirit awoke her, Melissa had no idea the time. The air was almost chilly. A hint of distant thunder mumbled against her chest and eardrums. A soft light had risen on the sagging porch and sifted through the rusted screen door. Sometimes thin, at times nearly solid, it never seemed to be light or substance. Sometimes the form had too many legs for a human or any proper animal. Other times, the thing had an insufficiency of parts. Melissa's saw it as a figure, a figure that at once walked, at other times simply pulsed softly, its edges drifting apart. The light that flickered in the room was not Will-o-the-wisp, Foxfire, St. Elmo's. Other things it could not be popped to Melissa's nearly sleeping head and were dismissed. What it was she did not know. Not at first. Eventually, even a Yankee from the Land of Lincoln knew enough to know a haunt.

The wraith seemed unsure. Sometimes it moved with the jerky gait of an old soldier on a long parade. Or it moved and didn't move at the same time, standing statue-still while the cabin crawled by, Melissa and sleeping B.A. merely passengers.

If a human person moved like that, Melissa would have said it was pacing, looking. It slipped through solids, waded among piles of Rafe's fragile magazines without turning a leaf. When it passed through the table by the hearth, the rough wood faded and grew solid, like an old skiff looming in the fog.

Melissa wanted to nudge her cousin awake. She did not, of course. Of course, the spirit that lit the air of the Boy's Room was that of cousin Rafe. She was certain of that.

"What're you sniffing at, you?" Melissa whispered to the ghost. At the moment, the haunt looked exactly as though it was doing just that, peering 'round, remembering, nosing something. Or looking for trouble, like boys would.

Remembering what, you? Melissa thought. "Life?" she asked aloud, again not aloud enough to wake her cuz. *What old life you looking for?* she wondered. *Seeing death, are you? Are you right now being blown to flinders on your Pacific island? Seeing other boys go to graves?*

The spook turned and drifted again.

You seeing the ceiling here, nights when you were a boy, alone? Melissa looked up and saw only shadows cast by the haunt's flickering light. *You remember the old outhouse, down there? You see me, back then? See me in your place, here and now? See the life you had and wasted and the life you don't have and want? You see me?*

When the haunt that *had*—just had—to be Rafe's passed through her body, Melissa's mind shut off for a moment. Passing through her, it felt like...

Electrocution, she thought. That was after, recalling. There'd been sudden vibrations that climbed her hand and arm. Like that one day she'd accidentally grabbed the bare prongs of a light cord. Him passing through was like that, she thought later, but the haunt's tingle was everywhere, a buzz that washed her deep. Her vision flickered, her teeth chattered. Every joint felt like exercise in Physical Culture class. Rafe's ghost—*goodness, call it what it is!*—never paused inside, but passed without effort. Melissa was transparent to him, a clear, clean window. He left a lingering of cinnamon, of cinnamon and cumin. Just that. *No!* Cinnamon, cumin and a whiff of chicory. The dry, ground, roasted root of the blue flower and, unaccountably, a whiff of charred cotton and other burnt up things.

Ghosts, call it that, spooks were unfinished business, life left over, never to be lived. She knew that at least. "What're you seeing?" she whispered.

At the wall of the shack, the thing seemed to climb a short set of stairs and sifted into the wood and daub. It stood a long moment, half in half out, drifted apart, drew together. Turned, seemed to look out, over Melissa's head.

She was less and less chilled by the old and impotent thing. She wanted to reach out, speak to this remnant of dead Rafe ("…a uniform of clothes, not even his!"), speak to what a fool boy he'd been, tell him… tell him that, well, life is for the living! That was it, the old thing! He ought to get on out of it. Life would go on without him and his old burnt up suit of clothes. Oh, yes, Melissa was curious, curious about *After*. Curious and, now she thought of it, relieved. There was something after. Maybe not a bright and golden place, no music and angels (which, to be honest, she'd always dreaded), but maybe Forever was not fire and torment nor awful cold and distant echoes either. Surely, though, there was a place where she would go when it was her time, a place in which she would *be*, for goodness sakes. Death would not be forever nothing, eternity, not a vast empty hole. The minute she died, she would not stop. Nor would death take her to some far-off Kafiristan or backside of the moon (or was it the dark side? She never could… *Oh for goodness sake*). Forever would not be a place she had never seen, never could see and about which, upon arrival at the Great Final Time, she might not approve. No, eternity would be a place like home.

Melissa turned to silly, pretty, sleeping B.A. Melissa was about to say, "Look, cousin. There's your brother, in his spirit world." She never said it. Squatting on B.A.'s cheek, breathing in that way they had, was a tickly crawly… *Oh, for heaven's sake, call it what it is*, she thought, a spider, wolf spider, the spit and image of that long-ago ground up soul-catcher. Why, every now and then, M'lissa Trish still saw that one peering with its thousand eyes bright in coal oil light, peering from the Sears book or scrabbling in the marble mortar. Now here, on cousin B.A.'s face, it was.

Melissa, out of bed in a shot. Chills climbed her tingles. The Awesome Forever was one thing. Spiders another.

Half-in, half-out, and half-up the wall of the Boy's Room, the ghost had stopped. There was a moment between them, Melissa felt, a moment when she looked at the old thing, then down at her cousin, spider and all, then back at the ghost. Melissa reached across B.A., reached to touch the brightness hanging above the floor. As she did, it reached down for her. They never touched. Too darn far. Just so, Melissa was comforted. *The worlds* might *touch*, she thought. She had feared that to be a ghost (and she smiled at how silly was the thought), she'd thought that to be a ghost would be like being the only person in a crowded room, someone always alone. Cousin Rafe's wander, him still aware, able to reach out to her, and her for him, comforted Melissa more than any minister's presumption of angels and song. The ghostly presence, there in the Boy's Room, was a guarantee of... well, of *something* after life.

A consolation she'd keep inside herself. She'd share it with B.A. later, when the hard immediacy of her brother's death had softened. Next time she came visiting, she'd tell.

Life grabbed Melissa. Nothing much happened. For a time, Melissa remembered the haunting as having been shared, that she and B.A. had both been passed through by the ghost, Rafe trapped by their spider, his spirit left to wander Tozier land for his sins. She remembered clearly (and falsely) a phantom truth, that she and Barbary Ann had hugged each other through that scary bright night in the Boy's Room. She remembered the hug, the talk of ghosts and whispered stories of lives that had had left too much undone in the world at death to go to heaven, hell or anyplace. She was comforted by these memories, however imperfect.

She told the story several times over the years, always with a laugh, at least with a smile, sometimes with a drink. Eventually, she buried the tale and refused to think it to life. Every few years, something in the senses, the smell of cinnamon, a shadow on the ceiling, a whiff of cotton scorched by a too-hot iron, brought a notion of wandering spirits to mind. Comforted, Melissa waited for life to happen.

After a few decades, she no longer smiled at the memory. She remembered the Boy's Room chill, the tingle as the spirit passed through her and beloved Barbary Ann. She remembered a lost spirit on its way. Its way where?

She didn't know.

She never spoke of it in middle-age. That's a lie. She spoke sparingly. A friend once asked if she believed in the supernatural. She asked over coffee and more or less to make conversation after a movie or reading a book. Mel thought, then told the story, now quite a bit different.

The friend cocked her head, looked surprised.

"That's the south," Mel said. "Magic."

"I'm amazed at you," the friend said, shaking her head.

Mel also told her analyst. He was neither amazed nor surprised. He asked what she made of it, the "ghost."

"Oh, I don't know," Melissa said. "Maybe there's a place somewhere in the world for me. Maybe I'll be able to reach out, touch someone sometime. You think?" She smiled. So did the analyst.

She was an old woman the next time she came south. Tozier land had long gone from Tozier hands. The family had spread, dissolved. By then, the town of Monocle had bulldozed itself all the way to the peeling Tozier house, gone through it and beyond. Brick buildings stretched along Roosevelt Avenue, the old Bay St. Louis canal road. By then, Miss Melissa Tozier was a woman grown old on a diet of deep fear, dark secret, and tiny sin. When she thought of it, she prayed; mostly, she did not. But there was Afterlife. She held that fact like she did the knowledge of her own heart's being. There was a future Forever.

By the time she stepped carefully from the bus at Monocle Station, she prayed only to be a quiet story with a happy ending. She'd come back because. Well, because she remembered being a little girl here and how wonderful it was to have been a little girl here, a woman child, a white girl in the south, such a one not expected to accomplish, not expected to be of much significance, content to be the pretty creature she'd one day surely become.

Mel had lived that expectation. Her day had come, gone, and now it was late. She barely remembered being silly M'lissa Trish, who'd held her cousin in the long ghostly night, her life still ahead. She remembered perfectly, her first fright and final contentment, seeing ghostly... Was it Rafe? All the pacing, the anger at an unlived life. She remembered the spirit's long looks, its climb up the wall, its descent, its climb again. The spirit she'd caught for vengeance-sake in that old mashed spider, angry at her, angry at the world.

Served it right, she thought. Lock her in dark, stink and fear. *Is that spook still here?* she wondered. Sixty years was nothing to a ghost.

The cab stopped at the heart of a black business district, long past its prime. The driver, a black man, sixty (*More? Who could tell?*), guaranteed, here'd been the junction of the old road and canal.

Nothing remained to remind.

The cab chugged at the curb. A few shops crammed together, a music store with noise, a burnt out shell next to it, then a frock shop also charred dead and gone.

"Yes, ma'am," the driver said. "That ol' canal bridge was somewhere, there." He pointed across the wide street. "B'yond, I remember. Bridge fell down, aw, must be thirty years ago. Canal's a sewer now. Cemented over."

Melissa stood washed in the smells of the neighborhood. She hugged herself despite the heat. The cab's idling engine tap-tap-tapped above a running cough. Hot oil reeked from under the hood. Cab wanted to go.

The driver seemed to know the city, been a boy here, he said, a boy during the War (*Older than he looks, who can tell?*).

Melissa embraced the sun and heat, didn't mind heat these days, even fierce southern summer. She peeled dollars from her wallet, all the while looking for the place in moonlight, in her past. She looked back toward where the scabby old painted wooden house must have been.

A run-down glass and aluminum-sided elementary school shimmered in the right direction, at about the right distance. The other way, where fields had stretched unexplored beyond Tozier land, a fast food parking lot roiled in waves of grease. Other smells came and went. The cab pulled hot air around her in its wake.

On the sidewalk, alone now in this strange town and time, Melissa turned. A squall approached, a cluster of boys, African American boys. They came with such loose purpose (she had no idea what) along the street (Tozier land, once). The boys were loud, they overlapped, hardly listened to each other. She cleared their sidewalk, fled three steps up to the door of the music shop.

For goodness! She's been around black people all her life, around them as equals.

They passed, laughing, spoke roughly, every other word, *that* word, they ignored, didn't see her. Didn't see her.

From the stoop she got her bearings. *If there*—she looked toward the restaurant—*if there was the land beyond Tozier's*, her head turned, *why* there *must have been the outhouse*. She chuckled at the memory. She paced mentally, from there to…

Then realized where she stood. She stood where the Boy's

Room had been. She stood where old Lady Ophelia had lived, conjured and died, where cousin Rafe spent nights, his last night a free boy, a living boy, staring at the ceiling where he'd doubtless been the night she'd trammeled up his spirit in the spider. She turned to look where it had been again. *What* did *I* do *with that spirit?* she wondered and laughed again. Then stopped. *An old white woman laughing on the street in the Negro part of town, heavens...*

She stood, perhaps, in the very place, sixty years along, stood, yes, above where she and now-gone cousin Barbary Ann had slept that last cool night of their lives, their lives together. She descended to the sidewalk, took a few steps toward the burned out frock shop. She stepped in space, crossed time, felt a sudden rush, a rush and tingle such as she'd never, *well almost never, never except for once, once before in her life,* felt. A tingle as if electricity moved through her. It chattered her blood. The tingle made every joint quiver like (oh, God) like her body tingled in Physical Culture class at school. And on the steps of the frock shop, a scent of burnt cotton embraced and entered her, a smell of old flames and...

Melissa Patricia Tozier stood three steps above the sidewalk. She looked back from where she had come. Wind whipped her hair, billowed around her face, whipped her eyes. A white ghost flickered in the breeze. Her. Her hair, body, an old, white presence in her own long-gone past.

Melissa looked down. Her cousin had slept by her side, a spider on her cheek. She had risen from the bed to stare at the spook. Now, she stood alone and looked down where they had been. No. Where both had been alone. Separate. Along the street stood the back house where she'd caught the spider. She (*almost*) saw the place, transparent, as though in a lifting fog. She could not see cousin Barbary sleeping alone in the night dark but she knew she was there. Their ghosts.

A cinder poked her eye. Melissa cocked her head, wiped her

eyelid, blinked. She staggered painfully against the doorway. The ghost she now was felt solid. M'lissa Trish Tozier from the Land of Lincoln: a thing caught and captured, spelled by her own self, a spider-spell she'd spoken in another century. She felt the living thing scrabble on her hand, heard it in the can, *tick, tick, tick.*

Now was the day that was supposed to be, the day poor stupid cousin Barbary Ann said to hope for, "a happy end to some happy, happy day."

The tale was winding down, not happy, not sad. It led from the back house beyond the Boy's Room, ran a circle and back through her. Went nowhere. She reached to touch the face she'd once been, glowing below her in sunlight. She could not touch it. Could not see it clearly. Could not be it, call it back, could not live it. Not ever again. Not ever forever.

LITTLE GIRL DOWN THE WAY

Erin was dead; dead, and her little body buried in the narrow alley where the rainspout spilled dirty water over the new concrete. The burial hadn't been a good job.

Erin stayed in the basement, the same basement she'd lived in the last years of her life. Mommy loved her. That's why Erin was here, because Mommy loved her, always loved her. Must have been her bad Dwarves, Erin knew, because day after day, all days alike, Erin slipped back into this small place in the basement. Day after day, all alike, she flopped face first into a growling rock grinder of lumpy pain; each day she fell, plop, into a sea of boiling do-do, got flushed, was snuffed and smothered, drowned in thick pee-pee, stinky diarrhea pumping up her nose. Every day she got tossed, heaved onto the broken cokebottle rocks of sharp light that caught, hooked and hung her, held her dangling, slipping by her gently tearing flesh, rip, rip, rrrrip, over the blazing hole of always.

That was just eye-openers and she was already dead.

She tried to cry. She couldn't. The dead cannot. Every day, all days the same, her eyes had no wet for it, chest hurt too much to heave, crying.

Even dead, she was hungry. Hunger made her stomach puff. Every now and then she caught something, something dead that scrambled across her face or arms in the cellar dark, scrabbled up

182

her legs. Caught 'em, sucked 'em down, slurp, the dead things fed her. Good the dead could feed the dead. Mmm.

Unless she puked, Mommy wouldn't know.

Right now, she had mice chunks and a hundred squirts of oozy bug in her belly. There was also most of a sock down there. There it had been, a long stretch outside her dog cage. It must have been from a time ago, something dropped in a corner, then, one day, kicked and left near enough for her to reach it.

She'd reached and reached and reached then taken it. It was small, so very small. Oh, maybe it had been her brother's oh, ohhh, ohhhhhhh, Baby's. She held it for a while, loving it, touching her face with it. Finally, hunger took her and she took it, a few threads at a time soaked in her nose blood. She let the strands trickle down her throat until: allllll gone.

That was long ago. And in truth she couldn't remember if that was when she was alive or not. There were other things, a few dirty things, down inside her, but not a lot, not so much that Mommy'd care.

What she fed on, she slurped. Jaw wouldn't let her chew. When she'd been alive, Jaw wouldn't let her cry, either. When she tried, Jaw made her feel like she was chewing sharp pieces of herself. Jaw was—she counted with her tongue—one, two, three, four—four places Jaw was broken. Tongue could touch and gently shift the broken ends, the bone beneath the skin; ear could hear it grate, grate, grate and make the shivering hot chill chatter all through her head. When she did, when she moved her bones like that, her shattered teeth bit, bit, bit, the swelling lips, shredded cheeks, and gnawed-on tongue.

Jaw minded her for Mommy. Mommy had made Jaw from her mouth. Wham, wham, wham, wham and there was Jaw.

That'll show me, she'd say to herself as Jaw snapped gnyang, gnyang, gnyang, down hard and pointy on all the soft places in her mouth. That'll show me, Mommy, she'd say as each bite slammed a hammerfall of agony against the back of her eyeballs! See, Mommy? she'd say very, very quietly and very, very fast. That'll show me! That'll show me! She whispered it aloud; maybe Mommy'd hear and like her more. She'd think it to herself, and maybe Mommy wouldn't hear and wouldn't hate her more. Jaw watched and minded for Mommy. Even when she died, Jaw watched Erin for Mommy.

None of it—pain, fear, missing her Mommy—helped her cry, though. She was dead. The dead don't cry.

Except for not being able to cry, being dead wasn't so bad. She'd hung on so to being alive! Mommy was right, she was a stupid bitch. And when it finally swallowed her, death was just the same as life. Same basement. Same Mommy. Same pain. What had she been so scared of? She was still safe down there. She just hadn't known.

When she'd been alive, she couldn't eat. Not the last few weeks. Once, when the cellar window had been left open in a dark wind, just to air the stink out of the goddamned place for Jesus's sake, and the rains had splashed down so hard, the mud had spattered and flowed thick dribbles down the wall, she'd caught some and sucked it down. The mud was cool on her lips, gritty. She could swallow it so smooth and it felt full and heavy in her tummy.

Mommy didn't like that! She found out and she didn't like that!

Today Erin puked a little snot and ooooo that hurt. The hundred Nasty Dwarves she knew were in her, inside her everywhere, started scraping, ruff, ruff, ruff, like that and got to kicking, kicking her with hard, sharp feet, wham, wham, wham, wham like that. They grabbed parts of her insides, her heart, her tummy, lungs, bones, and throat. They pulled and bent and hung, they stretched and bit and tore and made her hurt like she couldn't believe. They jabbed with knives and touched with fire and ran electric all through her. She'd hated the numb chatters of electric, how it made her go loose and poopy when Mommy'd run it through her, hated the way it made her slam, go whack onto the floor or against the wall, her head going boom, boom, boom. The Dwarves that lived in her had it all—fire, knife, and electric pain.

When Erin yelled, it was a tiny silent scream. She could hear it and that's what counted. Her broken bits poked her here, there, everywhere, tore out her cheek, her side, her arm. Bloody stuff ran out her poopy hole, but she screeched it to herself. She knew how much Mommy hated, just hated, that—when the bones showed, sticking out. But she couldn't, really, really couldn't shove the bloodred pointy things back inside, not again, not and keep the screaming to her-Goddamn-self.

So there she sat: forcing stillness, forcing her mouth to stop; Erin made it stop working against the jagged bony things that stuck out of her face the last couple of weeks, months, years.

She was dead and still she sat still. She remembered: Mommy didn't like a noise from her, mornings. She forced the silence of the grave over everything, willing herself to be dead again today as she had every day for days, weeks, months, years.

Even dead, she needed to breathe. Short pants did it. Deep breath hurt too much, made funny cracking pains inside. Little breaths—a lot of them—worked almost as good and didn't hurt as much. She took her first little sniffs of the day.

That accomplished, morning was underway.

Every now and then she knew a little light. Haze drifted through her like white air. Light hurt different than memory of life and the reality of this place, this Heaven, was it?

In the silent place she kept around her, she still stank. In the thank-the-Jesus dark, she still stank while she waited to be all the way dead again later, later—at night, maybe it was, when she was really dead. Like being asleep when she'd been alive. But when she was awake, she stank.

She felt the stinky dress still on her. Aw, it was still there. She still wore the dress she'd worn for weeks, months, years. The dress Mommy'd given her. The same old new dress from Sears that she wore forever, that her body was buried in out where the dirty water washed the crumbling concrete.

She remembered. Remembered the time when Mommy had come to see her and seen "what the fuck you done to that!" Mommy had seen the "Jesus Christ I paid good Goddamned money for and look what you done to it now" dress.

Now and then a living person would come, come to the basement, would turn on the light from upstairs and Erin would squint against the screaming shards the hanging bulb sprayed through her like spitting grease from a hot stove. That hurt, light did, but different from the day-by-day whap, bam, bong Mommy'd bring by later.

The person would move across the basement, do those things the living did. And when the person left, sometimes he'd leave the bulb on and the brightness would boil her away, day and night, until someone turned it off.

Sometimes, the living person would sniff, as though he smelled her stinky self all the way from the grave down by the rainspout. When this happened, the live one would shiver, hug himself, move quickly, finish in a rush what had to be done, trot up the steps, slam the door, and leave a silent chill behind as the lamp swung back and forth in the dark.

It was hard to see the living—they were little more than vapor—and even though their light and mist brought pain, Erin liked the times they came. Hard to see, impossible to touch. She could barely tell if these living ones were boys or girls, big people or kids. She had no idea what the living did, why they did it. Even when she'd been alive, she didn't know. Now...?

Every now and then, one of them walked right through her

and dragged a little piece of her upstairs, stuck to their shoe maybe or soaked into the hem of a skirt or caught like a burr on a pants leg. That little piece of Erin would move with the living, up in the day and light. She'd feel the outside day, just a little, like a splendid single note of a really pretty song. Then the note faded, whitened, died, and then the missing part crawled back to her, dirty dark and stinky, while she slept. When she woke another day, that little piece of her was sticking out, just a morsel of that day's pain.

That's how she thought of it anyway.

Every now and then something would scream past the high narrow window that looked outside, something so alive, something with small legs and shrill voices. Kids. Like Baby brother had been. As with all the living, she could hardly see these children, but they made her basement vibrate. What they did... they made her remember.

She remembered, back to before she'd come here, remembered when Baby So Sweet had first come home. Not like her. No. She'd seen Baby sleeping dearly, all the world quiet around him he slept so sweet. She went on tippytoes to Baby brother. She leaned over and kissed. Kissed his cheek. He smelled like milk. His cheek was warm and soft, something she wanted to taste, like something she'd remembered from long ago and she wanted now to taste him but all she did, all she ever did, was kiss his head and kiss his nose and kiss his cheek.

Then Mommy grabbed her arm and swung her around and around and smacked her on the wall, picked her up and told her good thing she come before she'd dropped Baby, told her good thing or she'd go out with the trash.

Even though Erin promised, promised Mommy never to come near Baby ever, never again, that was it, Mommy had had it with her. Mommy WAS planning to send her to school that year, Mommy said. But now? Not on her life. She WAS going to let her outside. But not now. She WAS going to let her have friends. But not not not not NOW. And she whomped her again on the wall and her arm bone, sharp and white, came through her skin and made a mess a Goddamned mess.

Then she went to live in the basement.

It was a long time till she saw Baby again. She almost didn't know him. He was almost as big as she was and he flickered by the window. His little legs flew by, a flickered blur of bright and shadow, but somehow she felt him pass. She shoved as close to the light as the dog cage let her. Squeezing her face against the cold metal, she could see one piece of sky and part of the wall of the house next door. The day was bright. A puddle of light soaked the floor and caught the corner of her cage. The heat of the beam licked her face.

Then the legs thudded past again and she almost felt the wind of their going. Like thunder. Like pounding pain, they ran.

After a silence, and all of a sudden, there was a face. It flashed into a corner of the window, clipping off her measure of sky. Her brother's face blocked most of the light and his shadow fell across her. She felt the cool of his shadow and could almost smell the memory of his cheek. But he was soooo big now. She stared at the giant Baby and his eyes, oh his eyes, were so black in his big round head, his eyes got sooooo wide and he shaded them with both his sweet little hands.

She stunk.

He yelled and yelled and in a moment he was whipped up and out of the frame.

Then there was Mommy, and Erin skittered into the dark corner of the cage and no, no, no, no, she knew she'd hurt. She knew she wouldn't know why fucking Jesus fucking Christ why was she so Goddamned bad? Why was she so...? She could feel it now...

This was when she was still alive, when she was the rat in the basement. Mommy told her that was what she was. To her, to Baby: the big, bad rat in the basement. What Baby'd called her.

Even after Mommy'd punished her for letting Baby see her, she'd remembered when Baby had first come home and she had touched him with her lips. She remembered the time when she had first, and for the only time, felt the cool life of his shadow across her eyes.

Ever after, once a week maybe, just once a week, she'd touch her own hand to her lip and close her eye for a moment, trying to imagine it was Baby's hand she kissed.

A long, long time later, the door to the cellar opened and it wasn't Mommy.

She'd been sitting. That's what she did most days. Then the cellar door opened and she scooted to the cagedoor so Mommy didn't have to get down and crawl to catch hold of her for Jesus's sake.

The cellar door opened and nothing happened.

A foot sounded on the stair but the light didn't come. In a little while the foot stepped on the squeaky tread. It didn't squeak like when Mommy stepped on it, no, it squeaked different.

It was gray outside and the world didn't make much light around her, but in the shadow on the stairs there was a small person. She had never seen a small person and she covered herself with her piece of blanket.

"Come out," the voice of the small person said. "I see you. You come out."

She peeked. The small person was near the cage. He was bigger than she was, but she knew he was Baby. Baby alone. She slipped her head out of the blanket and looked at him.

A beam of yellow light smacked her dead on the eyeballs. It felt like toothache exploding in her face. She screamed and her own voice scared her. It was like nothing she'd ever heard. It was just her but it was a ghost, a monster, a rat, yes a rat in the basement, and she was screaming from fear of herself.

Then Baby was screaming and the light fell from his hands and rolled on the floor. He ran. He clamored up the steps one at a time and the wooden door above slammed.

She screamed for a few minutes. Through Baby banging on the door, above, and his screaming and crying. She screamed into the silence that followed. She screamed for a little, and then she was quiet again because she knew Mommy would come.

Mommy came later that night. And that was the last day she lived. Before Mommy reached her Erin began whispering, telling Mommy she was really bad and she would never make another sound ever again. She wouldn't really, really wouldn't. She didn't sit by the door of the cage; she drew as far away from it as she could. She knew it was bad, but she was afraid.

Mommy was quiet, coming. She wasn't saying Jesus's sake and fucking Christ and Goddamn rat. She walked down and picked up the flashlight that had gone dark on the floor in the hours since Baby'd been down to see where rat lived.

She clicked the dead flashlight and put it on the bench behind her. She came to the cage and unlocked the gate. She got on her hands and knees and reached inside. Erin pressed against the farthest corner, saying, "no Mommy, no Mommy, no Mommy," but Mommy squeezed further and further in, caught her leg, and drew Erin forth.

Erin whimpered. She whispered no, no, no, no, no, no. She would never ever ever ever say anything again.

Mommy picked her up. She looked at her. Mommy was so big, so much bigger every day. Now she was the biggest thing in all the world. And Mommy put her hands around Erin's middle and pressed. Erin took a last breath and tasted Mommy's perfume and said, no, no, no. Then Mommy pressed more and more and Erin felt herself break inside, felt herself crack, felt sharp things stab her and stab her. Then she couldn't breathe, not even a little and in a short time, held close to Mommy, in Mommy's hands, she died.

That wasn't too bad, Erin remembered. There had been worse. When she'd spilled on the new dress from the Sears. That'd been worse. That had been a day! A whap, whap, whap, picked by the feet and spun, day. A wheee, and her face went wham-bong against the metal pole that held up the house from down in the basement day. That day, Mommy'd dropped her, "little fucker," Mommy'd called her, "crawl out of me, will you," she said. Then she'd shoved a rolled up newspaper down her throat until she nearly choked.

"You'll wear that thing until you wear it out," Mommy'd said, letting her go, letting her pull the paper out of her mouth.

Mommy sat on her for a while and hit her with a piece of coal from the bin. She hoped that showed her, Mommy'd said. She'd have to learn, Mommy said. And hit her. Learn to take care of things I give you. And hit her. Cost good money, these things. And hit her. She'd wear that dress. And hit her. Wear that fucking dress until Christ Jesus took it off her. Oh the dress was a wreck after that.

And Mommy had left Jaw to watch out what she did down there.

Then Mommy was gone, the door slammed and she didn't eat ever after. She didn't make any more fuss after that. Now that was a day.

Except Baby'd come down and she screamed and Mommy came and Erin died. That was another day.

Mommy took her body and put it outside with the trash. Just like she said, except she buried her where the rainspout poured. Nobody knew. Nobody had known she ever was; they knew less of her now that she wasn't.

Erin stayed in the basement. After a while she got used to being dead.

People came later, living people whom she could hardly see. They took all the things out of the basement. They took the dog cage and Erin had no place to be. In a little bit, Mommy came down and stood in the dark.

Erin wanted to cry, but the dead didn't do that. Mommy looked so beautiful. She was dressed for going. Erin knew it. Mommy looked around the empty basement. Finally she found Erin after looking long and hard, looked right at her.

"You better stay right here, young lady," Mommy said quietly. "You stay here or I'll be back for you. You hear?"

Then Mommy was gone.

How long ago?

Now, every day, all days alike, Erin came into the world, sat in the pain and waited.

The basement filled, then emptied, more people came, more things went.

One day, the basement was gone. Big machines rumbled through. The house fell. The machines rolled right through her. Light pounded down, dirt filled her and she rose to the surface. All her pains remained, pieces of her hung to the iron, to the men who walked right through her in daylight. She watched as her body was unearthed. She watched as people came and looked. She watched, sitting as close as she could to where he little dog cage had been, as people lifted her from the ground and put her in a bag.

"Bye-bye," she said as her body went away. "Bye-bye."

Night. She waited.

Day. The living came with more machines. They dug out her basement again and she found the old spot where she'd lived and waited the years for Mommy. The living built.

Days went along. All days, alike. The new basement was bright. The ceiling was white and smooth. Bright tube lights lit the place.

The living came and went. They passed through her like light through a window.

Then one night Mommy came.

Erin didn't recognize her at first. First, she was a shadow, something in the dark. The shadow was stick-thin, but Erin knew her Mommy.

Mommy was acting funny, too. Nobody was with them here in the basement but Mommy was struggling, fighting against something and losing the fight. Mommy never lost a fight. That was funny and Erin almost laughed. Somebody forcing Mommy! Despite her fear, Erin giggled a little.

Mommy screamed. Not words, a jagged something poured out of her.

The giggle dried up in Erin. She hid in the dark corner where the dog cage had been. The new basement was different, but she knew where it had been all those years. It felt so good to be in this place with Mommy again.

After the scream, Mommy didn't say a word. Not one word. That was not like her, either. Erin heard noises crawling around down inside her Mommy. Sobbing snuffles and gulps burped out. Mommy came forward, dragged, shoved, pushed, one shaking foot at a time. She was not moving on her own. It was as though people invisible were moving her like a big dolly. Erin wanted to go to her, to help her, but she couldn't, just couldn't. Oh, Mommy! Tears formed in the eyes of the little dead girl. Tears she'd not been able to shed since her death.

As the Mommy shadow wobbled toward Erin, thin moonlight from the window touched her. It didn't brighten but cut right through her and she staggered on. When she reached the place where the old light bulb had hung overhead for so many years, so many years ago, a hard streak of yellow light poured across Mommy's face. Mommy was hard and solid. Her skin hung in spotty folds. Her nose was a hook, thin skin over thin bone. Her beautiful green eyes were milk-cloudy marbles bulging from her pointy face. ...and her hair! Oh, her hair was stringy, gray. Mommy'd never been like this. Mommy was pretty. Mommy'd always loved her hair, her thick red hair, and would never let it go like that. And she was scared. Mommy was never scared. Her eyes were big. Mommy's eyes were steady and cool. When she got mad, her green eyes went dark and squinty. But Erin had never seen them wide like this.

Ohhhh! Mommy is dead, Erin knew.

Erin looked and, oh my, dissolving into being above Mommy, there was the bulb, there was the electric wire from which the bulb had hung, there was the old ceiling, the boards, beams and pipes. It all faded into being above Mommy and spread out above them both, spread to the corners. Then down the old walls flowed, down from where the ceiling ended, the old basement ran like spilled honey, oozing, covering. Erin remembered. Oh Mommy was mad when she had spilled honey at breakfast. Mommy had showed her! Face pressed to the pancake griddle showed her. She never spilled that Goddamned honey again, no sir.

The old basement reached the floor and crept across the new concrete, under Mommy's feet; the change washed over to where Erin cuddled with the corner's darkness. It rippled under her and when she looked again, there it was: Home. As it always had been and was always meant to be. Like loving arms, the cage spread up and around Erin, embraced her in its cool metal bars.

Erin peeked between the fingers she held over her eyes. Beyond the cage, there was Mommy and she was, oh, God, real as always and growing younger and younger. The red steeped through the grey hair that hung like weeds from Mommy's head. In a few moments, she was as Erin remembered. The thin body filled, became round and firm. Her face molded itself into the old shape Erin had always, always loved. The wrinkles around her eyes, above her lips, the loose skin tightened, fleshed the bones. She was growing pretty all over again.

Crunches came from Mommy, like tiny twigs breaking, like little bones snapping. Erin knew those sounds. And there were slurpy squishes as the old beauty blew her up like a beautiful Mommy balloon.

Mommy screamed all the while, then it was done. All done. All done and Mommy stopped screaming forever. The dead didn't scream.

Erin wondered. Had she been a bad little fucker again? She wasn't sure. Mommy was hurting and when Mommy hurt, it was Erin's fault, dirty little cunt.

Mommy stood under the old yellow bulb. Erin skittered toward the cage door, remembered what Mommy'd done the last time she'd come looking and her bad little bastard had tried to keep away. Erin waited by the door now, waited for Mommy.

"I was good, Mommy," Erin tried to say. Her mouth was broken though so she could only whisper. "I was good. I waited," she whispered.

Mommy tried to scream, but couldn't. Above the gurgles that she could get out came the sound of tearing cloth. Swish, swish, rip, rip, rip. Mommy's beautiful blouse, her skirt, everything she wore shredded and flew to pieces and she stood naked under the bulb.

Mommy's pretty little titties were all big now and sagging full. Her belly was swelling just like before Baby had come.

Oh, Mommy's going to bring home another Baby, Erin just knew it. She hoped, this time, she'd be allowed to hold Baby and kiss him and give Baby his bottle. Now that she was dead and now that Mommy knew what a good girl she could be.

The invisible people dragged one Mommy foot forward, then the other, then the first. They walked her like a rag doll, a beautiful, beautiful big rag doll, toward the cage in the corner.

Mommy pressed back, as if leaning against the people who weren't there, the ones who were dancing her out of the light and toward the cage. Her titties flopped; her hairy dirty-parts went open and shut, open and shut, open and shut as her legs quivered into the shadows.

Then, wham! Mommy slammed to her knees in front of Erin, the invisibles shoved her face down on top of the cage. Mommy's looked big-eyed down on Erin from overhead. Mommy made a strangled gulping, burping sound again as her bones and skin tried to flow around and through the bars. Her titties pressed against the cage door right at Erin's face. And they were so pretty. So warm and soft, so rich looking.

Erin wanted Mommy to stop hurting, wanted the invisibles to stop making Mommy hurt. She reached out and touched Mommy's breast. Mommy moaned and the breast strained against the wire bars. The brown titty tip grew firm, swelled; it reached toward Erin.

Mommy tried to scream.

"No!" Erin yelled in her dusty broken-jaw whisper. "Don't hurt Mommy!"

Erin leaned forward and pressed her lips against the straining titty and ohhh my, it felt so good to touch Mommy with her burning mouth. The nipple slipped so easy in between her shredded lips. Erin's jagged teeth massaged her Mommy's flesh and oh, her Mommy flowed, flowed so warm and sweet and thick into her, the Mommy milk surrounded her thick tongue, broken palate, shredded cheeks.

Erin closed her eyes. So good to suckle there again. She remembered. That's what she did, the little girl who was dead, she remembered. She remembered this very nipple from so many years ago. She remembered Mommy's hand supporting her heavy little head, cradling her body against her Mommy warmth and Mommy smell.

Erin's twisted little claws reached for the warm, fragrant breast. They closed softly around it. Oh, and it seemed so right for them to be there, the broken little fingers.

Erin wasn't aware, but now she leaned back. Mommy and her breast came with her. The little girl drew Mommy through the bars. The cold steel tore through the ghostly flesh, sending electric fires through every dead organ of Mommy's body. She tried to scream. Being dead, she couldn't.

Finally, the steel bars flowed through her and Mommy was in the cage with her little girl.

To Erin, the titty had a will. It knew how to feed and comfort her and her mouth bubbled with good milk, soothing, easing every part that ever hurt.

Soon, Mommy's arms embraced her once again. She felt herself grow smaller and smaller. That felt so good.

Erin's eyes closed. Through her lids the light bulb was red and sparkly black. Soon the light went away and all was dark. She felt mother heaving under her but that was fine. She felt her mother might be screaming, but no. Both were dead now and wasn't that nice? Both of them, mother, daughter, dead together.

The oozy things in Erin's belly, mouse chunks and thick bug jellies sucked from things in the dark, the nose snot she'd swallowed, the dirt, mud, the pieces of herself, the bone bits and teeth parts, the Baby's sock she'd taken one thread at a time, all that now flowed from her. When it started to come, it burned a little. But then the hurt stopped. It flowed and flowed and flowed from her from every part. For a moment, Erin worried that the stuff had gotten on Mommy. Then she stopped worrying. If it had, Mommy would have let her sure as shit know about it...

When it stopped, Erin was clean inside. Just Mommy's sweet, sweet milk still streamed into her from that pretty, pretty titty.

Mommy stiffened, then began to buck like a wild thing. Erin's eyes stayed shut and she soothed Mommy with her little hands and mouth.

"Mommy's dead. Mommy's dead," Erin said quietly to the invisibles making Mommy do these dumb and twitchy things. "She can't cry. Don't make her cry!"

Erin was still hungry. Erin got smaller. She felt herself snuggle so close and warm to Mommy, Mommy's flesh felt so nice and soft and warm. Erin pressed her mouth fully around the big, big nipple then she flowed inside. She flowed inside her Mommy where it all was dark and soft and warm and smelled so like food and goodness.

Erin laid her head on a softness in the dark. It was sooo easy. It didn't hurt to breathe anymore because she didn't have to breathe. Mommy breathed for her. Erin sighed so sweet and felt her mother try to scream again

"No, no, Mommy. It's okay. We're good. We're good."

Even then, Erin was hungry. A good hungry because food was there. She pressed her mouth to the fragrant Mommy flesh by her cheek and she kissed it, kissed it and licked it. With the kiss she felt her belly fill. It felt so much better. Later, she'd eat and eat and eat some more, eat until forever was over.

Mommy tried to scream.

"No, no, Mommy, we're together now. And this is heaven." Mommy tried to scream.

Erin had always loved her Mommy. That's why Erin was here for her now. Because she loved her Mommy.

Mommy tried to scream.

Erin slept. Soon she'd be awake and the rest of forever could begin.

A VERY BAD DAY

Later that afternoon, the world nearly came to a burnt toast kind of end. It did not, not just then. And that was a shame, because at that moment that was just the kind of thing Leslie would have appreciated. At that moment she had just been dumped by her third (and, for her, that was it, he was the final, absolutely last, no, this time he was really the last) boyfriend.

When she walked past *Chrysanthemum: Books—Used and Cheap*, she knew just how the stock felt. She barely paused. Then she saw the sign: Going Out of Business. *Chrysanthemum, going out of business, for goodness sakes,* she thought.

Books had accumulated in there for forty years. They had lain on tables jumbled together in a mathematically mystical way. Horror fiction lay cover-by-cover with cooking, European economics muddled alongside fairy tales and other self-improvement books.

In back, on the farthest table in an improbable corner, lay three books. Separated, they meant nothing. Taken together, these disparate volumes would have proved with fatal certainty that for the past quarter-century Earth had been in the thrall of the vanguard of an alien invasion force. The force was biding its time.

Really. The truth was in there as inescapable and incontrovertible as, as... well, as the fact of Leslie's having been dumped. Again.

Had she entered, had she browsed, had she gone back there, picked up each book—had she so much as glanced at the titles—had she lain the ideas those titles would have sounded, one against the other, inside her soul's brain, the tumblers would have clicked.

"Oh my goodness, my word, THAT is what it all means!" she would have said aloud.

She would have gone to her chum Daryl from *The Tribune*. He would have caught on like/that. He would have broken the story. The world would have known. The aliens' hand (well, not "hands," but you know what I mean) would have been forced and the world would have come to a char-dog, burnt toast kind of end.

Leslie, in her I-don't-give-a-rat's-ass mode, never went into Chrysanthemum. In minutes, a customer had picked up one of the three books, carried it for a half-hour then laid it on a table near the front. A second customer bought one of the others, took it home, where it would have ended inexplicably at the bottom of the hamper, below the stuff that never got washed. The third book? Who cares? It was pointless without the first two.

And, of course, Leslie's chum Daryl of *The Trib* was the prick who'd ditched her. The world was saved.

On the other hand, Leslie wasn't doing at all well. She went home and screamed for a while. Then she went to the bathroom and took off all her clothes. She stared at herself in the mirror on the back of the door as Wellington purred and rubbed 'round her ankles.

The view: Leslie: Red hair. Okay, not bad. A lot of people liked red hair. She'd cut it herself. Not a half bad job. A little

200

spiky on one side. The back? Well, who knew what was back there?

She sniffed her armpit. Not bad. She stared at it for a moment. Well, a lot of people didn't mind a little fur. She thought it was nice. Some found it sexy. Not everyone, apparently.

She lifted each breast by its nipple. Not difficult. They were breasts in concept only; she could have gone topless even at Oak Street Beach and not gotten busted, so to speak. No one would have noticed. Well, a lot of people like small. "Or say they do," the mirror said to her.

Below, down there, she was bushy. That looked sort of pretty. Red, airy. She fluffed herself, peered close in the mirror. "Pouty. Now, that's cute," the mirror said to her down there. She slid her hand between and gave her labial folds a little flub. Nice. The rest? She sniffed her flubbing finger. A heady cross-scent: sweaty butt-crack, Fulton's Fish Market. Well, some people did like that sort of thing. "Think it sexy." At the moment, she wanted to believe.

So did Welly, she thought from his urgent rubbing 'round her ankles. That felt nice.

The phone rang.

Leslie and the mirror had momentary jerks of the soul, an urge of the feet to get it. *Might be Dar...* Leslie thought.

"Fuck him," the mirror said. *Fuck. HIM. No. Don't* fuck *him,* they both thought. *Fuck 'm!*

She ignored the second ring and made an overall assessment of the woman in the mirror. Lithe. Muscular by miracle (she ate like a pig and never exercised). Youth and nervous energy accounted for that. She'd have to watch it in years to come. She gave a bitter, ironic little snort at the notion.

Okay, so that mirror-woman? A little bony. She has... knees, elbows. Breasts? She lifted them again, gently this time, supported them underneath. Which gave the whole effect dignity. With a little help, a pregnancy or two.

Oh, cut it out!

Wellington continued to nudge, more insistent. He nudged her toward the living room, the door.

The phone chirped again. *The hell with it*, she thought. *If it's Daryl, the hell with it. If it isn't... the hell with it.*

There was nothing wrong with her. Nothing, absolutely. She was, in fact, adorable. No Angelina-y, Scarlette-y sort of beauty, more along the Amy Adams-Ellen Page-Emma Watson axis. Smart, tough, a pal, a partner in a pinch and cute as hell.

Yuck, Cute! Yesterday, she would have groin-popped anyone using the C-word. Today: Cute was okay. She'd take cute.

The phone peeped a fourth time...

Okay, the phone was not Daryl. It was not even NOT Daryl. It was, in fact, radio station WLLB. Radio station WLLB, Classical 97.3, had absolutely nothing to do with Daryl. Had Ms. Leslie Groves of 831 Roscoe Avenue answered within the first four rings and if she had been listening to WLLB (She was.) and if she had been able to tell Freeman Yasgar and the 97.3 WLLB Classical Musical Firmament who had been the wife of composer Richard Wagner (She could. Leslie so admired Cosima Wagner and loved the romantic tale of the *Siegfried Idyll*, composed secretly by Richard as a Christmas present to Cosima and their newborn son... *Oh God, what a beautiful story.*) she would have won an all expense paid trip for two to anyplace in the world. The grim irony of *Trip for Two* would not have been lost on her but a change of place would have been just what she needed. In addition, the correct answer would have put her name into a pot to be eligible for a two-million-tax-free-dollar prize drawing.

And more about that phone call. In selecting the 2-mil-winner, Freeman Yasgar would have groped among the entries in the bowl and grabbed the card bearing the name of Mr. Willie

Luddens, 18 years of age, and the sole support of his slightly dotty mum and her thirty-two unaltered male cats. Before drawing Luddens's name from the pot, however, Yasgar would have had A) an overwhelming sense of his own power and of how that hand of his would alter, forever, some poor life out there and B) an itch in his right ear. Since this was radio (and not television, where Freeman *really* belonged, *damn it*), Freeman would have dropped Willie's entry, scratched his ear, then snagged the card of Ms. Leslie Groves of 831 Roscoe Avenue. The two million changes in Leslie's life would have caused Daryl to reconsider dumping her and would have given Leslie the wherewithal to flee Daryl and the horde of former and would-be suitors who would suddenly have found her allusive beauty utterly irresistible. She would have resettled anonymously in Dublin. In Dublin she would have met, been courted by, and given her heart to Middle Eastern oil septillionaire Musa Ben-Mustafa. At Leslie's gentle urging, Musa would have placed subtle but inexorable pressure on several warring factions within his home region to sue for peace with their neighbors and with everyone else. Dominoes would have fallen. A cessation of hostilities among the globe's organized religions would have cascaded from what would have become known as "The Dublin Accords." This, naturally, would have pissed off all the right people and dear, dear Musa would have been assassinated, thus precipitating Universal Armageddon. If only Leslie hadn't answered that damned phone!

Which of course she never did.

She debated, again, whether to shave her armpits or not. She decided not. The phone stopped peeping.

Thank God. No wonder Welly's so excited, she thought.

At about that same time, she also thought she might try being a lesbian. What did she have to lose?

(Do you want to know? I won't tell. Too depressing.)

There were three women of her acquaintance whom she knew to have had... experience. The first was Allison, tall, soft, lovely, sweet, feminine. You'd never know looking at her, but Leslie had it on several good authorities.

When Allison answered her phone, Leslie said, "Ho. Hi. He." Brain lock. Finally, "It's Les." She used the hated short form of her name. Today, she thought it might be a useful hint.

"And ho, hi, he there, back." Allison sounded pleased to hear from her. "What's happenin'?"

"Oh, Allison, Allison, Allison," Leslie sobbed. The sobs were only half-forced. "Daryl broke it off. Today. At lunch. Imagine? The Prick. Lunch. Not even dinner. I don't know." She waited. "I don't know. I just don't know what to do." She swallowed. She listened to the quality of silence on the other end. "Do you want to come over tonight and, well, sit with me...?"

No imagination. Graceless in the extreme. Just what Daryl had said about her: "You're graceless," he had said. Worse, he said, she thought she knew everything.

"I know, I know..." Leslie had said, half in jest, half without realizing the irony. Now the silence from Allison's end of the line was terrifying.

"Allison?" she asked.

"You want to go to bed with me," Allison said. A chilly, questionless way of saying. "Don't you?"

"No," Leslie said.

"No, I can tell. The idea. Where did you get the idea? I'm not. I have no idea where you could have gotten the idea I was. That I was that way."

Leslie had nothing.

"Well, okay. Goodbye," Allison said. "Okay?" she asked. Then she hung up.

"Damn. Damn, damn, damn. Damn," Leslie said to the damn dial tone. She was blushing. She felt it. She was also still naked.

And sweat-stinky. *I'm being needy*, she said to herself and made her second call wrapped in a bathrobe.

"Hi, Deirdre," she said when the line connected. "It's Leslie." She was getting better.

"Hi, Les," Deirdre purred. "I was juuust thinking of you. Feature that? Then the phone rings and who is it? It's you! Hiii..." She sounded at ease, comforted by her life. That was good. According to rumor, Deirdre would do it with anything mammal. Pretty and lithe and...

Good grief, Leslie realized, *Deirdre is, well, me*... Small, flat-chested, red-haired... Did she want to get involved with, with...?

"Uh," Leslie said.

"Les?"

"Oh," Leslie said, trying again. "What the hell? I wanted you to know, Daryl and I broke up. Just. I was, well, you know, feeling a little lonely. It's been a long time since, well, you know, since we were intimate, Daryl and I, and I was wondering. Thought you might like to get together. Tonight."

"Ohhhh, Leslie," Deirdre purred. "Have you accepted Christ as your personal savior, hon?"

Leslie stepped out of the shower. Her skin was smooth, hot, and red. Everything felt soft, smelled lovely. Her hair was plastered across her forehead. Squinting at the mirror, she thought she looked like a 12-year-old Irish immigrant lad. Cute. *Like a gerbil saved from drowning*, she thought. *Or a Calvin Klein ad*, the mirror said. A little heat under the voice. *All right, all right. Third time's the charm.*

She curled on the bed and dialed the third number. On the other end, the phone rang and rang. Then a click.

"Um, yeah?"

"Butch? Les."

"Hey, babe." Butch's voice was thick, groggy. In the afternoon. Just the way Leslie imagined lesbians at midday.

"Uh."

"Yeah?"

"Ee. You want to fuck?"

"What?"

"Fuck."

"You?"

"Huh?"

"Fuck you?"

"Fuck me? Oh. Yes. Now. Or maybe later tonight. Maybe?"

"Fuck you?"

There was laughter in the background.

"Yes..."

"Fuck no, babe. I like you, but not that way. I'd rather big tits. No offense. Sorry." There was more background laughter then Butch hung up.

Butch was one authority by which Leslie knew that Allison was, well, you know. Deirdre had been the other. In three calls, Leslie had exhausted her life's supply of lesbians.

Dykes, Leslie thought. She heard they liked being called dykes, or was it LGBTs now? Okay, maybe she could get her hair done.

Wellington stood on hind legs. He nudged Leslie's calf with his wet cheek and teeth then hopped onto the bed next to her. At a half-inch from her eye his burp was a fishy miasma that drifted up Leslie's nose. She smiled and waved away cat breath.

"Well. That's what I get for fixing you," she said. "Yes?" She snugged his ears.

Welly agreed. From the moment he had arrived on Earth, Welly had loved licking his scrotum. Licking his scrotum was one of the first joys he had ever experienced in an already long, hard, soldier's life. He hit dirt, discovered his scrotum, made his way to

Leslie's apartment, was taken in (as he knew he would be), and like/that, his balls were gone. He hadn't thought of that.

"Welly, Welly, Welly... Do you know how much I really, really, really love you?" Leslie purred and rolled him over to scritch his belly.

Welly knew.

You know, of course, that had any of the women on Leslie's short list accepted her offer, well, things would have ended differently. If, for example, Allison had agreed to meet Leslie at, "Oh, eightish, you know...? At how about *Tortue Perfide*? That new place on Clark? It's only great! No reservations! Just have to wait..." Allison, having received a last-minute call from an old boyfriend who'd just hit town and thought he'd give her old number a poke and, God-damned if she wasn't still there, would have been an hour and fourteen minutes late, which would have totally funked Leslie, who would have grumbled through the evening, wit-driven snides (at which she excelled) lobbed at Allison and the evening, which would have ended with Leslie in a dudgeon of tears and Allison in a flustered tizzy and off home, early, in a cab, alone. A week later, still fuming about men and women, Leslie would have seen an ad asking, "HEY, WANNA SAVE THE WORLD?" The ad sought volunteers to save rain forests.

Thinking, *What the hell, trees are better'n people*, Leslie would have signed on. Owing to her undoubted charm, her persistence and don't-give-a-rat's-rump verve, the effort, ultimately, would have saved the Amazon Basin. The resulting alteration in the world's climate would, finally, have tipped the scales, unexpectedly, to the warming trend that everyone but the oil companies and the Republican Party swore was coming. Yes: the polar caps would have melted, and, yes, the world's coastal areas would have drowned and yada-yada-yada. Repressions, interventions, hostilities, brutalities, tactical, strategic, and just-for-the hell-of-it bombings would have resulted and, at the end, global Armageddon, followed by cheerless nuclear winter. A few species of deeply sedentary sea slugs, some flightless insects, a handful of creeping things, and several cats (none of them cute) would have survived.

And that was only if Allison had said yes. Now if Deirdre had...

Well, there it is.

By 11:00 Leslie was having a long evening with old movies, chilled vodka, and Welly the cat. Fine. Welly had been brushed and lavished. He was still acting as though he had something much better to do, but that pretty much was Welly.

When the doorbell rang, Leslie was half afraid it would be Daryl suing for peace and trying for a break-up, make-up piece. Leslie staggered to the door, resistance prepared. When she flung it open, her robe came undone.

And there was Allison.

Welly gave Leslie's bare legs one last nudge and fled into the hallway and out the still-closing front door. *That is that*, Welly thought.

Leslie pushed halfway past a befuddled Allison to call Welly just as the cat's tail eked through the latching door. Leslie snuffled. Wide open naked, she finally realized Allison was staring at her. At her nakedness. At her.

"The cat's got out," she said.

"Oh," Allison said, and, "umm." Her hand waved like a swooning virgin's. The other hand extended a bottle of wine just under Leslie's right breast.

Leslie stared dumbly at it and her breast. "They're small," she said.

"Hiiiiii," Allison said, making the one syllable song sound like an apology. "I. Felt. So. Bad! At what I... Oh... you know!"

Leslie knew. And did not. Didn't matter.

No sense in speaking of what would have happened had Wellington NOT fled into the night, is there?

Later, gas log at full burble despite an unseasonable 82-degrees-Fahrenheit night, lights out all over the apartment despite both women's frequent needs to stumble to the loo, Leslie and Allison sat with their feet toward the flames. The empty Merlot bottle lay between them. Though Allison had shed herself of most of her unnecessary clothes, sweat poured down her nose. Leslie remained in open-robed shamelessness. They talked. Leslie's chin rested on Allison's shoulder. On two of the occasions when Les had dropped off, Allie had surreptitiously kissed her, once on the nose, the second time, on the upper lip. Feeling the soft fuzz that grew there, Allison's heart became an utterly captured province of little Leslie. She knew that... Oh, what the hell. Nose to nose, both awake, they kissed. Allison's hand, flickering nervously in the air (it did that when confused or aroused), brushed Leslie's left breast.

The Earth seemed to move.

In fact, it had.

As the day's luck would have it, the local-area Deity had chosen *that* moment to turn Her attention (yes, the feminists were right, God *was* a woman) on the Sol/Earth portion of Her domain. She had also chosen just that moment to turn Her attention to Leslie's portion of things. She noted with shocked finality what was going on, what had gone on and, worse, what was about to go on. So to speak. Worse yet, the Deity reached out and felt Leslie's thrill at the experience building in her, her joy, her, for lack of a better word, sense of "completeness" at the events building in that night (at least that was how Leslie would have described it later to her chums).

Now, the Deity truly loved all Her creatures. Leslie was no exception. Truth was in fact, the Deity had a bit of a crush on

Leslie. Go figure. She had a weakness for small-breasted redheads. Who doesn't? Deities are no exception. Read the Greeks.

Leslie and Allison? Well, that did it. More than She could take. At this moment certain Fundamentalist sects were also right. Today, at that moment, God did hate fags. Her anti-lesbian animus was trammeled up in some messy unresolved issues of self-loathing transference. All very sad, very nasty, and, to be honest, none of our business.

Full of wrath, the Deity took a moment. She slipped back in time to the Old Stone Age, scooted Herself way, way out beyond the Oort Cloud, found just *the* bit of wandering space junk that She needed, eyed Her shot, in spatial and temporal terms, and gave it a nudge. A flick of The Fingernail was all it needed.

"There," She said, more or less to Herself. "That'll teach you."

She then went off to pursue other interests and vanished from Earth's history, thus giving rise to the "God is Dead," flap of the 1960s. (She will, however, reappear briefly at the end of this story as just another visitor at a celestial equivalent of Club Med. You'll see.)

Back in Leslie's time, just as the tingle of Allison's first real kiss, first real touch, reached her vodka-numbed lips and Merlot-moistened eyes, the Deity's carom-shot from the Old Stone Age, which had wandered alone and cold throughout all of mankind's long march, crashed into Earth's upper atmosphere.

Allison gazed at Leslie.

Leslie stared at the end of her own nose.

Fortunately, the meteor was only the size of an olive pit.

"Oh, my," Allison said. Her lips reached for Leslie again. Leslie reached and gave herself, fully, to the touch, the kiss, the moment. She hoped she wouldn't hate herself in the morning. Somehow she already knew she would.

Unfortunately, despite its size, the damned thing was also a pure anti-matter black hole. It did not ablate to nothing as meteors mostly do. The teeny thing instantly turned everything it encountered to pure energy, released untold quanta of nastiness: heat, violently consuming plasma bursts... This is the stuff that powers the Starship *Enterprise*'s warp drives (by an unaccountable fluke, Gene Roddenberry had gotten it right). Now, the warp drive would never come to pass in human reality (even though the little girl who was going to do the original maths that would, ultimately, have led, irresistibly, to warp technology was at just that moment being born in a Mumbai slum).

Allison looked at Leslie as if for the first time. "Oh," she said again.

"Yep," Leslie said back. "The Earth moved..."

As said, it had in fact. The object punched through the air, bored a hole in the ocean off the coast of New Zealand, ate its way to the Earth's heart, then, finally, sucked the world right out of space and time forever and ever.

The sole survivors were Mrs. Carmine Luddens and her son, 18-year-old Willie.

Mrs. Luddens's 32 un-neutered male cats, the vanguard of the invading army from a distant galaxy mentioned earlier, feeling kindly disposed toward the old lady for having not removed their scrota, transported both Luddenses off-planet in time to avoid the insucking messy end of everything. A race doesn't get to have interstellar, cross-galactic invasion vanguard forces without the technology to detect nearby onrushing anti-matter black holes, for goodness sake. The troop recall had sounded *hours* before the final kiss that ended it all.

Out of respect for the Local Deity, the cats had not deflected the Instrument of Her Wrath. Instead they gave up their plans for world conquest as a bad idea. There were other options. As I hope you've now begun to realize.

Wellington (and of course that was not his real name—his REAL name was a batch of interconnected concepts, precepts, and moral/causal directions and inferences that by utter happenstance closely approximated the word "Dave") was back in his bunk with his buddies onboard the invasion craft and in his righteous skin once more, which would not have been cuddly-cute to anyone. Welly/Dave still missed the scrotum he had experienced for only a few earthly hours. It was one of the most uniquely useful biologic appurtenances he'd encountered in all his years a professional soldier. *Damn!*

The Luddenses? Their former cats planted the old lady and her son on a beautiful world in another creation entirely and left them alone. Willie Luddens kept his scrotum but never worked out what it was for. Mrs. Luddens missed the cats. The Luddenses' part of the story ends here.

(In case you wondered, the cats never told the Luddens family that they had very nearly been the big WLLP winners. Best they not know too much.)

Welly/Dave took a much-needed leave in another quadrant.

Steeping himself by an unheated slimepool, he met a spectacular (but strangely sad and somehow unfulfilled) minor Demi-Deity. She, too, was taking a rest to recover from a recent, well, bad experience. She and Welly/Dave hit it off far better than might be expected of a Demi-Urge and a common grunt. Even without a scrotum (such things had never been part of the old dating game in that quadrant) the grunt and the Deity had a great time. Of course, you know who She was, yes?

And you know what? Welly/Dave never realized how Leslie had connected the two of them. Even if the Demi- had mentioned the specifics, the coincidence of their link was on such a vast, such a, well, *cosmic* scale, neither would have believed it. And that very incredulity would have led to misunderstandings. Misunderstandings certainly would have…

No, the Demi-Doll said nothing about Earth, saying only that her last Creation was a pretty silly thing and just as well it had been disassembled. The rest was silence. But a great leave! Of course some things are inevitable, and following that...

Well, don't ask. It's best you don't know too much.

RAT TIME IN THE HALL OF PAIN

Outside, Kagen's Fine Jewelry was an island of gentle light in the soft California evening.

Inside, Alexander Winkler made a red mess of Kagen's manager's sharp wet face.

"Ah, ah, *former* manager," Alex thought aloud.

Kagen's was quality. Couldn't miss the fumed oak, spotless glass, the warm flow of indirect light across their surfaces. You felt the carpet's hush. "Real wool," Alex noted, probably aloud, deep wool that made you sink, sink so you wanted to come to rest and rest forever there.

"That's *Mis*ter Hillegas," the former manager said, frowning down his nose at Alex, who dropped him with a sharp shot from a three-foot handful of two-inch pipe.

Arrogant authority. Alex hated it. Rudeness of any stamp, anathema. Mother taught that. Her nature. She, a gentle woman, alone. If father hadn't gone off with the "other one"—the "her" of tearful evenings—when Alex was (*what was I?*) seven (*no, six*), things would have been so, so different for him and so many other *Mis*ter Hillegases. He knew that. Poor mother. What had she been thinking? Well, *mis*ters like Hillegas *seem.* They always seem.

Behind the counter, Alex straddled the still-twitching remnant of "*Mis*ter Hillegas." Thoughtfully, almost gently, Alex shattered another square inch of flesh and muscle with. The.

214

Pipe! Wai. Ting. For. Rat. Time. To. Come. 'Round. At. Last. For a moment the former manager's left eye dangled by the optic nerve from its splintered socket. The next blow crushed that pale wet thread and the eyeball flowed, winter honey, down *Mi*ster Hillegas's neck and settled, staring up at Alex from Kagen's good wool carpet.

Won't need that, Alex figured.

While Alex worked, Fat Marty held his cut-down boomgun on the clerks, a man and the woman. Marty's barrel quivered. The woman was a beauty. Alex wanted to look too. He venerated beauty but appreciated it at leisure and this… This was business. The woman was older than he, probably older than Hillegas, but by God, she was art! Probably deserved Hillegas's job. Oh yes, Alex knew she did. She was class. Hillegas? Greed, need, and attitude.

The other clerk was a kid in a daddy-suit, all wooly wrinkles, hair K-Y wet. The kid didn't belong. Not in Kagen's Fine. He smelled of sweat, gel, and loosened bowels.

Alex never broke rhythm. No, no, Rat Time, bless it, was almost, almost there. Another minute. Less. *Come on, comeon, comeoncomeoncomeoncomeon!*

Alex figured the kid in the too-big too-wooly suit knew he wouldn't make tomorrow. *He'll take it quietly,* he thought, *use all his guts to not beg. He'll be a Man, a sweaty man, a blind scared, piss-down-his-wooly-leg man but a Capital-M Man absolutely, a quiet good-bye good guy, yes sir, amazing that pretty woman to the end.* Alex snorted. *Yes. A co-worker, who should have been his boss.* He kept his eye on the woman. What a beauty she was, but Beauty had thrown up twice. She was all-over fear. Dread rippled on her like static. If there was a current to her terror, Alex realized, it was no doubt concern: concern for *Mi*ster Hillegas, the Hillegas family, something. Imagine. Or about the prick she worked with.

"Damn," Alex thought aloud, looking, "you should have

been manager." *Not Hillegas,* he thought. "He doesn't deserve you!" he said, and brought the pipe hard across the jagged stew of *Mis*ter's face. *Rude prick.* Oh yeah! Here it was, coming now: A Hillegas dance in Rat Time. *Rude prick probably GOT the fucking job because he was fuckin' connected. Right? Fucking somebody's daughter, Right? Fucking somebody's son. Yes? Maybe fucking SOMEbody somebody's-fucking-self. YES.*

Each stroke thrilled Alex's arm and he kept it, stepped it up. *Hillegas, Hillegas has something on that fucking Kagen-somebody.* Alex had a fucking feeling, a Goddamn motherfucking feeling, about that fucking guy and all the fuckin' somebodies it took to put together all the lousy deals that made a place like Kagen's Fine Fuckin' Jewelry spin like a well-fucked top.

In it now, Rat Time slithered up his arm, wrapped his shoulder. His jaw torqued shut, Rat Time tingling his head. His vision danced in Rat Fucking Time. Cracked a molar, once, he had, clenched down in Rat Time.

Mister Hille-fucking-gas did abso-fucking-lutely not deserve the fucking manager gig and Alex was always fucking right, always-on-the-fucking-A-track about those feelings. Well, this fucking paid him fucking back! Using both hands, his full weight swept down. The pipe end drove into the open hole where the exquisite woman's boss's supercilious nose had *Mis*tered for the last time just a few minutes before.

And now, as it always did, it ended with Alex dragged from the birth canal, dripping, clean, covered in new air and sucking freshness. His head rolled back. *Relax,* he thought. He relaxed. Caught the woman's eye. Wanted her to know, *I'm with you.* He understood, knew what she'd put up with from that. *Hill*egas. All those years. He shook his head, tired, smiling. He hoped the woman (*oh she was Beauty*) would appreciate this, what he'd done for her, before they married. Before he killed her. Whatever.

And, *aw jeeze,* Rat Time was over. Too bad. The

unconscionable bastard, Hillegas, had taken the edge. She'd be dull now. Business. A .22 to the base of the skull. Kid wooly wrinkles? The same. His partner, Fat Marty? Later, later, tomorrow, day after, sometime when the sweaty porker was jerking off, thinking of the Woman. Fat Marty, sent to hell, sins squirting. He shouldn't breathe in the same world as she, Fat Marty shouldn't. *Soon he won't.* She wouldn't be in the world by then, either, of course.

Rat Time over, Alex considered the future. The rest was business. For show, all for show. Jewelry, metal, money. Tokens in the game, how the game was scored.

Alex pushed himself up with the pipe. The pipe stuck out of whatshisname's face. *"Time for the game."*

He may have said that aloud because for the third time, Beauty puked.

Alex kept his foot to the floor. Highway white lines shot under; the roadway paint hissed as it passed. Speed chattered, amped him up to a place between sleep and terror, kept him sometimes more, sometimes less awake through grainy night.

The moon split the clouds and lit the layered haze that had settled in the valley into which he plunged. The rearview was black. He almost jumped, seeing his own eye lit by dashboard green in the corner of the mirror. Behind him and ahead were mountains, dark forests, deep glens. In these pale moments of moonlight and fog the old rock and forest whispered. *They're nearly dead*, he thought. *The east is a ghost*, he thought of the coast toward which he ran. Where the hell was he now? New York, P-A? Western Mass? Damn, he loved the east. *Moody son-of-a-bitch, this dead country.* The store out west had clinched it. (*Where? California? Yes.*) He'd had it with the west.

After Fat Whatsit, his partner barely remembered now, Alex hopped a Greyhound out of Berdoo, one breathing body among fifty-two. They rode a taut desert highway toward the mountains. He was surrounded by Mexicans, Indians, old ladies and drunks, pimpled soldiers and pregnant women riding alone. The bodies comforted, at first, brought warmth and scent. He leaned back in air-conditioned blue-glass comfort, lounged through miles of sun-soaked empty, breathing in the folk. He eased asleep, surrounded, supported.

When he woke, night hummed. He thought he was awake. In a while he knew he was. Greasemouth Marty, *Fat Marty, that was his name, Marty Mouth*, was garbage, a couple, three hundred miles back. *The store?* The jewelry job, yes. The name of the place? Who were the dead? Forget it. It was dollars. Not many. Enough.

Marty. Marty wasn't even an emptiness beside him. Marty was a negligible asset that had become a palpable liability. Partner? Partners made Alex nervous. They pinned you down. Partners were greedy, too scared, or, stupidly, not scared enough. Partners were whims with hands and anxious feet. Partners were mouths that hit and ran and never stayed shut. No, this was a business and the economic mantra of the day was *Downsize*. Reduce the eyes, shut the mouths.

Heck yeah, he thought, *after work a partner was just a witness.*

There always were witnesses. Someone somewhere always knew something and you couldn't kill them all. Much as you'd like to, you couldn't murder everyone.

Awake now, yes, in his Greyhound run to the east, surrounded in the dark glass night, the bodies breathed, each with its bouquet. Alex tasted the lives around him. He listened. They whispered. *Damn. Goddamn.* Their chatter climbed his spine. A murmur now, in a bit it would be Rat nibbles. Third Grade again. Miss Kerkauff again. On the way to Wednesday movies again, again marching down the hall between Robby Ringler and Brenda Hebhardt. In lockstep and under eye. And Rat Time would twitch 'round. Marty had barely done it for him.

"Oh, ohh," Alex moaned and wondered again if he really was awake. Another moan. He was.

"Y'okay, Mis-ter?" The voice drawled from an angular thing next to him. The quick light of a highway marker slashed across the voice's face. Bone thin and pimple-flamed, a greasy crew cut and snaggled-teeth. Sixteen, maybe. Country doofus, just like Alex. Good ol' Al.

"Y'okay?"

"Abso-tutely," old Al drawled back. *Aw Lord Jesus, yes.* Rat Time drawing nigh. And here he for sure was, *in the desert, wrapped in Greyhound, padded with Greasers.* "Indubitably, ol' buddy." He nodded thanks to Miss Kerkauff, who'd made him study his vocabulary. Words. They gathered the world so easy-like. He looked out above his own grin. Saw the uniform. Made like he just noticed. "Oh, hey, pardon, Sarge," Alex said. He considered: *Do I Rat Tango with Pimples here?*

Options flickered.

"'Cause I got some aspirins here, you're feelin' poor." Kid said. "I know how's I hate travelin' with the headache or the tooth. So, you need somethin', you lemme know, y'hear?"

The boy was real. *Probably real.* In a few hours, he'd be someone? His mother? His mother'd be talking or moaning make-believe, like she did.

"I surely will," Alex said. Even now, the kid in wrinkled khakis was becoming less kid, more Mom. He'd watched her, Mom, through iron curlicues at the foot of the bed. Seemed to Alex he'd stood all his childhood down there, watched a dozen daddies every night, the perfumed men who'd lined up for stinky-time with Mom. He'd watched through the bucking bedstead as her ass swayed, her smiling mouth gulped wet with —those daddies, square johns, rig pushers. Soldiers, *like Pimples here*, they all squinted at him while she slurped. They wanted to put out his light. Each one.

Mom never daddied no Mex. "Sure as shit ain't gonna trick with them, can't bother to learn English," she'd say, making hard eyes with potential daddies passing along the stroll. "Come here and ain't got the courtesy to learn our fucking language, expect we'll talk theirs. I don't wanna ever hear you speaking nothing but American, y'hear?"

No ma'am.

"Indian, either."

If he could see in the dark of the bus—better, if he could cut the lids off the eyes of the sleeping wetbacks and Indians around him, if he could shine a light and look—their eyes'd be the same as the white- and nigger-eyes that had stared him dead through those painted iron curlicues. All the same, Injun or Mex, they'd drain his light too if they could.

Considering the kid next to him: *The next stop? Talk him off, do him hard and wet, get back on, ride away? Or do him quiet by the john? Travel a distance with the sleeping dead, one among fifty-one? Then get off, casual?*

He considered. Soon the rats would crawl. He'd attend them when. Until? He'd keep them in check. It was dangerous to be not in control, hungry in the dark, surrounded by so much meat. The time would come and beyond that...?

Beyond? He laughed. There was no beyond, beyond that. Beyond Rat Time? The time when he had to go a little mad, like that freak said in that movie. When Rat Time came, it came for sure and always was obeyed. Obeyed, it always ended with someone—someone small or large, but someone—always, forever after, was always very very very dead. Then after, and for a while, he was this, what he was now, this perfect gentle man: resting, hunkered down, square-one. No. There was no "beyond" beyond Rat Time forestalled. A violation of physics, a contradiction in terms, the irresistible force, the immoveable object. Two factors that cannot exist in the same universe: Rat

Time and No Rat Time.

For now, he thought, *let's see how far we take it.*

"No thank you, Sarge," Alex said to the thin darkness beside him. "I'm fine. Just a dream."

And like *that*, the boy was saved.

A buzzer shouted. Felt it in his spine. The fuel light on the car's dashboard blinked. Thank the Lord. He'd have to stop. Too early for dawn, but he was riding near empty, and he'd have to pause.

A sign grew. "Food. Fuel. Rest. 17 miles." White on green. Then gone. The road flattened along the valley of a river he didn't know and couldn't see for dark and trees. Soon, a hazy light arose ahead. A nudge of the wheel eased him onto the gentle up-curve of the off-ramp. Eighty-five bled to zero as he rolled the last hundred yards into the sodium vapor island at the oasis.

Gas clicked into the tank and its good scent filled his head. He looked over the trunk and into the glass and aluminum cashier's booth. Three people crammed in there. Two guys, one working, the other, a buddy, with the buddy, a girl. Alex balanced: a fill-up and a rest or a fill-up and a dance? Depended. Now, Alex felt polite, soft. Now. He had no idea what the world would be like when the tank was full.

Now and then he had to go, get out. City, town, the place, wherever the place was, the walls of concrete, steel and too-bright glass, the asphalt floors or the fields of brown and green, the wide domes of blue sky, chrome sun and pointy black night, wherever it was the place would get behind Alex's eyes and shove.

When these days came, he'd remember Miss Kerkauff and movie Wednesdays in the dark. He'd remember the ratchet chatter of the projector, the scratchy black and white flicker. He'd recall the narrator's voice. The wooden slats of the folding chairs pinched his scrawny ass, his feet dangled from his skinny pins and made his butt go numb. On one side, fatty Stevie Hinnershitz's wool pants rubbed Alex's legs. On the other, Hazel Gensler's grape-pop bubble gum breath filled his hunger. Whenever he grew hungry forevermore, he had only to breathe and there would be Hazel and grape and he would fill. In front, Frankie Rhodes's hard white skull and damp crew cut waited. Frankie waited for the dark of the movie to turn, a bristly silhouette with knuckles. When the dark came, Frankie monkey-punched Alex's leg, knuckles going deep into his meat and muscle.

"That hurt like fuck?" Frankie whispered.

Alex said nothing. Mouth shut.

"We'll, s'posed to," Frankie said. Four, five times each period. Wham. Wham. WhamWhamwham. Movie Wednesdays.

He'd watch the wrinkled screen with the brown Rorschach water stain across the middle. He'd wait for the pain and keep his fuckin' mouth shut when it came.

Sometimes the movie was "Be clean, brush your teeth," or "Say please, say thank you." Sometimes it was "Work hard. Be good. Thank everyone."

He saw the rat film once. Only once. The narrator's voice, manly, smart. "Our world today grows ever smaller."

Airplanes, speeding trains, liners on the sea...

"The space between people narrows."

Cities. Traffic. Crowds.

The film told with pictures: Picture a rat in a cage. The cage is big. Picture a rat couple in this cage. Picture a rat family, a happy few, this band of rats. Sleek rats. Happy rat faces, clean bodies, scurrying, grooming whiskers. Mother rats nursing little ratties, hairless rat pups at suck. Mommy rat, baby rat, brother rats and sisters, daddy rat off to gather food. Beautiful. Home.

The picture dissolved; the narrator spoke numbers. The cage was fuller: a bustle of rat, a flow, and a marvel of rat efficiency. Roiling, busy rat paths crisscrossing, a Ratopolis, Rat Gotham. Rats carrying forth important rat tasks.

Another lap-dissolve, the narrator's voice went darker. The cage, once spacious, friendly, home and haven, now was jam-crammed. Packed rat-jowl to rat-butt, bodies clamored, claws raked bellies. Rats burrowed into corners or sat shivering, torn, dirty, crawled on, over, snapped at, shat upon and fouled. Rat faces in close up: terror, exhaustion. Breathless. Snarling. Big rats tore at small ones. Small ones ganged on old ones. Rats stole. Rats hoarded. Rats starved, shivered, thinned, failed, falling within inches of the food they'd gathered and held. Rats killed for nothing, yet nothing was wanting in the abundance of the cage. Rats murdered in fury while others waited calmly their turn to be torn, left twitching. The place was madness, this place, this lab-made hell.

In memory, the images are of teeth, fur, bodies, blood. All Alex hears is projector chatter and the smart, warm, passionless voice. Alex doesn't have the words, but the voice speaks of matricide, parricide, ratricide. This closing of the space between the rats has brought out the worst in ratkind, brought out the inner rat, brought forth Rat Time. There is one final image: a small rat in a corner, death around, his twitching whiskers, bloodied, his fangs dark with blood. Blood from where? Who knew? There was blood on his fur and nothing in the tiny bright eyes but patient waiting. That picture…

…flickered, and Alex's leg ached from Frankie's monkey punches, and the sound, the memory, the memory always was such a comfort to Alex. And Hazel's grape breath.

He touched her mouth with the shotgun barrel. "Open," he

said warmly. The barrel tapped her tooth. "Open," he said again, gentler still.

Tears ran down her nose and flowed onto the metal. She opened and he seated the blued hole in her mouth. "It's not like the movies," he said. He was careful. He didn't want to hurt her teeth with the little red-tipped sighting bead. Her lips closed involuntarily on the steel and she gulped, trying to breathe, swallowing deep in her throat like a cheap trick.

"Aw, the heck with her, anyway," Alex thought and said it aloud. "It's just something I want to see." He was awfully close to begging. A project, for criminy-sake.

Dad had been proud of his facility with science and numbers. "You'll be an engineer, a rocket scientist. Something. Jeeze, Alexander, the space program'll heat up again. There's opportunity out there, son." His dad had pointed to the workshop ceiling. "And I don't mean the dining room." They laughed together. Heck, Alexander knew that. Dad pointed to the stars. "There are worlds out there, chances no one knew in my day. If a guy's got brains—and education, don't forget that!" He tapped Alexander's head with the screwdriver blade, then tapped his chest with his other hand. "And the guts to make something of himself, that's the ticket. You have the guts to take the chance?"

Before he could answer, there was Mom, on the stairs to the basement, smiling at her two boys. "Dinner's ready, you pioneers!"

Aprons and smiles was Mom. How he always remembered her, anyway. *So what for all those worlds?* he'd thought. *Who'd want to leave here?*

Then Dad swept his arm around Alexander's shoulder and the two of them climbed the steps to Mom's fragrant kitchen.

Alexander bent his knees so the gun pointed toward the back of the girl's upper palate. "This is physics," he thought and said it aloud. "Like school." He smiled. But the girl was so gosh darned short he had to crouch, get darn-near on his knees to get it angled just so, so the wave front of expanding gases, the shot and unburned powder grains would pass at exactly the right place through her head. He never could get a decent lab partner, how the heck was he expected to...? He dipped deeper, bent to sight along the barrel, extended an imaginary line through her shaking, nodding, bobbing, gulping head. Her whole body quivered as he knelt in front of her. Kneeling, he had to say it, it felt... weird. Felt like church, like genuflecting. Fuck. Goddamn it, goddamn fuck it. For a moment, there was Father O'Donnell. For a moment, he flashed on Sister Marie George, smelled the chalk dust of her, the old spit and bad dentures. Why had the folks made him go to parochial school? God Darn, he really wanted to be in public school with his friends from up and down the street. Darn. He leaned into the kick as he squeezed both triggers at once.

As always, a shotgun blast in a small place was too loud to hear. He felt the concussion over his whole body. The tiles went red, black, and white. But he saw—YES—her eye sockets. They went empty! Empty in that fraction of a second before her head shoved, yes, *forward* onto the barrel, then jerked back and it was over.

That was the moment for this one. The moment. The moment her eye sockets went red, black, and empty, her eyeballs yanked out by the optic nerves, the whole package sucked out by the speed of shot passing, by the vacuum left as the brain vacated the open skull at supersonic, *wow*, speed drawing both visual—*God!*—stems out of her so fan-A-OK-tastically fast, spreading them with the pink gray brain against the—*oh fuck-fuck-outstanding-fuck*—back wall of the ladies' room. Then, *doggone*, he lost her in the moment. Then the moment was over and he had to get going. Back on the road, Rat Time in recess.

That had been where? The high desert west—no, east—of Denver. He'd ditched the Greyhound, waited at the stop for two days before getting a lift and by then the rats were swarming, a pot boiling over. They calmed, crouching, as soon as he got a lift. Pretty little girl. He took the person and her Ford when she stopped for gas and a pee. *Great experiment! Thanks, partner.*

He traded that Ford for another in Nebraska. North Dakota. Somewhere. He traded plates outside Minneapolis. Same year, same model, same color. *Ha.* Where'd he learn that? Reform school? That long ago? The Toyota? Along I-90 in North Nowhere, Indiana, near the College Football Hall of Fame. *Christ.* He swapped the Toyota for a Volvo. Cleveland. Near the Rock and Roll Hall of Fame. He swapped rides and rocked someone who'd roll no more. *Ha!* Boomtown Rat Time again.

He traded down to another Ford, a family wagon, in Cooperstown, New York at Baseball's Hall of Fame. A family, Christ, bad luck for them. If he hadn't been born in jail while his mother was waiting to take the gas for razoring his father to nothing, he might have let *one* of them live. Better dead than orphans. Didn't he know that. A favor. Fuck 'em. He had no feeling, one way or other, for any capital-F-Family. Shit, he'd let the friggin' dog live. Anyway, that family was not the poster-posers for Family-With-A-Smile! Bastards couldn't stand one another. Kids, dad, mom, none of them. He could tell. No wonder they offered him, a stranger, a lift to a filling station. Not a second thought. Figured Alex, maybe, would be one friendly face for a couple miles. *Bad call, Dad!* And Alex. *Yo!* On one fine roll. Bing. Bing. Bing. Bing. The whole one, two, three, four nuclear-warring family, one after one, one wonderfully squishy time. Cleaning out the gene pool. Wop-da-bop! Just outside Cooperstown, Crack! The Crowd Goes New York Nuts! Maybe he'd catch a ballgame sometime, somewhere. *A bar, maybe. Wow!*

He ditched the family boat a couple miles along. This was the good old crammed-together east. One jurisdiction shoved against another, one town across the street from the last.

He stopped at Canastota, still in New York, because he saw the sign for the International Boxing Hall of Fame. Amusing, this spate of museums, halls of fame. He let an elderly lady pick him up. A Chrysler. He let her live. He hadn't liked her that much but she'd sussed-out his story from the start. One sharp old lady. A bad boy, was she right? Like her last husband, yes? Ivy League, if she didn't mistake the look of him. Yes?

She was good. So few people realized that Penn was even part of the League. Huh! She dropped him two blocks from her home. He waited, then strolled over, hotwired the Chrysler and slid. She was a snob but he appreciated class. Like he did. Yes.

He laughed at the sign for the Basketball Hall of Fame in Springfield, Mass. He traded tags there—he liked that Chrysler—and tossed a goodbye wave to that Hall.

Then he was pumping gas and, oh God, it was wonderful being him. Free and on the open road, touching every museum along this highway of Halls. Didn't cost much and he'd met so many nice people. Last couple hundred miles, he felt he didn't even need a gun. The baseball bat he'd gotten... *Where? Yes, in Cooperstown.* The souvenir ballbat from Cooperstown was wholly adequate.

The pump nozzle was cold in his hand. The three young people in the booth looked warm, focused, slack mouthed, and tube-glued. By gosh he was glad Mom resisted getting a set. He'd complained, of course he complained. A kid's job. All his friends laughed over last night's shows the next day. Something to talk about. TV stuck them all together. Left him out. But Mom. She got him to read instead, encouraged him to pick up a couple musical instruments, learn a language or two. Made him, God bless her, made him want to take part in life, real life, "be part of the world!" she'd always said. To this day—and he hadn't played in years—he'd bet he could pick out a tune or two on the piano. Trombone? Probably not. That was how long ago? He chuckled. Young people today? He looked at the two boys and the girl in the cashier's booth. They know reality shows, soaps, sit-coms. *Faux* life, toy music. Trillions of images flicking across the night. All TV did was pile up heaps of people in rooms across America, the world, people alone or in twos and threes, but gathered by the ton. Gazillions of eyes, mouths, and armpits gathered and delivered, sold...

The pump clicked off. Tank full. *Time?* Could he go farther without Rat Time biting his butt? Should he bring it on? Now? Right here? Those wasted empty faces? God, give him the strength of character to know...

He hung up the hose, screwed on the cap. Over the trunk of the car, he saw the three faces in the booth, dead-eyed, licked by flicking TV color. They laughed.

"Huh," said Alex. His eyelids flickered.

Five miles down the road, he saw the first sign for the Hall of Pain.

Rain. Rhode Island, he was certain, but the states flowed together so. Every town, a black cocoon of brick and wood spun around a shut-down mill. *Jesus.* Dead buildings by nameless rivers. *Everybody sat down to die when the factory closed. Fuck yeah,* he knew what that was all about. He remembered Uncle Ben. Ben, who'd cared for him after Dad and Mum were killed on vacation. Little Al, what, maybe five? Life would have been...

Fuck it.

It was still raining when he stopped. The name of the town wouldn't stay in his head. Something-Tucket. Tucket was dark wet streets and left-over light. Tucket's streets were narrow canyons of brick warehouses, meandering coaster rides between houses that sagged this or that way, slate or brick sidewalks. Tucket was roads, cobbled or shattered, frost-heaved concrete, veins of tar sticking it all together. That was Tucket.

For the last hour he'd followed signs for The Hall of Pain. He cruised curved streets that slimmed to alleys, alleys that shriveled to paths and paths that died at brick walls or fenced lots. At every ending or turning, a sign: "See The Hall of Pain" or "Don't Miss The Hall of Pain," then an arrow and a decreasing number of miles then fractions of miles.

"This must be *the* place," he said aloud. The rain stepped up as he crawled from one island of yellow light to the next along the sad dark dead-ends.

This one ended at a river. Ahead was a black iron pedestrian bridge. By the bridge, a sign and an arrow: "*H LL F P N.*" Below: "Y r The e! His headlights kicked back from the white wall of rain and mist. He switched off. Across the bridge a black silhouette stood against the sky. His vision was grainy. Static sparks snapped in his blood; his body sang with exhaustion. Coffee nerves or Rat Time? He'd run too long. 3,000 miles at speed on I-buzzing-90, I-friggin'-80. Whatever fucking "I" he'd had to run, he'd run it.

"Stay or hit the road?" he wondered.

The museum was a square block of company houses, the lousy dumps factories rented to their workers month-by-month for damn-near each month's pay. The crummy dumps he and Uncle Ben lived in when he was… Through the rain-run window, the museum flickered. *Uncle? No Uncle.* Ben or otherwise! What the hell was that? *Nerves, yeah.*

He stretched, twisted. His spine popped all the way down.

"Hall of Pain," he said to the empty Chrysler. "Perfect. This is America."

A dim light glowed to life in an upper window of the building. With it, his blood rushed, flushed his vision clear. The chatter in his arms and belly steadied. "Ah," he said to the light, "a fellow human. Well." He remembered to lock the car as he walked away. Rain misted him like the body-hot sweat of bad work. No matter how tightly he clutched his jacket, the rain soaked his neck. The iron bridge was painted with shadows. Drooping weeds, junk trees, sumacs, ginkgos, grew, dripping, from the riverbanks, below. To his right, a smooth coil of water rolled over a spillway. The cataract pounded the stone bridge supports and transmitted the rumble to his feet. A suck of cold air washed him as the flood thrumbed downstream, down the dark.

"Great day for a field trip, Miss Kerkauff!" he shouted, his voice lost in the roar of waters.

The museum entrance was a stoop and a wooden door, one of a dozen, either way along the building. Above the door, a single bulb glowed yellow against mossy brick. The lamp was clear glass, like the streetlights he'd potted with his BB gun when he was a kid. He smiled. Then the thought, "What the fuck?" *BB gun? Jesus, no.* "Put your eye out, Allie," Aunt Florence said. Then another gut-punch: *Who in Christ was Aunt Florence?*

He tried the knob and *What the fuck?* It opened. He never expected it to, but it did and that pissed him off. Why the hell? Even this shit-house should be locked, at—he squinted at his watch—4:28 in morning. He was ready to kick, to smash a face... And, Jesus, there was nothing and nobody and Jesus Fucking Christ it was not going to be a good day for *some*body. Maybe a few somebodies would have a day of bad hurt and long forevers. Wait till he found the Manager.

Above the rain and rushing river, he heard a cry from inside, a sob. He listened, tuned.

Another.

"It *is* the Hall of Pain." His voice came back from the darkness. "Scare me, will you?" He stepped inside. And it felt so good to not be rained on. When he shut the door, the roar of falling waters was lost. A lamp came on overhead, then farther along. They made a trail of light. They didn't brighten the place, but he could see the path. Ahead, to the sides, a half-dozen paths maybe, maybe more, he didn't count. Hard to tell, but the ceiling didn't look right, too high, too high. But the floor—he bounced on the balls of his feet—good carpet. He liked that. Deep, solid underneath.

Above one corridor was a sign: "Those Who Suffer," it said, "Have Hope!"

Alex smiled. Above the smile came the sound, again the cry, a whimper from beyond the words. By God, he knew something of suffering, he did. He followed, alive now, tingling. The wonder of Rat Time: it posed no questions, it led and was reason alone, logic itself. *Bless those who cry.* Alex moved quickly from pool of light to pool of light. The whimperer ahead was one who knew the score, had no illusions left of life or of when death would come. The cry was the sob before the trigger. "Thank you," it said. "Please do it right, do it quick."

Alex was come to serve.

Passages intersected. He didn't care, didn't count. He followed his stomach. Rooms slipped by. Exhibits. Lives in mannequins, worlds in props and furniture. He glimpsed an amputation, a shattered limb hacked in flickering electric candle. The patient howled in silence, straining, frozen, from the blood-wet table, the saw poised for another bite of flesh, nerve, and marrow.

He'd seen better in life. Still, he almost tasted the loose-bowel stink in the air. An effect? Bad plumbing?

In other rooms, tortures, ancient and modern, the usual tools: flame, pincers, tongs, flesh-flecked rope and gore-beaded spikes, batteries and clamps. Accidents, industrial and domestic. Rooms of flickering solutions, many solutions, all failed, attempts that yearned for the perfection of finality. Photo montages tacked on cracked walls: holdups, murders caught on camera, dismemberments. Parents and children, husbands and wives, lovers and the damned of love. Or scenes of famed mayhem acted in silent film: local talent, Lizzie Borden, that swinging doll, her own Rat Time Two-Step blessing her. Crippen, Gein, Manson, Jones, and Dahmer, the wonders of Kosovo, Saddam and Sons...

And all lousy. None of it satisfied.

He wanted that voice, the still-wet meat-throat that led, the yellow-brick whimper down the halls of Pain. *Where are you? Where are you?* Through a window, dark: a man in gloom, a dummy man, slope-shouldered, by a bed. On soaked sheets, the newly dead— another dummy—legs spread, gown rolled, her whatchacallit place between her legs; she was a red crater, belly to knees. The guy? He held something. Something nice and red. Newborn, the thing, a baby. *Ah!* Alex had thought he'd done her with a knife, an ax, his hands, his teeth. But, no, no she had died of birth. Like his mother. Nice. The doctor, head hanging, hands blooded, held the life that had killed its mother. Frustration? Exhaustion? Disgust? Annoyance? Did he want to smash the little wet doll he'd saved?

"Fuck up, Doc?" Alex wished the doc were alive so he could kill him now, kill him to pieces.

The sob was near. A splash of light washed from an open door across the hallway. The sob was there. In there. Rats stirred deep, behind Alex's eyes, in his balls, at his jaws.

"Ahhh..." Alex walked into the light.

The room was a bright cube of no one. The sobs drained away.

"Ahhh..." His throat rumbled. He put a clamp on Rats about

to tumble. *It had* been *here.*

In the corner was a toilet. He used it. There was a sink. He splashed his face. There was a comfortable-looking chair, a refrigerator. The fridge was filled. He had a bite and it was good. There was a television. The bed invited. Every wall had windows, each window had curtains. He opened them one at a time. Nothing. Dark glass. One-way glass, he'd bet.

This was an exhibit. An exhibit in-process, in the making. *Me.* He sat on the bed and it felt good. It was still. So comfortable to sit on a thing didn't do 85-90 miles-per-hour. The ceiling was a transparent blue like summer. If he imagined, there were clouds. If he wanted, there was a breeze from across the, yes, meadow. *Damn.* This was a big room and his, no one else's. His room.

His door closed.

For the first hour, he smashed himself against the glass, the door. He shouted until he couldn't. Nothing gave, no one came, and he was bloody with effort. He dumped furniture, smashed it, looked for weapons. He could make knives, bludgeons, garrotes. Wonderful tools, but nothing to use them on.

He sat to think.

He thought nothing. He ate. He collapsed on the bed and pretended to nap. He'd catch whomever, prickbastard, cocksucker soon-to-be-dead-as-a-doornail motherfucking son-of-a-someone, sneaking.

No one came. Soon he slept for real.

When he woke the light had dimmed. Without glare, the room was almost pleasant. Personal rats swarmed his spine and loins, of course. They burrowed, rammed the inside of his skull. There he was. In memory the projector chattered behind him. Hinnershitz's wool pants prickled his leg. He ate deeply of Hazel Gensler's grape breath. Alone in his room, food, water, plenty of everything and he was going...

Going a little ratty. Jesus. Jesus. Jesus. Rat Time tunes and not a partner in the hall.

He whimpered and monkey punched a knot in the muscle above his right knee. *Good!* He clenched and hit himself again. He screamed. Again. Harder. Harder. He screamed. Sobbed. The sob. He recognized the sob. He'd known it before he knew it now. He was the expert on sobs, the tear without illusion, the cry that knew the score, the gasp before the trigger. Yes. He. *Alex, Alex, Alex. Winkler. Winkler. Winkler.* He reminded himself as he struck. All but his name slipped away. He buried knuckle in flesh, through nerve, struck bone. He called, "God! I'm a friggin' professional!" He bit his cheek to shut himself the fuck up. He shut, finally, the fuck up when he tasted meaty cheek, oozing salty, a morsel on his tongue. Then it wasn't bad. Wasn't too bad if he sat unmoving, so still no one knew he was nibbling inside. Just a knotting of the jaw, a quiver in the eye. But small. So small. Rat Time condensed.

Outwit the place. Ha! As long as there were no people, safe ones he could not get to, the other side of the glass, the door, as long as there were no people anywhere in this world, Rat Time would leave him the fuck alone.

He sat quiet, belly full, in good soft light. The window reflected him back at him. He saw Alex in the dark glass, Alex in the room. Alex, quiet. Maybe, in the distance, a tiny chatter, a shutter clacking (maybe). Open-shut. Open-shut. Ultra. Slow. Motion. Was it? There. Yes it was. A shutter. Each click, a picture. Each picture, a moment. Pictures mean people, people watching. Smart guys, scared guys, fat guys, beautiful women, pimply girls, tough guys, and guys just trying to help. Guys who'd disappear into the mass of rats around them. He hardly recognized himself among them in the flickering frames and pictures, those watching, and him, another rat in plenty.

Only his teeth moved. He chewed rich, slippery cheek meat, blood-salt seasoned. It hurt. Hurt like.

It's supposed to.

Each bite was a revelation of what pain, idealized, might aspire to. Each bite an apotheosis (Good word, a word to chew over. *Thank you, Miss Kerkauff*). Each bite a shot to take you to the stars on cold fires of dead-eyed physics. So far to go and so little of him, so little of this flesh to carry him.

Well, not so little. He still had (he counted): his lips, his tongue to work with. There were fingers, miles of fingers. Each hand had, *count them*, one, two, three... *Fourteen. Fourteen knuckles, each one a meal*, each, an ocean of pain to cross. He studied: a hand was a future, a planet of undiscovered pain to explore. And before the knuckles, the fingernails, each one hugging its meat. Each could be mined. *Oh, yes, fucking Hillegas, yes.*

Who were they, the watchers in the museum? Among those who would not be there: the Baseball Family, the Empty-Eyed Girl in the Ladies' John, the Sweaty Kid Who Would Be a Man, the Beauty Piece of Kagen's Island, his Partner, Fat What'shisname. And What'shisname, the Manager Mister, *Mi*ster Hillegas. They'd never be there.

He ran the trip in his head. Start to finish. There were more he'd forgotten. Where was he now? The beginning? Was he always here? No, no, he'd just arrived. Ah, that kid on the bus, the Greyhound out of Berdoo, the Doofus kid he'd left to breed, alive in the breathing world, he was out there. *Could he be watching?* And the Chrysler Lady. Oh, Chrysler Lady! He'd pay for them, oh the sins of so long life were not the deaths, oh no. The sins were those he'd left to live. So many. So, so, many. He'd pay for those, all those.

For now, he joined them. He looked at his image in the black glass: a small man, seated, quiet, a perfect gentleman. A man at rest on square-one, and, like everyone alive, watching. He was very, very, very, very, very, very good. And, he'd get better. He'd see to that.

THEN, JUST A DREAM

A kid walks. Late afternoon. All alone, he walks the rail line. Trees push close to the tracks, one side; the other, a graveled drop-off leads to more trees. Pine trees cover the hillside down to a river, maybe a lake, but something watery is off that side of the tracks and down there. He smells it, the water, the mud, fish, mosquito eggs; those smells rise from that side. He's walked miles. As long as he can remember the day, he's walked it. It's summer, late summer, not hot, but warm. Nice. No place to go from here but home. The smells, the feel of the gravel underfoot, the scent of creosote bubbled from the ties, it smells, yes, like home. Near-home. He's wanted to go there for…

Then, a soft click, metal, or a sound that would be metallic if it weren't smothered by leather and a soft foot, and he isn't walking. His foot is stuck. Now, he looks. The boot, his foot and ankle in it, is caught in a switch. A spur of a spur, the rails split at just where he was walking and a switch that he never noticed and hadn't seen closed just as his foot arrived there. Jesus Christ. Along some track, middle of nowhere, a guy's walking along, and the thing just closes, thump, like that. It doesn't hurt; it simply holds him. Fact is, he couldn't tell if it closed on him or if he just stepped in it and got wedged there. Doesn't matter. Point is he cannot get out.

The line, this spur, he'd been walking hasn't been used in…

He looks. Well, not for a long time. Grass, small trees and brush grow in the middle, between the ties, up from the rails; and the rails, they're rusty, like nothing had rolled on them in months, years.

So the guy... Call him what he is, a kid... The kid's not scared, not right away. Not of being run down and shoved to furious pieces by a train. Only thing worries him, how the hell's he getting out? How's he getting home? How's he going to eat? The more he twists his foot, the stucker he is.

He laughs. "The stucker." The switch, though, that's not moving, not opening. It's holding him like a retriever holds a duck: soft, but that's one duck that is not flying.

Takes him most of the afternoon to realize that unless someone comes, unless the switch opens, he is there, part of that track, for the duration.

Now the fact that this is most likely an abandoned spur of some out of use line is starting to scare the hell out of him. He could die there, a really dull, pointless death.

By the time the dark starts, he is halfway convinced this is a dream. He hopes it is, anyway, one of those things that, once you realize you're in bed, safe and stupid, you're going to wake up, go down and get you a sandwich and a beer from the PX.

He starts to believe the day, the place, the rails, the switch, his foot, really are pieces of a dream. He imagines a rabbit.

Doesn't a damn rabbit run across the track in the moonlight!

He imagines a howling wolf.

Yep. Beyond the trees, a pack takes up the cry.

He looks into the now-night sky. He knows a meteor will flash. And one tears a bright silent crack across the dipper.

He plays with the night, adjusting it.

Then he imagines a dinosaur nearby.

Nearby, the woods creak, crash, thunder. Trees groan, then explode. A hundred feet down the line a shadow like the world lumbers from the woods, crosses the track as a flesh-wrapped pile driver might and slip-slides the gravel down into darkness, the trees below. The dream shakes as it passes.

"Wow," the guy says, thinking of what he'd brought to the world, this dream. The damn rails still shiver. With the shiver, without wanting to, he imagines a train, a metal and fire thing, abroad on this abandoned, this unused, spur line. Can't help that. In the distance, the dinosaur cannonballs into the water and bubbles away, forever.

Into its place slides the sorrow of a steam whistle. In a few moments, pitifully few, the puff and chug of an engine rides the curve of rails. It's coming from ahead. The steel races toward him; the rails that hold him quiver, they breathe against his leg, tightening, loosening, but never giving up on him.

He pictures the train. It is an old friend, the train, black, a steam giant at full blaze, shadow and fire in night. He sees the length of it; the cars run bright with people, eating, dozing, talking, planning, dreaming. A hundred at least, a hundred people, all with places to go, promises to keep, business, things they'll do and undo at the end of the line.

The boy? He's still stuck. He imagines the switch opening, releasing him.

It does not. He comes quickly now to realize that in this dream, this world, you can't unmake the life you made. You can't take back the dinosaur, can't rezip the sky, unhop the bunny, unhowl the wolf.

And the train is near...

He thinks, maybe there is a bridge.

There is a bridge. Yes, he remembers. And he dreams it *out*. Dreams the gorge and the bridge across it a sliver of broken wood, down-bending steel, emptiness hung between the train and his trapped self! Then...

Then, he thinks, maybe. Maybe this dream is only the dream of someone. Someone on the train, the train heading his way is dreaming this. Maybe he's on board, home from the war, safe, and waking...

And the world is soft and too small, a compartment of a train, the train. It's night, his leg is asleep, the world is a window, a black mirror with only him and this little rushing room in it. Ahead, the engine whistle blows. They're going so fast that his compartment catches the shriek, devours, spits it pastward. The whistle blows again. His body presses into the seat at his back. The train screams with stopping, trying to at least, the whistle rushes on, 80, 90 miles per hour, all the steel and flesh around him strains toward zero. Working for stillness in a length of track too small to catch that much quiet.

Christ, what the hell? The young man looks out the window. He wonders. Is the bridge out? Ahead? Is there a bridge? A bridge, or something else, something on the track? And without thinking, he knows there is. He knows for sure there is a bridge but does not want to think about it. He knows for sure something else is there. The bridge and something. How high, how long, how deep, how rocky, how intact? And has he left the war, that place... Is THIS the dream...? Could this be THE dream? Could this be where he's not? Could THIS be something he should wake from? Or not? What the hell would happen if... if this is still not home, not a ride, not...

Then he wakes. And it was. A dream, a Goddamn...

SO MANY TINY MOUTHS

When the wind freshened, the mouths climbed the sky, played among the trees.

Earl Sooey sat in his shack, writing down. Like always. He wrote, *They eat top-down well as bottum-up. Don't matter nun.* He wrote like once, like long ago when he was barely a coot, back when the government claimed men were going to the moon. *Th whole damn world snackered by this bullshit. Cap Hainey, too.*

Earl saved that newspaper. Still had the damn thing somewhere. That was how many years ago? Earl was writing even then.

Now, he watched dark creep. Sand drifted in dog-high waves under and around his shack.

Dammed by sand and dark, he wrote, then added, *Forever dark is cumming.* Didn't matter, he figured. He figured the damn mouths couldn't see. *Even tho they got one of my eyes!* He swigged a little Beam and added *Ha-ha!* to what he wrote.

His eyehole itched and hurt at the same time. So many mouths, even blind, all they had do was open and bite, bite so quick and often that something would be there by and by to eat.

Blind mouths agenst a haff-blind man. That make an even fite? he wrote on *The Toms River Sentinel.*

"Even?" he said to no one, laughing. *Nuthins even wen th end is shur!* He wrote that down.

Earl wrote things down. Sometimes he didn't, but he had years of the *Sentinel* saved, saved to write on, writing his own wide lines of truth with black crayon overtop their damn gray lies. *Always sumthin gon to kill you,* he wrote over a story about some president and Water-whatever. "Now there's truth in that damn paper," he said to no one and swigged again.

He listened.

The air clacked, clicked, hissed. A dry rain of sand sifted over the shack's tin roof when the wind died; when it blew it scoured roof, walls, everything.

"Gobble, hobble, bobble," he said when the sand brushed the window. "Sweet nothings," he said. Sand making loving whispers to the glass.

Soon his windows were gone. *Turned!* he wrote. *All my windaglass gone back to sand!* He wrapped the plastic tarp around him tighter, hugged the bottle of Beam closer.

He wrote, *There're noyses in the air where they eat. They are...* He listened to noises in the air. By and by he wrote, *...are not like squirrel scratches inunder the eaves. Sand's eating noyses are...* He put on paper the sounds in the air. *Nik, nik, nik,* he wrote, *A millyun niks, is nite tonite.*

There were no squirrels now. *No squirrel in the Barrens,* he wrote. *An pretty soon, no Barrens, then no squirrel everware,* was the afterthought. "Do without squirrel, anyways," he said to his Beam.

The air was cool. His breath dripped down inside of the plastic he'd wrapped around himself. *That cold day in July everone talks of,* he wrote.

The mouths had come with the Fourth of July. He wrote, *Everone missed the end of the world.* Then added, *Cap Hainey an Buster Leek too... too much FUN I gess howlin at the moon.*

Moon! There had been a picture—made him laugh—he cut it from *The Sentinel* years ago, showed it around over by

Chatsworth. The damn picture was the astronauts standing on the moon in their suits. And there it was. The damn moon in the sky of the damn picture!

"Now, how can they be on the moon when the moon's in the sky, there?" he said. "You answer me that."

Folks, real folks, shook their heads. "Good catch, Earl," they said.

Cap Hainey looked. "Damn, Earl!" he said. "That's them practicing in their space suits there, out on the desert. See, it says them astronauts practicing for when they're on the moon, for crineoutloud. Sure that's the moon in the picture, that's where they're heading, Earl. Christ, it says right there."

Earl shook his head and saved the damn picture. *If ther on the moon how can the moon be in ther sky?* he wrote under it. Still made him laugh. Cap Hainey!

The end of the world started with the folks from "Filthydelphia," west of the Barrens. The family stopped on the day, Fourth of July itself, canoe strapped to their roof and dead lost. They bought a couple, five gallons of gas from his dipping barrel and he'd pointed their way to Papoose Crick.

Earl's old hunter dog ignored them. When their car had come crunching up the sand trail off the county road, the old bastard raised his head and sang a squeaky bass *ruff*. When the car stopped, he growled. When he saw their damn dumb faces, he farted and fell asleep.

The young dog was off on the causeways, in the wood. He didn't bother homing to see what the hell was with these folk.

"Help us with a little gas, there, can you?" the driver called. "Service station's closed over." The man turned to the little woman.

"'Chatsworth' was it?" The woman bent to the map crinkled in her lap.

"Yeah, Chatsworth. Buster Leek. Too Goddamn rich to work hollydays," Earl said. He squinted at the car folk. "Us Pineys gotta take our fun, too, you know?"

Two ton of plastic camping shit but forgot good sense. These folks were good and lost. The daddy's sausage hands were sweat-tight on the wheel. Pretty fingernails. Shiny.

"We're looking for, is it, the Wading River?"

"Yeah, the Wadin'."

"And the, what's it? Papoose Creek," Daddy said it like he didn't want to say it. "You heard of a 'Papoose Creek'?" He gave Earl a little nervous chuckle like he for sure didn't want to say it a second time.

The woman leaned over Daddy to look up at Earl, a white strip of sun grease war paint ran down her nose. She yelled slow, like talking to a damn Mexican. "We hear about Jersey's Pine Barrens in Philadelphia. So much history here." She shook her head like she couldn't believe it. "We want, you know, want the kids to see it, before, you know? To see the Pines before..."

"'Fore Cap Hainey cuts 'em down and rolls out them little prefabulous houses to sell?" Earl said.

The lady smiled. In the back seat, the kids did nothing, looked nowhere.

Earl started in. He gave them a little shit, spun tales, and charged a pretty penny for the gas. Penny? Hell, Earl charged what they call "an arm and leg" for a short five gallons of dewy low-test because Buster was closed for Independence. Son-of-a-bitch was good for something.

After dipping and shitting, Earl pointed them to the Crick. "That papoose-bottom water is good for what ails you." He winked at the man. "Make you strong. You know what I mean?" He looked at the woman. She snapped a picture of Earl with her little yellow camera box from the store. They paid and were gone. Like that.

Earl was going to tell them, "Watch out for that Jersey Devil." He was going to say, "What's the Jersey Devil? Why, doesn't he carry off folk in the night, his hundred teeth like needles clicking!" He'd written down that story years before.

He could've warned them to watch their damn campfires. Could have said, "Might look swampy wet there, but it ain't! Been dry for Christ knows how long. I don't want my shack and me burned through careless ways. Built this myself, aw Christ, back when Cap Hainey was a little shit. Back in the damn Depression, I been here that long, Cap getting richer, me getting older." He would have told them about Cap, his damn bogs, the nigger day-labors he jobs in for 'berry seasons.

But the damn people drove off, left all that unsaid. The car kicked a rooster tail of sand, slewed onto the trail and into the pines. Like that.

The old dog slept.

Earl laughed.

Then he kept watch through his back window. From sundown-on, Earl leaned against the glass, looking, looking toward the Crick, watching for sparks and tale-tell red-glowing the sky.

Night snuck from under the trees, across the sand between him and the woods. Tree shadow touched his wall and the dark crawled over him and into the shack, over Hainey's bogs, then was everywhere. The air stayed day-hot and the sky was pale and watery. That could have been his damn eyes, still, all he saw of earth and heaven that last night of the world was the forest and a few stars wiggling in the heat. Them and the Thing.

If there had been no folk in the woods, Earl would have sat his porch and taken the breeze off Hainey's bogs. He would have rocked, listened to the crick-crack and buzz of bug and the wing moan of the swallows as they fed; he could have sat and drew pinewood scent through his own and the dogs' familiar stinks mixed with the nearby whiff of frog, carp, and decaying water-life bubbling from the bogs and the far-away mossy sphagnum breath of cedar swamp steeping in the deep wood.

He could have had a good night, July the Fourth, gone to bed and died stupid like the world was going to.

Instead, he was watching out that damn bunch in the woods. Because he was, he saw the Thing—saw it come. Almost burned his eyes white. Like sunlight screaming, it set black shadows climbing the inside of his shack. He heard the coming Thing fry the air, felt it whomp the ground. For seconds, the shack shivered on its stone posts. Then the wind sucked out of him and deep thunder boxed his ears. The damn air punched his chest a second later and rolled across him, wiggled the flab of his face.

The old hunter dog jumped sudden and wild, looking, singing.

"Best write *that* down, what do you say?" Earl said. He wrote: *Stars shoot back!* He wrote, *July Forth the stars shoot back. A come. A big come!*

He figured the Philly folk were gone. Found later he was wrong. Figured the Thing had whomped down by Ong's Hat Cross where the Ford Sisters had their shack. That was that for them, he figured. Too bad. He liked those Ford girls.

Earl ran outside to look for fire sign.

Nothing but a glowing wake across the sky where the Thing had passed. He listened for the fire trucks to come shouting out of Chatsworth. Nothing.

Too much Independence fun, he figured. *All your money, Cap Hainey, and you don't even care about, about...* Took him a half-minute. "Don't even care about them poor people," he figured out loud.

In a few minutes the star trail was a blue smear down the sky. After a good half-hour, there were still no trucks nor men.

"Up to me," he told the old dog and humped toward the woods. Naught to it normally but tonight that hundred-foot walk was an uphill mile. Each step sank him to his ankles. Each step shoved backward in giving earth, like wading a running tide.

The black wall of the forest rose ahead of him. The dark place where the trees stood open above him whispered. "What's that?" he asked. "What say?" Little shit and grown man, Earl had never been afraid, not ever, of man, critter, woods, nor night. Pine-born he was and fearless was he.

Now the forest was a stranger; it whispered in a tongue he'd never heard. What was different? Something changed, but what the hell, he didn't know. He'd write it down when he did.

Twenty steps into the forest and the trees folded shut behind. The world—shack, bogs, and Chatsworth—was gone. Now it was him and the sand. The trees stood black and silent. Above, the pine boughs were black fingers against the blue ghost of the star trail. Even that soft light was spreading into the big night. He stood like a dumb-shit, like them folks from the city. Ignorant, new, lost.

Out of the forest came a ripple. Something breathed across him and the world rumbled. Earl's toes tried to grip the sand through his boots. Night's breath was cold, bad; a smell wrapped him. From down the trail a scream squeaked his spine. Wasn't man or woman; no animal he'd ever heard made that noise. Something, though, something clamped in pain was down ahead dying.

He tried to grab hold of it, remember the noise, the stink, for writing down later.

When a branch he should have known bit his ankle, when creepers he should have felt damn near snared his legs, when a heaved up root he'd stepped over for seventy years nearly tumbled him into the bog-feed, he stopped dead. Chill sweat covered him. Too much new. He'd walked the path to Papoose Crick since the Great Depression. It was become something else. Night's heat was gone (*and Christ, I should have brought th' lamp*).

He heard it, then. This time he could not forget.

He hadn't run since he was a boy. Men didn't run.

He ran.

It followed him.

Back to the shack. His hair stood wet with damp and chills climbed his bones.

He grabbed his crayon and scribbled, *Black sky.* He added, *Black forever everware. Everware suthins diffrent.* That was something he felt true but didn't know why.

Then he did. *The diffrence is it is diffrent!* he wrote. *Before: everthin was all the same, the same forever. Trees, paths, places, all ways the same. Now not. Now alls different.*

From his rear window, he watched the dark hole in black forest, the white sand path that led there. Everywhere difference, everywhere he listened—and he listened again to the night—even silence had a stranger's voice, and from the pines came the noise where the silence ate.

He woke when something thumped the shack's ass-end where his head lay. Fog had come while he slept and the shack was wrapped in a gray glow.

Another something whomped the wall. He laid his hand against cool glass. The fog on the pane shoved back. His hand tremored. "Can't see shit," he told the old dog. The hand pressed to the glass was veined, red and blue, thick skinned, crossed with scars and stories. The same, that at least. Nails, yellow, thick, chipped, dirty, after seventy years of night writing, his right thumb and first two fingers were black with crayon wax, the pinky edge of his hand was gray with news ink. Like always, those hands were truthful. And now they shook, *damn bastards.*

Another something whomped his wall and screamed.

Onto the porch went Earl, the old dog trailing.

The shack might have hung miles high in the air for all Earl could see of the earth below his own damn steps. He and the dog sniffed. To Earl's thinking, the morning smelled a little like fire—and something else too. Something maybe the dog placed.

What the hell, he thought, *90-something and afraid. Christ.*

Another whomp to the back of the shack. A flapping scream followed. The dog trembled against Earl's leg.

Earl gave the animal a shove with his knee. "Ought to by Christ take and shoot you, you old bastard. A 'fraid dog ain't useful."

The dog waddled toward the gray morning. He stretched his neck, took one step down, another. Then his body jerked and he sounded one long howling note. The bass end of it curdled into a growl as he scratched backward to Earl's legs. Dog-song echoed from the day.

This was a good old dog, lazy on his porch but one to fly, flapping ears and jowls, singing pretty into the trees and off the trail, taking long-leg strides ahead of roaring trucks and charging junkers bouncing after game. He'd run the night, unafraid of men, guns, or the tearing death of wheel, tooth, or claw, this old dog.

Now, the old bastard tucked and whimpered into the shack.

Another thing hit the back wall, another scream, more flapping from the mist. Echoes. Earl hear the old dog whimper. "What the hell?" Earl said.

The world stank a little like outhouse, something of old oil and gas—like them old fish boats by Egg Harbor. Fire scent still soaked the air and something else lay on the bottom of all those stinks.

"The fuck?" Earl said. Saying, it came to him. The day smelled, damn if it didn't, like sex. Once he caught hold, Earl reeled in. Damn if it wasn't the biggest part of the morning: the thick odor like that place women had. He remembered *that* damn much about it, anyway, *haw-haw.*

"You old shit," he said to the hound, "what good's a dog afraid of a little pussy?" The dog shuffled deeper into the shack. The flapping from the back sounded like someone shaking a wet sheet to dry. Two, three wet sheets, a dozen. Then another thud and more. Out of the sound came a stream of birds, big and small, running, reaching for the air. With them came fox, coon, squirrel, possum, a swarm from around the shack, from under it, the swarm flowed over Earl's roof, his porch and into the fog away from the woods.

Later, he tried to write down the sounds: birds so scared they forgot air had buildings and trees in it. Squirrel frightened enough to run with fox or any critter as would eat them standing still or on the run. He tried to write down cries so terrible as to frighten a chase hound. Some reason, broken flapping birds were worst.

Later, he wrote, *Birds will be last to go!* A minute after, he calculated fish might be, but didn't bother writing it.

Earl stepped off the damn porch. Two paces and the shack was a gray smear in the blank day. "A man could lose hisself a step from his own damn shack," he said. Having said it, he realized it was true. Inside, he kicked around stacks of *The Sentinel,* looked under some of the stinking clothes he figured on washing sometime, he scattered the pieces of his old radio hiding in under yards and yards of plastic tarp. He tossed aside tools, wire, pistons and rods, rooted among boxes, bottles, engine parts. He finally found the rope, good yellow stuff—the plastic kind the electric men used to stay the power poles over by the highway— two hundred feet, coiled neat.

He tied one end to the porch post, the other around his gut, then he stepped down onto the sand again. *Still like wading,* he thought. "Wading a running tide!" he said.

The shack disappeared, behind. Alone in the mist, he trudged through giving sand and payed out the rope. All around and overhead, the flap of wings, the rustle of paws and claws in sand continued. All invisible in the mist.

What the hell he was doing, he didn't know. He just felt the need to go, to look, felt he ought be on the trail. Whatever strangeness was here, it had come from the sky to his patch of wood this foggy morn. His duty, he figured.

He had forty, maybe fifty feet of nylon rope left on the coil when screams, a thousand of them, echoed from the mist. Some near, some distant, the screams held a thousand terrors, all on the move toward him.

A breeze stirred the stink of dirty sex. The air cleared enough to let him see the opening in the forest wall. That darker spot in the gray seemed a mile off. But that was the fog. It was close. Earl squinted. There was movement at the edge of his seeing. Sand, the forest floor rolled, moved toward him. Out of the screaming woods and rustling brush, the sand rippled. In slow-motion, the wave front crested, broke toward him, almost frozen but not.

The wave's breath came on the breeze: rotted meat and sex. The sand it was, that's what screamed the thousand, the million tiny voices. The sand and the things the sand was eating.

Nik, nik, nikniknik, the sand said a billion times above the hissing flow of coming tide.

From the trees, Earl's dog—the young one who'd been hunting when the Thing came down—the stupid animal now came dragging its ass end. The damn animal hauled itself from the pines. Where the wave crested, it collapsed, rolled head over ass, then stopped, stuck, sinking, in the rippling sand and devoted itself to screams.

From the shack, the old dog returned the call.

Whole thing took a minute. At the end, the dog was gone. For a few seconds it struggled, seemed to sink, sink slow, like a boat oozing under. When the hound rolled over, it was dead and no longer screamed. It continued writhing, being argued over by so many tiny mouths. The dog went side-up first, then belly up, ribs like teeth. Earl saw. No legs, no more, no more hind-end and belly. The thing was body cavity and bone, unwinding guts, dissolving flesh and blood seeping into the sand. The sand drank. The sand ate. The dog melted like ice on a grill and was soon gone. A minute, maybe two.

Earl wrote: *Sand cum from out of space.* He wrote it but knew that wasn't right. *Our sand made alive by...* He held the crayon above the page of *The Tom's River Sentinel.* His hand shook. What to say, what made the sand alive? He wrote: *That star fucked us shur.* Good an answer as any. *Fucked Mother Earth and made it live!* He was writing on the picture of the astronauts, the lie, back from that fake moon trip, sitting in their little trailer, talking with the president through the window. Astronauts all smiles and teeth.

The morning had stopped screaming, the mists cleared some. The wave rolled closer to Earl. He backed away, kept a good twenty, thirty feet of still earth between the living rolling sand and his own damn self. He could see a little now. Even so, he wound the yellow rope around his arm back to his porch. He hugged the post, the post he'd raised in the Great Depression.

The sand wave stopped a couple, three yards from his steps. It hushed, waiting. A pot set to simmer. He heard more than saw through the thinning fog, but the forest was moving, creaking, cracking. Trees, a few, then more, fell, rolled, tore the brush, the brush crackling in its own dissolving ways. He pictured the pines, falling, upended, rolling, sinking, eaten like his dog. A wind blew and the fog tore to shreds around him.

With the wind, Earl got a little of himself eaten. A grain of sand on the wind, a speck of grit to his eye. Nothing unusual in the Barrens. He blinked, wiped the corner, like always. From deep inside him, the familiar pain grew teeth. White heat grabbed the side of his head, fire flashed a bright hot needle inside his eye... One grain, but it ate fast and hungry; thing ate fuller than he could have thought.

That thought came and was written down, later. In the moment, the pain dropped him to his knees. He fell, hands first, on his porch. By the time he'd wiped the grain away, the eye jelly was gobbled, the lid nibbled through, eaten out. That part of his seeing was gone, gone for good.

Later, the sand wave swept forward, rolling slow like molasses in January. It surrounded the shack, rolled on by. Later...

Later, he wrapped his head in torn parts of his last clean shirt, took to wearing the goggles he'd kept when he junked the Indian cycle, 1942, wrapped and taped himself inside the plastic tarp. That's when he wrote, *Hell, there's always sumthin gon to kill you... mite as well be this,* which was as true as anything ever written down, he figured.

Later, the car came out of the silence, banged and screamed. It seemed a strange and alien thing. It rolled on metal rims, tires eaten, gone. The engine was over-racing, coughing toward a stall. But the spinning rims kicked sand every which way, sprayed tiny teeth into the air.

"Sand eats rubber!" he called to them. "But I guess you knew that," he said to himself.

The car folks stayed put; they screamed, but stayed.

Earl wore his new plastic suit onto the porch. He'd tied bricks to his feet with the yellow plastic rope. He whisked the wind-borne sand mouths off the porch with a flail of frayed tether.

The car's windows were near gone, pitted, holed.

"Glass turns to sand!" Earl yelled.

Shreds of nylon tent covered the holes where the windows had "gone over." "Guess you found that out, too," Earl said.

The car, the people screamed.

Earl couldn't see who was left. "Where to go? What to do, what, for God's sake, to do?" They all screamed.

"Give us gas?" someone yelled. "Pour us some gas, we'll take you too!" someone else yelled. Earl thought it was the man but who knew? The yelling was shrill.

"Sure!" Earl yelled. "Gotta charge you, though!" He laughed at that.

"For God's sake, help us out of here!" a woman maybe, maybe the girl. He couldn't see with his one eye, the fading light, the pitted plastic lens of the goggles.

"Where's 'outta here'?" he called across the sand. "Where're we going when the whole world's going over?"

"Please?" A squeaky voice. The squeak rose to "Pleeeease!"

"Gas is there, son." Earl pointed to the drum. It sat where it had yesterday and for fifty years, on its stone base. "Hep yourselves. Day-after holiday special!" He felt a needle-sting as a hungry mouth nibbled his nose. He swatted the bite and left a smear of blood inside the plastic suit. "Fill 'er up!" he yelled and couldn't help laughing at the thought.

He laughed again.

The family danced inside the dying car. They shouted at him, themselves, the world. What was going on, being decided behind those tent flaps? Who'd sacrifice? "That's it," he said aloud to himself. "Bet you're figuring, 'Now how far can we get on this tank and no tires?' or thinking, 'How much gas can I dip till they eat me to the knees?'"

He didn't figure the man with the pretty nails to give himself for eating. The woman? Not likely. "Send the boy!" Earl yelled. He was wondering how damn desperate the folks were.

He stood to watch.

Earlier, he calculated why he was uneaten.

Back in the Great Depression, he'd built this shack just right, kept his sill beams off the ground on stacks of flat rocks, old granite. Even so, the sand was eating the cabin now. He couldn't miss that. It was at the wood. He heard. The mouths were at rest now, but when wind stirred, sand flew. Where each grain nested on something living or once alive—log, blade of grass, or critter—the sand ate; it ate and didn't fill. A grain here, a grain there, it nibbled, gobbled, roof, wall, floor and, sooner or later...

He wrote down: *Nik, nik, nik a billyun times all ready. Billyuns to go before.*

Earl watched through the day. When the sun sat on the western sawtooth ridge of trees, the sand began to stir again. *Waking for nite*, he wrote. The frozen wave began to murmur.

Not a bird, a bee, nor critter moved that Earl could see, just the ground itself, crawling on its mouths. Earl dozed, downing Jim Beam to kill the pain. His eye, his nose, his head. He slept not well, but hard. He woke alone. *Dog gone*, he wrote. Then laughed.

Brick shoes were smart, he reckoned. Keeping wind-drift sand off his floor, out of the way, became impossible. Too much, too damn much wind and the sand, too small, too much. The plastic tarp he wrapped himself in got worn as he walked. Some of the mouths wriggled in. When they came, they ate. *Nik-nik-nik* at his shoes. Finally, he put something between him and the floor. Something sand didn't eat. *Brick*, he figured, brick would work. Knocked a couple off the base of his kerosene heater. That was that. Fine as frog fur.

From then to the end of the world, Earl clumped, *thud, thud, thud*. Made him laugh.

In sundown light, Earl kept watch from his porch. The damn folk never drove off. Never tried. No one tried to fill the tank.

They sat, revving now and then. Now and then the inside
screamed. Sometimes the screams were at him. Every so often
the car shimmied, someone inside dancing, fighting, humping.

Sundown, the car went still. The engine chugged through last
light. When the crawl of shadows touched it, it coughed twice,
raced again, then shuddered still.

Earl listened. A voice inside. One. Crying.

Earl took a last sip of Beam. "Go on home, now," he told the
bottle and tossed it. Not light enough now to see, but he heard
the whisper of the sand, the urgent chatter of the glass as it
shivered into a billion parts, the parts making friends with the
sand.

The voice from the car still cried. An hour after dark, it
screamed. The scream lasted a minute, two. Maybe three; Earl's
clock had stopped. Then the car went quiet.

Later, he gave attention to the trees, their noises as they fell.
After he was gone, Earl figured, pretty soon after, he figured, the
trees would be gone too. *Fuck 'em*, he figured. Damn trees. All his
life. The mother of splinters, burns and broken chairs. Tried to
put his eyes out, to trip him all the years of wandering the forest,
wanted to crush him when he felled them. Trees might outlive
him now, but not by much Goddamn them.

Grass and cranberry, sphagnum moss and fern, other living
shit, they'd all go down the mouths.

Fuck trees and the horse they rode in on, he wrote down. Almost
the last thing.

For a second he thought about being proper buried. Then he
laughed. *World swallows you anyway. Might as well lik this*, he wrote.

That was the last.

The wind freshened, blew through the empty windows. Earl
looked up. The grains scoured the wood. *Nik, nik, nik.* Earl
gathered the plastic tarp around him. Keep them out long as he
could. He looked to the noise above, the roof beams crackling

like small arms fire. Pieces of rafter fell, dissolving as they dropped. Through the holes, the stars shone bright.

At last, he pictured the world, the whole damn thing spread below. Like he was one of them astronauts, a real for Christ sake traveler in the outer space. He and the sand were real astronauts. In his mind's eye Earl saw the world. He looked down on it like the papers said the astronauts in space had done. *Ha, ha.* In his mind's eye Earl watched Earth shrivel, all the living, all that was growing green and climbing, all critters, people. He watched it shiver and go down, rolling in sand like that dumb young dog. He watched it all go down the tiny mouths. How many grains of sand was there? All around the world, how many tiny mouths?

From where Earl stood—wrapped in plastic, tethered to his shack, peering through his goggles, breathing slow—his mind's eye saw the world reshape and flatten... in his mind's eye, looking down.

Damnation. He hoped that would be the way. Everyone gone when he was gone. Buster Leek. Cap Hainey, the pickers in the harvest. Folks in Filthydelphia. Folk everywhere. All gone soon after him he hoped.

When it came, the pain was pure lousy. Soon it ended. In just a minute. Maybe two.

JEREMY TAKES HIS TEXT FROM THE LIVES OF THE SPIDERS

The door shoved Robideaux back inside where was whiskey warmth. Blues, like a bad tooth, shook his soul; the pretty noise made him wish, *save-me-Lord*, for a night of temptation not resisted. Still, Robideaux shoved back. On the street, cold, night, and sleet drove him against that fearsome door. *Drunk out again*, he figured. *Who care?*

Preach' Robideaux, jangling among the lowdown dives of wherever this sure'nough town was. Somewhere lights burned bright. Not here. Somewhere his barge rode Mississippi swells, tied, tight, and taking on. *Amen to all that till morning.* Robideaux, nothing to do except make his witness to the bottle and the bottle's folk—*Lord's work.* Amen to that too. Preach' Robideaux, taking his text from the lives of working folk, talking the Lord and drinking long, showing himself no better than they, no sir, none.

Guitar Blues behind him died. Whispering sleet shivered Robideaux. Looking, he could not certify his way to the tow. He sucked night, drew creosote and old oil from the railhead across the way. The river'd be a silence on one corner of his compass. He turned, turned around and around. From the hiss and chill, a sliver of warmth oozed from the south. Robideaux licked his lips. Head, like radar, top of Cap'n StDenis's bridge, turned that…

…way, and…

…there was the guy. Death for sure.

"Evening, sir," said Robideaux.

"*Whoo-eee*," said Red-eyed Death, chattering, about to fall, guitar sack slung on one shoulder. Dead eyes leaned close, went wide. The dead mouth worked pale gums. The eyes leaped Robideaux like wolf spiders, swallowed, ate his head, his whole self, and Robideaux figured...

Bad ride, Jeremy figured. *The world couldn't shake so, fuck no.*

He opened the eyes. Dark poured in. He took a breath. The world stunk like something for sure gonna blow the fuck up: diesel fuel, gasoline. Smell made his lips go dry, his tongue tasted... The tongue was named Robideaux. He remembered that. So was the rest of him, Robideaux too. Robideaux was wrapped in a greasy sheet and scratchy blanket and there was, fuck, what? A push from behind, a load of power making the whole damn place go rumbling somewhere Jeremy didn't know where. His teeth chattered. Robideaux's teeth. How the fuck he sleep through that? He did not, purely did not know, but sure enough, everything moved, Robideaux, the bed he was on, the room he was in. First fucking impressions.

Through Robideaux's eyes, dark gave way to dirty light. Crusted windows, other bunks stacked along the wall, mess everywhere. Another stink lay inside the gassy reek, a stink of bodies, sweat, unwashed clothes. Nobody in those clothes. No, he was alone. He was it. *What the fuck?*

Second thoughts.

Number three was "Where the Old Lady?" He groped floor by the bunk and there she was, dear old thing. The guitar lay safe, her bag wrapped around, soft rope held her snug, the rope Jeremy slung over whosoever's shoulder he had at whatever time. Jeremy had walked earth with that guitar, the last, what, hundred-some years? Long for a Traveler to carry any one damn thing. Travelers took whatever body, left what was left behind.

That, *fuck him Jesus*, was the extent of his fucking memory, *God be praised.* That, and he knew how to play her, that old she-box of a wood guitar. He knew *that* fact all the way to Robideaux's balls. Another couple seconds and he had the guitar out of her sack, hugged to this belly and cheek. He touched up her strings, made her quiver so-pretty. He whispered with her for a little. By and by she reminded him where was this dirty thumping room and who was this Robideaux he's walking 'round, traveling inside.

Jeremy remembered, finally, a bar, a bar someplace. He remembered this Robideaux, a rouster, a rouster in a bar. A bar where? Bar in Cairo. Say it right, like they say: KAY-ro. Cairo, what? Cairo, Illinois. Fuck yeah. Felt more better now he's talking through the old girl; guitar made him easy.

And where they were, was in some boat, some big boat.

Robideaux's voice sat by Jeremy's heart. It said, "The Lord defend." A whimper. "I take my text from the lives of the saints and dem marted souls."

"Shut the fuck up," Jeremy said with Robideaux's mouth. Baritone. "*Hhmmmmm,*" he hummed. "Nice," he said. He touched greasy linoleum with Robideaux's bare feet. A throb climbed the legs, settled in the balls.

RmmmmHmmmHmmmHmmm, the throb said. Big. The tow, the boat, was talking. That's where they at: on the tow. Robideaux, Jeremy aboard, barging on the Mississippi.

Traveling, his Jeremy brain said...

"...home," Robideaux's body said.

RmmmHmmmHmmm, the room said. Two thousand horses of Cadillac Marine shoving downwater. Where to?

Robideaux knew.

Christ All the Mighty, they're going home to the Easy. New Oy-uns and Fat Tuesday coming sure.

RmmmHmmmmHmmm, Engine growled, quivered his dick, Cadillac engine, stuff of song. Jeremy sang, *"Cadillac's drivin' deep waterdown... shovin' long twa'ed Easy Town..."*

"Fuck your saints," Jeremy said to Robideaux. "Take my text from the sweated bits of pretty ladies." Robideaux's calloused pads brushed a cathouse roadsong in the left hand. The right gave the tune a delta-driving Cadillac shove.

Before the first eight rounded, a square of light opened across the room. A breath of swamp and fish washed in. Above the smell—good by Robideaux's lights—a cut of blue sky sang out: *Hello Robideaux! Who you got witchoo, Robideaux?*

Jeremy laughed.

A shadow in the doorframe said, "Fuck, Preach'? You playing wit' music, and we bahgin'? Get you black ass topside, see Cap StDenis, wha' say?"

The door cracked shut on the voice.

Jeremy's first day, traveling Robideaux: When Robideaux wasn't bucking so to toss Jeremy from his flesh into Nowhere-Nowhen, the man was working, in a sulky way, hauling ratchet on the web of cables and couplings kept the tow laced tight, a quarter-mile of steel barges, fifteen stinking holes in the water. They carried grain this trip. Their tow-mule, a pusher boat, a little home with big engines, pilot house above it all.

Preach', his body, knew barging. So Jeremy gives Robideaux his head, just a little, takes walking-round lessons from the Preacher: Robideaux works, Jeremy tastes the life. Suited a Traveler way-fucking fine.

The world smelled older, further south they towed. Day and night, Robideaux's nose worked like an old blind tickhound dreaming long-gone hunts. Warmer, wetter, the days never give up the stink of barge. Jeremy, his soul, tasted living things everywhere. He itched at the universe of cells in the barges beneath them, each grain a tiny life dying in ferment. Dark vermin, fattening in the steel bellies, crawled so lovely in Jeremy's dreams.

When he could, Jeremy walked Robideaux to the fore. There, the air was not yet steeped in boat stench. There, the bow wave rose from the flat iron face of the fore-barges. Smooth and green, the 10-foot-high liquid snakes curled into morning mist or evening dark, both sides.

Robideaux was two ways. Times were, Jeremy had to grip, keep Preach' from throwing himself overboard with the despair. These times, the man'd moan and sigh, preach on his sins and cry the casting out of devils.

The other men shook their heads.

Other times, Robideaux walked smug and chuckling. Those times, Jeremy purely wanted to jump into another someone entirely, bash Robideaux's big black face with his own wrench, *Wham.* That notion had its wonders. A long while had come since Jeremy'd done the murder game and been hung up to swing for it or got sat down to sizzle before jumping out and into another blinking face nearby. *Ah, yes.*

But this one, this preacher? Jeremy wanted to burn him out from his dick inward. *Whoo-ee.* Sometimes, midnights, after day had frictioned Robideaux scant, Jeremy latched tight. They sat in the fore-barge while night swallowed them. Small towns came and passed sparkling with life and silence along the dark shores then winked out around a riverbend. Jeremy played and preached with his old guitar. The men in their bunks, aft, or in the wheelhouse, heard the music from the dark, ahead. He knew that, knew they shook heads, wondering what going on in that nappy haid of Robideaux's since Cairo?

Fuck them.

Bad disaster almost got them just once. The way it happened: Robideaux, walking barge, checking lines, fore to aft, staring down at oily cable, rusty steel and big-toothed pawls, paying no heed to the one beautiful bright blue and golden day around. Nothing happening. Then something happened. Jeremy looked up and saw a thing. Thing sparked and gave him wonder. High and all 'round, the air was filled with bright threads. Little things. They drifted over, ahead, across their bow, their wake. How long had they been barging through them? He didn't know, he'd been looking down at cables, chains and such. Mile on mile they shoved through the pretty things on the wind, so silver-flashing, way, way up.

"*What is that?*" Jeremy said.

Robideaux didn't say.

Jeremy tasted, touched life around him. They lived, each thread a little life, an urge, a yen to go, to be. He stood dumb wondering, said, "What IS that?" He tried to catch one as the boat floated through like a dream. "What the fuck is that?" He jumped and yelled but couldn't catch-hold.

Aft, in near-disaster, none of the others noted the crazy Preach' jumping, yelling.

At just that time, the tow was riding the chop of the main channel, a busy stretch of water. Just prior, they'd woven through a delta-maze of chutes and runs. They'd dodged other tows, northbound, and slipped by slower moving southbound commerce. To that, add the tidal rush running upriver from the Gulf; its easy swell flexed them, soft and dreamy, along their thousand-feet of bound-together parts and pieces.

In all that, one cable worked loose, enough to put a gap between three barge and number six. This little whoopsie slip, a hundred-ton steel mouth, opened man-wide slow, then closed down, *chop*, like that.

And there's Jeremy, wondering into the sky, reaching for bright threads and Robideaux, not tending barge business underfoot.

Then of course, it was Swede Lewis near got himself gummed in half by that steel maw. Would have if he hadn't slipped all way through and only caught himself, last second, by a dangling chain, feet dragging almost in the rushing river till the other men could pull him out, portside. Robideaux's fault. Ratchet man. He allowed the slip get loose. Big dumb nigger.

On the dock at payoff, the men were eyes and growls, Swede Lewis, worse than most.

The Captain, Mister Raymond StDenis, thank you very much, jostled Robideaux aside. "Have woids wit you, Robideaux," he said. He held the fat pay envelope saying "Robideaux" in big letters out of reach. Snapping and breathing, Captain said, "You tink we takin' you, come next trip up and back? You tink I'm takin' a man who leaves he cables woik loose between my numbers tree and six bahges and looses me almost a man's laig, *snip*, off like dat?" He snapped his fingers under the big man's nose. With a bit less snap, Captain added, "Even if it was a bitty dumb-sumbitch Swede who'd have gone chop off his *udder* laig later, jess showin' the story, how it happen." Captain was a bitty guy, too, but he could be big with mean. Then the snap was back. "Even so. You tink I gone take you back?" he said right in Jeremy's nose. The money envelope waved, waiting for Jeremy to answer him back some ways.

"No, sir, Cap'n" Jeremy said, "I purely do not expect it, Mr. StDenis. I sure was a fuckin' mess, this trip."

It was the Captain then, not expecting Robideaux to be so easy about it all, who stood back shuffling. "Now Robideaux. You, there…" Captain said, "*got* to get yourself shut." Then he stopped saying.

Jeremy figured Captain was thinking about what it was Robideaux had to shut himself from.

"You get youseff shut of dem *woman* problems, Robideaux, you pure must," Captain said. "Damn," he added. "You get youseff right 'fore you come back to woik my river, y'heah?"

Then, like that, he gave Robideaux his money.

Women problems? Well, who didn't have women problems, he was a man, man problems if he was a woman? People were such a fucking bore, people were. Jeremy's laugh nearly seeped from Robideaux's hung-down head. Robideaux was near jumping, near yelling, *"No, sir, no sir. Ain't women's. Got me a bad spirit what took me down in Cairo, trying to stick me in some dark place where there ain't no God A'mighty, and is gone ride me till he wear me out, toss me aside like a wore-down boot. It ain't me, Captain, it surely ain't me, I pays attention, my woik."*

Which he never said; Jeremy gripped Robideaux and made him take his dressing like a man. Then, reluctant, like he didn't for real deserve his pay, Jeremy took the envelope. "Yessir, I hear you, Cap StDenis," Jeremy said. "No mess of a man need work your tow, Cap." Jeremy threw Robideaux's truck-sack over one shoulder, hung his old lady guitar from the other and headed, sad and slow for looks, toward the city.

Captain StDenis yelled down over the dockside's banging cranes and growling donkey engines, "Y'get yourself right, now, y'hear? Get y'self right and we glad to hev you back 'nuder trip."

Jeremy smiled and nodded.

"'Sides, Preach', we used to dem songs you been making since Illin-wa."

"Yassir, Captain," Jeremy hollered out, deep day washing up his nose from town. Then: "Cap'n, oh Cap'n, one more ting."

He waited till everyone had turned for listening. "Fuck y'all to a fare-thee-well. You, your boat, all who work the boat, all the boats that work the river you float on, the world you crawl across and the God that grinds you up like the meat you truly are. Fuck you each and every one." A whimper squeaked out Robideaux's nose. "'Kay, Cap?" Jeremy added. A tear rolled down a valley of Robideaux's cheek. Jeremy threw a smile, tossed a wave. The captain and the men stood round-eyed. Swede Lewis most of all. And Jeremy was gone. *Some fun* in sweet-home tonight.

Two things, now. One, even after humiliation, his bridges smoking ruins, Robideaux was home, and two, Jeremy had no idea where the fuck he's at. The river was small. On the tow, everyone knew this Robideaux Jeremy walked in. Jeremy was Robideaux, who tended cable and held the barge together, big dumb preaching man as got himself drunk in every lowdown the whole Mississippi way. Being him, there? Easy.

In the big world, now, he was just another laid-off, paid-off river man with a guitar, come down for a dirty time, catching at Mardi Gras.

Robideaux was kicking. Jeremy hadn't traveled anyone, man or woman, with so much thrash in him, not in half a thousand year maybe he hadn't. Took some fight to make those big feet go where Jeremy wanted. Other side of that was, Jeremy didn't have any particular place he wanted. If Robideaux eased north, though, Jeremy figured, he ought to bear south. Pain in the ass that was, but there 'twas. Oh, yes, he'd have to hurt this Robideaux.

By and by, walking got easier.

"Give up?" Jeremy asked.

Silence.

"Robideaux?" he said.

Nothing.

With walking, walking got easier. The warm wet town carried blood heat. A million men, a million women gathered, bumped, shoved, jiggling, to have each other in screaming carnal ways. One good long juicy hump, *Whooo-eee*, that was JUST what it was, coming. Good times in a good place.

Might be this Robideaux was not a young man, but he was, for sure-enough, a man and Jeremy strutted him on the *Vieux Carre*. "Thank you, Robideaux," he sang out, jostled by a passing wave of flesh and sweet eyes flashing him and his old lady guitar. Flesh everywhere. The stinky places between a million legs breathed in with a swish, exhaled musk and magic. Each bumped another, going, coming, rushing here or, sweated for the night, waited to rub a stranger there. Each rub gave a little hint, a glistening sniff of what might be had, might be—later, sometime later—but tonight for sure.

Good time, this. And this wasn't even it, not yet, not at all. Yet this was good. For a Traveler, this town, this time? Bring it *on*. Jeremy could about use up this Robideaux in one grand night, easy to find heart and legs and eyes in some other man or woman in the swollen silence Robideaux knew would come by magic after Lenten midnight swept the town, amen.

Crushing bodies carried him through narrow ways. The breath from every peeling building smelled...

...Jeremy pulled heavy through Preach's nose...

...of old mold and plaster, bugs and iron, like cellar damp and niter-frost, of sweat and a seven-night-stained bed. A reek of old times, when the world was hungry, sharp and bloody, filled him at every breath.

The smell, too, was a smothering wash of spice, not half a bad smell.

Sky was scarce on the narrow streets, a slice of late day blue, steeping in sundown red. Iron balconies trailing shadows set off the color. Above them, pretty twilight hid the big black, deep forever tarted up for fun. Music slapped him ever which-way as evening settled over the Quarter. Tunes thumped ahead, behind, or came down through louvered shutters from tall bright rooms above the street. The noise was tin, tingle, and rumble, distant booms and screeching toots and brashes. The guitar hummed at his back, now. She wanted out. Wouldn't be hard, finding a place to let her wood and steel go loose.

He went into a place. Set down, had bourbon whiskey. A few minutes and someone asked, *Can you play that thing, or's it just deadwood there?*

"Deadwood, sir?" he said, not understanding. "Deadwood, this?" he said, petted the wrapped guitar. "Why, she a breathing thing."

Yah, but can you play it?

"Mostly she play me," he said. "Heyaw, yaw, yaw..." Then he played, his eyes gone knives. Eight bars made him a star. A couple numbers, he was famous. When he left an hour later he was a legend, a drug they'd never tingle to again, not there.

An easy town and easy times, and Jeremy was feeling— Robideaux was feeling—heavy 'round the groin. Oh, yes.

Dark had deepened while he'd played. Shooting crackers let a stink of spark and powder now. Beads filled the air, spinning. Rings and coconut flashed. A throb tingled him from Robideaux's feet to behind his neck. It wanted. He wanted. Bodies pressed him, each a life, a story, a world to go to and be in. He yearned to reach and be them.

But he was tongue hungry. The bouquet of roiling oil and flaming spice breathed on him from a dozen places, this street, that street. Behind wide doors and tall windows, wood fan blades shoved the boiled perfume of crawdad and hot boudin to him. Red bean juice and andouille filled the air. *Hmmm-mmm...* Time to feed this Robideaux corpse. Jeremy turned on a whim, rode the notion through a door, like *that. Daddy Boil's.* Old Mother Guitar mumbled at his back; must have liked the joint.

Daddy Boil's was nearly full, not quite. Nobody paid note as he slipped Robideaux into an ass-warmed chair beside the stage next to the john door by the far wall. A flow of bodies flashed in and out, looking, yelling, catching one another, leaving someone, then banging back to the street and the party roaring out, beyond. Jeremy settled him back among stomachs, groins, and legs. For a while nobody cared that Robideaux waited to feed.

At the bar, backs and elbows. At the far end, a round and shiny church lady poured ass over both sides of her stool. An old whore, waiting. She never turned but her eyes glowed white in the mirror, other side of the bar. She stared into her own darkness and sipped tea, listening.

A good place to start, *Daddy Boil's*, yessir.

By and by came a pretty girl covered in sweat and pissed at him—the particular him of Robideaux. "You play that thing now, Preach'?" she shouted over the beating juke.

"Yuh-huh," he said. He was known. Robideaux had tricked him here. He smiled the man's pretty best. "I surely do." Jeremy's Robideaux eyes drank the girl, so obvious.

"Since when you take that up?" she yelled. "Give up the preaching now, old man?"

"Since always is when," he yelled back. He unwrapped the guitar, loving the touch even with Robideaux's hands. "Since the Trojan War and long before." The strings hummed when the cover-cloth brushed them, sliding off. In light, the living blaze of the wood pulsed in the heart of its grain. "She proud, huh?" Jeremy wiped the strings and looked up and down the woman. "An' I ain't showing you no old man, li'l girl."

A run of firecrackers prattled in the street. Robideaux's left hand pricked the frets; thick black fingers flicked the steel strings. The guitar matched the night's song, just a chuckle—enough to show this pretty piece of woman that "old man" Robideaux was the for-sure goods. "See you, there?" he said. He didn't even tingle with that pitiful effort, music to a firework night. "Nothing to that. And I don't give up no preachin' neither, now, you see?" His right hand axed out five church chords, loud. Heads turned. "Still sermonizing. Taking my text from *Mardi nuit*." He resolved the church he'd conjured in the air, let it dissolve to cathouse buttermilk. God-chords pumping a fine wet fuck. *Whoo-hoo...* the crowd laughed. Some crossed themselves with a shiver. The tea-drinking lady turned her blind face to him, cocked her head.

Jeremy smiled Robideaux's big eyes at the sweet sweated girl by his table.

"So then," she shifted her hip and looked at Robideaux's hands, "suppose you'll be wanting to make arrangements? Pay your drinks with playing, now? An' if that, well then that's a thing you gotta take up with Daddy Boil and Daddy Boil ain't here, so there."

Jeremy had already fished down his pocket and grabbed the envelope of money. "I pay," he fanned the bills across the table, "American folding. I play when I want and not for nothing, neither, girl."

She ran to bring a mess of food, trailing smiles and the fine perfume of sweat and laig. When she lay down his plates, she hovered to admire Robideaux's way with food and those big hands working. *She's thinking,* Jeremy knew. So, too, was Robideaux. That much he knew.

Daddy Boil came, trailing a hail of calls and the spit of shootin' cracker. The street gave him up with a grudge and Daddy filled the door. Then he stopped, sniffing like with a smell of something old, long-gone but real familiar. Then Daddy squeezed through and ate the oldness right out the room, filled it with his own self, then some. "Where dat man? Where is dat one?" Daddy shouted. "Where is dat Jeremy?" he called, head rising from his neck like a fat black cobra.

Onstage, Jeremy was snugged down and riffing, stroking the neck of the guitar. All for himself, but the room was in love.

Daddy's voice took the room, Jeremy with it—who tingled at his name, his by fuck real name of Jeremy, who no one in this room, in this *town*, should know. No one anywhere should see him, Jeremy, wearing Robideaux like a skin-suit, *no one but oh fuck, another Traveler.*

Then Jeremy looked and saw *old Father Goddamn, himself.* Jeremy, for-real pickled. "Aw, fuck," he said aloud. Daddy boomed so no one heard. Bodies made a wake around him, saying "Where yat?" or "What the hell, nigger!" Then, quickly, "Goddamn sorry, Daddy Boil," or, "Shit, Daddy, din't know 'twas you," voices sorry to be alive in the place Daddy Boil wanted to be.

But shoving toward the stage, Daddy was in no mood for mad. Inch-thick fingers wagged gold. Beads and poppits snaked around his arms and neck. He smiled white and gold; purple, yellow, and green rainbows, baubles and sweat sprayed as he threw to the crowd.

Jeremy squatted inside Robideaux, watching the unlikely approach of another Traveler.

The big head rumbled deep laughter, "*Ho, ho, HO,*" and, "*Ha, ha, HAAA.*" It called, "*Heya, heya, HEYA,* you got yousef kotched, for sure you did, Jeremy Fuck-face. Let yousef be traveled, you yousef, trying to travel *him…*" Daddy pointed at the Robideaux Jeremy wore. "Preach' there traveling *you* all the way to Fat Tuesday and some Gumbo *Gris-Gris* for to salt your tail like some garden slug. Ho, the Big Dark be hungry for you, Fucked-faced Jeremy."

"Goddamn," Jeremy said by way of greeting.

"Ay-yez," Daddy yelled to the crowd, "you hear dis? The Queen of the Iris's tossed out her t'ree carat diamon' ring wit' her poils, Sattiday past, an' nobody ain' find it yet since. Riotin' in the streets ovah deah, y'heah?"

Jeremy's music was forgotten in the suck of bodies chasing three-carat riches through the door.

Daddy Boil turned to Jeremy. "Ain't no ring been toss'd, but it one good rumor, huh?" Close and personal, Father Goddamn's Daddy-voice sounded like a millwheel. His head shook with the joy of it.

The laugh became a steel smile.

"Been a time, Goddamn," Jeremy said.

"Has indeed," Daddy nodded. "A decade? No, I lie. Two."

"Ireland," Jeremy said.

"The Lebanon," Daddy winked, "but who's arguing? Lemme hear some of that good old stuff, Master Fuck-face. Gimme that old minstrel lay from the foist Crusade, what say?"

Jeremy obliged the old, old creature inside Daddy Boil. The guitar wailed for Father Goddamn and the few slouchers, too drunk—and the church lady, too blind—to go hunt diamond rumors in the streets. They heard the music of the Elder World, a ghost's prayer, cried in a tongue common two thousand years gone, words called out in market cities along the eastern trades, or spoken in places where desert waves broke against sandstone gates, or whispered across campfires when frigid night breathed *wolf* from dark forests.

The drunks turned to squint. The Church lady sipped. Jeremy finished.

"Maire Laveau," Daddy Boil called. His voice loosed dust from the ceiling tin. "Maire Laveau," he said when the pretty lady came running, "you forgive this po' dumb preachah man his bill of fare for the night, y'heah?"

"Paid," Jeremy said.

"True it is, Daddy," Maire Laveau said.

"Huh," Daddy said. "Well that I owe, you providing free entertain' an' all." The Daddy smile slipped from behind old

Father Goddamn's knife-edge grin. "Come with me Jeremy, and we'll have a drink. The old stuff. Upstair."

Through the kitchen, where lean, tired men lolled after the crowd's quick departure, cigarettes dangling long ashes. When Daddy steered Jeremy through their sweat and smoke, they twitched, being busy, but the big man paid no heed. Then, up a spice-soaked stair, round a dark corner and up another few treads to a room.

The room was high and wide. To Jeremy, it was cramped. Room enough for Father Goddamn and his furniture. Robideaux and the guitar squeezed in behind.

Daddy lit a candle and poured two pulls of thick green liquor. "Play s'more of that sweet old stuff," he said over the noise from the street. "Let me to more'a that Jeremy noise." Daddy laughed again.

The bitter essence of old time rose from the liquor; the scent of wormwood filled Jeremy's heart.

"Oh, Daddy Boil…" Robideaux started. Jeremy shut him out of it. "What're you fucking doing here, Goddamn?" he said.

"What am I doing?" Goddamn slipped from behind the Daddy Boil face. He spilled a touch of the Red to Jeremy's drink. It spun clear in the glass. "Same's you, Vatachela. Traveling."

Jeremy bristled. Long years since he'd heard his old name. He sipped. The bitter touch of worm' made him tingle, numb and alive together. "High-profile traveling. You settled like a citizen, living big."

A touch of Daddy edged his voice. "Comforts and joys, Vatachela." He poured another slop of absinthe and laced it Red. "Been the Daddy Boil here, near ten years, J-boid. Since the Lebanon, I think." The fat man sat back. Watered silk cushions lapped him like a loving tongue. "Comfort. Joy. The way you taste time, feel its flow." He sipped. "You understand? No you don't," he added without a pause.

Tight-stretched, Jeremy stood in the center of the room. He held his guitar by her neck.

"An' han't it been a time?" Daddy said. "Tell you, this the fines' city in this half-round woild." Goddamn sipped. "An' you? You criss-crossin' de oith? On the bum. Hoppin' into one, eatin' up another? And now..." Daddy Boil laughed again. "All that bumming and hopping and you ain't loined nuddn'. And now you gets dragged here by dat... dat *Robideaux.*" He leaned forward and spat the name ahead of his laugh. "Robideaux taking you to conjure the Jeremy out of him; he going to shove you inter the big Dark for the long Forever." He sat back. "Thought you'd like to know."

Jeremy tingled. "You warning me, Goddamn? You love me same's I have respeck' for you." He sucked green, poured another. "You just another eater of flesh."

"Mebbe absinthe makes the heart grow fonder, Jayboid," Goddamn said. Another *ho ho ho* filled the room. "You got respeck' for no one and no thing," he said, the cushions sagged around him. "Trouble Jeremy, trouble is. Nothing make you love. You travel, you go nowhere. Don't live the life you have, don't use the lives you take." Then there was Daddy Boil again. "And you gots yourself a pickle now, nigger; cotched holt a mans as wants to live, a mans as believes in his heart all the magics of the woild he given."

Fireworks crackled. A wind carried a whiff of flesh, old food and fresh night. Jeremy felt the stars above burn through smoke and scent. He heard the old Earth grinding on its axis. Daddy smiled through sweat and rolling skin, his eyes creased all way back to his hair. "And that living man's gonna blow you the fuck outta him and t'row you de hell off this oith." Daddy's eyes narrowed, laughing. "I'd feel sorry for you Jeremy, I purely would, if you was woith it. But you..." He looked up and down Jeremy.

Father Goddamn's heart tickled like a bug every which way over him.

"...you jess a small thing," Goddamn said, "been aroun' a couple dozen thousand year and soon be gone, 'fore anyone knows you was even heah, none carin' that you left." The smile drained to nothing. "Won't remember you, myself, Vatachela."

The absinthe was body-warm in his mouth. "We see," Jeremy said, smiling Robideaux's lips. He backed toward the door. "We see."

Daddy Boil stood, filled the room. Outside, the night blew steam. "Will miss your music, though."

In a second, Jeremy was in the dusty hall, heading for the dark. Daddy's voice followed. "Hey Robideaux, you hear?"

Jeremy, on the steps down, gripping the guitar by her neck...

"You get shut of that old Traveler man inside you, Robideaux, and come back to Daddy Boil's, y'heah?" The voice shook the walls.

Jeremy, in the moldy stairwell, then running through the bright hot kitchen...

"Come back alone, I get you fed, drunk and laid. *Ho, ho, ho*, you hear? All on me."

Goddamn's voice shook the building. The cooks looked up. A dozen eyes covered him. An ash hissed into the roux.

Jeremy, out the back and up the alley...

"Come back alone, an' I'll sure take care of you, Robideaux. You know Daddy Boil pays for nuffin' he doan gotsta, but I figure: this, he gotsta." Father Goddamn's laugh followed over Mardi Gras.

The old town wrapped Jeremy. The sidewalk bucked like the tow in the chops of a wake. Some places, rain and centuries had worn all away leaving the old, old dirt of the Earth.

Daddy's voice gone, Robideaux commenced shouting. "Help
me! Help me!" He called to the masked world reveling around
them. The world laughed.

Jeremy dashed into a wall. "Take that!" he whispered to
Robideaux. Blood ran down his face.

"Help me, Lord!" the man called and tried to run them to a
line of dancing men.

"Show us your tits!" Jeremy called to the men.

They laughed and did!

For a thin moment Jeremy felt the urge to ditch this body,
leap into a dancing man. *No, Goddamn it.* He did not, would not,
no.

They ran.

Now, as before, Robideaux hauled left when Jeremy heaved
right; Robideaux urged full ahead, Jeremy spun 'round, turned
back.

Half a short block from the blinking blue emergency light,
Jean Louis's Charity Hospital, he snatched them shy of the glow
that washed down from the cross above the old wing.

Then Jeremy, off into the dark streets beyond where…

Robideaux ran them to a mounted cop leaning in his saddle
like *The Thinker.*

"Devil got me!" Robideaux shouted. "Ho, ho, ho!" Jeremy
added to Robideaux's scream, cry-eyes flashing.

"Ho, ho to you, too, sir," the cop said. The horse farted.
"Wanna keep movin'?" cop said. "Sir," he added and waved
Robideaux on.

Jeremy heard *fucked up nigger*, beat unspoken in the cop's
heart.

"Thank you, sir, thank you muchly," Jeremy said, Robideaux
gibbering. "I be one fucked up nigger, I sure do, sir. Surprised
you don't just whomp me upside my haid."

Jeremy stumbled them down the way, chuckling, sobbing, running, walking. The dark way widened to gaping holes between old buildings. The buildings soon dissolved leaving flat earth and ruins, broken brick and glass, either side of the broken street. Here and there a building. Mostly, though, empty stretched to the distance, the distance vanished into silent night. Robideaux took breath in this place. He sobbed. Jeremy let the man have his cry, fed on it.

"I runs to the Rock..." Robideaux blubbered.

"Rock doesn't hide you." Jeremy's song bounced across night silence in the dead city. Jeremy grabbed Robideaux, shoved the man's face, their face, to the black glass front of a boarded bar. *Baby Doll,* the sign said. Robideaux's face pressed *Baby Doll*'s window.

"Now you're gone stop. We gone stop."

In a minute Robideaux's breath settled. Ahead a squat silhouette loomed against a few milky stars. Two bell towers, either side of the building. The roof between them sagged.

"That a church, Robideaux?" Jeremy said. Robideaux's heart tingled. *Sanctuary,* the tingle said. "You taking me to church, old man?"

Robideaux, he said nothing.

"You want church?"

Robideaux said nothing.

"We'll go church, then."

The shadow of the place loomed then swallowed them in stone and damp ruin. The doorway was a black opening. Inside, the smell was old smoke and mold. Arched vaults let into the walls, one row atop another, flanked the narthex. The empty chambers glowed green with phosphorescent moss. White niter gathered like colonies of coral.

"*Bad gothic,*" Jeremy said. "Never liked the mode. Heavy, dull. Dead now, gothic. This 'bout as dead a place as you'll find,"

Jeremy whispered then let silence hover. "I do believe this was a cemetery. Am I right, Robideaux? I disbelieve old man God's at home. Not even the dead left here. Gone with the wind. Sure this the church you want?"

Robideaux's body chattered as it had in the chill night of Cairo. Soft stars ruled the air and the broken land surrounding. Creepers cascaded the walls. In summer sun the place would have been a torrent of goldenrod in a mist of fronds. Now, the vines were tense and dark. Small things crawled within. Dry leaves quivered with living shadow: rat, possum, snapping palmetto. Life crackled winter dry vines under starlight and in deathglow from the vaults.

"Stop in a spell? Do our Stations, be on our way? Do a murder, shall we? Shall we do worse?" Jeremy walked Robideaux into the nave. Passing, the vaults breathed old death. Glass crushed under the big man's feet; wisteria curled his ankles. "There are things can be done, you cannot dream of doing, old man. The ways of life, the how of death. Such fun. Such fun."

Deep inside, still air hung. Starshine sifted between roofbeams. "Chatter, chatter, chatter," Jeremy whispered to the rustling walls and Stations of the Cross. "Chatter, chatter."

They stood by the broken face of a blooded Christ. "Oh, God!" both shouted to the swallowing empty.

Nothing returned but the rustle of creepers and an old scent of herb and distant flame.

"I'll have my time with you," Jeremy whispered. "Think haunts and bugs fright me?" Jeremy whispered. "Send me off in a sniff of incense and the breath of long-gone priest?"

Robideaux cried tears.

"Maybe the devil," Jeremy whispered. "May he be scared of saints and holy places? Maybe the devil is. I ain't."

Robideaux, to his knees.

"Might as well give up, br'er Robideaux," Jeremy said. "It's just death."

Tears flowed warm across Robideaux's cheeks.

"Just flesh, old man. Life letting go and you not in charge," Jeremy whispered low. "The common tragedy. I can give you one great way to go and no mistake. Even God can't get you for it, 'cause it's me wearing you. You end. Then you go..." Jeremy pointed to the starry above. "Go clean to reward eternal."

Robideaux and Jeremy sucked long breath, snuffled salt snot.

"Unless I give you," Jeremy whispered to Robideaux, "at the very last, a taste of some dark something. Something you truly, truly want... a taste of the best sin you can think of. Now what might that one thing be, Mister Robideaux? That one thing will kill your soul forever? Hmm?"

"Two-Bit!" Robideaux called out. "Two-Bit Suze!" he called again. Past the altar, a door opened. From the dark came a flicker, a shape, a rattle of stones. "I take you to a place, Brah Jeremy," Robideaux said deep in hard misery.

The shape croaked, "I hear you, Robideaux." The light exhaled a power of stink. The scent caught Robideaux.

"Aw, fuck," Jeremy said and down they fell, winked out before Robideaux hit ground with his face, *splash*, on the chill church floor.

Jeremy felt Robideaux's blood pounding against the bindings.

The church lady looked inside Robideaux with milk-blind eyes. "Oh," she said, caught a glimpse, Jeremy dodging through caves of Robideaux-meat. She crittered down Robideaux's eyes, past the bloodshot; she jerked down his optic nerve and to the deeps. Past all flesh, there was Jeremy.

"Who you?" She padded 'round. "Who you?" she said, touching with the liberty of the blind. Robideaux, tied to the old lady's stinking bed, the whole place foul with her body and dead

church. Somewhere near, flame licked the ceiling. From its heat came bad old scents, herbs he hadn't breathed in half a thousand years mixed with words, the dusty ashes of nuns, priests, and sinners tumbled together with words. "Who YOU?" the mama Gris-Gris shouted, shaking all of Robideaux.

"Easy, lady. Fuck!" Jeremy said aloud.

Old Suze took back at his word. "Robideaux's a man not used to language." She sniffed, looked deeper, walked round the Preacher—inside and out—feeling for the limits of the traveling critter inside the man.

She smiled, toothless but for one long chopper in front. "Why, you nuffin' down dere, you." She leaned back and laughed. "I seen dead mans walking with spirit, but you? *Hoo...*" Her breasts rocked, laughing. "You hain't got *that* much life in you," fingers, a teeny way parted. "You some old thing, never lived at all."

"I'll show you life power!" Jeremy called. He shoved the bindings to their limit. He oozed from Robideaux's eyes, a lightning flicker snatching at the old lady.

She dodged, slippery like a filly girl. The rush of her made Jeremy hurt with its flicker-flicker. Back into the meat of Robideaux he went...

Who flopped, *whomp*, on his back.

"Power?" She leaned over, showing blind white eyes. Her chuckles breathed foul down Robideaux's nose...

Who sucked her in before Jeremy could stop him.

Mamalous's breath hit Jeremy like desert wind. Sand and ice abraded him to the heart. The taint of her kicked, blew him sideways, whichways. "Power?" the old lady shrieked. "You got what stren'th this man's got is all. You got what you wearing, you."

Jeremy thrashed.

Two-Bit Suze allowed it. Finally, she looked down. "Who you be ridin' this fine mans? Who you, wearing him down to nuffin, huh? Who you at ALL?"

"Fuck you, lady," Jeremy said. He strained Robideaux's tethers. He rose a bit, danced a sweated moment in the fire's flickerlight, Robideaux's dick flapping, balls flopping. Then, "Aw fuck you," and he lay still. Smoke from the dark, pot steam filled Robideaux. Half offal, half like coming home to rest, it was. Half like death and half like juice and whorehouse sweat.

"Fuck you and this body, too!" he shouted at the limit of Robideaux's fine baritone. From nearby, the old guitar buzzed in sympathy.

Nude, the old woman was not beautiful. In firelight, her parts and places danced too alive, too much; too much, flesh and sinew. Soft canyons opened, shut. Runneled flesh rolled in oiled waves. Not beautiful, but she was life—the human end of life. She leaned over Robideaux. "Oncet I was a fragrant joy." She smiled. Her smile gave Jeremy leave to touch.

He did not.

"Oncet this was wonder, delight measured out to all who had the price." Her smile deepened. "No longer, you old spider thing?"

Jeremy shoved Robideaux against the bonds. The bonds held. Jeremy prayed, "I've been alive a dozen thousand years and more. I've been everywhere, done everything."

"An' now, gots nowhere to go. Your limit's this Robideaux." Two-Bit Suze's flesh rose and fell. Her breath filled Robideaux. She stared deep, blind, no care Jeremy rode there, below Robideaux's eyeballs, ready to spring.

"Robideaux," she whispered in the man's ear. "Gone to cut you, now, open a vein. In a little bit you bleed to death, you hear?"

Despite Jeremy, Robideaux nodded. His voice came through tears. "Hear."

"Life'll flow 'way, Robideaux. When it does, you be daid and so that old spider thing inside. You hear me, now?"

He nodded.

She held a razor to the firelight. "It just be a nick and won't even hurt. There."

He felt the chill cut. He felt the warm as blood flowed. He heard a soft pour running from Robideaux, caught in a bowl by Suze. Suze's blind eyes pressed down, her scouring breath.

"Want me, critter? Come for me."

He could not. Couldn't find his way into her blindness, into her herbs and the words of knowledge.

"Cain't catch me, y'old daid thing," Suze whispered, "you got nuffin left." Then to the man, "Still here, Robideaux?" she called.

"Hyere," he whispered.

"Spider? Of life, you empty. You nothin' at the bone. You hunger for somewhere else, wanna be someone other. Thas what lets you grab and go walking 'round. All you gots leff is the empty. Now we waits," she said. She settled squat astride Robideaux. "We waits your death."

Jeremy flickered in the cold wind of forever. Darkness waited in the hole, below, in Robideaux's mortal guts. It opened like a drain and spinning there, the universe, big, dark and always.

Robideaux spoke. "On the tow, Jeremy," he said, "flashing threads? Spiders they was. Bitty spiders and that wide river to cross. What they done, they done. Climbed a tree, each and ever one. Spun theyselves a thread, let it fly like a sail. And when the wind was right and persistent, they lets go their perch. You take you text there, brah' Jeremy. Find you that persistent wind, brah' Jeremy, an leggo. Let go."

Jeremy felt the man's soul widen to the size of the big bright river in the gold old sun and blue, blue sky. The two of them,

Two-Bit Suze and Robideaux, were singing a storm and weather blew and blew. Oh, Jeremy hung, hung on for life, for dear eternal life he knew was his, he hung tight, looking, not finding, a home anywhere round.

Then he did. Saw a place. *The* place. He picked his place, then, remembering the spiders on the river air and hoping they knew what-the-fuck, Jeremy let go.

Not alive, not exactly. Wasn't warm, it wasn't cold. Tight it was and there was something. Familiar. A sound, but without ears he felt the sound everywhere that was he. Jeremy recognized the sound. It was his sound, his voice, a hollow buzz. It hummed a hundred years and more. The life here all around him was the life, the lives, he'd given this worn wood and varnish, glue and steel. All around a billion cells, old, dry, once living cells, the hollow wood of an old, old tree, cut, shaped, formed and carried. Played. Played and maybe loved…

Old Father Goddamn, still traveling Daddy Boil, leaned at the glass. The big man stared, then laughed.

Robideaux stood next to him, fine again, alive.

"Tole you, Daddy," Robideaux said. "Told you dere he was."

"You told me and dar he is," Daddy said. "Dar he is."

Jeremy heard. Not with ears. Vibration washed, made him quiver like pond-ripple. The laugh lapped Jeremy, warm and chill. Jeremy buzzed in Goddamn's laugh. He conjured it in his heart, the Jeremy heart, translated it to: "Haw, Haw, HAW."

Jeremy tasted dust, light and…

Daddy Boil lifted, turned him 'round by the neck. His strings sang dissonant with Father Goddamn's touch.

Daddy's face peered down the big old hole in Jeremy's belly. "An I thinkin' you was gone from de oith." Daddy's voice rang him. "Well, you mebbe loin sum'in from dis all, Jeremy Fuck

Face?" Daddy's voice touched Jeremy's body, Jeremy hummed with it.

The face was gone.

"Want to play him, Robideaux?"

"No sir, Daddy, I pure do not."

"Aw, go 'head. He played you right fine. He sure can't hurt you now, locked in wood…"

"No sir, Daddy, please. I want no more to do."

Daddy again: "Well, mebbe I should buy dis my own damn self," Daddy said to the clerk. "Buy and keep it locked somewhere, someplace, a long time."

Daddy turned the old guitar around, ran his hands over the grain. "Naw," he said, handing it, gentle, back to the clerk. "Onliest mans I know can play such a fine thing as this here old piece of woik, ain't in a strumming state right now. You keep it. Some soul bound to come 'long and 'preciate what 'tis."

Daddy watched the clerk return the old guitar to the high glass closet where dust lay settled.

"Fine instrument," the clerk said. "A hundred-thirty, hundred-fifty years old."

"You keep him safe," Daddy told the clerk. "I pay you and you don't show him to nobody. Nobody but what loves the music can be made on such a wonder. Someone who loves, y'heah dat?"

"Yes, sir. Someone who loves."

Daddy peeled money bills from a roll. "Yes sir. This old man guitar be oining his traveling, next time." He said that to the clerk. To Jeremy, he said, "Yes, sir. You woik for your traveling, next time, y'heah?"

CORDWELL'S BOOK

What I write of my experiences I swear is the truth. The rest? I don't know. John Cordwell loved a story and, "A story," he always said, "is best told tinkered, sar. Yes sar. Tinkered."

I write that and I hear John in his "Seventh Earl of Muffington" voice. John was not an Earl and there is no Muffington except in a foul tale or two, but being both *very* British and not-an-earl-of-anything was also part of the Book of Cordwell, that special creation, his life. His tale, a thing he tinkered all the time. Not lying, you understand, simply enhancing the experience of being John Cordwell for the credulous unenlightened.

Tinkering.

All right. The Red Lion is a bar. A pub on Lincoln Avenue, Chicago. A red pin in the map of my life. I've gone steady with the place since I moved here from the east in the '70s of the last century, already a theater-head, a director, looking for work. In those years, Lincoln Avenue was a respectably seedy diagonal slant of Northside real estate, bars, booksellers, coffee shops, folk joints and blues clubs, edgy record shops, the places that gathered the shuffling, the sweaty, the hip, and the giggly, the black-eyed pop-girls with shy smiles and belly button bangles and those who fed on them all.

And theaters. Lincoln Avenue cut through what then was America's theater wonderland: Steppenwolf, the Organic, St. Nicholas, Body Politic, Victory Garden. That was the heyday, the high-water mark and Holy Golden Age of brash theatrical life and blood that was Chicago, alas. Alas, Chicago.

The area also had a reputation for the weird.

Across from the Lion is the Biograph Theater. In 1934, Gentleman Johnny—John Dillinger—spent the last two of his earthly hours-given watching *Manhattan Melodrama* at the Biograph. Then he and his Lady in Red walked onto Lincoln, into Chicago night, and was blown into history by G-Man Melvin Purvis. It is said when the wind swirls from the west to make the shadows moan, Dillinger still loiters on the Avenue by the brick wall at the alley where he fell, a scent of the Indiana fields on which he grew up, rising, drifting.

Well, I don't believe in ghosts. *Didn't.*

Then, the Red Lion Pub was bright white and rose red, two-and-a-half stories and a peaked roof. Built a few years after the Great Fire, the Lion is flammable as a soul. Defiantly wooden, the place droops. It would sag southward or lean to the north if not flanked by a pair of solidly respectable redbrick businesses. A new generation has recently painted the Lion an indefensible black and white at which John might have snorted and called the design "a damn Nelsonian checkerboard."

The year I came to town, the Lion was a natural watering hole for theater creatures such as I whom, you see, require large quantities of nightly beer and daily approval. The Lion offered both.

Inside, it's two floors of nooks, small rooms, and shadowy coves where smoke hangs and dreams are smelted, shaped, and blessedly forgotten. It is a place of low ceilings where narrow footpaths between stools and tables breeds cautious intimacy—and requires social agility and grace to match.

The publican, John Cordwell, was…

No. The temptation is strong, but I'll not say he was Falstaffian—though John Cordwell had charms in common with that *other* John, Sir John. Cordwell was a big man, stood well above 5-foot-4 and almost as much across. Like Sir John of the *Henrys*, Cordwell had been, in his time, a warrior—a pain in the ass to those he fought and those he served—an artisan, a lover, a teacher, a wise man, a rogue. He loved big things and beautiful women. He loved to shape lives and bring people together. He loved drink and art and words and buildings.

Buildings, yes. He'd been involved in what he called the "last formal unpleasantry with the Hun." As a prisoner of war, he escaped frequently and was captured frequently. As a result, he'd made a grand tour of Europe, trucked from one Nazi chateau to another, one escape-proof camp to the next. One of these Boche-sponsored road trips took him through Dresden. Though he saw it between the slats of a cattle lorry, Cordwell fell in love with the Rococo marvel and stone filigrees of that magical city, thought it quite the most beautiful manmade place on earth.

A few hours after his departure the place was pounded to rubble—his chaps, the RAF, at night and the American 8th Air Force by daylight.

Like most British families, the Cordwells had been touched by war throughout the century. His grandfather was wounded at Gallipoli in the first round of incivility with the Hun. Two great uncles were killed at Paschendale during one of the battles of the Somme.

John's brother was a London cab driver during the Blitz.

"The Blitz. The Blitz." John stared somewhere between the ceiling and his top-shelf Irish. "What we found of him was a metal button from his jacket."

In those days, to fly, to be given a plane and command, one had to be an officer. To become an officer, one had to be a gentleman. At least one had to be passed for a gentleman by an RAF Board of Review. Other officers. Gentlemen all. Cordwell, you understand, was not a gentleman, not to the manor born. But Cordwell was also determined to fly.

At his interview, he out-fustianed the board. When asked what he might like to fly—*if* he were allowed to fly—Cordwell replied without hesitation, mustache aquiver, "Oh, bombers, sir, no question of it, heavy bombers! Hit the Hun where it hurts. Get the bally war over quick as that, what?"

"Wizard, Cordwell," the inspector said, "jolly good. Take a letter, Miss Wren: 'Dear Adolph, might as well surrender now, Cordwell's flying heavy bombers.'"

"Now that," John said years later in the pub he'd made on Lincoln Avenue, "*that* was Theatre!"

John survived the enemy, his own officers. He survived the theater of war, emerged with tales of captivity, tales of pigs as pets and being rabbits on the run. Oh it was Wizard fun and it was awful and he lived. It's what John did: he lived to tell it all.

He came home, became an architect, married an American, moved to Chicago, and built, built, built.

Then he made the Red Lion.

When I came to Chicago from the east, the Lion was a nest for a burgeoning corps of actors who fancied themselves in the Shakespearean line.

As an easterner, I considered Shakespeare—the classics, in general—to be my province, a place where practical stagecraft merged with scholarship. You see, I *like* the stuff, don't feel it needs improvement.

Midwestern Shakespeareans seemed all headbash and rock and roll. For them, it seemed less performance, more like day labor in an abattoir.

Okay, shut up, Larry. The point is, I wasn't expecting much when I caught the first preview of *The Tempest*, the premiere work of a group calling itself "Will's Jolly Crew," performances under the stars, on the Red Lion's roof garden, beneath the spreading arms of Cordwell's ancient oak.

A word: this "ancient oak." It is not so ancient and definitely not an oak. A city weed tree, the thing grows in the crack between the pub and another building. When it reaches the roof garden, though, the thing does seem to have come magically up through the Lion. The trunk writhes and twines to spread a leafy canopy across the deck outside the second-floor dining room. Very nice. From time to time, when nested birds shat upon his patrons' fish and chips, John threatened to cut it down. He never did. It remains. John was allowed his eccentricities. Anyway, he loved that tree. "Grounds the place, you know. Connects it to the world!"

I had to admit, for *Tempest*, the simple setting—night and tree—was effective. Even so, I wasn't expecting much.

The production blew me away. Simply stated, the director stepped aside and let the play sing.

It sang.

Despite the whimsical familiarity suggested by the company's name, the actors of Will's Jolly Crew knew their stuff. By the end I was in tears, weeping, in part, because the play always makes me cry. *Tempest* is Shakespeare's last script, a farewell to the worlds of magic he created over that short, extraordinary life. After this, he retires to Stratford, lives, a wealthy man, then, soon, dies. Even on the page, Prospero's final speech moves: He breaks his staff, he drowns his book then says, *"Now my charms are all o'erthrown, And what strength I have's mine own—which is most faint…"*

The other reason I was bawling: reality had hit me. These people were *good*, at least as good as I. Better, maybe. Oh, feh! It's truth: in theater, no one is happy unless A) he's on top, *and* B) his best friend is in the dumpster. These weren't my friends.

I sat. I stared at the empty playing space, at Cordwell's tree. I blunted my disappointment with a fourth pint. A moment later I noticed another audient, also still seated, also in tears. That was it for resemblance. He was an anti-me: I, young. He, not. I, tall. He, tiny. I'm… Okay, heavyset. He, not so, no not a bit. I am fully furred—haired, bearded, *et al.* He was naked as a molerat.

We sucked the dregs of Cordwell's thin bitter English beer, though, and both shed salt tears, I, for the passing of Shakespeare's magic and because the butt-end of my illusions was kicking me in the nuts. He, for whatever reasons old men sob in the night. We both stared at the stage.

The director's dad, I thought, and gathered my things. I was heading toward the aisle when, around me, the lights went out. From behind me, where the little guy still sat alone, there came a glow. The light was cold, oh so cold, and cast my shadow across the seats and among the branches of the tree. I froze. I turned.

Four pints in three hours do nothing, I repeat, do nothing to my head, heart, soul, or eyesight. They also cannot make little old men incandesce in sweet summer night.

I yelped out one of the seven or eight queeps or whimpers actors tell me I make when I suffer and hide it from them. The old guy must have heard. He jumped and gave me a look as though I were an avalanche come down upon him. "Ach!" he said and fluttered out like a candle in the wind. The scent of something smoky wafted toward me in the sudden dark.

"I do apologice for dat," he said. His accent? European. Northern. German, perhaps or somewhere east of there. He turned to the dark stage again. "Yes. For dat, I do apologice."

"No problem," I said.

"Dis iss most remarkable…" He seemed to seek just *the* word to describe the past two hours. "A most egzeptional…" Still seeking.

"Play?" I ventured.

"No. A most remarkable *Trans. Fig. U. Ration.*" He was proud of that word, savored its parts. His smile broadened at each syllable.

"'Transfiguration.' A good way to put it," I said. Humoring the gallery never hurts. "Transfiguration is what an actor does…"

I swear: he glimmered when I spoke this minor flattery. *Glimmered*, pulsed, once, twice, three times, then again, then went out.

"I dank you, so wery much," he said. His broad smile showed no teeth but something glistened in the dark of his mouth and I didn't look there again. "Dank you, greatly, but no, no. Dat? Dat shadow show? No, no. Not dat. Dat vasss…" He shrugged, squinted. "Dat vas, ah, well, delightful, but no. I mean dis…" He gestured. "Dis wholeness, I mean. Dis place…" The sweep of his arms took in the roof, the dark tree and stage, the restaurant at our backs, the Red Lion, below, it also seemed to encompass all the times I'd had there, maybe all that was to come in the dark, ahead of me down the years, down the years to…

No. All right, still, the whole place was gathered by that one gesture and stuffed into my heart.

God, would that I'd had HIM for my Minneapolis Mephistopheles *and not Rick Bloody Bolig*, I thought, *Jesus*.

He smiled, nodded as though I'd spoken what I'd only thought. "Yez?" He'd come to a decision. "You see it, too? What *Cord-vell* hass fabricated here…" He spit John's name and slobbered on it. "Ahh. Ach…" annoyance growing, "Ach, ach, ach, achachach…" His *achs* fluttered into a pizzicato back-throat growl. He finished coughing that vocal hairball and drained his pint. "I cannot see Mizter Cordvell. No, not tonight." He turned to me. "You vill. For me. You shall give him diz," he handed me a wooden box, "ding." The box was the length and a half of an index finger, two fingers wide, one deep. "You vill tell him, John

290

Cordvell, dat diz ding no longer shtands between uz. Dat ding you hold? Yez? Yez you will."

My mouth was open. I shut it then said, "I?"

"Yez. You," he said.

"I may not see John. Not see him tonight. No. I hadn't planned to."

The man had gathered his coat, umbrella, Marshall Fields bags. He walked toward the stage. "Ya, ya, ya, ya, yayayaya. You vill. You say it now, wiz me: 'Diz ding...'"

"This di—thing..."

"Wery gut. 'Diz ding,'" he pointed with his chin at the box, "'no longer shtands between uz. Hm?'"

"Yes. The thing..." I waved the box. "No longer shtands... between us. Between you and he..."

He looked at me as though I were a bright puppy. "Yez. You go now. He vill be dere. Turn 'round so you do not zee me go. Yes, go. Go on."

I did and he must have gone. The tree rustled and a cool breath crossed the back of my neck. The next thing? The L was passing a block away and I was the only one on the dark roof.

Between the deck and the bar, the little guy drained from me. It wasn't natural but the Red Lion was like that. Not natural. I mentioned it. The place has a reputation. There were stories, stories I never credited. Okay. The joint's haunted. Not that I believe that. *Believed.* All right. What I felt was that the little guy had slipped down the tree and flowed into the world. Or something. And time had shifted. That too. The first I was aware of my actual going, rooftop to bar, was when I reached the landing in the stairwell. Okay?

Oh. The stairwell. It's a funny place. On a ledge above and facing me on the landing was a wooden shield. On it is carved the face of a lion. The stairwell ceiling is twelve, fifteen feet overhead. From it a fan turned slowly, stirring the shadows.

Pictures of the Queen, other pictures, Napoleonic frigates and such, lined the wall. Shadows licked them. Dark evenings, and this was a dark evening, going up or down this stairway can be… delicate. When he opened the place, Cordwell had hung a plaque to his father's memory on the wall beneath the lion's head. It's still there. Tonight the plaque glowed in the ambient light from below and from the high window above. Father Cordwell had died years ago in London. His grave remained unmarked. John had made this place in America as a memorial to his father who had loved the life and the spirit of pubs, the communities they gathered and nourished.

The plaque opened something, so the story goes, and since that time, the Lion had gathered a reputation. It was the most haunted bar in Chicago. That was saying something. This is a haunted city.

Okay. I don't believe any of this. Didn't. The little guy was probably some Polish pal of Cordwell's from the war. I shivered and scooted to the light and warmth below.

Actors were mingling, spreading compliments, tossing off sweat, sharing loudly, feeling about, in equal measures, for return praise, a jolly put-down, the next gig.

Too sharp, those memories from my actor days. I shivered again. Tonight was a triumph for the Jolly Crew. Tomorrow and tomorrow would be the days after. This Shakespeare-upon-roof? Grand fun, yes, but also it was Equity waivers work. All for free. The rent would come due and be paid by the next McDonald's ad; the haircuts, headshots and resumes, food, beer, visits to the shrink would all be courtesy of the next chorus boy stint—"O-K-L-A-H-O-M-A" at Pheasant Run Dinner Theater, *if* they were lucky. If not? They'd be behind some bar, not belly to it.

Tonight, though, in the Lion? They ruled the world. I didn't want to stay. If the play had been a crock, I would have made nice with Prospero, Ariel, Miranda. I would have mingled, angled, wheedled, worked such wiles as I possess, gotten next to the producer, made self and *bona fides* known. I'm not a nice person. The play, alas, had not been a crock. It had been sublime. Even Trinculo and his pal, whatshisname, they'd been exquisite. *Rats.*

Then I heard John. "I learned, you see," he intoned to Caliban, "that your moral tale must be wrapped in a good song. *You* know that. A good song and a funny story. Shakespeare knew, by God. And that is why we love it all. Why we cry with him. Why we learn from him." He dropped his voice to a whisper audible in Kankakee, "This thing tonight, now, *Tempest.* It's just the politics of old age, you know. That and a bit about education and family, all wrapped in magic, love and good song and dance. Yes? Yes!"

John.

Right, I said to myself. *I'll hand over "dat ding" and be off. Off to find another career. Another life. Somewhere. Further west.*

I slipped between Cordwell and a hutch of street-bunnies who seemed unable to stop touching Ferdinand with their noses.

Colin, Cordwell's son, was behind the bar. The world's best bartender, Colin juggled jokes, patter, orders to the waitress, balanced laughter and business as only a great publican, to the matter-born, can do. He was—is—brilliant at the art.

I ordered another pint. Got it. Placed the wooden box on the bar. At first lull, I *ah-hemmed* John.

"Ah," he said, turning. "What'd you think?"

I thought.

I believe—believed—that it is never good simply to love something. Such love always must be tempered with analysis and *kvetch.* "Sagged at the top," I said. "A great storm. Then that first island scene, well…" I hated having loved this production.

"Well, yes!" Cordwell said. "It's all that stuff. Then it gets into it and, by God!"

"Yes. It sang," I said. I hated myself.

"Ha!" he said. "Yes. It sang. Good."

I handed him the box. "From a friend of yours," I said, "at the show. Said he had to leave and could I give it to you. He left. I've given it to you."

Cordwell turned the box over. His vast nose wrinkled. His eyes crinkled. The box looked small.

When I made to leave, Cordwell stopped me.

"Have you *any* idea what's in here?" he asked. He waved the unopened box under my nose. "Any idea at *all?*" The box seemed to offend him, as though he knew that I knew *just* what was in there and, by God, sir, he wouldn't have it. No, sir, not a bit of it!

"Damned Bavarian bureaucrat." He tipped his head back and looked along the hump of his nose at it.

I remembered my line. "He said to tell you, 'This thing no longer stands between you.' With an accent, but that's more or less it."

"Yes, yes, yes…" Cordwell was slipping into fustian mode, as he must have with the RAF officers' board, more British than God, donchaknow?

"Let me show you, young fella."

So saying, he opened the box. I almost heard a boom of kettledrums, a growl of bowed basses. Inside, a metal something gleamed in barlight. The place faded. The background of actors, fans, and dreams withdrew.

Not really but this was a cinematic not Shakespearean moment. Inside the box, nested on a piece of charred khaki cloth, was a bullet. It looked newly cast and polished, yet I knew it was from the war, the Second War, as John called it, World War II.

"Huh," I said or something like.

Cordwell picked up the thing, held it from point to cap, between thumb and middle finger. He handled it as though it were of vast import and impossibly fragile. He turned to me. The brass casing caught a spark of warm light from the lamp on the end of the bar. The glint flashed in John's eye.

"The nerve of the fellow," he breathed. His dudgeon had softened. "He wasn't even supposed to be there, you know? You know that?" Cordwell turned the thing, hefted it, gauged its weight, looked at it point-on, then from its rear. "He was a substitute. Making-do because it was wartime. Damn the fellow anyway. His fault."

He laid the bullet on the bar.

"You know, don't you, what this damned thing is, eh?" He was speaking because I was there, not because I was important to him or that I hear the tale he was about to spin.

Because I was there I answered. "A bullet," I ventured.

"Right…" There was more expected.

"I'd say… .30 caliber?" A guess.

"Thirty."

"Maybe?"

Cordwell hefted it again. "Caliber thirty. Yes." He knew he wasn't going to get a savvy answer from me. "I'll tell you a story," he said and put the shell, slug-up, on the bar. "Colin!" Cordwell ordered a quarter-gill of Irish whiskey and sat it next to his pint of Watney's. He flicked both ends of his mustache with the knuckle of his index-finger then bolted the whiskey. "There," he said, "now…"

He was wound for a good one.

"That bullet," he said, pointing with his chin, "is my bullet. Meant for me, here." He touched himself over his heart. "See?" He pointed to the markings along the shell casing. "That, sir, is me, my number. Go on. Have a look."

I shoved my eyeglasses an inch or so from the round. There was a number. Fine lines engraved on the brass. I read it aloud, and as I did Cordwell spoke it with me.

"A thing one doesn't forget: one's *number!* The one that, when it's up, it's bloody well *up*. Don't care how old you are, what war you were in, you carry it forever." He tapped his chest again. "Turn out Beowulf's crew from the ashes, ask them their rowing numbers, and by the Lord Harry, they'd know 'em to the man. To the man." He picked up the round and turned it again. Again the light caught his eye. "One's number." He repeated the number. I'll not repeat it here.

"Beginning of the war: everything was shambles, I can tell you. Not enough of anything: men, weapons, ammunition; everyone a bit of shy about who does what to whom. Well, the very same was true of the *Small World*."

That's how he put it, as though anyone would know instantly what he meant, "the Small World." I crunched my nose a bit and must have looked confused.

"Let me put it to you this way," he said. "The wee-folk, as the Irish have it, 'the kingdom,' Faerie, the glamour world, don't you know? See, they're no more ready for war than is the smelly mob. Us. At the beginning it's all chop-chop and never a by-your-leave. Things have to be done and they are done. Not well sometimes, sometimes bloody badly, but they get acted upon."

I took a long sip and found the glass empty. A full one sat next to it.

"Take for instance the Hampden bomber. Damn fine ship. What I flew, Hampdens. Four-man crew, tight little piece. Kept losing them. Long narrow tail had a way of falling off when hit with too much at one time. Well, that's war. Mind you, the Hampden was a bit elderly. Came along in the '30s. A grandfather of a plane, you might say." He smiled and licked his lips. "And now this is a *thing*. They looked just like one of Jerry's kites. Yes. The damned Dornier, the Do. 17. Our own chaps kept shooting us down. Bloody embarrassing. 'Anything to report, flying officer?' 'Oh, I say, sir, either I topped one of Adolph's 17s or, by God, punched Old Reggie's mess ticket.' 'Ah, bad show…'"

Cordwell did that, burst into playlettes. Good at it too.

"So there we were. We flew at night, you know? Yes. And this was early in the war. I was observer. November. November 7, '41. We were over Belgium. Yes, we were going to bomb, but first we had to fly this long-wide triangle between the *Paix de Calais* and two other checkpoints. We're there principally to draw Jerry fighters and ack-ack—that's anti-aircraft to you Yanks— from our Wellingtons flying the main show into Berlin that night."

He squinted as though I'd sneered at something. "Now let me tell you, sir: Observer! Observer was a term left from the First War. Not to brag, but the observer is the busiest man in the aircrew." He ticked off the observer's jobs. "He's co-pilot, navigator, bombardier, nose gunner, and if there was time he brewed the tea and did what-have-you."

"Sort of a stage manager?" I ventured.

Cordwell beamed. "Exactly!" He tapped my pint with the rim of his. "All right. During approach, my station was in the nose. Picture this: I am squatting in a Perspex bubble. I see myself reflected on this curved surface all around…" He reached out his hand ahead, as though touching his reflection a half-century gone. "Below is the ground, ahead, the night. You're surrounded by whatever's trying to kill you: fighters, flak, birds!" He laughed, then became serious. "No joke," he said. He paused long enough to let me know there was another tale *there*.

"Tony Gordon. Old Tony was the pilot. His canopy was above and behind me. There was a top gunner-slash-radio operator and behind it all, the tail gunner. "Now, we were on the landward line of our triangle, over Belgium, still carrying a full bomb-load. A flight of Wellingtons goes over on its way to the show. 'Ta, loves. Good luck. Give 'em a bit for us,' and then…"

Cordwell's mouth and eyes froze, wide open.

"Then one of our fighter lads drops down—support for the Wellys, you know—and has a go at us. Well, suddenly it's not so funny, eh? Shot by one of your own.

"We did a few light-and-fancies, he flipped a few up our tail, then was gone. I reckoned he'd sussed that we were the home team and fled to avoid embarrassment and vile language.

"That, or as I found out later, he'd run out of ammo." He waved the cartridge in the air. "After that we caught a cross-fire from two ack-ack batteries. Barrage lights had us fixed so Tony dropped to the deck—ack-acks are useless at low-level—and there we were." He looked at me. "Been to Belgium?"

I shook my head.

"Bloody country's like Kentucky. Flat as prairie, then you're in the mountains. Point is, we ran out of prairie and a mountain tore our tail off.

"Okay. We crashed. Fiery mess. The tail broke off and the plane tore itself to pieces for a half-mile down a valley before going nose-first into a hill. We survived. Tony dragged himself out, then helped the other two. The tailgunner was injured so badly, the Germans repatriated him. Imagine that. Well, it was early in the war.

"There's no good reason why I survived. I'm jammed in the front, the plane's on fire, everything's a twisted mess and unexploded bombs. I had no idea where I was, how to get out. And Tony, bless him, Tony climbs back on the flaming wing and, I swear it, he talks me out. By the time I'd gotten myself to where he could grab hold of me, the plane was about to blow. Still had our bombs, did I mention? Then we're out and running and then we fall and it blows.

"Now I am on my knees watching it all. 'Am I dead...?' I ask. 'You're not if I'm not,' Tony said."

"Wow," I said.

"Indeed," he said. "Now here's the thing, you see. I wasn't supposed to have been there."

I blinked.

"You don't understand at the time, but later you find out. Damned Bavarian Bureaucrat. I was to have bought it. Killed. Earlier. Our fighter lad was to have put *this* in me." He held up the .30-caliber round.

"Colin," I said, loudly.

"On me…" Cordwell said and went behind the bar, tapped each of us a draught of bitter. "Tony, I reckon, was supposed to have gotten out, away. Gone back to England, escaped, maybe been killed. But I was alive in there and he came back for me.

"We were captured, taken to a Luftwaffe night fighter HQ. Big stone chalet. I walked into this large room. Pleasant place, I thought, warm, other pilots—German, of course, but what of it? They were sipping beer and eating apples, and there across the room—I looked—stood this shredded fellow, strips of skin, burned flesh, shredded flight suit, still smoking. 'Poor bugger,' I thought, then, 'By God,' I said. 'By God, that's me.' And it was. A mirror.

"Quick as you please, those Jerrys, those pilots, came over and they carried me to their table. Gave me beer and harvest apples. November, you know."

He leaned on the bar and turned the bullet in his hand. "Cradled me in their eight arms and carried me to the fire. They gave me beer and apples and talked to me kindly. And I realized, 'I like these fellows…'" He didn't finish.

"It was still during the war, the first I heard from," he jerked his head toward the upstairs, "from our friend. He wrote to me, if you can imagine. Through the Red Cross, if you believe it. A long letter in which he apologized, said he'd been on temporary assignment, transferred from the east—I never asked from where—in charge of a draft of his Folk whose job it was to 'write the history' of the war. 'Write the history!' By which he meant it was their job to inscribe numbers on the munitions that," he made a vague, un-Cordwell gesture, "the shells that had chaps' numbers on them. Our little friend was a manager, *Gruppenfuhrer* they called 'em—you wouldn't believe the bureaucracy of Faerie, by the way—anyroad, he was in charge of a whole passel of the Wee People from all parts of everywhere at the beginning of the war, drafted to keep up with demand, donchaknow? Takes skill, I have heard—from him of course, to tinker together that sort of an operation. Supply blokes, craftsmen, dogsbodies, shipping clerks. A huge operation and put together overnight. Even *they* don't work that quickly."

He looked me in the eye. I think he was daring me to snicker. I nodded.

"His letter said an error needed to be rectified. My number had been on a cartridge. Said cartridge intended for Hurricane such-and-such from Fighter Command Squadron so-and-so; the details went on and on. Point being, that Hurricane was to have peppered us and, me personally, through the chest—he cited just where on my person it was to have entered, what damage it was to have been done, where it was to have exited..." He touched himself again. "I was, you see, officially dead. As official as those buggers can be. History, you see.

"He bungled it. The shipment never went out, ended in a warehouse somewhere, whatever. The point being, this slug and my chest never met, and that luckless fighter bastard who'd had at us over Belgium... Well, he ran out of ammo. Like that. Without this." He placed it on the bar.

We stared at it.

"His bookkeeping was off. Drove him mad. He followed me all through the war, through everything. I was a pretty active prisoner, I guess you've heard, something of an escape artist. He kept missing me, camp to camp." He stared at my eyes again.

"Dresden. You know? Missed me by thirteen hours. I'd been and gone."

"You mean Dresden was bombed just to get...?" I started to say. Then decided not to.

"Dresden. Yes, one of the reasons I went back to architecture after the war. Wasn't going to, but it seemed as though I owed it, somehow. Drink?" he said. "This one on you?"

I nodded, paid. He poured. We drank.

"He's been following. Through the '50s, '60s. I was a character in that POW escape film. You knew that one? Yes? Yes. My character's killed in the film. Shot in the chest. Ha! His doing, I trust.

"He keeps writing. Suggesting things would be better for all concerned if I were to let that bullet find its place. Something about history, time or the way things are supposed to be. Rot, I say, petty bureaucratic rot. Just to have paperwork balance. You know, I could tell a tale... But I won't."

He drank off the pint. "I think I've adjusted damned well for a dead man, eh? A man who should be dead, anyway, which, according to him, is the same thing."

I nodded.

"Now that's a true story," he said.

I didn't doubt it. And I didn't tell Cordwell that night but the little man seemed to have come to appreciate the value of that missed delivery over Belgium. I think he had liked the play. Maybe he had appreciated the night, the roof, the tree, the street, the Lion.

I wanted to tell that to Cordwell. I didn't. After John died in the '90s, I told Colin.

Colin is now the Eighth Earl of Muffington, but only behind the bar. He has that .30-caliber round but doesn't much look at it. The Shakespeare troupe nested a while in John's pub, under John's tree. Then it grew and moved on. It and I are doing fine, just fine, thank you very much. And that about Dresden, for cripes sake. I do not believe. Not that.

THE LAST SCOOT AT SKIDOO'S TAP

"No fangs." The old guy's voice was sandpaper and whiskey. I awoke. "Fangs are whatchacallit?"

I didn't know.

"Literary conceit is what you call it." His laugh was a rusted screen door. "I knew that all along," he said. "See? Stories about them," he pointed at my book, "they're based on Lord Byron. I know that, but you?"

I was surprised to hear Byron and *literary conceit* from…

His throat cleared deep into his chest. Booze was on his breath, his clothes; it seeped from his skin. "Lots of *conceits* over them. Coffins? Sometimes. Stakes, crucifixes?" He snorted. "And garlic. Who likes garlic anyway? That about blood? Well, there's blood and then…" A passing truck wiped out the rest; the lights caught a tobacco-brown smile among gray whiskers. No fangs. Then it was just road hum and the dark.

"That about being invited? That's halfway right."

"What?"

"'What?' Being invited's what. What it is, is it's *you* who needs an invitation. You see?"

I said nothing.

"No? Don't mind if I sit here, do you?"

He already was seated and I hated sleeping away a night on a long ride.

"Something else." He dropped his voice. "They float, the real ones. Flames on black water." He pointed again. The cover of the book was lurid elegance, silk, flesh, fangs and a discrete drop of blood. "Other than that, that book could be about the guys. Old friends."

I'd grabbed the book from a rack in the terminal in Pittsburg before boarding. Had me asleep before the Interstate. I was dead to the world when the old guy got on, I guessed at some middle-of-the-night place between Youngwood and Mount Pleasant. He was my seatmate now and we were far west of Philly.

"A long time ago," he started, "oh, the names are changed, like they say. 'Course, you know that."

I knew I'd hear his story. I did. I'll tell it my way.

Brewer. Nice place. Red brick everywhere. A hard working town now out of work. A mountain, river and rail yards. The rails come from everywhere. They funnel into the valley between Nesquala Ridge and Mount Bohn, run through town, screw up everything, then sort themselves at the yards. The yards were miles of steel and rolling stock, engines, switches, and depots. They stank of creosote, coal dust, and smoke. The men who worked the yards were seen only at a distance.

"They were, therefore, very small men," he said. "When they got close, they became fathers, uncles, brothers. See?"

I did. He—*they*—were kids then. The kids came from what he called the East End. Proud of it, too. Called themselves *Enders*.

"The End's where people lived when they couldn't live anywhere else. Not much to be proud of, I guess. Still."

The rest hung.

The End was east of the yards. Stenawatt High School was at the top of Spring Road. Named after someone. Spring covered a hell of a hill. At the bottom it leveled out at the Pacific Theatre. Just past the theater were the yards.

"During the War, the yards worked forever. After? Not so much." A rusty chuckle rumpled the last couple words.

Spring Road ran beneath the yards through a subway underpass. Back in the sun, the road climbed a steep quarter mile.

"'The Nutcracker,' Keegan called it for reasons obvious."

Skidoo's Tap sat on the western top of Nutcracker Hill. Two floors of Pink PermaStone, fake stone in genteel colors. "Some people's idea of class." A snort. "Hiding the brick is as common as coal soot in Brewer. Pitiful, but Skidoo's had a thing: electric eye doors going in and out, a very big deal in Brewer, 1954. Sucked us in, anyway!"

Turn right onto Thorne Way where Spring topped the Nutcracker and it was a short block to a place the old guy called "Chucky B's." I didn't ask. Figured I'd find out.

Past Skidoo's and Thorne, Spring ran a mile of rolling dips up and down and finally down to the river. This was the West Side—the nice side—of town.

"The guys always pedaled like hell down Spring from the End. Hit level at the Pacific full-throttle, make the light, you hump through the subway quick as *that*." His fingers snapped. His breath came heavy, telling it. "You did not want to be under there too long." Phlegm cracked. "We all knew that. Even before that day." He laughed another whiff of booze my way. "Smelled like dusty fart in there, see?"

The subway was a half-mile of burn-out lamps. Exhaust from cars, buses, flatbeds out of Lieberknecht Mills filled the space from the vaulted ceiling down. Spilled fuel and oil, animal or industrial waste, dissolved ash and cinders leeched from the yards above. The stuff oozed through cracks in the ceiling. The ooze hung in gray stalactites or ran phosphorescent ribbons down the walls or lay curled in shit-pile stalagmites in the gutters.

"Who knew what the hell was in there? We never stopped to look. The guys pumped and set up a howl going through. The

'Ender Holler,' Keegan called it. Sometime a pretty note, sometime a long bad scream. Anyway, hump through, you made the Nutcracker easy as pie. Coming out, making that hill sometimes…" He stopped for a breath. "Sometimes it was beautiful, busting the 'Cracker. So perfect. Times a guy wouldn't break a sweat or even have to stand on his pedals. Push it right, you float over the top, Earth drops away, your head's light, and for a second you're *Destination Moon*. Weightless, you know?" He took another breath. "That day, it was beautiful. The 'boes on Skidoo's corner hooted and smacked each other. Celebrating."

"'Boes?" I said.

"'Boes! Hoboes up from the jungle, far end of the yards out by Chucky B's. Must have felt they got a workout just watching us five float the 'Cracker that day. 'Boes. Cripes, listen. You'll catch hold."

As he told it, Skidoo's electric eye door opened that day. "Out sucks dead smoke, old breath, stale beer," he said. "Then Short Draw and Daryl, they tumble out with it, rolled down the three concrete steps onto hot pavement. PD, who's waiting with the bikes, about crapped himself. The 'boes, they scatter. Halfheart's last out the door and he's onto the tussle. A mess of pups dumped out a box! Shorty and Halfheart untangle. Daryl lays dead. A little blood, mainly nose blood, that was common blood for him and didn't need a tussle to get it going," he said.

"Shorty and Halfheart shook him. To bring him back up, you know? Finally, the kid *whoofs* one big stinking burp and his eyes flop open. Cripes! Halfheart yips like a girl. Shorty blurts something Indian and let go. He's fast. PD crabs backward till he runs into some hobo's standing-there legs. He's screaming 'Oh God, oh God. Sorry, sorry! I'm sorry!' PD was always sorry.

"And Daryl? Daryl lays white eyed."

I got another whiff of Greyhound America as the old guy leaned close. "Eyes, see, Daryl's eyes are like the Martian cavewoman in *Rocketship X-M*. Blind white, you see?"

I did not.

"Yeah. The movie. She wakes up and there she is, a Martian surrounded by Earth guys, our heroes. Her eyes are all whites. Bugging out. At us, us Earth guys, see? Suddenly *we're* the monsters from outer space. You get it? The guys from Earth! Guess that was us for Daryl at just that minute. Monsters. You get it?"

"No."

"No. Too young. Well, the guys were nose-on to a pair of round blank eyeballs. That's strange enough. Then the blue parts wiggle to the surface, like rising from the deep.

"Halfheart's squeaky, 'You see that? You seeing this?' Squeaking.

"Shorty whispers something, '*mucking-doggie*,' sounds like. It's *Lenni Lenape*, which is what he halfway is, and has no translation.

"Later, PD says it was like seeing your answer float up in the Magic 8 Ball. You know what *that* is, right?"

I nod, forgetting the dark.

"Right?" he says. "Hey. You interested?"

Except for road hum, the bus is quiet. We're awake, so's the driver. We're rolling through the wildest of Pennsylvania's mountains. "I'm interested. And?"

"Yes, yes, and. And I thought you were dead to the world like everyone. And later, the ones who're left later, they agree: this is *the* big thing. All their lives, nothing's going to touch this. See? Being an Ender is to face an assumption one day. What is that assumption? That assumption is: nothing happens. Well, the usual tragedies. But this? Forget kids, weddings, going to jail, going to war, *this* would be *the* memory."

I ask. "What the hell are a bunch of kids doing in—"

"In Skidoo's Tap, a bunch of kids? What're a bunch of kids doing in Skidoo's Tap? That, yes?"

"That."

"I was about to say. Running a scoot, we kids were. 'A scoot?' you ask, all in innocence. Wrong question, I reply. What question should you ask, I ask?"

"What?"

"'What?' No. 'Who?' is your question. 'Who the fuck were you?' you should ask."

I say nothing.

"Since you ask, I'll say what. First, we were Enders, which, as mentioned, involves some assumptions. Still, we're kids and not allowed in a bar, not legally anyway. This is Pennsylvania, after all. Also, Skidoo hates us. That, second, is one of our assumptions. What did we think he hated about us in particular? We're uninvited kids is what. See? Poking somewhere we're not supposed to be, that's the nutshell of being an Ender. And, third."

There was a moment.

"Third, we were different. Different, yeah, from everybody else in the world. Who isn't? Anyway, we're young. We're stupid. Dumb enough to think we'd beat the assumptions. Stupid, thinking that scooting places none of our business would make us..." Another pause. He put his stink inches from my face. "We were stupid because we were, okay?"

A moment. "So, 'Who?' you finally ask." He sounded more relaxed. "By name there was *Halbherz*. That's German. Written down it looked like it should be 'half heart' so everyone called him Halfheart, which sounded like 'Hey fart!' the way the guys said, which he hated. Halfheart's old man had been a Kraut. Mean as a snake but dead by this time and thus a good Kraut, but who cared? Though *that* is a story by itself! Halfheart said he was glad his old man was out of the way and nobody even wondered if that was true or not. Short Draw told him once, 'Half Heart? That could be an Indian name. If you want.'

"Halfheart said he didn't.

"'Just an offer,' Shorty said. 'Wouldn't be a very *good* Indian, anyway. Name of Half Heart.' He wasn't pissed, he was just making a point.

"That was *Short Draw*, our name for him, or Shorty. Shorty was known as Little Beaver by others. Why? He was little and he was an Indian. Outside of us and some others his name was Roscoe Beverage, which nobody called him except teachers but which is why all our guys called him Short Draw in honor of a nickel beer or for when the bartender didn't give your Yuengling an honest pull." He laughed that same in the chest creak. "Keegan said that. Halfheart thought that was about the funniest damn thing ever said. Laughed and laughed till someone, Keegan probably, told him 'Fuckin' don't *die*, will you!' Shorty was only half an Indian on his mom's half but he also looked like Red Ryder's kid buddy, Little Beaver, so that all came together.

"There was *Daryl* who was Daryl or sometimes Darly, and if you knew Daryl you'd know why. The guys sort of *had* to be his friends. Lanky, doofus, hair every which way, big apple in his Adams, big feet, glasses of course, ears. Said things over and over.

"There was PD. Pete Durance. It was Peter, but who wants his guys calling him Peter? So PD it was. Sounded like Petey the way it was said.

"And there was Keegan, Jackie Keegan. There had been his brother, Rory. But Rory. Rory was dead that summer. Which is the point.

"That's it, the guys, and at this time they're all about to make the big fucking move!"

"Big move?"

"The big *fucking* move. The move to Stenawatt High is the big fucking move."

"Which one are you?" I ask.

He sucked air. Let it out. "'Which one?' Which one? Huh. You figure it, which one. Now for your scoot. A scoot is this."

"It's going someplace where you're not supposed to go. Right?"

"Going a place you're not supposed to. Right. You're learning. East Enders west of the tracks, they'd be going to Pendora for baseball. That's okay. Maybe to the CYO dances at St. Maggie's. Okay too. They might go to Mostly's for pop, funny books or whatever. Truth told," he said, "Mostly's had nothing on a half-dozen fountain stores up the End, but summer days, the guys stopped at Mostly's for a Pepper or to snake a look at the funnies before heading up Thorne to Chucky B."

"What is that? Chucky?"

"Chucky B, Chucky B. Hold on about Chucky B, I'm about to get there." Another rusty laugh. "'Plenty 'a room for us all,' Keegan'd say, 'no waitin' at the Chuck!' Then, Keegan, he'd smack someone, Halfheart or Shorty, up the back of the head, punch PD in the arm or Daryl, whoever was around. They loved it. But I'm talking scoots." He stopped. "So, you tell me. What's Chucky B's?" he asked.

"A playground?"

"Yeah. A playground."

The story went on.

There was a great view of the mountain, the yards, the whole East End from the stoop at Skidoo's Tap.

"'Boes hung there day and night, enjoying the view, waiting."

"For what? Waiting?"

"For what waiting?" he said. "For what might you think?"

"Work, booze, handouts? I don't know."

"'I don't know I don't know.' But yeah. That's, yeah, what we thought. But no."

"Well?"

"Well, an invitation is for what," he said.

Another 18-wheeler Dopplered west; its diesel horn came and went into the night.

"You still want to know about that last 'scoot'?

I did.

"Skidoo's, see, was mystery, adult stuff. Get it?"

I did.

"Whenever that eye-door opened, out comes smells as mentioned, most of them bad, but still… But still no matter what stink oozed out, those 'boes and roadies—what Keegan called them, 'Knights of the Road' before you ask—those 'boes and roadies went on point, sniffing, waiting…"

That rusty hinge cracked in his chest again.

"Daryl had it right, first time. First time we biked to the west top of Spring Road.

"'Jesus,' Halfheart said, looking at the 'boes that first time.

"Shorty gives one of his Injun grunts.

"PD shakes his head.

"'What the fuck they so happy for?' That's Keegan.

"Then Daryl. 'What the fuck they so happy about?' he says. 'I don't know what the fuck,' he said. 'I don't know happy, but hey, looks like, I don't know, but what the fuck, looks like they're *hopeful*.' A second's dark and quiet. "He talked like that, Daryl," the old guy said, "but hopeful was what they were. All those busted mugs are all sudden, happy pups. Dirty 'boes, stumblebums, and hay bags they might be, but that door opens and every one's styling. 'What the fuck?' Yeah. That door goes *whoosh* and they're buttoned up and spit-combing. Then," he leaned, his voice went low, "then, see, one maybe gets the call. And in he goes. Then, *whoosh*, see? The 'boes left out? They'd had a whiff, a couple bars of tune. Then the look fades and it's back to the view till next time.

"'Yeah, *hope* was what the fuck,'" says Daryl.

"'More like flies to shit,'" Keegan says.

"See? Everyone figured Skidoo's was just another road to Schnockertown."

"Schnocker…"

"…town. Yeah. A Daryl word. First time he said it, Keegan just looked at him. Didn't noogie him, so it stuck. Anyway, that door opened, it was always cool, fragrant, and the tunes never stopped."

"How'd you know?"

"'How'd you know?' You ask 'What?' then 'Why?' now we're off to 'How?'" He took a breath. "The scoot is how. After the busting the 'Cracker we'd drop bike—sometimes—right at the 'boes' feet. No thinking, no talking, just drop and dash like/that! Up those three steps, break the beam, scoot and scream. Grab a couple, three-seconds of Kool-Air, suck a snootfull of the other half, hang peepers on the clientele, swing 'round the eye-pole inside, then scoot the *out* door, howling all the way.

"Pissed him off, Skidoo. Regulars'd turn to look. Daylight'd catch their ugly mugs. Women, too. 'Hay bags,' the 'boes called them, so we called them too. That was fun, knowing the bags saw you. Didn't matter how ugly, there was always that something about women, no matter. You know?"

I did.

"Now, Keegan's the mother duck, see? First in, last out, he watches us pass. Then he sticks his chin out, and like it's some big choice, he calls to Skid, 'Make mine a fist of John Daniels.' See, he's Bogey or Raft, so familiar he calls it by its given name of John."

I laughed.

"Us too. Halfheart doubled over every time, funniest thing he's ever heard.

"Then, like Keegan's had a second's thought, he says, 'And what the hell, Skid, set up the house.'

"By then, Skid's yelling fuck off. Keegan though, he waits for fuck-off number two, like he doesn't get it. Then, real disappointed, he says, 'Damn, Skid! I don't even know why I come here.'"

I laughed again.

"Then he strolls. Not a scoot, a walk with a little swagger, like he belonged. You know?

"Keegan," the old guy said. "Down on the sidewalk he'd take a bow, hoist his jeans, you know, like Cagney. Something. Very even, Keegan was, very smooth. Always was, before Rory. Hell, even after!"

Another bus passed heading west.

"This day now, we scoot. We're in. We're out. Door's open as usual. No Keegan of course. We wait. We listen. The 'boes stare down on us. We hold our bikes like they're our precious dicks. Halfheart's working up a laugh. Then nothing. Nothing. Then the door shuts—*whoosh*—Keegan's still inside. We wait, we wait, we look, we wait. We don't know. We don't know. We drift. We look back. Nothing.

"There's chatter, 'What could happen?' That's Halfheart. He's got Keegan's bike. We drift half a block to Mostly's stoop. 'He gets served, he's in for it.' That's Shorty, the non-Indian half talking. PD leans close, whispering, 'Keegan's got no money, guys!' Like it's a big secret. Halfheart gives him the face. 'Skid ain't serving him, you maroon,' he says like Bugs. 'He'll bum-rush him, call the cops maybe, who cares? Keegan don't.'

"'He got no money!'" The old guy coughed up a laugh. "Master of the obvious, PD was. Truth, though. Someone always tipped Keegan his Pepper, comics, whatever, and no one ever mentioned it again. Jesus, the guy was an orphan. Anyway, Skidoo never called cop. Cripes, no. So, this, what I'm telling about, the bad part, this starts at Mostly's after that scoot. We're outside because old man Mostly doesn't like us Enders touching his comics he might 'actually *sell* for some Goddamn money, for

Christ sake!' That was Mostly. Anyway, it's summer. Hot as summer, anyway. Anyway, we're not in school. And Rory, Keegan's kid brother, he'd just drowned at Squaw Lake—what we called it, the pond up at Chucky B's. Viewing, funeral, all that, that was long over, long enough over so you could talk about it without Keegan getting, you know?"

"Too bad," I say.

"Too bad, too bad. Not much to say about Rory drowning except he did it. Disappeared late afternoon, then showed up late that night at the bottom of Squaw Lake, Chucky B's, for the cops in fish waders. Full of water and nibbled on by carp. 'What a loss.' 'Such a waste.' 'Kid drowns in a cemetery,' everyone says. 'How ironic,' everyone says. Okay, they didn't know the word but they recognize irony. Just shook their heads, you know?"

"Cemetery?" I said. "You said Chucky B's was a playground."

"I said? *You* said. I exaggerated. Chucky B's is the Charles Bynum Cemetery. Big old place. Miles to hang out in. Hills, trees, little ponds, dark paths. Goes back to the Revolution. So Halfheart, Short Draw, PD, and Daryl are by Mostly's. Sweating and swearing. Waiting for Keegan."

The old guy slowed to a cough. I figured another digression. There was.

"I have to mention. About this time, up from down by St. Maggie's comes this woman. She's young, thin, and she's pushing a baby carriage, a big one. She goes by. Everyone goes quiet, like something holy's going on. The cart is full of babies, three of them, a year apart maybe. She's maybe new, maybe visiting someone, I don't know, nobody'd ever seen her. I give a peek-around. None of the others are moving.

"She's not old. Old *enough*, 20 maybe 22. And she throws a shadow, going by. I feel the cool of her shadow. I feel the cool of it to this day; swear I do. I smell her: sweat and baby stink, yeah, but another, a smell of sweet, sweet girl like flowers or something nice and something else. But her shadow's like the light and we're the one's casting the dark.

"Then she's by and everyone pretends nothing's happened. Halfheart's picking gum out of his sneaker treads. Short Draw's staring the way she came, no expression—even half-Indians are like that. PD's squinting at the sky like he's remembering something."

He leaned toward me. "See? Everyone's somewhere else, not there on Mostly's stinking hot step and thinking, not about Keegan, but...

"Then Halfheart says, 'Hey, girly, you want another one?' He's quiet; no one hears but us. He says it like he's asking if she wanted a second dip of chocolate or something, but we know what he means. No one but us. Shorty goes very non-Indian. Even PD makes to pound the crap out of him.

"Then Daryl. Daryl says, 'What?' Meaning, 'What do you mean?' Meaning, 'I don't know what you're talking about.' Meaning, 'Want another what?' Like he didn't know where kids came from. Which maybe he didn't.

"Halfheart gives Daryl the eye like he doesn't know if he should tell him or kill him. So the moment's gone. Someone laughs. Then there's Keegan."

A small town passed at a distance in the dark. I see two lights. A gas station, a small man in the window, everything blue in blue bus glass and a soda machine on a corner. That was the other light. They drifted by. Then the place was gone forever.

"And?" That was me.

"And Keegan came up the street from Skid's. At least he looks like Keegan, at least looks like something wearing a Keegan suit. He passes the girl, he walks through her or she through him, cart, babies and all. Well, maybe not.

"'J'see that babe?' Halfheart says. 'Want to know what I said? I said...'

"Keegan doesn't want to hear. He doesn't hitch his jeans, he doesn't spit—no one spit like Keegan—he takes his bike, looks nowhere. 'I'm gone,' he says to no one. And he's down the street toward the bar. By then the girl's around the corner or down the hill, anyway she's nowhere, and when Keegan gets to Skid's, he leans the bike toward one of the 'boes. Words follow. We don't hear the words. After the words, like he said, he's gone."

"Where? Inside?"

"Where inside? Inside. No scoot, he walks, climbing steps to a noose.

"'Gone? I'm gone?' That's Daryl yelling like he does at us but never at Keegan. 'I'm GONE! You're not gone, Keegan. You're here, you're us! You're not gone!'

"Then Daryl drops bike and he's after him, still shouting. And *whoosh*.

The old guy coughed again. "The rest wander up to the corner and now I gotta hang hog." Like that, he was off to the back.

I watched the dark out the window. Not much to see in the Alleghenies in the deepest part of night. Whatever's out there, it's imaginary.

A stir of air freshener and he was back. "Finally Halfheart and Shorty, they go in after them." The old guy wrestled with the seat. He settled. "Leave PD with the bikes and the 'boes and *they're* off. *Whoosh*.

"And?"

"And? And inside, it's like always. Juke tunes and stink, gloom and bar art. Halfheart stays in the beam at the door. Daylight has his back. Shorty runs to the center, way past the eye pole, farther than any of the guys had ever been before. There's no screaming. What's to scream?"

The old guy's looking out the window.

"Nothing out there," I said.

"Yeah. Nothing. Then, like I said, out they came. Tumbling. Daryl's white eyes. Eyes fill up. Then everybody asks everything, wants to know what's going on, what's happening, where's Keegan, what the fuck? Then Daryl's off. He looks around and he's up, heading to Chucky B's. Heading to the Place the others figure."

I begin to ask.

"Don't ask," the old guy said. "The Place is our place up in Charles Bynum's. Out the back, near the fence and woods, a big old yew tree, trunk like a thousand brown bones rising, branches thick as a fat man, twisted like an arthritis, reaching, far out, drooping, then red creeper tying it all to ground. A tent, a living tent, our tent. The oldest thing in the Chuck, that tree. Our 'Angel Yew,' Daryl says. We hung there. A guy could sit and be, read a comic, suck a Pepper, cool and quiet. Peek the world. What world there was.

"Anyway, Daryl's no athlete. Nuts get cracked pedaling the 'Cracker; they're his nuts. Now he's walking up Thorne, the rest pedaling after. He wins. You remember what it was, running? Back then? Your body knew where it all was: ground, bumps, the next step, the next jump? Everything worked, feet barely touch. Push earth with your toes and you float and fly, nothing to it? Remember?"

"Maybe," I said.

"Maybe that's what Daryl looked. Only he's walking. And the rest, they're shoving cranks like starting a cold climb up the 'Cracker. Halfheart and Shorty, they're coming fast. So's PD. But Daryl's through the gates, up the road, into the trees. He's past Squaw Lake and gone. Vanished.

"The guys get to the Angel Yew. No Daryl. They hang like doofuses. How long? A while. Then Daryl. He claws through the vines and there he's standing, draped, low branches frame him. It's like they want to…" The old guy clenched both fists under his chin. He held an imaginary something close.

"Daryl's not twitching. Not blinking. This is, what? Tops, it's fifteen, twenty minutes after Keegan's 'I'm gone.' The others are panting like mutts. It's near sundown, see? The air's turning cool. The guys are sweating like pigs. Then, 'Christ!' Halfheart says.

"'Shh,' Shorty says. 'Cripes!'

"'PD sat and stared.

"'They got me,' he said, Daryl said.

"'Got?' That's Halfheart. Shorty kicked him.

"'I think.' He looked at himself. He brushed his shirt and pants. He touched a spot on his shirt, kept rubbing.

"'Christ.' Halfheart again.

"'Probably not, though, huh?'

"'What?' Halfheart again.

"'Mom. She probably won't kill me for messing myself. And they probably didn't get me. They had me then let me go. I'm sure.'

"'They let you?' Halfheart said. 'Hell no! We came and got—'

"'Shh!' Shorty says.

"'I almost vanished,' Daryl said. 'I could see through,' he held his hand to his face, 'or thought I could.'

"Halfheart now shouts up his nose, 'O! Kay! What's! Happening!?' Like he's talking to a Jap can't speak English.

"Shorty shushes. 'Where were you?' he says.

"'Rory's,' Daryl says.

"'And?' That's Halfheart again. Yelling.

"'And…' Shorty says.

"'And there is Paradise,' Daryl says."

The old guy turned to me. Something sparked in his eye.

"'There is Paradise,'" he repeated. "See? Daryl was looking for words. 'There was a place…' he says finally, 'not heaven but a place…' He went looking for the word again. 'Someplace forever, someplace maybe they don't boot you, no one ever rags on you.

Paradise. It wasn't real, I'm sure of that. I think they were taking whatever was real out of me and leaving me with...'

"'Paradise,' Shorty said.

"'I ain't ever gonna see no Paradise,' Halfheart said. PD whacked his leg. He grabbed the spot and started in again but PD smacked him again.

"'Yeah,' Daryl said. 'They gave me Paradise for a little bit. It was big, a place like heaven. But...'

"Suddenly PD's cussing. PD never cusses. He forgets about being PD and shouts, 'What? The Fuck? Happened? In Skid's?' It's like Halfheart talking Jap. 'Where? Is fucking? Keegan?' He's shaking.

"'Fucking Keegan?' Daryl says. 'Fucking Keegan, oh, that's complicated.'

"The story comes. The story's this. Daryl is up the steps, through the electric eye, *Whoosh*. Another *Whoosh* and it shuts, light's gone. Just beer signs and jukebox, Como crooning, and some other sounds. And the other sounds: American Shuffleboard goes clink, thunk.

"That's first. Then it's sawdust, peanut shells, something whatever goes crunch under Daryl's feet. That's next. Como quits. The juke goes hiss-hiss-hiss. Daryl's still yelling, 'Keegan! Keegan, you're not gone!' thumb up his butt like always but with the dark and now just a hiss-hiss from the juke, he's winding down, winding down.

"But see? No one's drinking, no one's talking. Skid's not calling 'fuck youse' and no one's actually playing American Shuffleboard. So the clinks and thunks are what? Imaginary? Yes. And something else. The air goes from cool to cold, not conditioned, this is the shadow under a summer thunderstorm and the stink isn't rummy bod and shit-streak clothes, it's worm, it's rot and open cellar. The juke hiss blends with the clink, thunk and it becomes a voice. 'Who invited you?' the voice says. It's maybe Skid. Probably not.

"'Keegan?' Daryl gets out a squeak.

"The regulars turn. They are not as remembered. 'It was like reading small print,' Daryl says later. 'The space, the stink, the voice, the faces. You squint at it, it clears.'"

"And it was?"

The old guy took a breath. "'Dust,'" he says, letting it go. "What Daryl said. Daryl, he's standing in shadow and vines in the Place. He's with the guys. Everybody's safe. And he says it was 'vapor like dust,' he says, 'dust out of the walls, the floor, coming out of the juke, the john, it's sifting from the ceiling, pouring from the bottles, out the taps, overflowing the glasses, the ashtrays. It's everywhere, it's dissolving out of the air.'

"'Like dew does,' Shorty says.

"'Like dew does!' Daryl says. 'Out of air. Bright and alive. Dust like vapor and it's rolling toward me.'

"'Like snow snakes!' Halfheart shouts.

"Everyone looks at Halfheart.

"'Yeah. Like at the beginning? And snow starts? Just light stuff in the wind and it rolls? You seen it, curling like them sidewinders in...'

"'PD punches Halfheart. Halfheart punches PD back. 'I didn't see no dust in there anyway,' Halfheart says, 'or dew, fog, or what-the-fuck!'

"'Go on, Daryl,' Shorty says

"Daryl uses a lot of words now. What it came to was dust, vapor, whatever, was everywhere. 'Gathering light,' he says it's doing. 'My light,' he says, 'my life.' And the bar, Skidoo's, that's becoming nowhere."

I verify. "Nowhere?"

"Like it doesn't exist. Like maybe it never did. The regulars stand, looking at Daryl, who is now not saying 'Keegan, Keegan' or anything. They are 'bright and shadow,' Daryl says, 'bright like they've got fire oozing out of them and what's left of the world is black stuff rising all around. Sewer water black, thick.' Daryl squints at his sneaks. He's trying to see a long way away. Then he goes on, says their light makes them hazy in the vapor or dust or what-the-fuck. The rising dark swirls around them, and them, they're being carried with it. 'Floating,' Daryl says. 'Flames drifting on night,' is what he said."

He pointed at my book again. "But like I said, all that's literary convention.

"So, they float toward Daryl. Daryl, as mentioned, is in the middle of it all, thumb up his butt.

"Then. In the corner. In what would have been the corner if the world had corners anymore and, I don't know, maybe in that last second before, Daryl catches a peek at..." the old guy thought for a second, "at 'real people,' what Daryl said. 'Boes, regular guys, the ones 'invited.' Them and Keegan. Real people. And this is the thing, this is the main thing: 'Next to Keegan, is Rory,' he says, Daryl says."

"The dead kid?"

"Dead Rory, yeah. Rory, dead, there with Jackie, his brother, our Keegan. There they are, the Keegan brothers, one real, the other not so much. A flame, a small one, that was Rore. A small flame embracing its brother."

"'Then, time changed,' he said, Daryl said. 'One look at that dead kid, time wasn't real no more.' What he said. 'The room was already not real. Now it was, I don't know, a dream of burning and the burning was all around...'"

The old guy was quiet.

"Yeah?"

"Yeah, yeah," he said. "I just realized," he said after a second, "this is a road. We're on a road, a mountain road."

Ahead, the road rushed toward us, in white dashes under us.

"Okay. Skidoo's is fading into something not real."

DRINK FOR THE THIRST TO COME

"A dream."

"Yeah, a dream. Daryl said. The people—except for Keegan and the 'boes—were light and dust..."

"Vapor!"

"And light. Yeah, vapor and light. 'And the darkness they float on is night. Or time and the world,' Daryl said. The inside of the bar became outside and outside it was night, quiet night with stars. 'And a long road,' Daryl said. 'The way unrolled down a hill then up. Like our mountain if our mountain went on forever and didn't have houses or people. The road goes down and down like the Nutcracker if the Nutcracker was forever,' he said that too. Then he said, 'The road is silver in starlight. Then they touch me,' he said. 'They touch me.' That's Daryl. 'I felt them, cold, they took me. I feel their flame, it's cold and it comes into me. And they take. They take and I am on the road. And I don't mind, see? The road unrolls like coming down from the End faster than ever but not having to pedal, not even a little. The world passes, mountains, trees, they whisper, and the sky is dark and silver,' he says. He says, 'It's like an old movie, a negative in dark silk and old snow,' he says, 'and I'm going farther and farther from...'"

The old guy stopped.

"What?"

"Oh, cripes, he didn't know what he was getting farther from! From 'the beginning,' he says, but he didn't know. He never did know, not until..."

"Where was he?"

"'Where was he?' Nothing. He was there. He was in Skidoo's. Get your questions right. 'What?' That's your question. What're they sucking from him? I'll say. They're taking whatchacallit? The *real*. Like I said, there's blood and then there's blood. They were taking day and night, they're taking parents, school, hell, taking us, the Enders, taking the End, the good shit and the lousy, all

the crap of being alive, being in Brewer, all the shit of being
Darly, being one of the guys, being a no-one among nobodies.
All that's draining out of him and into them. And he's happy to
let it go, glad to be rid of being smacked by Keegan, by everyone.
He's stupid and glad to be rid of having to go to Stenawatt next
year for bigger smacks, happy as hell to see the back of Mrs.
Feinerfrock, whom I haven't mentioned, nor will I! He's jumping
over all that shit."

The old guy looked at me.

"But you know, you add up all those jumps, all the crap living
shovels you, and you got half, no, maybe *most* of a life. But he
doesn't know that. Not then. And he was happy to be on the
road to..." He stopped.

"Paradise?" I said.

"Yeah, where forever happens. 'Paradise,' he says. And that's
far, far from the beginning.

"Then *Whoosh*. The door blasts. Sunlight slams. In runs
Halfheart, in comes Shorty, the Enders to the rescue. Halfheart's
in the eye beam, letting in the sun. Sunshine rips it all to hell.
Shorty's shouting Redskin, Halfheart's yelling Kraut, stuff he
heard in picture shows at the Pacific. Daryl is saved. Snatched,
thrown out the door, he and Short Draw. Halfheart behind,
flying, ends on top. As I said."

"Well," I say.

"Well, well. Daryl's eyes swim up from Paradise, like I said,
and we're back and up to the Place and the tale being told."

"Keegan? And Rory? The ghost of Rory…"

"Is not a fucking ghost. No more than." He took a breath, let
it out. "I was to say no more than I am, but I'm not so sure I'm
not."

"No," I said. "No, you're real."

"Yeah, yeah, and a swell fellow too. But Rory was dead. No
more to him than." He looked at me. "What's left after we've

left? Huh?"

"Memory and lies," I said.

He looked as though I'd frozen him.

"Memory and lies. Yeah. Or lies and illusions. But there they were. Solid. Out of the grave, all the regulars. Back from years ago and sitting in Skidoo's drinking and waiting."

"For?"

"For someone with too much of the real. Someone who needs an invite. You know?"

"So what'd you do?" I said.

"What'd they all do?"

"About your friend? Keegan?"

"Oh, Keegan. Yeah, I guess the guys killed him." It came simply.

"You?" I said.

"The guys. Yeah."

He explained. Evening. The air had chilled. The guys sat in the crawling dark under the branches of the Angel Yew in Chucky B's. They wondered what to do. After telling his story Daryl was sort of there, sort of not. The rest wondered what to do. Night came. They were still there, still wondering. Finally, they left their bikes sheltered at the Place and walked back to the bar, still wondering what they'd do.

"That walk through the cemetery, it wasn't scary," the old guy said. "Always was before, thinking about ghosts and whatever's coming. What a boneyard's supposed to be. You want a little bit, right? Now?" There was that rusted chuckle. "Now it was black grass, white stones, trees. The pond where Rory drowned was just black water and white carp. A smell like rotted mud. The fish splashed now and then. A little of Rory in them, I guess. There were rabbit screams. Owls taking rabbits. But see? The guys were headed to Skidoo's. Another scoot, the last scoot, they figured. They didn't scare. Like the end of *The Wild Bunch*, you know."

I didn't.

"The corner was almost empty, like never before. Lonely. That pretty view of the End by night, wasted. Home lights all along Spring Road running up on the far side of the yards. "'There's my house,' Halfheart said. And there it was, his house and the others'. All the houses of the East End climbed, one over the other, till they reached Stenawatt High. Above them, the mountain was dark until the sky and then were stars.

"All but one of the 'boes had gone. He was an old one, tears crying out of him. He's curled by the steps. The steps are still sun warm. He's hugging them. 'Please,' he says, 'please leave it be.'

"'Please, please?' Daryl says. 'Please what, please? There's Paradise,' Daryl says, 'then there ain't. Once Heaven gets to you, what the fuck, you're a goner. We have come to save you all!' Someone snickered. Halfheart."

"Daryl," I said, "he sounds, forgive me, kind of nuts."

"Daryl? May be," the old guy said. "But he'd been there and come back. So let me finish this. Let me finish."

I did.

"In they went. *Whoosh*. Into dark, into a stink of freezer meat gone off. No Como, no Stafford. Just scratches learning to talk. Their feet crunch. They run on what no one could see, but what they all knew."

"Sawdust, peanut shells?" I said.

"Yeah, sawdust and peanut shells," he said, "in the real. But now, in what Skidoo's was becoming, it was spider, snake, roach, and bone. Living twitches cracked, skittered under their sneaks, tried to slither or carry them with. But it was air that stopped them, not crackles or speaking scratches. Thick air yanked tether on them and they dead-stopped at the edge of the dark that Skidoo's was oozing.

"Halfheart, it was, who lit a match. A barn-burner. He lights it with a thumb and a smirk. There's a headful of sulfur, a flare, then there are eyes everywhere. Red eyes of the regulars, white eyes of the real folk off in Paradise, and a million small eyes on the floor, walls, the ceiling. Who knows what eyes they were. And the guys, their eight good eyes, two behind Daryl's specs, I guess, in Halfheart's matchlight. A quick bright second, then it all fades. A single match working to light Forever."

The old guy was breathing heavily. "You okay?" I said.

"Yeah. And sadness, not terror. Oh fear, yeah. Fear-sweat down the back. But the heart of that place was sadness. The sadness went on and on as the eyes faded with the matchlight. Everything ever lost? Everything not gotten to get lost, every assumption come to pass, there it was. A sad song, one you can't sing. In here."

I didn't need to see him touch his chest.

"Shorty yells, 'There!' Shorty points. Halfheart turns. Another match flare, more sulfur. Eyes brighten again. At the far end of seeing, there's Keegan. Keegan's smile, anyway, and a shape. Aside him, behind and half above, is Rory. A dream of Rory, soft and waterlogged. Too long with the fish then too long underground. He's attached. He's melted with Keegan.

"Light hits them. Like Halfheart's barn-burner was a searchlight. Their shadow hits the wall, Rory's arms around his brother. What passes for arms among them: shreds of a best suit, bones, muscle, hanging sinews and mist, smoke, maybe for effect, snow-snakes like Halfheart said. Them and other critters, white and gold carp, smooth, fat. Rory's arms. They wrapped Keegan, the still-alive brother. And Keegan? He says nothing. White eyes. He's there and another somewhere with his brother. Family. Warm. Time, home, and, yeah, I guess love." The old guy gave a sudden snort. "Orphans!" he said. "Sadness."

I said nothing.

"Halfheart jumps back. Rory and Keegan are afloat, they're

still. There's just a drip, drip, drip where Rory leaks pond or whatever. The drips flow down Keegan and spread.

"Halfheart tries to see more with his match. That Siamese shadow does a slow hootchie, like a stalking snake in *Jungle Jim*, like Yma Sumac warbling in *Secret of the Incas*, like…

"Then everyone, all of sudden, everyone gets it. Same time, I guess, everyone realizes Rory, Keegan, they're bait and the hook's setting good.

"PD is the one who went for it, PD who apologized for everything. Imagine. PD runs at them, like he's going to, I don't know, snatch Keegan, save him from that embrace there in Skidoo's Tap or wherever the hell they were. And the others follow. Daryl at ass end, Daryl who'd had a taste and for the first time in his life knew what was what.

"Halfheart's match gets close. Rory and Keegan's shadow spreads. Their darkness fills the wall, the sky, whatever. They withdraw, Rory holding his big brother. He opens. He's a kite, a sail. And they fly. They fly into their own shadow, high and out of reach. Except for PD. The leap of his life. He catches Keegan by the sneak and he's off with them, dangling, hanging, slow.

"There are voices, sounds, but I guess voices. Words, language I don't know, not German, which we all knew a little of, not Polish, not Dago or Indian.

"Then we're out. Outside, running after, following hard. Out somewhere, a place we'd never been, a place where nobody'd been. Except it was…"

The old guy looked at me, just eyes for a few seconds. A few seconds of eye can be forever on a dark bus, at the end of a long story, middle of the night.

"Except outside was the corner, Spring Road, the underpass. Okay. We were all still standing in Skidoo's Tap. Sure, sure. But where we ran was that road into starlight, the world Daryl told us. We're on that road to forever, nothing holding us like Rory held Keegan and Keegan's sneaks held PD. We ran. Like topping the Nutcracker, like the first time a run takes you whole and you know you're free of gravity, earth, body."

"Yes," I said.

"Yeah, then we're under. The subway. Something like the subway. Smelled like the subway…"

"Dusty farts," I said.

"And antique piss," he said. "Then that smell of meat, dead meat and old. Rory and Keegan, they're ahead and we follow them up the wall curving onto that arched ceiling. We're small things. Animals or bugs running upside down, we leap old stars or burned out lamps, we find old holes in the world up there, we burrow into the ceiling's cracks and we wiggle, follow Keegan and Rory and dangling PD through…" He thought for a second. "Funny, you know. All the years gone since then. I've thought about it. But this now, this is the farthest I've gotten into it. Aloud. You know how it is? To yourself a thing's one thing, saying makes it something else."

"Yes."

"So. It's dirt, rock, root, and grubs. All that flows by as we wriggle. Rory, Keegan, and PD are just ahead. The world sings. And we flow, now. No wriggles or running. We're riding the rails, bottom of the rails, under the steel rails of the yards, we're sliding a greased track to someplace ahead, someplace forever, and…

"And I don't know who it was who stopped. Stopping was a son-of-a-bitch. Fall down a well. Try to stop. It all keeps moving. Remember *2001*? The falling keeps on and on.

"But someone was a hero. Someone said, 'No!' Put on the binders. Saved us all. We stopped, then there we were."

"Where?"

"Hell, I guess it was. Or heaven. Same thing. That Rory and Keegan shadow that ate the world, the darkness that became the world? That big thing zoomed down to a pinprick and—"

He stopped again.

"For Daryl, it was a forest. Trees tall as mountains, thick as skyscrapers. 'Great dignity'—what he said later, looked like 'old Gods reaching...'" The old guy raised both arms. His hands nearly touched the luggage rack. "They reached over the world and shaded Earth from the sun. Shaded Daryl from the sun. Shadows spread everywhere. Living patterns. Bright and dark all around, whole worlds in bright, others in dark. Daryl. He wandered those worlds for, he didn't know, hours, years. There never was another place like it, there never were sounds like those that fell from the crying sky and breathing trees, sounds, songs, voices. Daryl. He could taste the smell of the world. He's just a little bitty bug, a little pinch-thing, scrabbling along, then flying, dreaming worlds, worlds that grew and grew until he's just another little bug chittering up the trees again.

"And the best was, he felt like these great old people..."

"The trees?"

"Yeah, yeah trees. They were great old people I think they were, great quiet old people, but they knew me. They knew I was there, and they were teaching, giving me..."

"What?"

"Whatever I needed."

I understood.

"All the guys had stories like Daryl's. Later, they all talked. Were warriors, pilots, kings... Well, you know. Heaven stuff. Stuff you always want and know not to expect."

He was quiet.

"Then Halfheart lit another match. Another heroic act unprecedented in all the world's braveries. Then PD. PD lets go of Keegan. Gave up, a hero. PD falls from them to us. Then everyone died. Died or something, anyway there they were. All the guys but Keegan. And the guys were in Skidoo's surrounded by regulars, the regular faces from the stools, whiskers, and hay bags. All around. Arms, rags, bones, old flesh. They all reached out. A hundred scoots but they're close now, close to touch, close to smell. Bones and hanks of hair reach to embrace as though the guys had been invited. Dead meat reached out like that octopoid goes for Flash Gordon... Like dead Rory held his brother, Jackie, our Keegan.

"I don't know if it was Halfheart's light or what." He tapped my book. "Just matchlight, not sun, but the rags and bones and hanks fell away. And Halfheart hit the beach at Normandy. He was over the bar. He's smashing bottles and rivers of whiskey flow, alcohol fills the air. He screamed movie Kraut, Shorty hooted Indian, PD screamed 'Sorry! Sorry! Sorry!' like a war-cry. Everyone shouts their own personal scoot-and-run. Thumbs and matches were everywhere. Lights flared. Fire, fire everywhere. And we ran, everyone ran. Not Keegan. Not Rory. Not the regulars or the invited. They were flames. Like I said. Flames drifting on the dark. The stink of John Walker ignites. *Whoof!*

"Then, *whoosh*, the guys are out and down the steps. Flames suck out on a rush of Skidoo air. They writhe like snakes, they rise, jaws snap night.

"The guys ran like hell. Hell, we were kids. Scared shitless kids. Fearless? Not us. Bravery's over. We'd just killed. Keegan at least. Our Keegan. Others. 'Boes and whatever. We'd torched Skidoo's. Rory, the rest and regulars were already dead. You know... See? Thing about them," he tapped my book with its lurid cover, "they have gifts. Plenty of them. They're old. They're powerful. But they're weak, too. In the end, they're just smoke and memory. Ashes and dust."

He leaned so the smell of him was close, comfortable. "When someone like you is near, see? They burn. They're fire in the night. They take and take and take you running in starlight. Send you flying to some paradise you want so much you'll leave your pain for them to gobble-gobble. Well, fuck them." He pressed a finger into my chest. "That pain in there, that's *you*, the pain. The stuff that makes you alive. See? See, life's beautiful, but the world? Oh, the world's shit."

"Maybe not me," I said. "Do I have pain? Too much 'real'? Nah. So what happened? To you small felons, I mean?"

"So what happened? We murderers, we ran. Back to the Place. Bikes still there. Still dark. We walked them, ran them all the way around the yards, across the tracks downtown. Fire trucks coming everywhere to the conflagration, top of Spring Road.

"From the East End it looked like the world was dying. Fires are scary to kids. Something old, something that always was, is going away, becoming light and heat then ash. We walked roundabout and were back on the End in time to catch dawn and the fire dying."

The bus downshifted, slowed.

"Caught hell for being out all night. All of us. 'We're watching the fire,' we said. 'Nah, we never seen Keegan.' 'Nah, no idea where he was.' Played it smooth. When we visited the pit we were shaking, Halfheart chattering too loud about being quiet, keeping shut if we knew what was good for us. The hole where Skidoo's Tap was, was…" He took a moment. "Was there for as long as I knew. Three concrete steps on the corner. Climb them, look one way, there's the view. Turn 'round, there's a hole in the world where Skidoo's was. An old tunnel, maybe. Brewer is on old limestone. Old limestone has caves, you know. Anyway, Skidoo's fell in, down to nowhere. Halfheart said once, maybe the last time he ever said anything to all of us, he said, 'Wonder if my old man's down there? I hope,' he said, 'hope he fried.'

"Never did find out the why of them. How. What. Something at Chucky B's maybe, something Indian and old in the old ground around Brewer, you know, great spirits, some bullshit. Why'd they come back? What gave them the power? Just

Brewer's small men hanging 'round after the dance. You know? Anyway.

"Anyway, one by one all the guys did what was not expected. They left. Scattered."

The bus stopped, hissed. Outside was blue and dark. Yellow lamps lit a block-long platform topped by corrugated rust. The terminal was shingles and shadow, a thing from the 1920s, a single story and a clock. The clock had no hands. No one waited for train or bus.

"Brewer," the driver called, "all for Brewer." The door opened. *Whoosh.*

The old guy was up. He had no luggage.

"I know who you are," I said.

"Nah, you don't. Names are changed, like I said."

"Like you said. One more thing?"

"One more thing? Well?"

"Never mind," I said. "I'd ask the wrong thing, anyway."

"Anyway, I'll tell you: all the guys stayed gone. I guess forever." He smiled in the blue. "Maybe not. Hey. Enjoy Philly," he said. He was out the door and headed north and the bus pulled out.

I had time.

We were on the turnpike to Philly when I let night and flame float me, carry me through the darkness, back.

Not hard to find. The old guy stood by a flat spot on the hill above the quiet rail yards. He never saw me. Never saw the snow snakes, the other critters of air and dark. Never felt the embrace, the drawing out. Maybe at the end. I took him, was full, and was back in my seat on the bus before Philadelphia.

I was going to ask about the girl, the carriage, the babies. But I didn't have to.

FINAL WORDS

If you are content with the stories, if you don't care to know from where these things came, so be it. I hope you've enjoyed them. If you want to know something of how or why they were written, here you go. Let's begin at the beginning.

FROM *A NATION OF ASH*: **DRINK FOR THE THIRST TO COME**

I am the loneliest guy at the dance so I'll fox-trot with whoever asks. The title story is typical of several in this collection: I was asked to write it. This one was made-to-order as part of a shared-world anthology-to-be, a collection of ten post-apocalyptic tales by ten authors.

I had worked with the editor before and he knew I was a writer for the City of Chicago. He suggested my offering might center on our city's new Emergency Management and Communications Center.

Reasonable, intriguing.

Despite being a Geek (with no Geek *bona fides*) I'd never had occasion to tour the EMC. I got the okay from my Commissioner and scooted over to the West Side (Chicago has no East Side) to get an insider's look at the Center. The place was intriguing, almost exciting. More than that, I cannot say. I will say the EMC is big, scary, secure-looking as you might imagine such a windowless bunker-like command and control center to be. It is state-of-the-art air-conditioned hardware humming away in darkened rooms, serviced by chilled wetware.

Homeland Security restrictions aside, however, somewhere along the tour I realized I didn't want this story to be nuts and bolts, a tale of by-the-numbers survival; I did not want to focus on beleaguered City workers bureaucratizing the end of the world. Christ, that's my daily job. By the way, in case you think nuclear holocaust will exempt you, the Feds have contingency plans for the distribution of mail and the collection of taxes in the wake of Armageddon.

In my mind, then, the EMC of my submission would be a shell, maybe the beginning and end-points of a quest. I like quests.

Researching the apocalypse, I came to realize the similarities between a landscape stripped to the skin by nuclear winter and the Dust Bowl of the 1930s. The photographs of what we now know as "haboobs" and the first-person accounts of survival and death by dust from that time convinced me that something of that world had to be part of the story. By the way, for a personal look at absolutely avoidable human misery, I recommend Timothy Egan's *The Worst Hard Time: the Untold Story of Those Who Survived the Great American Dust Bowl.* I can tell you, our hero's Long Walk from Texas to Chicago would probably not be possible in conditions as described. Okay, miracles happen; that's part of what horror is: the wondrous meeting the unthinkable. Another book of immense help was Jared Diamond's *Collapse: How Societies Choose to Fail or Succeed.* So too were Michihiko Hachiya's *Hiroshima Diary* and John Hersey's *Hiroshima.* For the shape and tone of *Drink...*, I re-read Alexander Solzhenitsyn's *One Day in the Life of Ivan Denisovich.*

The plot is a basic quest story with both victory and defeat at the end of it.

The Chicago sites are real. Johnny's IceHouse is across the way from the EMC. The Deep Tunnel, one of the largest civil engineering projects in history, is being built beneath my feet as I type. The opera house? Still there. The Turandot gong? That too. The Expressway? Still streaming. They wait.

This story's history? Until now it was a virgin, untouched by human eye. The shared-world anthology for which it was written never happened. That happens.

THANKS FOR YOUR MEMORIES: **ROOT SOUP, WINTER SOUP**

At this writing Tycelia and I have been married eight years. We have known each other for a half-century. We met in an empty room in a college town in eastern Pennsylvania, dated for a short time then lost touch. Forty years on we reconnected through an article in an alumni magazine. At the time, she was teaching French in Maine and I was writing for Mayor Daley in Chicago. At first, our courtship was two chums catching up by email. We wrote every day; we shared news, thoughts, and, as boomers will, we reminisced. Tycelia is from Mississippi. Her childhood was filled with tired old places, hard folk etched with histories and memories of food. One day she mentioned she was slicing parsnip 'fingers' for a root soup.

I was off.

Where Cordelia comes from is a mystery. Without being specific, the voice of the story is southern though Cordelia could be from any place at any time. She is a woman with a past, deeply wronged, scarred by someone, left damaged to live and be a small monster in a tiny world. She lives beatifically and embraces goodness as only a true monster can. Her place in the woods is taken from a place in which a philosophy prof/friend of mine lived in the year before I went into the service. That old house in the woods was one of the most haunted places I've ever entered. See, it had been a station on the Underground Railway before the Civil War and…

Damn. I have got to do something with *that* place sometime. I'll say no more except: that haunted little house in the woods, that name, Cordelia, the image of chopping fingers for a root soup… That was enough.

ZOMBIES IN THE TRENCHES: **WIND SHADOWS**

Again, I received an email from an editor who invited me to submit to an anthology. This time, Zombie stories. The other invitees formed an impressive list. I was honored. I'd recently been nominated for a Bram Stoker Award by the Horror Writers Association and, for the second time, had been beaten for the award by the same guy. That's probably why I said yes.

I've never been a fan of zombie entertainments. I'd never written a zombie story. I'd read only one zombie tale. Even zombie films (excepting *Shaun of the Dead*) left me, forgive me, cold. Still, it was an invitation. I had no idea what I'd do but, hell, I had six months to do it in.

I re-watched a few Romero films, read *How to Survive a Zombie Attack* and some other things. Two months in, and no good ideas presented. Hell, I had four months.

What was my problem?

I don't like working the old tropes. That was my problem.

One Sunday afternoon Tycelia and I were wandering around Hyde Park, Chicago. We stepped into one the bookstores that services that rather idyllic University of Chicago neighborhood.

Tycelia headed for the foreign language section. I bungled about. For no particular reason—which is the salient feature of bookstore bungling—I picked up a long, wide, and not-so-thick book called *Harry's War: Experiences in the 'Suicide Club' in World War One*. *Harry's War* is a facsimile of a self-illustrated diary kept by a British soldier named Harry Stinton. Harry had been a so-called "bomber," a ground soldier trained in hand-grenade warfare, during the First World War. I bought and devoured it in a day.

The almost casual acceptance of violent death surrounding Private Stinton suggested a direction.

I research by immersion. It's very non-academic. I eat books, take no notes, try to catch the feel and flavor of a place, an era; I try to hear, to touch. When I can smell that world, I begin to write.

Smelling the "First War's" trenches is no fun.

The draft was more than 13 thousand words. I cut. I submitted. The story was accepted. Then, the project was delayed in favor of another book-to-be in which the editor was involved, something called *A Dark and Deadly Valley*, horror and dark fantasy set during World War II. He thought that since I had a feel for war stories I might have something for that one.

I did.

The zombie book was further back-burnered when the editor opted to do yet another anthology. This was to have been a shared-world work, ten authors tethered to a single universe, one in which humankind barely survives a nuclear war. He asked me to be one of the ten. My contribution to this effort eventually would be called *Drink for the Thirst to Come*.

The zombie book never happened. The authors retrieved their stories and groused to each other. I put *Wind Shadows* aside and never tried to sell it. Face it, it's too zombie for straight markets, not zombie enough for the shuffle and moan crowd.

Every now and then, though, a wind blows across the fields and I run into one of the authors, ask about his or her contributions to this and other books that never were.

Now you've read my contribution.

A strange thing: until I considered it for this collection, I'd not read *Wind Shadows* myself. As a writer, yes, reading as I went, reading as I cut, pared, adjusted, proof-reading. But as a member of the audience? No. Interesting experience. Hell, it must be a zombie story, it was accepted into an anthology of zombie tales. Okay. It is about the dead animated by... Well, by something. It wasn't until I finished reading it that first time as an audient that I realized it's about what war does. War takes people to a place, below; it brings them to that blank wall, to themselves. The other side of which is something unseen, unseeable for most of us this side of the grave. It gives a warrior a hint of that something that lurks beneath us all. In World War I it was called shell-shock. Now we call it Post Traumatic Stress Disorder.

My war was Vietnam. My wartime experiences were mild compared with the people I write about. Still, I could tell you stories...

ONE FROM THE ID: **IN A DAINTY PLACE**

My father never went to war. I'm an only child. The "dainty place" was a lie I told my grandmother.

In a Dainty Place was the jump-off point for a novel set in the world inside the wall. The novel, still pending, is set in a medieval milieu mixed with the made-up family stories our hero tells his kid brother. The book begins in the world of the wall and *In a Dainty Place* is back-story, revealed as the story progresses.

I almost know where this story comes from. I am sure that in writing it I was ridding myself of something that had niggled since I was a tot. That something was the side hallway of the large old house my parents moved into when I was five. The hall was a long, dark splintery place where aged vacuum cleaners lived and where—don't ask me why—the British lay in wait for me.

Okay. Ask.

Okay, I'll tell. I could read before I went to school. Not bragging, it was an accident. My grandfather used to sit me on his lap and read to me. Stories, poetry, whatever. Granddad would read and I'd follow his finger as it touched the words. I learned that certain places his finger touched made certain sounds come from Granddad. The sounds were stories. The stories were wrapped in the words.

Granddad liked Edgar Allan Poe. At that lap-age I honestly thought poetry was so-called because Poe had written it, all of it.

One writer with a silly name, Longfellow, wrote a poem about Paul Revere. The poem was a rush of terrifying sounds: belfry arch, muffled oars, midnight ride. In it were graveyards and horses galloping the night of another time, across a younger land. The hero, Paul Revere, rode to sound the alarm to every Middlesex, village, and farm, calling them forth because monsters called the British were coming. The British of the poem came from a black hulk silently afloat in the dark harbor, they loomed out of the mists of the river. Having loomed, they landed and marched with a steady tread through the town…

Our town?

No, no. A distant place. Boston.

In my mind the British were too awful to see. They were large, dark, hairy, and smelly, they came by the thousands and crouched in shadows and dust and hid among Electrolux hoses in the unlighted hallway that led to our attic stairs.

Why there? In that corridor was wallpaper similar to that described in the story. Not as detailed but it was from an older time, a different place. It was from that wallpaper that I annealed a terror of "the British" with a fear of blood hunting.

As mentioned, I have no brother or sister. I am my own sibling. I am Raymond. I banished me to that wall, the place of blood and death bordered by deep forest, distant villages and, somewhere invisible, to a castle of my own making. I built that room, the dainty place within. I filled it with the machineries of wonder...

Oh, yes. That.

Once upon a time, the rods for our kitchen curtains vanished. My grandmother had taken down the curtains to wash them and left their spring supports on the table. They vanished.

Where had I put them?

I didn't know. Truly. The taking of and hiding the things had slipped from my five-year-old consciousness and the rods truly had vanished. Magic.

I finally admitted I'd hidden them. I didn't remember but it seemed better to confess.

Where were they?

In a "dainty dish" I insisted. Which notion I suspect I'd cribbed from the nursery rhyme, "Sing a Song of Sixpence." Eventually, I allowed that they were in a dainty place rather than just a dish. I stuck to that. For weeks, I insisted I'd put them in a dainty place.

Eventually, someone found them in the junk drawer in the kitchen. I did not remember putting them there, I do not remember. It must have been magic.

RAF LAKENHEATH: **AT ANGELS SIXTEEN**

"It is well that war is so terrible—lest we should grow too fond of it." —Robert E. Lee

1966 through 1969 I was in the U.S. Air Force. For most of that time I was in England, some of it near Cambridge, most of it in London. At 24 in that era of Vietnam I was older than most just entering the ranks but still, I was a kid. Now and then something from those years will pop up and I write. Typically, I mothball what emerges. Why? No idea.

I wrote this story when another writer and I thought we might package and sell an anthology of war-themed horror. I dipped into memories and out came RAF Lakenheath near Brandon, Suffolk, England. The night I drove there from London, the farmers of Suffolk were burning chaff from their fields following the fall harvest. When I got to the Heath, USAFE (United States Air Forces, Europe) was conducting a practice alert and RAF Lakenheath was locked down. I spent my first night in-country in the base jail, safely out of the way of colonels and master sergeants who wandered the evening dropping smoke bombs and telling people they were dead and their posts destroyed. Apparently, the brig was not part of the game and we FNGs were out of the way.

My eventual home on base was a World War II-era Quonset hut, a corrugated steel structure that looked like a silo lying on its side and half buried in the earth. Most of the guys assigned to them hated the huts. I loved mine. I had my own little room at the rear of the building, my own kerosene stove. My own back door opened onto a field where cattle grazed. I even had my own cow who greeted me mornings at the fence. A hundred yards beyond my cow was a forest. What's not to like?

Lakenheath hadn't been a base during the Second War. It had been a target. German night raiders tasked to bomb RAF Mildenhall, about 4 miles away, were expected to pound the dummy flightlines, mock aircraft and bogus buildings of Lakenheath.

The core of *At Angels Sixteen* came from an article I read when I was about 10. *Boys' Life, Reader's Digest,* not sure which. The story was about a man who survived a fall from an airplane. He survived in circumstances much as the German doctor posits about our tail gunner in the story.

I didn't buy the explanation when I was 10. Obviously magic saved the guy, but you're free to accept the Nazi version of the story.

B-17s. I love them. I got a ride in one at an air show in Reading, Pennsylvania when I was about 7. There were plenty of the old war birds doing such work in 1949. One or two still fly. The noise, the smell, the bone-chatter was magic, magic to the core. See? We boys love the machinery of warfare. It isn't until we're grown that we realize that combat is terror, boredom, loss, flesh, and pain.

There's the story. Our proposed anthology never came about and I never submitted it until the editor of the zombie book-that-never-was asked if I had any World War II-centered horror/fantasy tales for an anthology to be called *A Dark and Deadly Valley.*

I did.

FIRST VOYAGES: **SOME STAGES ON THE ROAD TOWARD OUR FAILURE TO REACH THE MOON**

There once was a sub-realm of science fiction called First Voyages. These were stories of mankind's baby steps off-world. Cyrano de Bergerac wrote one, *ditto* Jules Verne and countless more. Kids of my generation had Lester del Rey's *Mission to the Moon* and Robert A. Heinlein's *Rocketship Galileo.* We had films too. I can't tell you how many wet summer afternoons I spent in my Uncle Jim's Lyric Theater in Chester, PA, watching *Destination*

Moon and *Rocketship X-M,* a first voyage that does not end well for the intrepid explorers.

Yes, this story is autobiographical. My dad was not killed in Korea or any war. Reinhart's name was not Reinhart. The hat had a major's gold oak leaf on it and had been my Uncle Bonney's and he remained alive long enough to divorce my Aunt Ida and move out of all our lives. I did pray to be the first guy on the moon. I drew countless pictures, made hundreds of plans. There was a well traveled-in refrigerator carton in our basement. Other than not getting to the moon, that's it. In the '80s of the last century, I had occasion to pick up Buzz Aldrin at O'Hare Airport and deliver him to a book signing at THE STARS OUR DESTINATION bookstore in Chicago. That's as close as I got.

Some Stages was written because my writers group, Twilight Tales, decided to hold a benefit on the second anniversary of the loss of Space Shuttle *Columbia.* The goal was to honor not only *Columbia's* but all astronauts, cosmonauts, and dreamers who died trying to kick our monkey asses out of the cradle and into the real world, the universe. Twilight Tales regulars Jody Lynn Nye, Richard Chwedyk, a few others, and I were asked to read something personally meaningful at the event. It was a good evening. We heard a few first voyage pieces by Heinlein and others. Money was raised for the families of the *Columbia* crew and we spent time together over drinks and good tales.

Jody and I wrote original tales. Her story was excellent and, as you might expect, featured a space-faring pussycat.

Mine was the story you just read.

DeAngelo is younger than I, but we both planned for ours to be the first feet on the moon. I was in 7th grade on the evening of October 4th, 1957. I'd been to my eye doctor and came home bespectacled, a four-eyed flight-school wash-out to-be and learned that the Soviet Union had beaten us to space. Like DeAngelo, I felt my country had been cheated out of its proper place in history. That night, like DeAngelo, I decided, hot damn, I'm going to fix that.

There was no cat.

"Reinhart" and I stayed friends throughout grade school and junior high and fell out much later over Carol Devine and because he remained a gearhead and I…?

Well, I'd fallen in love with distance.

"Reinhart" and I planned many trips to the moon, the planets. Then we became convinced that dinosaur bones lay just beneath the surface in the cemetery near our homes. Who needed to mount expeditions to the Gobi Desert or anywhere? We had Charles Evans Cemetery. We sifted through tons of damp soil gravediggers had conveniently put aside for us. We found suspicious things, things that may have been… who knew what? We found meteors, which were most probably bits of slag from the Carpenter Steel plant not too far from there. We found curious markings on sheets of shale. I was convinced Neanderthals had lived in our town and had sketched saber tooth tigers and wooly mammoths on those slabs of yellow shale. Better yet, perhaps those shadow blots were… Well, maybe, perhaps, might have been… Could they be accidental "photographs" made by a marvelous coincidence of ancient lightning and the magical chemistry in the soils of Reading, Pennsylvania!

Eventually, "Reinhart" explained the fissiparous nature of shale and how intrusions of impurities into… Well, something. And that was that and…

And maybe I never forgave his explanations and maybe Carol Devine wasn't to blame. I recognized, finally, that we'd taken separate paths to our personal stars. See? He wanted to know. He wanted accuracy about rocks, bones, and rockets. I wanted the rock I held in my hand to have had ghosts within.

What I said about falling in love with distance. That's not

quite right. I had fallen in love not with the stars but with the space between stars. The moon? It was great. Other planets? Wonderful. But like many travelers, I fell in love with the going to rather than the being there. Science and its handmaiden, engineering, were about smoothing it out, turning a voyage to the moon into a trip to the grocery store.

Wrong. Obviously wrong. A lot of people hung their soft and fragile asses out there. Quite a few had to die to earn us our first trip off-planet.

I didn't lose interest, not exactly. When Neil Armstrong set foot on the moon, I was living in London, not serving in DaNang. My across-the-hall neighbor, a producer for the BBC, and I sat on the edges of our seats. I thrilled to Armstrong and Aldrin's descent and touchdown. Then… "Tranquility Base here." Ahh! He nicknamed God's place! No longer part of a distant planet, where the Eagle landed was now a Base. Humans are there. Americans. I waited for the first words on the surface. There they were. *Small step. Giant leap.* Good but rehearsed. Nice sentiment. His next words were about soil compressibility. Important, things Reinhart would have drooled over. The dream was concluded. Reinhart had beaten me to the moon and Carol Divine.

It also occurred to me that night in London, that all the books on that first voyage had now been written. There'd be no more *First Men in the Moon*, *The Moon Is A Harsh Mistress*, *Rocketship Galileo*. Our first voyage was now history. And it was, well… kind of dull.

Apollo 13 changed that for a bit, but the dream was over. We beat the Russians and, cripes, what a lousy reason to make history.

Understand. I am not saying I was disappointed that Armstrong, Aldrin, and Collins's flight hadn't been a disaster, but the DeAngelo in me really wished that something had been lurking in the space between here and there, something no one had counted on, something the Reinharts hadn't factored in.

When I thought to write a story to commemorate the loss of the crews of *Columbia*, *Challenger*, or *Apollo 1*, the dead of *Soyuz* and other losses along our way, what I really wanted to memorialize was the dream that took us to the edge. Too many of us are left, still looking toward the horizon or into the shadows.

Back to Buzz Aldrin. He'd been scheduled for a bookstore appearance. At the last minute, I was the only one with both car and time enough to get and deliver him. When I got to O'Hare, he was walking down the onramp, bag in hand, about to hitch a ride. I gathered him. "Fine thing," I said, "you can send a man to the moon but you can't pick him up from the airport." He laughed. He did that easily for a man who'd almost been left by his hosts to find his own way. I had an hour or so of gridlocked privacy with the second man on the moon, the man who had in fact uttered the very first words on the moon. Look it up: "Contact Light. Okay, engine stop." Significant here is that in that hour, I met a guy who was earthy, human, bright—this is the guy who taught NASA orbital mechanics, the guy who suggested using water submersion for zero gravity training—this was the ultimate Reinhart. And I found that he had as deep—if not a deeper—capacity for dreaming than DeAngelo.

Well, Buzz wasn't the first on the moon either.

REAL GHOSTS: **THE BOY'S ROOM**

For me, *The Boy's Room* is the most disturbing story in this collection. It is also one that was rejected for publication, turned down not by distant editors but by one I considered (and still do) to be a friend.

The story was written for an anthology called *Spooks*. Ghost tales. Simple, yes, but there I was, bitten in the ass by my avoidance of tropes. Cripes, the world will not end if I write a vampire story featuring the toothy undead, or a zombie story with shuffling corpses.

Tycelia and I had just married, our fortunes newly merged. She was going through pictures, telling stories of life in Mississippi. She mentioned a part of an old home-place the family called "the boy's room." The place was a separate shack behind her grandmother's main house where some boys of a boy-heavy family of brothers, step-brothers, and half-brothers could sleep. There are photographs. The name tweaked my fancy and I melded the pictures and her stories with some of recollections of sleepovers at cousins' places during my own summer holidays in eastern Pennsylvania.

What makes this story so disturbing to me? The ghost is not that of the boy, Rafe, or of the old conjure woman; it isn't the spirit of anyone dead in the common sense of the word at the time of the girl's experience. The ghost of the tale is Melissa, her life attending her from her own empty future of missed opportunities.

With age, that strikes bone. At 60, a lot of looking-back accompanies forward-peering hope. These years I catch echoes, glimpse earlier iterations of Larry; I see him in his hopes and wishes. He knows deeply that such and such a thing will—no: must—absolutely must happen.

And I know now, of course, it did not and so dearly wish I could reach back, advise, nudge, speak to that life that is still alive in me.

As said, my friend did not buy this story. As said, the story still makes me shiver.

BECAUSE I HAD TO: **LITTLE GIRL DOWN THE WAY**

This is a ghost story. It posits the not very original notion that heaven and hell are the same place, depending on who you are. It's also about love in some form or another. It was written quickly, in a passion, fast as I could type it. Here's how it came to be.

I write for a living and I write because I want or have to. For a living, I write for the City of Chicago. When I write fiction, I write because a notion has popped into my head and I think it's pretty neat.

Sometimes, though, I write out of passion. Some scream. I write. Anger, fear, sorrow, hatred. The pieces that come from these screams are frequently harsh, brutal, nasty. I call them my "Vile Tales" after a comment I once made to a friend about a story of mine called "Catching."

She called it "erotic."

"It's not erotic," I said. "It's just vile."

There are a lot of these. Typically, they begin with a person in crisis and often end in mayhem, blood and pain.

"Little Girl Down the Way" is one of these Vile things; it comes from sorrow and anger. Here's where the anger came from.

I live on the Northside of Chicago. Wrigley Field, where the Chicago Cubs play, is three blocks to the north. Lake Michigan is three blocks east. During the season, my neighborhood, Wrigleyville, becomes... Remember in *It's a Wonderful Life*, when Jimmy Stewart wishes he'd never been born, his guardian angel shows him a world without his influence? Potterville! That's my neighborhood: sports bars, frat-rats and bunnies. In winter it's just a place where the overcompensated come to hoot and puke out the butt ends of youth.

In the decade before the housing bubble busted, Wrigleyville

348

was undergoing a facelift. People with far too much money and far too little imagination wanted to move here. They came because this had been a place they prowled when young, a place to get drunk, to get laid, to piss unchecked in alleys.

When they came back to live, they looked up and said, "We can't have this...!"

They are not the source of my passion.

A malignancy came with yuppie infestation: 19th-century frame houses were dissolving; overnight, cheaply-built, enormously pricey faux-brick condos arose in their place, a form of urban cancer that both destroys our collective memory and offers us a glimpse of mid-21st-century slums-to-be.

But this isn't from where my passion that formed this tale comes either...

One afternoon, late in the 20th century, I was driving up the alley. I passed a muddy pond where a house and garage had been the day before. The site was surrounded by yellow crime scene tape. On hand was the usual cast: police, paramedics, plain-clothes bureaucrats, photographers, rubberneckers. The demolishers had uncovered the bones of a small body at the end of the walkway from the old house to the alley. The corpse was the body of what was presumed to be a 2-3-year-old girl. Apparently, she had been there for many years. Decades.

The old, sad tale went to the papers and disappeared.

Three years later, the story oozed back into the news. Chicago homicide had not given up on the little girl; they had done their job of speaking for the dead, a yeoman task when you consider that the victim the murder-police had to speak for in this case was about 50 years into her measure of eternity. The story returned as a page 5 news item: on her deathbed, a woman in Nebraska confessed to having killed her child in Chicago, in this place, now gone, in the late 1950s. The details were scant but moving by the bareness of their bones.

The woman had been identified and been found in hospital dying of congestive heart failure. When questioned, she confessed to having given birth to the girl in the late 1940s and had kept her a secret from the world. Reasons? No reasons. Or if there had been a reason, it probably derived from some unrecognizable form of love. See, when the mother became pregnant again, she kept the little girl locked in the basement to keep her new child from... From what, remains unknown. Love, of some unimaginable species.

While the remains found just down the way from my apartment seemed to have been those of a 3-year-old, the girl had actually survived to about 7 years then was murdered by the mother, maybe in a rage, maybe not, and, having confessed, the woman died.

The son that had been that mother's second child, now in middle-age, was surprised to learn that he had had a sister and had shared that house in Chicago until he was 3 or 4 years old. Then he and his mother had packed and moved by night.

The view from our second floor porch looks down that alley. The little girl's former burial site is less than 100 feet from my back gate. I wasn't living in Chicago when the crime took place. I was just a kid then, a reasonably well-adjusted, all-too-coddled kid growing up happy, and not, in Reading, Pennsylvania. I don't know what I was doing when the 20-pound 7-year-old became a corpse. But in my trailing years I shared a back alley with the little girl and that view from my window, down the way, and the changing shape of the neighborhood has always made me feel connected. We were neighbors, I guess. I grew up in a small town and people close to each other are neighbors, damn it.

The story was written more than a dozen years ago. I put it aside and read it publicly a few times—in Chicago, at a World Horror Convention in Denver. I tried to sell it once. It didn't sell. I understand. It's got problems. It's too long, it rambles. But it is one of those things I won't fuss with. Finally, an editor who had heard me read it asked me for it and published it in early 2008 in an anthology of tales by Midwestern writers of the dark called "Hell in the Heartland."

The Little Girl is complete; her story is told. The Chicago Police spoke for her; now, I let her speak for herself. It's not a story for enjoyment, but I hope it touches you as her story still touches me.

Well, maybe it'll get you up and moving around the room, that at least.

"NOT WITH A BANG BUT A WHIMPER": **A VERY BAD DAY**

Very little needs to be said. I was asked to contribute to a pet-themed anthology. I had two cats, Mozart, a tabby-Siamese blend, deep blue eyes and haughty as hell and Wolfgang, a gray, sweet-tempered former boy who was a surprisingly swift mouser.

There once was a bookstore nearby, something like the one in the story. It had everything and they charged too much. Then it closed and I missed it.

When I considered how much mystery-life was to be found in a cat and how mathematically magical was the amount of information to be found in so vast a place as the now-gone bookstore, I started to write. I had also just been dumped and wanted to memorialize that fact. Leslie is my go-to character for shifting things out of my own life and dumping them into someone utterly unlike me.

The end of the world? Catholic guilt.

CORRIDORS OF NIGHT: **RAT TIME IN THE HALL OF PAIN**

There was such a film. I saw it in elementary school. The twitching images never left me.

Rat Time... is one of my "vile tales"—the vilest of which are not included in this collection. This one wriggled into my head during a road trip to a World Fantasy Convention in Providence, Rhode Island. Marty Mundt and I drove, Chicago to Providence, 983 miles, with pauses for input and output only. Twelve hours. Most of the night driving was mine. When the world is a rushing tunnel of strobing median perforations, when your companion is a sleeping lump, when the world's only voice is an F.M. stranger who fades in, then crackles away, when you push the speed so your nerves keep you quivering awake, then oddities begin to peek in at the periphery. Somewhere in Ohio I realized we'd passed signs for a strangely large number of "Halls of Fame." Travelers of I-90 not in a highway fugue-state might pause to visit the College Football, Basketball, Rock and Roll, Baseball, Professional Wrestling, and Volleyball Halls of Fame. There are others I no longer remember, all along a thousand linear American miles.

Back in Chicago, I began a generic tale about a guy riding the I-90 corridor who stops by these places and does dreadful things. At some point the fame/pain pseudo-rhyme suggested itself and there it was. Who better to be memorialized in a so-named hall at the literal end of his road than a serial killer?

I apologize to a junior high buddy, now, alas, no longer with us. His name was Winkler and he was a quirky old pal. Like many of us in the middle-years of youth, he reinvented himself with wonderful regularity.

I wanted my killer guy to carry a squeaky, non-threatening name and "Winkler" it was. I also wanted him to wake in each

352

cycle of murderous urging with adjusted versions of old memories. And there he was, Alex Winkler, monster.

Where to leave him at the end? Where to memorialize, to punish him? In himself, of course. In himself.

I CAN BE BRIEF: **THEN, JUST A DREAM**

I once read this story aloud in a heartbeat under five minutes. A joke among my friends is that my titles are longer than some people's stories: *God Screamed and Screamed, Then I Ate Him. 'What Do You Know of the Land of Death?' Clown Said One Night to the Haunted Boy. She Was Washing Her Frock When Winston Churchill Came Galloping Out of the Mist.* By publication time, that last one became *Children, Invisible, Watching from the Great Darkness,* but you get the idea.

Not surprisingly, I'm not much for "flash" fiction, tales developed and ended in 500-700 words. I certainly never intended to enter the flash fiction competition at the 2007 World Horror Convention in Toronto. I was going to hear some friends read. That was it.

While slicking my hair in the room before the event, though, I remembered a thing written a year or so before, one of those notions that nudge you when you're doing something else. I dug through the computer and there it was: *Then, Just Dreaming.* Fifteen hundred words. I skimmed it. The skim took more than five minutes. The contest limits readers to five minutes and "not a heartbeat longer."

At first look, the thing felt like one of those shaggy dog tales everyone writes in junior high, ending with, "and then I woke and found it was all just a dream."

Come on, I said to myself, *even goofing around you wouldn't have written that.* I re-read and realized the thing needed a second (maybe third) reading to make its way inside the reader. It's a true nightmare, one folded on itself.

I'll let you decide what it is. What I thought at the time was, *Damn, flash fiction should not require a study guide.*

I trimmed it. Trimmed some more. Not hard. Even at 1,200 words there was flab. *Screw it.* I printed it, went down to the lobby, crossed out a few more lines then let it go. *You can't do flash fiction, Larry. Hell no.* Peter Crowther was one of the judges along with Ed Bryant and Nancy Kilpatrick. *Christ no. You're not going to get up drunk and...*

Did I mention? This was one of my beer and vodka nights. They happen at conventions.

I stuck the "Dream" in my pocket and went into the ballroom to hear my chums. Chums saw me coming. Chums chuckled.

"Santoro. Flash Fiction. Mutually exclusive concepts," someone said.

"No, no. Just here to watch."

Perverse as I am, though, I sign up. Being with the beer and vodka helped. I sit. Some read. My name is called. I go to the lectern. The assembly calls out, "On your mark! Get set!! READ LIKE A MOTHERFUCKER!!!" Tradition.

It is not that I motormouth the tale, I keep it brisk. I begin quickly because near the end I know there's a moment when I need a long beat of dead air to give what follows some weight. I establish a pace quick enough to make even a short pause seem like a deathwatch. Later beats lend themselves to breathless rushing and there, indeed, I read like a motherfucker.

I speak the tale's final word, "Goddamn…" as the timekeeper puts his hand on my shoulder. I am in, out and under five by less than a second.

Others read. The judges retire. We drink and cuss. They return.

I do not take third place, which I halfway hoped for. There had been some really good writer/readers. I do not take second. I'm done, I think. I do take first. The world is turvy, topsy-wise. We've fallen into another version of the Big All.

The prize? Bragging rights, basically. But I am pleased and honored so here I am bragging. I read like a motherfucker.

Since then, the story has been podcast in Great Britain by the StarShipSofa. It won the StarShip's "Best Short Fiction" award for 2009 and was published in StarShipSofa Stories, Volume 2, in 2010. Now it's here. I hope you enjoyed it.

JERSEY, 1950-SOMETHING: **SO MANY TINY MOUTHS**

My first-hand knowledge about the Jersey Pine Barrens is 40 years out of date. Let me go back even further, to Pennsylvania, 1950-something. Summers, Dad, Mom, cousins and I would hop into the old man's green-over-cream '53 Bel Air hardtop and point the grille toward pre-Trump Atlantic City. We'd make the Delaware crossing into Jersey on the Chester-Bridgeport Ferry and two hours later a half-dozen layers of winter skin would have blistered to a sweaty peel and Steel Pier salt-water taffy would have yanked that year's fillings out of our heads.

Before we became beach-blanket brisket though, we had to cross Jersey. I spent those 60-plus non-air conditioned miles in the Chevy's back seat meditating on undertow or skewering a bare foot on the tail of summer's first horseshoe crab. Being thus occupied it wasn't until years later I noticed that most of trans-Jersey was trees.

Later still, I learned those 60-some-odd miles, the whole of central Jersey in fact, was a geopolitical entity called the Pine Barrens. As explained by my elder and savvier cousin Fred, the Barrens was dark and scary woods inhabited by inbred six-fingered folk who lived in caves, prayed to odd and grubby gods, made their own gas from pig shit, and ate lost travelers. They called themselves "Pineys."

Much later, I made a now-long-gone documentary film about the region called ...*Where the Sun Never Shines*. In making it, I found Pineys, sadly, to be garden-variety Americans. Your personal demons can inform whatever image that concept conjures. The Pineys I met were independent-minded and didn't care to be fussed-over about where they live or what they do. They do a lot for themselves, things most of us gave up doing a generation or more ago (That, about pig shit and gas? It's true). Their world is deep forest and truck-wide sand trails; it is small streams and cedar swamps, abandoned bogs and the smell of decay and sphagnum moss. The tales they tell outsiders are curious and spooky. Of course.

Navigating the Barrens was tricky. Now we'd use our iPhones. Then we felt our way among the trees by dashboard compass, odometer and Geodetic Survey maps. Place names still dot those maps: Ong's Hat, Batsto, Hog Wallow. All that lived in those invisible towns was stillness, a sense of the once-was and never-will-be hung in those clearings and shallow hollows that once were lived-in places. An outsider who arrived at one of those named abandonments, who stood at a five-trail wideness in the forest and turned his eyes four-ways into that old, old darkness around, most likely felt the lurk of the strange behind and ahead. I'm sure of it.

Despite squatting at the concrete heart of the Megalopolis, there are economic, political, and social reasons why the Barrens remains green, relatively human-free, and unimproved. These reasons are not part of this tale's fetchings.

Point is, I liked the area. I admired the people and, despite the arrogance of youth, I learned a little about them.

Another thing I learned: it's a hard place to get right. My film never caught it. Later, I set a story, *Veterans*, in the Barrens. Later still, having sold two screenplays, I adapted *Veterans* for film. *Veterans*, the Movie, remains unproduced. Worse, in Dreamland terms, it remains unsold.

One supremely good writer I know set a much admired story in the Pines. He missed it. One of the best episodes of *The Sopranos* was set there. The show's city-bred wiseguys were money-on as strangers in a strange land, but that episode, *The Barrens*, shot in a generic woodland with no spirit of the Pines, lost the chill of the place.

When I was asked to submit to an anthology of tales on a theme of fang and talon, the Pines entered my head. I guess I wanted another shot at getting it right.

Okay, thought I, the salient features of the Barrens are trees and sand. Trees with claws? A cliché. Sand with teeth? Well…

The editors passed on *So Many Tiny Mouths*. They were right to do so. That version focused on the tourists from Philly. I guess I was still sitting in the back seat of Dad's Chevy. I read the story in a few public venues. A friend asked to buy more or less this version for an online prozine he was publishing, so there it was. Most recently, Great Britain's StarShipSofa.com podcast a recording I made of the story.

So here it is, re-thought, in ink, on public paper for the first time. I hope I got the Pines right. I wouldn't bet on it, though. As I said, it was 40 years ago and the Barrens is an elusive place.

By the way, Earl Sooey, the coot through whose eye we watch the world end: He's fiction, coincidence. Really.

LIFE ON THE RIVER: **JEREMY TAKES HIS TEXT FROM THE LIVES OF THE SPIDERS**

My writer's group, Chicago's Twilight Tales, used to throw an annual Mardi Gras party at the Red Lion Pub. One year the chairman of the group asked some of the regulars to read something set in New Orleans. Having been asked, I wrote this tale.

Jeremy suggested himself to me because vampires and "walk-ins" seem to be a part of the atmosphere of New Orleans. Understand, I've never been there. Always wanted to go but the several times I've planned trips, the plans became undone, the most recent undoing courtesy of Hurricane Katrina.

I do know something about river travel, though.

One dark and drunken night after my return from the Air Force, a buddy and I decided that we had never had an adventure. Exciting things, yes, had happened to us, but nothing ever of our own volition. We decided it would be just swell to go down the Mississippi River on a raft. Okay, a small boat, no cabin, nothing fancy. We'd start at the Golden Triangle in Pittsburgh where the Ohio begins. We'd ride the Ohio for its full 981 miles, pick up the Mississippi at Cairo, Illinois, then slide down to the Big Easy. Simple.

We bought a 14-foot sky blue jon boat, a shallow flat bottomed thing with blunt prow and stern. When fully loaded with outboard motor, fuel, camping supplies, clothing, food, and us, about three inches of freeboard remained.

Research begun and concluded the same drunken night the urge took us told us that the Ohio trucked along at a comfortable several miles an hour. We had visions. Huck and Jim would drift through sunny days and starry nights of the soul. Gentle water would lap our gunnels as froggies courted along the shore. Friendly tow-barges would wave to us as they slipped by. Our little putt-putt motor would be used only when a quick hurry was required to take us here or there along the way.

Currents are funny. Their substance is deep. After our put-in below the triangle, we found our expected downstream flow toward the Gulf of Mexico was more of a generalized upstream drift toward Pittsburgh. Even near-swamped, our little flat-bottomed boat reached barely 11 inches below the surface. The consequence was, we skimmed the river, skewing, sliding here and there more at the whim of breeze than current. Heavy rowing or the engine was necessary simply to keep us heading west and south.

The first tow-boat scared the bejeezus out of us. Out of morning mist there came a quarter mile of diesel-pushed steel, bellowing, two barges wide. The blind monster threw an eight foot high bow wave that spread across the river like a green rolling mountain. Imagine the view from a blue aluminum hole a bare three inches above the surface.

Less than five miles from our put-in we went to shore, set up camp, reappraised this volitional adventure.

To say "shore" is to idealize the land along the Ohio west of Pittsburgh. Conjure a slurry of mud and cinders capped with a six-inch mat of oil and other industrial effluvia spread along a sumac-crowded railroad right-of-way. We camped, rethought, regrouped, slept, and to our credit (or disgrace) continued the adventure the next morning. It was a cold night. I didn't mention:

this was October, heading into November. We did not dare build a fire the night before for fear of igniting the river or the land or both.

We never got to New Orleans, nor to the Mississippi. We did make Kentucky. We had many adventures and were jailed only once and that in Bellaire, Ohio for attempting to enter a VFW Post while wet. That's a long story. We did not join a drinking companion we met in West Virginia as he headed out to find his girl, who had started dating a biker gang while he was in the Nam. He had a loaded .45 in his belt and dynamite in his truck and invited us along to watch. That also is a long story, which I will someday tell.

The spiders are real. They happened damn-near as written.

A TALE FROM THE RED LION: **CORDWELL'S BOOK**

There is so much true and accurate in this story that I almost need not tell you any more. John Cordwell is gone now but he lived and his story as written here is mostly as it was lived. He was among those who made a habit of escaping from the Germans during that Second unpleasantness with the Hun. John was a character in the film *The Great Escape*. There are documentary films about him and the other POWs who made that audacious escape. Escapes, actually. The reality is more remarkable and more improbable than that shown in the theatrical film.

"Cordwell's Book" came about because a bunch of us were drinking in the upstairs room of the Red Lion Pub in Chicago one night. Eventually the talk came around to the idea of doing an anthology of stories centered on the Lion and written by writers who hung out there. "Like us," someone said. "*Tales from the Red Lion,*" someone suggested, "like Spider Robinson's *Callahan's Cross-Time Saloon* but different, see?"

Seemed like a good idea.

As mentioned, I'd fallen into the place during my first week in Chicago. I was a theater guy from the east and the Lion was a place where theater folk hung. John Cordwell was a bigger-than-us-all presence in the bar and I was shy around him. I liked him and the place and was learning to like that time of my life.

One summer evening, I saw a remarkable production of one of Shakespeare's plays on the roof garden—it was not *The Tempest*—and met a swath of good people as a result. There was great talent there and then.

That's the core of the story.

I learned of John's wartime experiences from John and, after John's death, heard more from his son, Colin, who *is* a great barman and who told the stories almost as well as had his father. I kept the facts and mixed them with a bit of implausible froth and fairy tale-telling and published *Cordwell's Book* in *Tales from the Red Lion*. I revised it for a second edition of *Tales...* and I fussed with it for this effort.

Those who know about such things say the Red Lion Pub is one of the most haunted spots in Chicago. I know people who have had experiences. I have not, not preternatural ones anyway.

At this writing, the Lion is a sheer hulk. Unavoidable decay and expensive repair estimates forced Colin to close the building. The notion was to raze it and build a new Red Lion on the spot. Then came the crash.

At this writing, the shell remains. And the memories. The memories, bless them. Bless them all, they're alive.

DYING'S EASY. HORROR'S HARD: **THE LAST SCOOT AT SKIDOO'S TAP**

This is more about me as a writer than about where *The Last Scoot...* came from. Where the story came from is simple. My wife suggested it.

"Look at this!" A well-known book dangled from her fingertips. "Write a vampire book," said as though asking me for the last time to take out the trash.

Now, I have friends who have written vampire stories and were very happy with their lives.

I said, "Sure," then, perversely, I wrote this.

Here's a life-rule: Nothing will be what you expect. Nothing real, neither will vampire, zombie, man-wolf, or any creature of the night be a thing you'll recognize. They will come from the literal dark, blindside you, and do things you cannot imagine.

I believe that a writer of the strange has a responsibility to that truth and to the creatures that support him.

The vampires of Skidoo's Tap inhabit a grubby part of creation. They drink not blood but life itself. They take not what we hold dear, but that which we are happy to forget. They take pain, the drear of life. In return, they offer paradise, a heaven of non-being.

The trap of course is that pain and tedium are the artists of the beautiful. The dreary slog through life provides the contrast that allows us to see, touch, feel, smell the wonders of it all.

From where did Skidoo's Tap come?

When Tycelia made her suggestion I was working on a novel. Not horror, not exactly fantasy, the story is set in small-town pre-JFK America and deals with a band of kids who set out to grab death by the tail and toss him.

The vampire story began in the same town. My town. Railroads did run through it. There is—was—a Skidoo's taproom there. It wasn't called Skidoo's but it was as described. When I was 12, my genteel gang of non-Ender hooligans did weekly scoots into the joint. We ran screaming in, around the electric eye pole and out the OUT door. Doing so we caught whiffs of beery, smoky, sex-charged conditioned air then hooted all the way to our theater on the far side of our yards. There was a subway viaduct. We also had a gathering place in the cemetery.

That's it.

I started there. I'd gotten about 16 thousand words into the thing before I realized what I was writing. Inefficient way to work, I know, but I do love to hang out in those grubby places of the mind. When I found where I was heading, I went back and fussed. The story went from 16 thousand to just over 9 thousand.

This is one of those stories that I wrote and never tried to sell. Sorry, Tycelia. I know vampire stories can make big money right now but that's dependent on people actually liking the damn vamps, finding them cute, sexy!

So there. The stories are yours and you now know, more or less, where they came from.

A final word. I don't plan for the most part. I begin, typically, with a notion and a person, an image, a face. When I have at least a person in my head, I begin writing. Most of the time I've no idea where the path is or through what country we'll travel. For example: I was walking in the neighborhood today. I saw a sign in a store I've passed many times. "WANT TO LEARN MORE ABOUT ROBOTS?" I was returning from a visit to my doctor. I wondered, what if a robot stopped in because…

Well, because.

See, my process might be summarized best by the 13th-century Persian poet Rumi: "Respond to every call that excites your spirit."

I hope you've been excited. Now excuse me, I have the call. *The shop was in a dark part of town on a narrow, unclean street...*

About the Author

Award-winning writer and narrator Lawrence Santoro began writing and reading dark tales at age five.

In 2001 his novella "God Screamed and Screamed, Then I Ate Him" was nominated for a Bram Stoker Award. In 2002, his adaptation and audio production of Gene Wolfe's "The Tree Is My Hat," was also Stoker nominated. In 2003, his Stoker-recommended "Catching" received Honorable Mention in Ellen Datlow's 17th Annual "Year's Best Fantasy and Horror" anthology. In 2004, "So Many Tiny Mouths" was cited in the anthology's 18th edition. In the 20th, his novella "At Angels Sixteen," from the anthology A DARK AND DEADLY VALLEY, was similarly honored. Larry's first novel, "Just North of Nowhere," was published in 2007.

He lives in Chicago and is working on two new novels, "Griffon and the Sky Warriors," and "Mississippi Traveler, or Sam Clemens Tries the Water."

Stop by Larry's blog, At Home in Bluffton, at:
http://blufftoninthedriftless.blogspot.com/

and his audio website, Santoro Reads, at:
http://www.santororeads.com

and you can find him on Facebook at:
http://www.facebook.com/lawrence.santoro

CPSIA information can be obtained
at www.ICGtesting.com
Printed in the USA
BVHW080803090620
581030BV00001B/27